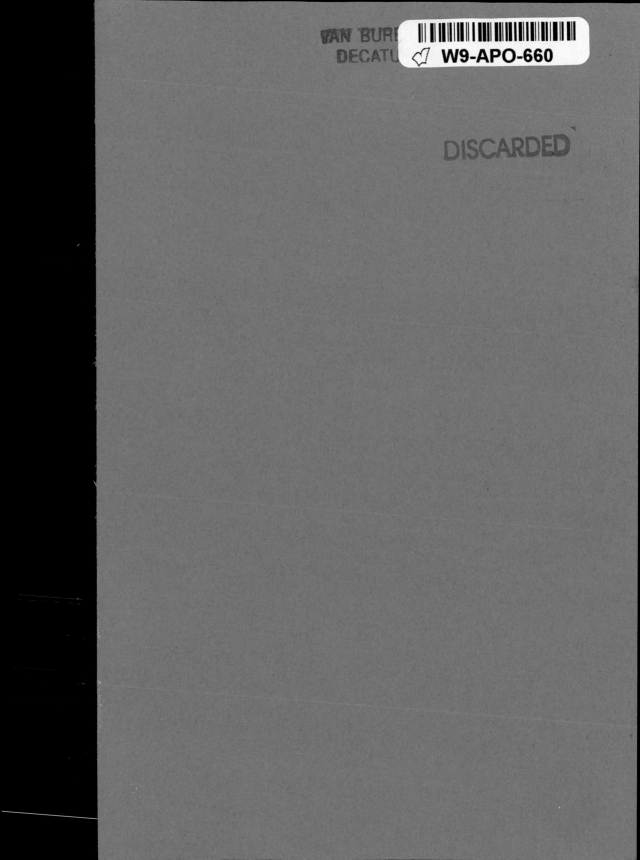

THE COLD NOWHERE

THE COLD NOWHERE

A JONATHAN STRIDE NOVEL

BRIAN FREEMAN

Quercus

4/14
BAT

The

Quercus

New York • London

© 2013 by Brian Freeman

First published in the United States by Quercus in 2014

Any member of educational institutions wishing to photocopy part or all of the work for classroom use or anthology should send inquiries to Permissions c/o Quercus Publishing Inc., 31 West 57th Street, 6th Floor, New York, NY 10019, or to permissions@quercus.com.

ISBN 978-1-62365-131-2

Library of Congress Control Number: 2013913391

Distributed in the United States and Canada by Random House Publisher Services c/o Random House, 1745 Broadway
New York, NY 10019

Manufactured in the United States

2 4 6 8 10 9 7 5 3 1

www.quercus.com

For Marcia

PROLOGUE

Despite the ribbons of blood on his face, which were as angry as war paint, the man on the bed was still breathing. She hadn't killed him.

He lay on his back, sprawled in a tangle of bedsheets. His unbuttoned dress shirt exposed a flat chest, winter-pale and hairless. His pants puddled around his ankles. He smelled of cigar smoke and cologne. The whiskey bottle he'd opened lay tipped on the floor of the old stateroom, dripping Lagavulin onto the emerald carpet. He still clutched a crystal tumbler in his hand. Her blow had come by surprise, knocking him off his feet.

Cat slid a flowery cocktail dress over her nude body. She wanted to be gone before he woke up. She grabbed one of her cowboy boots from the floor. Its heel was slick with blood where she'd swung it into the man's temple. She shoved her foot inside, and the leather nestled her calf. Her legs were lithe and smooth; young legs for a young girl. She reached into the toe of her other boot, retrieved the chain that held her father's ring, and slipped it over her head. She fluffed her nut-brown hair. Reaching into the boot again, she curled her fingers around the onyx handle of a knife.

Wherever she went, whatever she did, Cat always carried a knife.

She felt a wave of desire—as tall and powerful as a tsunami—to unsheathe the blade and plunge it into the torso of the man on the bed, slicing through skin, tissue, organs, and bone. Up and down. Over and over. Thirty times. Forty times. A frenzy. She knew what he would look like when she was done, butchered and dead, a slaughtered pig. She could picture herself spray-painted with his blood, like graffiti art in a graveyard.

She'd seen that painting before. She knew what knives did.

Cat hid the blade in her boot and left him there, unconscious. He wasn't worth killing. She felt sick from the images popping in her brain like fireworks. She headed for the bathroom, sank to her bare knees on the cold tile, and vomited into the toilet. She flushed down the puke. When she felt steady on her feet, she hurried down the steps and escaped outside, where the elements assaulted her immediately.

She stood on the deck of the giant ore boat *Charles Frederick*, but she wasn't at sea. This ship didn't go to sea anymore. It was a museum showpiece, locked away from the open waters of Lake Superior on a narrow channel in the heart of Duluth's tourist district. The long, flat deck, like two football fields of red steel, swayed under her heels. The ship groaned like a living thing. Wind off the lake made a tornado of her hair and sneaked under her dress with cold fingers. It was early April, but in Duluth, April meant winter when the sun went down.

Dots of frigid moisture beaded on her skin from the flurries whipping through the night air. She hugged herself tightly, shivering, wishing she had a coat. Her heels clanged on the deck as, feeling alone and small, she picked her way beside a rope railing sixty feet over the water. When she looked down, she felt dizzy. Her eyes darted with the quickness of a bird, alert to the shadows and hiding places around her. She was never safe.

Cat located a hatch, where steep wet steps descended to an interior room that was like a prison of gray metal, with huge rivets dotting the walls. The room was dark and empty. On the far wall, snow blew inside through an open exit door. She exhaled sharply in relief; all she had to do was hurry to the ground and run. She bolted for the door but at the gangway she stopped and nervously studied the deserted street below the ship. Her boots were on a metal landing in the water of the snowmelt. She wiped wet flakes from her eyes and squinted to see better.

Then, with her heart in her mouth, she froze. Even in the bitter cold, sweat gathered on her neck like a film of fear. She backed into the shadows, making herself invisible, but it was too late.

He'd seen her.

He'd found her again.

For days, she'd stayed a step ahead of him, like a game of hopscotch. Now he was back and she was trapped. She pricked up her ears and listened. Footsteps crunched across the gravel and ice, coming closer. She ran to a steel door that led to the mammoth cargo holds in the guts of the ship. She tugged on the door—it was heavy—and slipped through it, closing it behind her. Looking down, she saw only blackness; she couldn't see the bottom of the steps. The interior was cold and vast, like she'd been swallowed down into a whale's belly. She was blind as she descended. The air got colder on her wet skin, and the wind made muffled shrieks outside the hull.

When she finally felt the bottom of the ship under her feet, she inched forward, expecting open space. Instead, she bumped against walls, and wire netting scraped her face. Her fingers found grease and peeling paint. With no frame of reference, she lost her sense of direction. Her eyes saw things that weren't there, mirages in the shadows. Objects moved. Colors floated in the air. Vertigo made her head spin, as if she were on a catwalk instead of safely on the ground.

Something real skittered over her foot—a rat. Cat flailed and couldn't stifle her cry. She collided with a stack of paint cans, which clattered to the floor and rolled like squeaky bicycles. The noise bounced around the walls, rippling to the high ceiling in ghastly echoes. She dropped to her knees, tightened into a ball, and slid her knife out of her boot and clutched it in front of her.

The door high above her swung open. He was here. A flashlight scoured the floor like a dazzling white eye. The light, passing over her head, helped her see where she was. She was crouched behind a yellow forklift in a maze of makeshift plywood walls. Twenty feet away, a corridor beside the hull led from the cargo hold where she was hiding. That was the way out.

Cat waited. She heard the bang of footfalls. He was on the floor with her now. His light explored every crevice, patiently clearing every hiding place as he hunted her. She heard his footsteps; she heard his breathing. He was on the other side of the forklift, no more than six feet away, and he stopped, as if his senses told him that she was near. She rubbed her fingers on the knife; her sweat made it slippery. She aimed her blade at his throat. His light spilled across the dusty floor in front of her. He took a step closer, until he was a dark shape beside the wheels of the machine.

She saw the light glinting on his hand. He held a gun. Cat's breath shot into her chest, loud and scared. She sprang up, slashing with the knife, but as she lurched toward him her wrist collided with the cage and the blade dropped to the floor. Helpless, she charged, taking them both to the ground, landing on dirt and scrap wood. The gun fell, and the flashlight rolled. Cat jabbed with her fingers and found his eyes. She poked hard, and when he screamed she squirmed away, scooped up the flashlight, and ran.

With the light bouncing in front of her, she sprinted down a narrow passage. He scrambled to follow, but she heard him lose his footing and fall. She widened the gap between them. The passage opened into a second cargo hold, and she saw another set of steps, which she climbed two at a time. Her mouth hung open, gulping air. At the top, she bolted back onto the ship's deck.

She was out of time. She took off the way she'd come, beside the rope railing with the water far below her. The metal was wet, and she skidded, trying to stay on her feet. He was already closing on her again. She heard his running footsteps behind her, but she didn't look back. She sprinted on the slippery steel like a clumsy dancer, until she reached the end of the boat and had nowhere else to run. She stood at the stern, with the massive anchor chain beside her and the wind and flurries stinging her face from the midnight sky. The steel floor thundered, reverberating with his heavy footfalls. He was almost here. He almost had her.

Cat clasped her fists in front of her face and stared in despair at the harbor below her. Then she did the only thing she could do.

She flung herself off the ship into the ice-strewn water.

PART ONE
RUNAWAY

1

Jonathan Stride knew he wasn't alone.

He arrived at his cottage on Park Point at two in the morning and realized that something was wrong. It was instinct; nothing looked out of place on the street. There were no cars in the neighborhood that he didn't recognize. His eyes flicked across the trees and shadows around the house, but he saw nothing to alarm him. When he listened, he heard only the intermittent roar of Lake Superior beyond the crest of the dunes. Even so, as he locked his Ford Expedition and headed for his front porch, he went so far as to slide his gun into his hand.

Instinct.

Nearing the house, he spotted footprints in the snow. The prints were small, maybe size seven, and whoever made them was in a hurry, not trying to hide their approach. He tracked the running prints across his lawn and along the dirt driveway that led to the back of the house. He examined the cottage windows from the yard but saw no lights. If anyone was inside, they were waiting for him in the dark.

Stride headed for the rear door of his house, near the grassy trail that led to the beach. He let himself inside onto the screened porch. He eased his leather jacket off his shoulders and draped it over the garage-sale sofa he kept out back. He shook snow out of his wavy hair. Leading with his gun, he opened the inner door that led to his kitchen.

The house was colder than usual. He heard a whistle of wind. He left the lights off and walked quietly, but the floor timbers in the 1880s cottage were never silent. They groaned with each step, announcing his arrival. It didn't matter.

"I know you're here," he called.

No one replied.

He followed the kitchen into the dining room and eased around the corner into the living room. The cold fireplace and his red leather armchair were on his right. Sofas and throw rugs took up the middle of the room, near steps that led to the unfinished attic. The open space was empty. The room was dark. He heard the wind again, loud and agitated, blowing curtains in a spare bedroom immediately across from him. He rarely used that room; it was filled with dusty bookshelves and notes on cold cases. He crossed through the threshold into the bedroom, where the old floor slanted downward, like a corridor in a fun house. He spied a broken window, with glass littering the floor and lacy fabric billowing in and out of the night air like a ghost.

The bedroom was deserted. Using a penlight on his key chain he studied the glass and saw a spatter of blood on the shards.

"You're hurt," he said aloud.

He went back to the living room and eyed the doorway to his own bedroom on the opposite wall. She was hiding there. He'd already decided it was a woman, based on the footprints. There were other rooms in the house—another small bedroom in the corner facing the street, the attic, the tiny bathroom—but he could make out damp tracks on the carpet leading toward his room. Halfway across the floor, he saw beige cowboy boots that matched the tracks in the snow.

"I'm coming in, okay?" he said.

Still nothing.

He examined his bedroom. The comforter had been yanked off his bed. The space on either side of the bed was empty, but his closet door was closed and latched. It usually swung shut by itself because of the slight tilt of the house, but he never actually pushed it all the way closed. He turned the antique metal doorknob and pulled hard. The closet door opened with a shriek.

He turned his light to the floor and saw a huddled body wrapped tightly in the blanket from his bed. All he could see was her face. Not a woman. A girl. A teenager. She stared up at him, eyes wide with fright. Her long brown hair was soaking wet, plastered to her face. She was wracked with trembling, and her skin was blue with cold.

Stride holstered his gun. He turned on the closet light and the girl's eyes squeezed shut.

"My name's Stride," he told her. "It's okay. I'm not going to hurt you. I'm a lieutenant with the Duluth police."

Without opening her eyes, she nodded. She already knew who he was. The blanket slipped, and he saw bony bare shoulders.

Stride squatted in front of her. "What's your name?"

She opened her eyes now and he could see how brown and perfect they were. "Cat," she said.

"Hello, Cat. Can you tell me why you're here?"

She didn't answer right away but he could feel her reaching out to him across the dusty space. He could feel her fear and loneliness and he knew without her saying so that she had nowhere else in the world to go. Finally, she whispered to him, as if it were a secret to keep hidden.

"Someone's trying to kill me," she said.

The flannel shirt he'd given her draped almost to her knees. She wore a pair of Stride's white athletic socks and roomy shorts. Her hair was dry now, and her skin was pink and clean from the bath. She clutched a mug of tea with both hands as they sat at his dining room table. One of her fingers was bandaged where she'd cut it on the broken window.

"Sorry about the shirt," Stride told her, smiling. "The woman who used to live here, Serena, she's a lot taller than you."

Cat shrugged. "It's okay. I like it. It smells good."

The girl stared into her tea. He had a chance to study her features. Teenagers always had the prettiness of youth, and Hispanic women were particularly attractive, but Stride thought that Cat was one of the most beautiful young girls he had ever seen. Her bone structure was like a sculpture, with high cheekbones and a chin that made a sharp V. Her face was small; so was her body. Her chestnut hair tumbled in broad waves to the middle of her chest, and he could see a gold chain glinting between the buttons of the shirt. He hadn't seen her smile, but he could tell by the way her lips turned upward that she would have a pretty smile when she used it. She had a petite, slightly rounded nose and dark eyebrows that were arched in innocent surprise.

Even so, she wasn't innocent. He knew that. The ravages of street life were already creeping into her face. He could practically measure in months how long she'd been hanging out in the industrial areas and near the graffiti graveyard under the freeway overpass. She was malnourished; he could see that in the dark circles under her eyes and in the way she'd devoured the turkey sandwich he made for her. He'd smelled alcohol on her breath, and he assumed she used drugs. Probably synthetics, which were the street drug of choice. Her expression was melancholy, and in a few more months it would become cynical. She was still young now, but she would soon be old.

"I'd really like you to go to the hospital, Cat," he said, not for the first time. "I left a message for my partner, Maggie, to come over here right away. She and I can take you there."

The girl shook her head emphatically. "No! I told you: no way, no hospital. He'll find me. He always knows where I am."

"I'm concerned about you. You should be checked out."

"I want to stay here. I'm safe here. I'm fine."

He didn't push her. She was skittish, and he was afraid she would run. "Listen, a buddy of mine named Steve Garske runs a clinic in Lakeside. We go back a lot of years. He's my own doctor. Can I have him take a look at you in the morning?"

Her eyes brightened. "Dr. Steve?"

"You know him?"

"He volunteers at the youth shelter downtown. I've seen him a couple times. He's sweet."

"Good. I'll take you to see him. Okay?"

Cat nodded. "Yeah, okay."

Stride took a swallow from a can of Coke. He was a self-acknowledged Coke addict. Capital *C*. "What happened to you tonight, Cat? Are you ready to tell me what's going on?"

The girl glanced at the dining room windows, as if she expected to see the face of her stalker framed behind the glass. She was like a deer, alert and swift. "I was at a party on the big ore boat in Canal Park. Some bigwig rented it out."

"Do you know who?"

"No. It was a bunch of car dealers."

Stride frowned. It took clout and money to get a private party on the *Frederick*. "Why were you there?"

"They needed girls." She chewed a fingernail and looked guilty. "It was me and a few others. We were the entertainment."

"What kind of entertainment?"

She shrugged. "You know."

"How old are you, Cat?" he asked.

Her pretty lower lip bulged. "Eighteen."

Her eyes looked like a kid's eyes again, trying to get away with a lie. "I'm not going to arrest you for anything," he said. "I want to help you, but I need you to trust me, and I need you to tell me the truth."

He knew he was asking a lot. For girls like Cat, trust was a foreign thing.

"Okay, I'm sixteen," she said. "I tell them I'm older. Nobody asks questions. I'm pretty, that's all they care about. The sex stuff . . . it's just a way to get money, you know? The guy tonight, I didn't even do it with him. I—I hit him. Hard."

"Did you hurt him?" Stride asked.

"He was bleeding, but he was okay."

"Why did you hit him? Did he assault you?"

"He wanted me to do things I don't do. Not anymore. I mean, I'll sleep with guys, fine. What's the big deal, it's only sex. But not other stuff. I won't do that again."

"Stuff?"

The girl explained. Stride hid his disgust.

"The man you hit, is he the one who tried to kill you?" he asked.

"No, after I hit him, I left. I just wanted to get out of there. This man was waiting for me outside the ship and he chased me back inside. The only way I could get away from him was to jump into the harbor."

Stride leaned forward. "You *jumped* from the deck of the boat?"

"Yeah. It was so cold. My dress tore off. I swam to the Canal Park side, and I ran. I figured he'd try to come after me, so I just kept running."

"It's more than three miles. You made it all this way? In the snow?"

"I stole a blanket out of a car on the street," she said. "That helped."

Stride liked the spark of life he saw in this girl, regardless of the things she'd done. Cat was young and small, but she had courage. Serena would have said he had a weakness for women who needed rescue. "This man who came after you, do you know who he is?"

"No."

"What did he look like?"

"I never saw his face."

"Why do you think he's trying to kill you?"

"It's not the first time. He's been after me for a while."

"He has? Are you sure?"

"Yeah, it started about three weeks ago. I was back home for a while. I'm in and out of there, you know? I slipped out my window one night, and when I came out of the woods, somebody ran after me. That was the first time. I was lucky, because a bus came by, so I hopped on. I could see him down the block behind me."

"But you didn't recognize him."

"No, it was too dark. I've been bouncing around since then. I stayed with my aunt for a few days. She rents a place at the Seaway, but you know what it's like there. They'll rat you out for a Snickers bar. I thought someone was watching me again, so I bolted. Then last week, I was hanging out at the shelter on First Street. I took a walk in the middle of night. I do that sometimes. It was Sunday, nobody was around, but a car took off after me. He almost ran me down as I crossed near Sammy's."

"Did you see what kind of car it was?"

"No, all I saw was the lights. The engine sounded like a sports car. Anyway, I've been running since then. I thought maybe I'd lost him, because I didn't see anybody all week. Until tonight."

Stride thought about what Cat was saying and what he saw in her face. She was scared, but he had no way of knowing if any of it was real. When you came and went on the streets, sometimes bad people found you. When you drank or did drugs, sometimes your brain took detours and got lost. It was easy to get paranoid. A string of odd incidents, even if they were all true, didn't add up to a conspiracy.

Cat was smart. "You think I'm crazy," she said.

"No, but I do have to ask, have you been using anything? Maybe synthetics like bath salts? Those drugs can cause severe reactions, including paranoia and hallucinations."

"I'm *not* using," Cat insisted.

"Never?"

"I didn't say never. I've tried things. I didn't like what they did to me, so I quit. That's the truth. I haven't taken any of that stuff in months. It all happened just like I said. This guy is trying to kill me."

"Do you have any idea *why* someone would want to hurt you?"

"No," she said. "Not a clue."

"Has anything out of the ordinary happened to you recently? Did you witness anything bad? Were you with someone who might not want the relationship exposed?"

"I don't think so. I mean, I can't think of anything like that."

He gave her a reassuring smile. "We'll figure it out. We're going to have to sit down and go through everything you've done and everyone you've been with recently. Are you okay with that? You'll need to be honest. You can't hold back."

"You may not like some of it," she said.

"Don't worry about that. It's pretty hard to shock a cop. Anyway, I want you to get some sleep first. You've had a tough night. Get some rest and then we'll go see Steve at the clinic."

"Thank you, Mr. Stride." He saw her smile for the first time, and he was right. It was as sweet and warm as the sun coming out from the clouds.

"Can I ask you something, Cat?" he said.

"Sure."

"Why did you come here tonight? How did you find me?"

The girl played with the gold chain on her neck. Her eyes got misty. "I looked up your address a while ago. My mother told me that if there was ever a time in my life when I needed protection, and no one was around for me, I should go to you. Find Mr. Stride, she told me. She said you'd help me."

"Your mother?"

"She died. You were there."

Stride was confused. He looked at Cat and saw a teenager, like any other girl. A stranger. Then he looked at her again and saw a familiar child hiding in her face. He knew her. Ten years ago, she'd been a six-year-old chasing butterflies between soaring evergreens. A six-year-old with messy hands and pumpkin pie on her mouth.

A six-year-old cowering under the porch behind her house, her face frozen in terror.

Cat.

"You're *Catalina*," he murmured, as he realized who she was. "Catalina Mateo. Michaela was your mother."

"You remember her," she said. "I knew you would."

Stride pushed back his chair and got up with a start. The reality struck him like a blow to the chest. He went into the living room, where it was dark and cool, and he took a loud breath, which felt ragged in his lungs. His face taunted him in the antique mirror. Short, messy black hair, swept with gray. A day of rough stubble on his chin and cheeks. The brown, brooding eyes, feeling everything, showing everything. He could feel the furrows in his weathered forehead deepen. Not wrinkles anymore—furrows. A storm washed over him. He felt his age. He sat down in the red leather armchair in the shadows, and he saw her face again. Michaela.

He'd never gotten past the guilt of what happened to her. For a decade, she'd been his nightmare.

And now this.

Catalina. Cat. Michaela's beautiful little girl, descending into the lost life of prostitution. A runaway.

"Mr. Stride?"

She stood framed in the doorway of the dining room, with the lights behind her. She came toward him tentatively. When he read her face, he knew they were both thinking about the same night. Remembering her mother.

Cat slipped to her knees and Stride folded her into his chest and hugged her with the tenderness he would give a child. Ten years had passed, but she was still a little girl. She was fragile and warm in his arms. He wanted to change the past for her and make everything right. He wanted to restore what she'd lost, but that was beyond his power. He couldn't undo what was done or erase his mistakes. All he could do was make a promise.

Not to himself. Not to Cat. To Michaela. A new promise to replace the one he'd failed to keep ten years ago.

He would rescue her daughter.

He would save her.

2

The girl had vanished again. She was smart.

He threw down the garage door with an angry jerk of his wrist, shutting out the noise of the wind. With the door closed, he stood in perfect blackness beside the snow-crusted Dodge Charger. He switched on the light, which illuminated the concrete floor, with its mud and grease. The garage was neatly organized. Metal shelves. Tools on pegboards. Chest freezer. He grabbed a plastic gasoline can and topped off the Charger's tank. Gasoline spilled onto the wool of his gloves, raising pungent fumes. Despite the cold air in the detached garage, he felt sweat under his winter hat.

He'd spent half an hour scouring Canal Park and the streets surrounding the city's convention center. The girl had to be freezing. She had to be scared. There were moments when he knew she was close—he felt it—but wherever she was hiding, she kept out of sight.

Smart.

He gave up on the search as it got late. The Charger was stolen. It wasn't safe to stay in the tourist area longer than necessary. He didn't think the girl would call the police, but he knew that they patrolled the Canal Park area through the overnight hours, and he didn't want them eyeing the Charger with suspicion. A car slowly making circles through the deserted streets attracted attention.

He headed back to his hideaway in the forested lands north of the city. He could park the Charger, take his car from the garage's other stall, and go back to his real life. Shed one skin, put on another.

He slid open the second garage door and studied the woods outside before he made his escape. He was sheltered from the highway, and it was a lightly traveled road. No one could see him. The owners were snowbirds; they wouldn't be back for months. He had to be cautious about neighbors noticing tracks in the driveway, but few people lived year-round on the lonely back roads, and the wind and snow would cover up his trail overnight. This had been his lair for a month. He would be gone long before anyone discovered it.

His phone vibrated in his pocket, demanding attention. He knew who it was. Only one other person had the number for this phone.

"She got away," he said, answering the call.

There was no reply. He could hear mixed emotions in the silence. Terror. Relief. Then finally a voice: "Maybe we should just forget about her. Maybe it's okay."

"It's *not* okay," he said.

"The girl doesn't know a thing. Let her go."

"We can't. Don't you get it? She's a bomb waiting to blow up in our faces."

He heard another long, tortured pause.

"So what happens next?"

"She disappeared again," he replied. "She's on the run. You need to find out where she is."

"I already told you exactly where she was going to be tonight. You said you would handle it and you didn't. You said it would be over by now."

His gloved hands squeezed into fists. He didn't need blame. They were way past blame. He couldn't believe that one teenage girl could put the entire scheme at risk.

"Just find out where she is," he repeated angrily.

"How do I do that?"

"That's your problem. And do it fast." He hung up the phone.

He was breathing heavily. It was true; it should have been over by now. A teenage hooker had outsmarted him. He'd let her sneak through his grasp again. She should have been in his hands weeks ago; she should have been dead and forgotten. Once she was out of the way, the trail would be buried like dirt over a grave. They'd finally be safe.

He told himself he still had time to fix this. No one was asking questions now. No one knew the girl's secret. Even so, the clock kept ticking. A month had passed. The longer he waited, the more chance there was for things to go badly. Someone had already made the connection and, sooner or later, others would follow, as long as the girl was out there. The dominoes would fall, snaking their way back to his doorstep. He couldn't let that happen.

Time to go. The outside woods were deserted. The street was empty. Real life.

Before he got into his car, he spotted the chest freezer on the far wall. He couldn't help himself. He checked it again, the way he'd checked it a thousand times, lifting the lid, feeling the frost envelop his face. The body was a horrible thing, rock solid, like an alabaster statue. It was odd how he still expected the eyes to pop open, the mouth to form a scream as it gasped for air. He wasn't a monster; he felt regret. Sometimes there was no way but the hard way.

Some secrets couldn't be allowed to come back to life.

He shut the lid of the freezer, leaving the body to feel the burn of the ice. It was a tight fit but there was enough room for one more inside. The girl was small.

3

"Go with me on this," Maggie Bei said. She sat on Stride's kitchen counter, kicking her legs and sipping hot coffee from a cardboard cup. "I think a sausage McMuffin with egg may well be the world's perfect food."

Stride glanced at the clock. It wasn't even six in the morning on Saturday, and it was still dark outside. He'd been asleep for two hours, but the noise of his partner in the kitchen had awakened him. He opened the McDonald's bag and saw a second sausage McMuffin inside, which he took out and ate ravenously. "I think you're right," he said.

"It's the little slice of cheese that does it. I love that. And the egg that looks like a hockey puck. I could eat these every day."

"You do."

"No, some days I get those little breakfast burrito things." She popped the top of a can of Coke with her fingernail and handed it to him. "You look like you need caffeine, boss."

"You think?" Stride said. He still wore his jeans from the previous night and the same wrinkled dress shirt. He'd kicked off his old boots, and he felt the coldness of the floor under his feet. His head throbbed, but the fizz of Coke was like aspirin.

"Sorry it took me so long to get over here," Maggie went on. "The phone didn't wake me up. Weird."

He wondered if that was true or if she'd chosen to ignore his call.

The tiny Chinese cop hopped off the counter onto her big block heels and sat at his dining room table. She wore drainpipe jeans and a tight red Aerosmith T-shirt that barely covered her stomach, despite the morning chill in the cottage. She acted as if nothing had changed between the two of them but, in fact, their relationship was strained. For years, she'd shown up with breakfast two or three times a week. He'd wake up and find her reading his newspaper, eating from her McDonald's bag.

It had been nearly two months now since she'd appeared in his kitchen. Two months since they'd pulled the plug on their brief, misguided affair.

"Long time, no see," he said.

"You act like it's been three years, boss. We're together every day."

"You know what I mean."

"I do, but my weekends have been busy lately, okay?"

"Okay."

He noticed that she didn't explain what she'd been doing, and he didn't ask. He suspected she was seeing someone new and didn't want him to know.

"So who's the girl?" Maggie asked. She gestured into the living room as she chewed on hash browns. The door to the smallest bedroom in the cottage, which was in the corner facing the street, was closed. Cat had spent the remainder of the night in one of the twin beds there.

"I peeked inside when I got here," Maggie went on. "She was asleep."

"So was I."

"Yeah, well, I didn't wake you up, did I?" She added pointedly, "Not anymore."

"Mags."

"I know, we said we weren't going to talk about it. Pretend like nothing ever happened. Zip my lips." She pulled a red-tipped fingernail across her bright lips and winked at him. It was a joke, but with Maggie there was usually a dagger behind her jokes. "Anyway, she's pretty. Who is she?"

"Her name's Cat Mateo."

Maggie had a near-perfect memory for details and she didn't hesitate to pull the name out of her brain. "Mateo?" she asked. "As in Michaela Mateo? Is there a connection?"

"Her daughter," Stride said. "Cat was just a kid back then."

"I remember. Well, that explains the pretty part. She's got good genes."

"Yes, she does."

"At least on her mother's side. I don't even want to think about what little pieces of Marty Gamble are swimming around inside her."

Stride frowned at the reminder. Marty Gamble was Catalina's father and Michaela's ex-husband. Cat was the only good thing to come out of their violent relationship. Stride wanted to believe that Marty had left no imprint on the teenage girl in the corner bedroom, but bad seeds had a way of spreading like weeds.

Maggie watched his face with concern. "Is this going to be a problem for you, boss?"

"No, why should it?"

She rolled her eyes. "Because I was there. Because I know you."

That was true. Maggie probably knew Stride better than he knew himself. She probably knew him better than Serena, even though he and Serena had shared a bed for most of the past three years. Stride and Maggie had been partners for well over a decade. When he'd first met her, she was a book-smart police grad, with a stiffness born of her childhood in China. She'd done a turnaround over the years, developing a sassy mouth and a taste for hot clothes. She was the size of a doll, short and skinny, with golden skin, a diamond stud in her bottle-cap nose, and a bowl haircut that looked like a mop. She'd dyed her hair as red as an Easter egg a few months earlier, but her hair was black again now, hanging over her eyes. As he watched, she blew her bangs off her forehead.

Stride was older than his partner. He was knocking on the door of fifty, and Maggie was staring at forty. Age didn't matter. She'd had a crush on Stride ever since she met him, through his first marriage to Cindy and then his love affair with Serena, years after Cindy's death. It was a crush that should have stayed nothing more than a crush, but sometimes life was messy.

Five months ago, they'd made love. Neither one of them had meant for it to happen; it was a product of desperate times. The consequences had rippled through all of their lives like a rogue wave. His life. Maggie's life. Serena's life.

"So what's Cat's story?" Maggie asked.

He explained what the girl had told him in the middle of the night. "She thinks she's being stalked," he concluded.

"Do you believe her?"

"I told her I'd look into it."

Maggie stared at him over the steamy top of her coffee cup. "Sounds like a job for Guppo, boss. Or one of the street cops. Not you."

"This is personal, not official," Stride told her. "She came to me for help."

"So what are you going to do?"

"I want to have Steve Garske check her out and make sure she's okay. Then I'll drop in on the *Charles Frederick* and see what I can find out about this party last night. Maybe someone saw something."

"You want me to come with you?"

"Actually, I was hoping you could run a background check. Cat's still a minor. I know she had legal guardians back then, so where's she supposed to be living? Has she had any arrests? I'd like anything you can find."

"You don't trust her."

"I didn't say that. I just want to know what's going on in her life and how she wound up here."

"She's a sixteen-year-old hooker, boss. Hookers lie."

"I know that, Mags."

She didn't miss the edge in his voice, and she held up her hands. "Sorry, you just looked like you needed a reminder."

"Michaela had a sister," Stride went on, ignoring the jab. "Dory Mateo. I left her a message."

"Dory was a big-time user in those days," Maggie said. "I busted her a few times."

Stride shrugged. "I want to talk to her and see if she knows anything that might be useful. That's all."

"Meanwhile, what happens to Cat? She stays here with you? That's a really bad idea."

"That depends on what you find out. Until I know she's safe, I want to keep her close to me. If I put her somewhere, she'll run."

Maggie crumpled the empty McDonald's bag into a ball and rolled it around under her finger. "Listen, boss, I know you don't want to hear this, but I've seen this movie before. After Cindy died, you weren't always thinking straight. You made some big mistakes. Now you're sitting here all winter without Serena, and along comes a girl who reminds you of one of the worst tragedies of your career."

"So?"

"So this is lousy timing. I'm not sure you can be objective about Cat. You think I don't know what her mother's murder did to you?"

"This isn't about Michaela."

"You're right. What happened to her wasn't your fault, and neither is the fact that her daughter got dealt a lousy hand in life. Bad things happen, boss."

He didn't say anything, because she had him dead to rights. Maggie got up and cleaned the table and shoved the wastepaper into the garbage can under the sink. Her movements were quick and angry but she stopped herself and stared through the dark window, letting her frustration bleed away. She wandered back to the table and stood behind him. He felt her fingers massage his shoulders, and then she pulled them back.

"Have you talked to her?" she asked.

He knew who she meant. Serena.

"No."

"Why not?"

"And say what, Mags?"

"Blame me for what happened. That's the truth."

"No, it's not."

Maggie sat down next to him and stole a sip from his can of Coke. "You've got Guppo coordinating with Serena on the Margot Huizenfelt case. Why not do it yourself?"

"Because there's no Duluth connection."

"So? You don't need an excuse. You don't think she'd welcome your help?"

"No, I don't."

"Call her anyway."

"Look, Mags, I appreciate—" he began, but his words were cut off by a wild scream piercing the morning quiet of the cottage.

"*No no no no no no no no no no! Stop! Stop! Stop!*"

The noise was as shrill as the cry of an animal being torn apart, alive, in the next room.

It was Cat, wailing in terror.

Stride bolted out of his chair, spilling Coke in a river. He ran toward the closed bedroom door, with Maggie on his heels. When he hit the door with his shoulder, it flew around on its hinges, nearly separating from the frame. The little twin bed was on his right. The room was empty except for Cat, whose eyes were wide and fixed, her body convulsed as if electricity were rocketing through her veins. The blanket was on the floor. She flailed back and forth, swinging her hands as if tormented by a swarm of wasps.

"Cat!" he shouted, but she didn't hear him.

"*Cat!*"

He grabbed her wrists. She erupted with ferocious strength, dislodging him and knocking the pillows and nightstand lamp to the floor. He held her again, wrapping his arms around her body as she battled to get free. Her chest was bathed in sweat. Her heart beat crazily. He didn't think she was even awake. He whispered her name, and slowly, she ran out of struggle as he held her. Her cries died into whimpers. When he eased her back onto the bed, her eyes sank shut and her body shrank into her chest. Her arms and legs squeezed into a fetal position. He retrieved the blanket and slid it over her. She murmured into the mattress, but he didn't recognize what she said.

"Jesus," Maggie whispered.

He left the bedroom door open as they left. Outside, he spoke softly.

"Something's happening to that girl," he said. "She needs help."

"She needs a shrink." Maggie's face was grim.

"After what she's been through? Wouldn't you?"

"It's not just that."

Maggie held up something in front of his eyes. It was a butcher's knife, long and sharp, dangling from her fingers. He recognized it. It was *his* knife, taken from the wooden block in the kitchen.

"Where did you get that?" Stride asked.

"It was under her pillow. It fell when she fought back."

"Cat had it?" he asked.

"That's right. Did you know she took it?"

"No, she must have gotten up during the night."

"She could have killed you with this."

Stride didn't say anything. Maggie handed him the knife and he stared at the blade, which had a sharp edge as deadly as a machete. She was right. It would have cut him open and run him through nearly to his spine. If Cat had attacked him, he would be on the floor now, bleeding.

Dying.

"Be careful, boss," Maggie warned him. "I know you want to help, but you don't know what's going on in this girl's head. She's dangerous."

4

A battered silver Hyundai parked on Superior Street across from the clinic in Lakeside. Its tailpipe popped like a gunshot. A short woman with dark skin and bottle-blonde hair crossed toward the building in short, quick steps. She wore a down coat, torn blue jeans, and black boots with high heels. Her sunglasses shielded her eyes, and she kept her head down as she came inside the waiting room.

Stride recognized her and met her at the door. "Dory?"

Dory Mateo, Michaela's little sister, stripped off her sunglasses. Her eyes were bloodshot and tired; her skin was as worn as leather on old shoes. He knew she couldn't be much more than thirty, but she looked fifteen years older.

"I'm Jonathan Stride," he added.

"I remember you," she replied. "You look the same. More gray hair, though."

He smiled, because she was right, but he didn't need the reminder. Her own hair was cut in a messy bob, and he saw black roots. Stride was lean and strong and over six feet tall, which made him nearly a foot taller than Dory. The Mateo women were all small.

"Can we go outside?" she asked. "I need a smoke."

"Sure."

He followed her into the cold morning air. There was no sun, only slate clouds. It was Saturday morning and there was little traffic on the shop-lined street. Lakeside was a neighborhood on the north side of Duluth, a few blocks from the shore of Superior. It was quiet, without even a bar for the after-work crowd. If you wanted a drink, you went elsewhere.

Dory lit a cigarette and let out a raspy cough. "So is Cat in trouble?"

"Why would you say that?" he asked.

"A cop calls me, I figure she's in trouble." She eyed the clinic. "Is she okay? She's not hurt, is she?"

"She's fine, but I'm having a doctor check her out."

"What happened?"

"That's what I'm trying to figure out," Stride said. "When did you last see her?"

"I don't know. A couple weeks? She stayed with me for a few days but then she took off. She didn't say where she was going."

Dory's face twitched. Stride could see that she was self-medicating. They picked up women like her off the downtown streets every night. Frostbitten. High. Often naked and beaten.

"Cat says you rent a room at the Seaway," Stride said.

"Yeah, so?"

"Rough place."

"You think it's by choice? I don't want to be there. I had a house in the Hillside, but I lost it. Goddamn banks."

"You have a job?" Stride asked.

"Off and on. A girlfriend hooks me up for events in the Cities. You know, selling T-shirts and key chains and posters and shit like that for bands. I crash with her when I'm down there."

"T-shirts?" Stride said dubiously. He doubted the merchandise was limited to clothes. Whatever a concertgoer wanted, someone was there to supply it. "Nothing under the table?"

"Hey, what do you care? It's Minneapolis, not Duluth. Anyway, I had a decent job for a while. I answered phones for a construction company until I got laid off. Since then, I take what I can get." Dory threw her cigarette on the ground, where it smoldered. She shivered and zipped her coat.

"You want to go inside?" Stride asked.

"No, clinics freak me out."

He gestured at a bench in the dormant garden beside the medical complex. They sat next to each other, and Dory stared at the gray sky. The wind was cold, mussing Stride's hair. He couldn't see much of Michaela in Dory's face, unlike Cat's, which echoed her mother like a mirror. The ten years since Michaela's death had been hard on Dory, but she'd had a bad life long before her sister died. She'd been a chronic addict and runaway during her teen years, and Michaela had tried and failed to get Dory to reform herself.

Dory snuck a glance and saw him watching her. "You're thinking about my sister," she said.

"That's right."

"Michaela liked you," she said.

"I liked her, too."

"She talked about you a lot. Those pirate eyes of yours. She liked your eyes."

He said nothing.

"I still miss her. She never bailed on me, no matter how stupid I was. It's not her fault I was a fuckup. I didn't want her help. I didn't care about anything back then."

"How about now?" Stride asked. "Has anything changed?"

"I have ups and downs. Mostly downs lately."

"What about Cat?"

"Hey, I'd do anything for that girl. Anything. I don't want her to have the kind of life I've had."

He thought she was sincere, not just mouthing the words. Whatever her other failings in life, Dory loved her niece, but love wasn't necessarily enough to change anything. The two of them already shared the wrong kind of parallel lives. They'd both lost parents at a young age, and they'd both headed down bad roads as they got older.

"Do you know she's been hooking?" he asked.

Dory's face was stricken, but she nodded. "Yeah, I begged her not to do it. When I had money, I gave it to her. Not much, but it was something. Whenever she was with me, I made sure she stayed off the street, but I'm out of town a lot. And Cat, sometimes she just leaves and I don't know where she is."

"What about the couple that took her in? Her guardians?"

"Cat won't say anything, but it's not good there. I get it. It was the same for me bouncing in and out of foster homes as a teenager. I wish I could have taken her in myself back then, but you know what I was like. She was better off without me. I guess she still is."

"Did you try to get help for her?"

"Sure, I did. I took her to see Brooke at the shelter downtown. Brooke's a friend. I told Cat that if I wasn't around, and she didn't want to go home, she should go there. You know how it is, though. There are abusers everywhere who take advantage of these girls. And Cat, she's so beautiful. That makes it worse. She's a magnet with that face of hers."

"She won't stay beautiful for long," Stride said. "Not if she stays in this life."

"You think I don't know that? I had a sweet face, too. I know what I did to myself, you don't need to remind me."

"How long has Cat been heading downhill?" Stride asked.

Dory shrugged. "Two years, I suppose. Since she was fourteen. That's when she started running away. She'd show up at my door, or I'd come back to the city and find her sleeping in my bed at the Seaway."

"Did she say why?"

"No, but I figured the shit with Michaela and Marty was finally backing up on her. You can't go through something like that and not get screwed up. Sooner or later, she had to pay the price."

"How bad is it?"

"Hey, she's still a good kid, you know? She's not far gone like some of them. That's why I thought Brooke could help her, but you want the truth? I'm scared to death."

"Drugs?" Stride asked.

"Yeah, sometimes."

"Do you supply her?"

Dory leaped to her feet. He thought she was ready to slap him. "No! Never! You think I would do that to my own niece?"

"I had to ask."

"I never give her anything!"

"You're not clean, Dory," Stride said. "You think I can't tell?"

"Yeah, okay, it's been a shitty year, and I'm circling the drain. If that's what you want to hear, fine. But Cat? No way. She never got so much as one fucking pill from me."

He sat her down again. "I'm sorry," he said.

"I wouldn't trust me, either, but it's the truth."

"Who has their hooks into her, Dory? I need a name."

"I don't know. It could be anybody. Try Curt Dickes. Greasy little bastard. He's a janitor at one of the hotels in Canal Park. Word is, he's been fixing tourists up with the local girls. Cat mentioned him a couple times."

"I know Curt," Stride said.

He and his team knew most of the repeat offenders by name. Curt Dickes had been on his radar screen for ten years, ever since Stride caught him coming out the rear door of the Great Lakes Aquarium with half a dozen stolen stingray pups in a tank of water. The kid came from a big family of girls. He was the little brother who always got into trouble. He was mostly a petty thief and con artist, but if he'd expanded into prostitution, Stride needed to talk to him.

"Listen, Dory," Stride went on, "Cat thinks someone is trying to kill her. Did she talk to you about that?"

"Yeah, I didn't know whether to believe her."

"Why not?"

Dory hesitated. "Look, Cat's pretty scrambled upstairs. You and me, we both know why. Some days I don't know what's real with her and what's not. I'm not sure she knows herself."

"Can you think of a reason why anyone would want to hurt her?"

"Most guys don't need a reason to hurt street girls," Dory said. "You know that."

"I want to check on some things she told me, but I don't want her on her own when she's done. I'm afraid she'll take off again. Can you make sure she stays here until I get back?"

Dory looked at the clinic building and frowned, but she nodded. "Sure, whatever."

He stood up to leave but Dory tugged on his sleeve. "Hey, Stride, can I ask you something? Why are you doing this for Cat?"

"It's my job."

"Yeah? A lot of cops would dump a girl like her at county and forget about her. Is this because of what happened to Michaela?"

"Partly," he admitted.

Dory lit another cigarette and shook her head. "Michaela wasn't perfect, you know. I warned her about Marty. I said he'd keep coming after her. She didn't listen."

"It wasn't her fault," he said.

"Yeah, maybe not, but I blamed her for being so stupid. I blamed myself, too. If I'd had my head on straight, I could have done something to stop him. As it is . . ."

She closed her eyes. Her lips squeezed into a thin, pale line. He could see guilt licking at her insides like flames. He knew what that was like.

"I have to go," he said. "Believe me, Dory, I'll do whatever I can to protect Cat."

Dory opened her eyes. Her face darkened, not with anger, but with sadness. "Like you protected her mother?" she asked.

5

Stride lived in a place that never forgot the past.

Duluth was a small town masquerading as a big city, and small towns had long memories. Fewer than one hundred thousand souls lived inside its borders. It sounded like a lot, but for a native, it was nothing. When Stride dragged a middle-aged man to the drunk tank, there was a good chance it was someone who'd gone to Central High School with him. When he found a drowned child in the Lester River, he usually knew the parents. It made the job harder and the wounds more personal. He couldn't see the people as strangers. They were neighbors and friends.

Other towns tore down the past and built on top of it. Not Duluth. The terraced streets that rose off the shore of Lake Superior still boasted Victorian homes that dated to the early part of the previous century, when shipping and mining had made the city a glamour town. The wealth of that era was long gone but the houses remained, decaying like sorrowful echoes. The same was true of the Canal Park factories near the water, even after they'd been shuttered and converted into shops and restaurants for the tourists. You could still see old industrial names etched into the building stone, like DeWitt-Seitz and Paulucci.

When something did get torn down in Duluth, people complained. Where Stride lived, out on the sliver of land known as the Point, which divided the harbor from the wild waters of Superior, the shabby old lake homes were slowly disappearing, replaced by condos and hotels and new mansions. No one liked it. The house where he'd lived with his first wife for twenty years was gone. Every time he crossed the lift bridge over the shipping canal, he remembered the homes and the faces of the people who weren't there anymore.

He'd spent his whole life here. It was an extreme place, like a frontier outpost on the border of the Canadian wilderness. Tourists flooded the town for the brief, warm summers, but the endless winters defined the city and gave it its fierce beauty. For months the waves of the great lake made ice sculptures on the beach and the smaller lakes simply froze into roads for fishermen. Blizzards buried the empty highways, and Alberta winds swept snowdrifts up to the rooflines. Living here was harsh, but Stride couldn't live anywhere else. When he'd tried, he always came back. This was his home.

Locals boasted that Duluth toughened anyone who survived the winters, but Stride knew that it also made you old before your time. You couldn't fight the elements and not feel the damage to your body. You couldn't weather the storms and not get broken. There were other, less visible scars, too. The more time he spent in Duluth, the more he learned about keeping things inside. You hung on to the pain and locked it away. You stayed closed off to the world. After a while, it became a way of life.

Serena had complained that he kept every death harbored in his soul, and she wasn't wrong. He never forgot the people he'd left behind. To Stride, loss was like the parade of giant ore boats coming and going through the city's ship canal. Every boat arrived weighted down with black cargo, and every boat had a name.

Like the one in his mind dedicated to Michaela Mateo.

"Private party," the guard told Stride, holding up a beefy hand to stop him as he boarded the *Charles Frederick*.

Stride peeled back the flap of his black leather jacket, revealing his badge pinned to the inside pocket. "I have an invitation."

The guard swore under his breath. He looked like a tackle on the UMD football team, with a blond crew cut, no neck, and a huge torso bulked with muscle, not fat. He was young, probably not even twenty years old. He wore red nylon shorts despite the cold morning, holey sneakers, and a gray sweatshirt with a logo advertising Lowball Lenny's used cars.

"What's your name?" Stride asked.

"Marcus," the kid told him.

"You been here all night, Marcus?"

"Yes, sir."

"Tell me about the party."

"I don't know anything about that. They hired me to make sure nobody crashed. I stayed down here. All the fun was upstairs."

"Who hired you?" Stride asked.

Marcus pointed to his sweatshirt. "Lowball Lenny. You know, Leonard Keck. The car guy. This was some big celebration for his top salesmen. He brought them in from around the state."

"Was Lenny here himself?"

"Yeah, but he left early. He was gone by eleven o'clock."

"You saw him leave?"

"He walked right past me down the steps. Had his F-150 parked across the street."

Stride wasn't surprised to hear Leonard Keck's name in connection with the party. Lenny was one of the richest men in the northland, thanks to his string of Ford dealerships and his commercial real estate developments around the state. He'd served on the Duluth City Council for a decade. He was also a close personal friend of Stride's boss, Kyle Kinnick, the chief of police. The combination of money and political power, and a relationship with K-2, made Lenny believe he was bulletproof.

"Let me guess," Stride said. "The girls arrived later."

"Girls?"

Stride was getting impatient. "Marcus, you play for the Bulldogs, right?"

"I do, that's right."

"Your parents won't be too happy if your scholarship gets yanked, but that's what happens when you lie to the police. Understand? So don't play dumb with me. I know there were girls here."

Marcus's face reddened. "Okay, yeah, about a dozen girls showed up before midnight. Some guy brought them in a van."

"Who?"

"He was a little guy, skinny, with Hitler hair. Lots of cologne."

Stride nodded. The description sounded like Curt Dickes.

"I'm interested in one girl in particular. Small, Hispanic, brown hair and eyes, very attractive."

"Yeah, I remember a girl like that," Marcus admitted. "She was hard to miss."

"When did she leave?"

"I don't know. I didn't see her."

"Were you here all night?" Stride asked.

"Well, I grabbed a nap after midnight," Marcus admitted. "I figured all the guys were busy with the girls upstairs, and I had a tough practice yesterday."

"Where'd you go?"

"There are beds in the crew quarters on the stern. The party was on the other end."

"Did you see or hear anything?"

"Nah, I crashed. I sleep like the dead. I set my phone to get up in twenty minutes, but I blew through the alarm. I was gone for an hour." He looked nervous. "Don't tell anybody, okay?"

"I better not find out you were with one of the girls, Marcus," Stride said.

The kid shook his head. "I wasn't. No way. I got a girlfriend, sir, and she'd rip me a new one if I messed around."

"Good."

Stride left Marcus and took the stairs to the main deck. He stood alone outside, surrounded by the long expanse of red steel. The *Frederick* was small compared to the thousand-foot freighters that now traversed the Great Lakes, but it was still an imposing boat. He shoved his hands in the pockets of his jacket and followed the starboard railing toward the fantail, where Cat said she'd run from her pursuer. Puddles of melted snow gathered on the metal deck. Cold wind swirled off the lake.

At the stern, where the massive anchor chain slipped into the water, he saw no ice choking the channel, but the water temperature could be no more than forty degrees. He imagined Cat throwing herself toward the canal. He knew what that long second felt like before the frigid impact. He'd gone off the side of the Blatnik Bridge between Duluth and Superior the previous year during a police chase and nearly died of the fall. Panic attacks had dogged him for months. Even now, the height made him dizzy.

He examined the channel. Near the pedestrian bridge, he spotted something caught on one of the wooden posts where pleasure boats tied up during the summer. It swished and eddied with the movement of the waves. When he squinted, he saw what looked like flowers opening and closing on a sodden mass of fabric. It looked like a girl's dress.

Cat's dress. She'd been in the water, just like she said.

Stride backtracked the length of the boat. He reached the multistory superstructure of the bridge, and the door to the guest quarters was open. He heard laughter somewhere above him. He followed two flights of steps to an elegant half-moon-shaped lounge. He found half a dozen men inside, drinking whiskey from crystal tumblers and playing cards. Once upon a time, rich men had stayed here. Steel company presidents. Army generals. Congressmen. Now boys who made too much money came here to pretend to be their fathers.

One of the men had a gauze pad taped to his forehead under messy blond bangs. The man, who was well dressed and in his midthirties, sprang up as Stride walked in. "Who the hell are you?"

"Police," Stride said.

The laughter stopped, like switching off a record player. The car dealers clamped their mouths shut in nervous silence. The man with the bandage adopted a showroom face. He grinned and finished his drink, as if the arrival of a cop were nothing more than a chance to make a sale.

"Always a pleasure to meet one of Duluth's finest," he said. "How can we help you?"

Stride pointed a finger at the man. "Let's talk."

The man with the bangs spread his arms wide, pleasant and helpful. "Sure, whatever. Let's get some fresh air. Another gorgeous Duluth morning out there. Guys, don't look at my cards."

They exited the lounge onto the landing of the upper deck. The car salesman leaned his elbows on the white railing and lit a cigarette. "So what's up, Officer?" he asked. "Why the little visit?"

"Lieutenant," Stride corrected him. "I hear there was a party on the boat last night."

He saw a flicker of concern in the man's easygoing face. It wasn't hard to imagine what he was thinking. *The girl talked.* He was debating in his head whether to shut up, lie, or confess.

"Yes, it's our annual sales award banquet," the man said, with a false air of surprise. "I'm the top salesman at Keck Ford in Warroad. Conrad Carter, that's me. You need a new vehicle, Lieutenant?"

"Where'd you get that wound on your forehead?" Stride asked, pointing at the bandage.

"I slipped. Banged my head. Footing's pretty treacherous on this old boat."

"I heard that a girl hit you," Stride said.

"Yeah? Where did you hear that?"

"She told me."

"Someone told you that? No, it's not true. Besides, if someone knocked me in the head, that would make me a victim, wouldn't it? I'd be the one pressing charges, and I'm not. So what's the problem?"

"She was sixteen," Stride said.

The car salesman's face froze in dismay. "Sixteen? Really? Well, you've definitely been getting some bad information, Lieutenant."

"I know there were girls here last night, Mr. Carter," Stride said.

"Okay, sure, some ladies decided to join us. What's a party without female companionship?"

"Paid companionship?"

Conrad blew smoke from his mouth and crossed his heart with spread fingers. "You mean prostitutes? No, no, no, Lieutenant. There was no money changing hands here. Definitely not. If you have good-looking guys and free booze, you can always find women who like to have fun."

"Where did the girls come from?" Stride asked. "Who knew they were going to be here?"

"I really have no idea. Party planning's not my thing. Maybe some-one spread the word at the bars downtown. Maybe there was a flyer on the bulletin board at UMD. Word travels fast."

"Did you talk to Curt Dickes?"

Conrad smiled. "Curt who?"

"He brought the girls."

"I wouldn't know anything about that."

"So who would?" Stride asked. "Are you saying Mr. Keck arranged everything? I'll be happy to tell him you said so."

"That's not what I mean," Conrad replied quickly. "Don't put words in my mouth."

"Then let's try this again. Who arranged for the girls?"

Conrad drummed his fingers on the railing. He squinted over Stride's shoulder at the lake. "You know, Lieutenant, I think I've said enough."

"You know which girl I'm talking about," Stride said. "Young, pretty, Hispanic. She was here. She hit you."

"If this girl was here, and she was underage, then she faked her way on board. Nobody wants kids at a party like this. It kills the mood, you know? As for me, I never saw her and I never touched her."

"You never solicited anal sex from her? Because she says you did, and that's when she knocked you out with her boot. Right there, on your forehead."

Conrad threw his cigarette onto the deck and stamped it under his foot. "I told you we're done, Lieutenant," he said coldly.

"Someone was waiting for this girl outside the ship, Mr. Carter. She says he tried to kill her."

"*Kill* her?" he said. "That sounds pretty crazy to me."

"Did you see or hear anything?"

"No, I didn't, and I think you better consider the source. A sixteen-year-old girl crashes a party to get some free drinks? And then starts throwing around wild accusations? If you ask me, she's running some kind of scam."

"A scam?"

Conrad gestured toward the men in the lounge. "That's right. My friends and I, we're successful, we've got money. I don't need to tell you how much money Lowball has. A street girl looks at that and thinks, 'How can I get some of that for me?' So maybe she figures she can blackmail somebody."

"Is that what happened?" Stride asked.

"Nothing happened, Lieutenant," Conrad replied. "Nothing at all. I already told you. Whoever this girl is, she's a liar. You can't trust a word she says."

6

As Stride descended into the cargo holds, his boots made a hollow echo on the iron grid of the stairwell. Wire-encased lights strung along the hull of the ship illuminated the huge space. Gray riveted walls rose to the high ceilings above him, and moisture squeezed through the hatches overhead and dripped to the steel floor like music. He smelled closed-in dankness that had gathered over the winter months.

He'd been on ships like this throughout his life. Access to international waters through the Great Lakes and the Saint Lawrence Seaway sometimes meant that smugglers tried to ferry illegal cargo via the giant freighters. Drugs. Weapons. Even people—usually desperate immigrants bought and sold by human traffickers. Over the years, investigations in tandem with the FBI and Homeland Security had taken him onto the water many times.

His own experience with the ore boats went back to his childhood. His father had worked as a seaman and had often taken Stride aboard with him when he was in port. Stride had been five years old the first time, awed by the boat's vast size. The ships had never completely lost their magic for him. There were days when Stride thought he would have been happier here on the boats than he was with the police. Then again, there were also days when he remembered what the lake had taken from him. A December wave on Superior had snatched his father into the sea, leaving him and his mother alone. The loss had broken his mother's spirit, and for himself, it had been the first loss of many to follow. That was one of the reasons he lived on the Point, to be closer to the ghosts of Superior.

From nowhere, a rat, alarmed by his presence, scampered into a pile of wooden beams. He had no idea how a rat could cross from the land to the ship, but rats were smart. They always found a way, and there were plenty of hiding places down here. He saw plywood walls throughout the massive hold that had been used to create a Halloween maze for children. Posters about Minnesota shipping and mining were covered in plastic and stacked in piles, ready to be unveiled for the tourist season. Tools and machines lay scattered like debris.

In the light, he could see to make his way, but for Cat, being here in total blackness would have been terrifying.

She'd been here. Just like she said.

Directly in his path, he saw the yellow forklift where she'd hidden. He stepped through standing water to get a closer look, and in one of the puddles he spotted a metallic glint reflecting off the light overhead. He squatted and used two fingers to extract a six-inch knife with an onyx handle from the water. He held it up by the hilt and examined it, then deposited it in a plastic evidence bag from his pocket.

Everything on the boat backed up Cat's story, despite Conrad Carter's denials. She'd struck the man who wanted to violate her. She'd dropped a knife in the cargo hold as she charged her pursuer, and then she'd fled into the water to escape.

He also thought: *A knife.*

This was the second time he'd found a knife connected to Cat. When he'd confronted her about taking a knife from his kitchen, she said it was for protection. In the places she went, in the things she did, her life was always at risk. That was true, but it still felt wrong to him. He didn't like the idea of Cat obsessing over knives. She should have been terrified of knives; she should have associated them with blood and evil. She should never have wanted to hold one in her hands.

Ten years ago, her father had stabbed her mother to death while Cat hid in the frozen night outside.

"So how are you?" Dory asked.

Cat didn't answer. Her mind was reeling. She smelled the acrid smoke of Dory's cigarette. Her aunt smoked cheap Indian cigarettes from Arkansas. They were strong, like road tar. She hadn't smoked in weeks, but she wanted one between her lips now. "Can you spare a cig?"

Dory looked at her strangely, but she thwacked the pack on her palm. The ivory tip of one of the cigarettes nudged out of the box. Cat slid it into her hand and rubbed it between her thumb and forefinger. She put the unlit cigarette in her mouth, and her fingers trembled. Dory offered her a match, but Cat shook her head.

"What is it?" Dory asked. "What's going on?"

Cat didn't want to say anything. Not now. Not to Dory. "Nothing."

"You know, you could have called me. I would have come to get you. I'm here for you, baby."

"I didn't want to put you in the middle of this."

"The middle of what?"

Cat shrugged. "Whatever's happening to me. If somebody keeps coming after me, who knows, maybe they go after you, too. I don't want that."

Dory looked away. Cat could see in her aunt's face that she didn't believe her. It was drugs. Or it was a lie. "You and me, we don't need anybody's help," Dory said. "I won't let anyone hurt you. Didn't I promise you that?"

"Not this time."

Dory bit her lip, annoyed. Cat didn't mean to hurt her feelings, but she had open eyes about her aunt. Dory wasn't strong. She was in over her head. She was like a figurine riddled with cracks, ready to break apart if the ground shook under her feet.

"Who is this guy you're afraid of?" Dory asked.

"I don't know."

"Did you do something?"

"Like what?"

"Whatever. Steal something you shouldn't. Fuck somebody you shouldn't."

"I didn't do anything!" Cat insisted, eyes blazing.

"Except you said you don't know, right? So maybe you did. You should think about it."

"I have."

"I'm just saying. Everybody does things they regret, huh? Everybody makes mistakes they wish they could take back. I'd cut out my heart to go back and do things right."

"You think I wouldn't? But not this time. This one's not about me."

"Okay." Dory reached over and stroked Cat's hair, the way a mother would. "The doctor, he checked you out? You're okay?"

Cat eyed the street. She said nothing. She told herself she wouldn't cry.

"The doctor?" Dory repeated.

"Yeah, sure. I'm fine."

"You don't look fine."

"I'm okay, can we drop it?"

"Whatever you say."

Dory tossed a butt into the frosty grass. Cat took the unlit cigarette out of her mouth and handed it back to her aunt, who slid it between her teeth and lit it.

"You don't have to stay here with me," Cat said.

"I told Stride I would. He was afraid you'd run."

"I won't."

"Yeah, well. I'll stay anyway."

Cat wished Dory would go. She wanted to be alone. Stride was right, though; she might run. Sometimes it wasn't even a conscious thought. When she stayed in one place too long, she got claustrophobic, like she was in a box and had to get out before she ran out of air.

"Why Stride?" Dory asked. "Why'd you go to his place? You don't know him."

"Mother liked him."

"That doesn't mean anything. She liked your father, too. She didn't see who he really was until it was too late. A fucking beast, that was Marty."

Cat frowned. "Stop that. Don't talk like that."

"Yeah, I know. Nothing bad about Marty. Jesus, Catalina." Dory grazed the chain on Cat's neck with the back of her hand and Cat shrank from her. Her aunt's face looked sunken, almost gray. "You think it's so smart going to a cop?"

"I trust him."

"Cops are trouble. I don't care what he tells you. You always have to watch what you say, huh?"

"He's trying to help me."

Dory shook her head. She looked like she wanted to say more, but she didn't. Cat felt bad. She reached out and put a hand on her aunt's leg. When she squeezed, she could feel bone, as if Dory were eroding under the weight of the world. *I'd cut out my heart to go back and do things right.*

"I thought about killing a man last night," Cat told her. "I almost did it."

Dory took the cigarette out of her mouth. Her eyes narrowed. "You?"

"It would have been so easy. It scared me."

Cat explained about the car salesman on the boat. What he wanted to do to her. How she hit him, how she held the knife and thought about plunging it into his body. Make him bleed. Make him die.

"Sounds like he deserved it," Dory said.

Cat shook her head. "No, it was me."

"You still carry a knife, huh?"

Cat's arm dropped to her calf, and her fingers slipped inside the leather of her boot. She'd found a knife inside a drawer when Dr. Steve left the room. The handle was stainless steel, cool against her skin. The blade was sharp and open, so she'd wrapped it in a piece of gauze.

"Yeah. Always."

"You know what they say about knives and guns," her aunt said.

"What?"

"You keep them around, sooner or later you find a way to use them."

Cat forced a hollow smile at Dory. She thought: *Vincent.*

7

"Don't make me."

"You're safe, Cat. You're with me. You trust me, remember? Tell me what you heard that night."

"I didn't hear anything."

"Cat, that isn't true, is it? You were there. You can't be free of the pain until you remember."

"There's nothing. It's blank. It's always been blank."

"Your mother."

"No."

"Your mother."

"No, please."

"Relax, Cat. It's safe. I'm here. No one can hurt you. When you wake up, you'll be at peace. Now tell me about your mother."

"Scr-screaming. She was screaming."

"Screaming what?"

"STOP STOP STOP STOP STOP STOP No no no no no no."

"More, Cat."

"No no no no. . . oh God. . . oh God. . ."

"What else did your mother say?"

"Please. . . I'm dying. . . I'm dying. . ."

"Your father was there, too. What did he say to her?"

"*Vincent, no. Don't make me.*"

"Your father, Cat. What did he say? You have to trust me. You have to do this to be free of the past."

"*He. . . he said. . .*"

"Tell me."

"*I'll kill you I'll kill you I'll kill you I'll kill you I'll kill you.*"

"Good. Tell me more."

"*You fucking bitch, this is what you deserve! You cheating whore!*"

"Go on, Cat. What happened next?"

"*Silence.*"

"I don't understand. Is it over?"

"*Silence.*"

"What's happening, Cat? You're still under the porch. What do you hear?"

"*Footsteps.*"

"Footsteps? Whose footsteps?"

"*Where's the girl?*"

"What? Who's talking?"

"*Where's the girl?*"

"I don't understand. Tell me what's going on, Cat."

"*Where's the girl?*"

"Cat? Come back to me, Cat."

"*I'll protect you. It's okay. I'll protect you.*"

"Who's talking, Cat?"

"*I'll protect you.*"

"Cat? What's happening? You're safe. Trust me, Cat, it's Vincent. Talk to me."

"*BANG.*"

"What's going on, Cat?"

"*Oh, no, no, no. He's dead. They're both dead. Oh, God.*"

"Your father?"

"*He killed him.*"

"What? Who?"

"*Sirens.*"

"Talk to me, Cat."

"*I'll protect you.*"

"Everything's okay. What's my name, Cat?"

"*Come out, it's okay.*"

"My name, Cat. Who am I?"

"*Stride. My name is Stride.*"

8

"So?" Maggie asked as Stride climbed into her yellow Avalanche, which was parked beside the ship.

Despite the frigid morning air, he lowered the window. He liked it cold. "Cat was there. She was on the boat."

Maggie nodded but otherwise didn't react. Her fingers drummed the steering wheel as Guns N' Roses played on the radio. It was a big truck for a little woman, and she needed blocks to reach the pedals. She drove insanely fast, and the streaks and grooves in the paint testified to numerous collisions. Sergeant Guppo had suggested that the truck be registered as a weapon with the Bureau of Criminal Apprehension in Saint Paul.

"Anybody see anything?" she asked.

"No, they were busy with the other girls."

"Whose party was it?"

"Leonard Keck."

Maggie stopped drumming. She clicked off the stereo and gave him a Billy Idol snarl with her upper lip. "Lowball Lenny? Seriously? That sucks. K-2 will want us treating him with kid gloves."

"Yeah, the story is that Lenny left before the girls arrived. Convenient, huh?"

"You think he hung around for the fun?"

Stride shrugged. "Everybody knows Lenny's a playboy. I saw a condom wrapper in the lounge on the upper deck. Who do you think gets the top floor in that party?"

"Okay, so what about Cat?"

He held up the evidence bag with the knife. "I found this down below."

"So you think this is legit? Someone really came after her last night?"

"I don't see any reason to think she's lying."

"It could be a random assault. If someone saw a bunch of girls boarding the ship, this guy might have waited to see who came outside. It doesn't mean anyone was targeting her specifically."

"That's true," Stride said, "except for the other incidents she told me about. What did you find out about Cat's background?"

Maggie didn't need notes. It was all in her brain. "Nothing much that you don't already know. Catalina Mateo, sixteen years old, daughter of Michaela Mateo and Marty Gamble, both deceased. Her mother had no living relatives other than her sister, Dory, who was deemed unfit to care for the girl. Her father's parents were alive, but were elderly. Custody went to a cousin of Marty's, William Green, and his wife, Sophie. They were named Cat's legal guardians and still are. They have a house in West Duluth near the Oneota Cemetery."

"What's the story on the Greens?"

"Sophie Green is a secretary in a real estate office in Superior. William Green does highway construction labor. We've had reports on him for minor stuff, fights, drunk and disorderly, the usual busts for someone who hangs out at Curly's Bar. I also found a couple arrests for him in Minneapolis in the last three years."

"For what?"

"Solicitation," Maggie said. "The most recent was a month ago."

"What about Cat?"

"It's what you would expect, boss. The girl is vulnerable. I talked to the principal at Denfeld, who says Cat is absent from school as much as she's there. Too bad, because the principal thinks she's smart as hell."

"Arrests?"

"Nothing yet, but don't kid yourself—she's spending a lot of time on the street. I described her to Guppo and he remembers seeing a girl like that in Lake Place Park where the homeless hang out. I also called Brooke at the shelter on First, and she says Cat is a regular. Guppo and Brooke both said the same thing. Sooner or later, something bad's going to happen to this girl."

"That's what I'm trying to stop," Stride said.

Maggie said nothing, but he watched her face turn sour.

"What's going on with you, Mags?" he asked. "You obviously don't like this girl. Why?"

"I don't know anything about her. Neither do you."

"She's the daughter of an old friend. She's a good kid in trouble. Do I need something more than that?"

Maggie shrugged. "Do whatever you want. You said it's personal, right? So it's none of my business."

"Except you're giving me the cold shoulder all of a sudden. It feels to me like this is about something else."

Her golden face swung toward him. "Meaning what?"

"You know what I'm talking about. Is this about Cat, or is it about you and me?"

"There's no you and me," she retorted. "We tried, we failed. End of story. We said we weren't going to talk about it anymore."

"Yeah, that's what we said."

Stride stared at his partner, whose fists were clenched around the steering wheel of the Avalanche. They'd been friends for years, as close as two people could be without being lovers. The trouble was, that had all changed. He knew things about her now that he was never meant to know. He knew about the birthmark on her upper thigh. He knew that she slept facedown in her pillow and somehow didn't suffocate. He knew that her ears got bright pink as she reached orgasm. Those were things he couldn't put back in a box. He couldn't will the knowledge out of his head.

Years earlier, his wife, Cindy, had warned him how easy it would be to break Maggie's heart like the porcelain pieces of a Chinese doll. He'd lived by that advice for years, but now he'd done what he always swore he never would. He'd gotten involved. He'd let it end badly. He'd wounded her in a way that no other man could.

She read his face and knew what he was thinking. "Spare me the sympathy. I'm a big girl."

"I know that."

"We fucked for, what, six weeks?"

He didn't answer her. She was trying to make their brief affair sound unimportant by swearing about it. She wanted to pretend there had never been an emotional bond between them, which wasn't true at all.

"We were good at the fucking part," she went on. "I liked it. Did you like it? Or was this all in my head?"

"Sure I did, but it's not about that."

"I know. Look, it happened by accident. We both blew it. We knew this was never going to work out, and it didn't. I don't regret giving it a try, but I know you do. I'm sorry I screwed up your life."

"I never said I regretted it."

"You didn't have to. Your poker face isn't as good as you think, not with me. Whenever we were in bed, Serena was there with us, and not in a fun way."

It wasn't really funny. They didn't laugh. He knew Maggie was right.

"So what now?" he asked.

"Now we move on. We go back to the way things were."

"Just like that?"

"I can if you can," she said.

"Okay."

"Okay. Done. Let's forget about it."

He didn't think anything was that easy.

"Are you seeing someone?" he asked.

"Does it matter?"

"I'm curious."

"Okay, yes, I'm seeing someone."

"Anybody I know?"

She sighed. "Fine. Remember Ken McCarty?"

"Sure. Is he back in town?"

"No, but we hooked up a couple weeks ago when he was here to get some evidence from the property room on a larceny case in Minneapolis. For now, it's just sex. Nobody knows about it, and whatever you do, do *not* tell Guppo. I'll never hear the end of it."

"Ken's pretty young, Mags," he said. It was a joke, but it was the wrong thing to say.

"Six years. He's six years younger. I tried older men and that didn't work out so well for me."

He acknowledged the jab but didn't poke back. He checked his watch and opened the door of the Avalanche. "I've got to pick up Cat at the clinic."

"Say hi to Steve."

"I will." Stride stepped down onto the street and looked back inside. He stared into the eyes of his best friend. "Can we really get past this? Are we good?"

Maggie shrugged. "Yeah, we're good."

But they weren't. He wasn't a fool.

9

"Well, well, if it isn't Jonathan Stride," Steve Garske announced, glancing up from the computer monitor in his examining room. He stripped his half-glasses off his face and eased his lanky frame backward on the rolling chair. "Usually, I need a crowbar to get you into my office. As long as you're here, how about you turn your head and cough?"

Stride chuckled. "You put on those gloves and I'm heading for the door."

"Uh-huh. You're overdue for your physical, buddy. Again. One of these times, you could save me the trouble of calling your assistant and scheduling an appointment for you."

"I can hardly wait."

"No, you can't, and you won't. We're both turning fifty soon. You know what that means. The big poke. Or as the joke goes in the medical biz, 'I told my doctor I didn't need a colonoscopy, and he told me to shove it up my ass.'"

"Funny."

Steve crossed his arms over his chest and gave Stride his best I'm-the-doctor frown. "I *will* see you here before summer, end of discussion. Got it?"

"Okay, boss."

Stride knew better than to argue with his friend.

Steve got up and stretched his arms over his head. He was able to lay his palms flat on the ceiling. At six feet five, Steve was one of the few men who towered over Stride. He was lean and casual, wearing a T-shirt and ratty jeans under his white coat. He walked with a slight stoop from a bad back. He had blond hair that needed a trim, and his pale skin was burnt red from a week in the sun. His nose had started to peel. Steve was a workaholic like Stride, but he allowed himself a seven-night cruise to the Caribbean twice a year.

"So how was Nassau?" Stride asked, pointing to Steve's T-shirt, which showed the sky bridge at the Atlantis Casino.

"Paradise. A week down there feels like a month. Time stands still. I really need to do a Kenny Chesney and move down there permanently. Play steel guitar in my swimsuit and get drunk on mai tais with the island girls. That's the life."

"You say that after every trip."

"I know, but this time it's different. This time I'm really going."

"You say that every year, too."

"All right, fine. I will live in cold, gray Duluth forever. I will be shoveling snow when I'm ninety-two. Happy? Anyway, you should come with me in the fall. A getaway would do you good."

"Maybe."

"When was your last vacation?"

"Every day in Duluth is a vacation," Stride replied.

"Uh-huh. Sure. This fall, buddy, clear your calendar."

Stride smiled and held up his hands in surrender. "Okay, okay."

He knew that Steve was right. He was overdue for a vacation, and Steve was probably his oldest friend. They were lifelong Duluth boys who'd met as teenagers in the mid-1970s while they were jumping off rocks into the deeps of the Lester River during a hot August afternoon. They'd bonded on late-night runs to the House of Donuts and down-and-back trips to the state fair on Labor Day before school started. That was a time when Stride still imagined he'd spend his life on the ore boats and Steve had a dream of making it big in Nashville. Their dreams didn't survive the end of high school, but their friendship did. They'd stayed in touch while Steve was in medical school, and by the time he'd opened a practice at a clinic in Duluth, Stride had signed on as his first patient.

Steve had been his doctor through difficult times. He'd seen Stride and his wife through Cindy's infertility treatments and then her cancer diagnosis and her swift, terrible death—a time in which Maggie and Steve were about the only people on the planet who kept Stride from sinking into a well of depression from which there was no escape. They still saw each other every few weeks to hang out, fish, hike, play Sara Evans albums, and get drunk on Miller Lite and bad memories. They both lived on the Point. They both loved country music, and Steve still played in a country band that did weekend concerts in dives all over the Iron Range. As men, they were completely different. Stride was closed-off and intense. Steve was as open to the whole world as an unbuttoned shirt and utterly unflappable. Even so, they shared the same passion for the place where they were born.

"Maggie says hi," Stride said.

"Uh-huh. Seems to me I haven't seen her big yellow tank parked outside your cottage lately. Am I right?"

"You're right."

"Her choice or yours?" he asked.

"Mutual."

"Yeah, well, that's no surprise. I love her, but I never did see the two of you together. Now Serena? That's another story. You should get that woman back in your life."

"When's the last time you had a date, Steve? You're like a priest doling out marital advice."

His friend crossed himself and sprinkled imaginary holy water. "It mattereth not, my child. Do as I say, not as I do. Remember, I may not have sprouted the Garske seed, but I come from a family of nine siblings and God knows how many cousins, so I've seen more affairs, fights, breakups, reunions, marriages, divorces, births, and deaths than you will ever see in your shrinking lifetime."

"Probably true."

Steve twisted the chair around and sat backward with his long legs jutting toward Stride. "Look, you messed up with Maggie. You nearly died going off that bridge. Your head wasn't screwed on straight. Serena will understand."

"I'm not so sure," Stride said.

"Are you planning to wait forever to talk to her? Are you that stubborn?"

"Probably."

"Well, you still love her, don't you?"

Stride frowned. "Is this inquisition going to last much longer? Because it feels like the colonoscopy has already started."

"Fair enough. I'm done meddling."

"Can we talk about Cat now?"

Steve waved a white paper on his desk. "Ask away. I had her sign a release for medical and psych records."

"Cat told me she'd seen you before. Is that true?"

Steve nodded. "I volunteer over at Brooke Hahne's shelter. I'm over there twice a month helping with the homeless and the street girls. I do physicals, screen for STDs, drugs tests, AIDS tests, the basic stuff. I saw Cat a couple of times last year. Nice kid. She doesn't have the streetwise attitude yet, not like some of them."

"So how is she?" Stride asked.

"Given what she's been through, she's actually not in bad shape. I've seen a lot worse. That won't last, though, unless she gets into a stable living environment. She's got a home, but she keeps running away. That has to stop."

"I'm talking to her legal guardians this afternoon. Did Cat give you any idea why she keeps bolting? Is something going on at home?"

"She wouldn't tell me. I asked, and she shut up. The good news is that she looks clean in terms of disease. No STDs despite her risky behavior. I'm running an AIDS test to be sure. Substance abuse doesn't appear to be extreme. She admits she's tried synthetics, but claims she hasn't done it in months. As for the harder stuff, she says no crack, no coke, no heroin, and I didn't see any track marks or scarring in her nasal tissues."

"She has nightmares," Stride told him. "Extremely severe ones. Possibly hallucinations, too. Could that be the synthetics playing with her head?"

"Possibly. I don't have the equipment here to test for it. If she's under the influence, sure, you can get hallucinations, tremors, seizures, extreme agitation, spikes in blood pressure, any of which comport with the girl you found in your closet last night. As I look at her now, I'd say it's not drug related, but I can't rule it out. Remember, I knew Michaela, too, so I know what Cat went through as a child. You'd have to figure nightmares come with the territory."

"Crazy as it sounds, I hope the stalking isn't a delusion," Stride said. "If it's real, then at least I can help this girl."

Steve reached across and took Stride's shoulder. "She's not a girl, buddy. Don't be naive. Cat's very much a woman. She's probably slept with more people in her young life than you have."

"That wouldn't be hard," Stride replied with a small smile.

"You know what I'm talking about."

"I do. What else can you tell me?"

"You spotted the malnourishment. She hasn't been eating well for weeks. Also, there are numerous old bruises on her legs and torso. She claims she was beaten up by another of the street girls several weeks ago, but it looks to me like there was more than one beating, and it goes back more than a few weeks."

"Like when she was home?" Stride asked.

"The injuries are consistent with abuse."

"That would explain her running away."

"Yes, it would," Steve said.

Stride frowned. He remembered the little girl in Michaela's backyard, and she deserved better. She deserved a different life. No matter what he'd said to Maggie, he also knew that it was his own fault.

"This one's not an ordinary case for you," Steve said. "I get it."

"You're right."

"So what are you going to do about her?"

"Legally, she belongs with the Greens. They're her guardians, but I want to find out what's going on in that house before I drop her back there. Dory's still not an option, and I'm not comfortable putting her in the hands of the child protection system until I know whether she's genuinely in danger."

"You may be taking on more responsibility than you realize, Jon. We've both seen kids like this. No matter what you do, Cat may run away again. Teenagers like her do stupid things, and sometimes they pay the price."

"I hear you, Steve. Really."

"I hope you do, because I was waiting to tell you the most important thing. It's urgent that she change her behavior immediately. No drugs, no drinking, no smoking, no fighting, and a better diet. I want her back in to see me this week. She and I have a lot to talk about."

Stride closed his eyes in frustration. He knew what Steve was going to say, but he asked anyway. "Tell me."

"Cat's pregnant," Steve said.

10

Cat's skin glistened as she emerged from the bathroom, wearing a silk robe that Serena had left behind. Her hair was wet. The gold chain around her neck sparkled as it dangled into the swell of her chest. Her body carried a floral smell of soap and shampoo that wafted through the cottage. She saw him on the leather sofa and smiled at him, and as it had before, the warmth in her smile made him melt. She planted herself next to him with her feet tucked underneath her body.

"Thank you," she said.

"For what?"

"For helping me."

Her head sank into his shoulder, as if they were father and daughter. Her familiarity unsettled him. It was too quick, too strong. She had invested her dreams in him in the space of a few hours, and he wasn't ready for it.

"Did Dr. Steve tell you?" she said, with a tiny frown. "I'm going to have a baby."

"He did."

"I suppose you think I should get an abortion."

The word sounded cold and jarring out of her lips. *Abortion.*

"I would never tell you that," Stride said, "but you're also very young to have a child of your own."

"I know. Mom was young, too. Not as young as me, but young."

"There's always adoption."

Cat shook her head. "Give up my child? I won't do that."

"Well, you still have a little time to think about those things. You're not far along. Right now you need to get healthy and stay healthy. That's the best thing you can do for your baby."

She looked up into his eyes. Her own eyes were big and brown. "Will you help me?"

"I'll do what I can, Cat." He added, "Do you have any idea who the baby's father is? Do you have a boyfriend?"

"No boyfriend," she said. "I think I know who it was, though. There was a guy a few weeks ago, and he had a problem with the condom. I remember his face, but I don't know his name. He was a tourist. I bet he wouldn't be happy to see me again."

"We can try to find him."

"I don't want to find him," Cat said.

"He could be forced to pay child support. That would help you."

"No, if he knows about it, he can take her away from me. I know who wins and loses, and girls like me always lose. He'd take her away, or he'd make the court take her away, and I want to keep her."

He heard steel in her voice that reminded him of Michaela. He liked her toughness, but he was a realist about the economic odds she faced. A street girl having a child rarely ended happily.

"I visited the ship," he told her. "I talked to the men at the party."

"Did anyone see who chased me?"

"No."

Her face fell. "Oh."

"I found your knife in the cargo hold where you lost it."

"That's good. See? It happened just like I said." She added, "Can I have my knife back?"

Stride shook his head. "I need to keep it as evidence."

"Oh. Sure. That's okay, I already—" She stopped.

"You already what?"

Cat shrugged. "Nothing."

Stride studied the teenager's face. She looked away. Her legs unfurled, and she pulled a foot nimbly into her hand and chipped red paint off her toenails. He eyed her boots on the floor. "Give it to me," he said.

"Huh?"

He got off the sofa and dug inside her boot. The first boot was empty. In the second, he found a medical knife, its blade swathed in gauze. He tightened his fingers around it and frowned at Cat, who grew teary. "You stole this at the clinic."

She bit her lip and nodded. "I'm sorry."

"I don't like the idea of you carrying a knife," he said.

"I already told you. It's for protection."

"Is that all it is?"

"Sure, what else?"

"Have you ever used it?"

Cat tugged her robe tighter across her body. "No! What are you saying?"

"I was wondering if you'd ever been with someone where you felt threatened."

"Not like that," she murmured, but teenagers were bad liars. She was hiding something. He sighed and sat down next to her again.

"Listen, Cat, if I'm going to find out who's stalking you, or if you're in any danger, I need to know what's really going on in your life. You have to tell me everything."

She nodded earnestly. "Sure, yes."

"You said this started three weeks ago with someone outside your house. Is that right?"

"Yes. Well, sort of."

"Did something else happen before then?" Stride asked.

"Not really. I'm not sure. The thing is, I heard that somebody was looking for me. One of the street girls, Brandy, told me about it. Brandy's a real head case. Crazy eyes. I saw her down near the graffiti graveyard and she cornered me before I could get away. She told me someone was asking around about me and I better watch out."

"Did she say who?"

"No, I figured she was just messing with me, you know? Then, a week later, I saw someone at the house. That's when I started to run."

"How can I find Brandy?" Stride asked.

"Talk to Curt. He knows where all the girls are."

"Curt Dickes?"

Cat nodded. "Yeah."

"You shouldn't hang out with him."

"Oh, Curt's not so bad. He's greasy but funny. When I need something, he helps me out."

"That's not the kind of help you need," Stride said.

"Yeah, I guess."

Cat climbed off the sofa and Stride gestured at the spare bedroom, where he'd left a few bags of new clothes from Target. "Why don't you go get dressed? I want to talk to the Greens and check out the area around your house. You can come with me."

Cat froze. She crouched in front of the sofa with her hands on his knees and shook her head frantically. "Don't make me go back there! Please, I don't want to!"

"I'll be with you," Stride said.

"No, just let me stay here. I'll be fine."

Stride watched the pleading in her face. It was as if he'd suggested putting her in a cage. He didn't tell her his real concern, which was that she would be gone when he returned. Without someone watching her, she would become a runaway again, lost somewhere in the wind.

"Okay, listen," he said. "There's a young woman house-sitting one of the mansions down the Point. Her name's Kim Dehne. I'll see if you can hang out with her while I'm gone."

"I don't need a babysitter."

"Kim's not a babysitter. I'd just feel better if you weren't alone. You'll like her."

Cat twirled her hair around her fingers. "Yeah, okay. Sure. Whatever."

"You leave home a lot," Stride added. "It's not safe to be on the streets by yourself. It puts you in dangerous situations. Why do you do it? Why don't you stay with the Greens?"

"I don't like it there."

"Are there problems?"

"Everybody's got problems."

Stride pointed at her bare calf, where her skin showed the fading colors of an old bruise. "Someone hit you. Where did you get that?"

"Brandy," she said.

"Why did she hurt you?"

"Because that's who she is."

"Does anybody else hurt you?" he asked.

Cat didn't answer him. She swiveled nervously on her knees and pulled a strand of hair through her pale lips. "Can I ask *you* something?"

"Sure," he said.

"Why are you alone?"

"That's a good question."

"You weren't alone when my mother was alive."

"No, I was married to a woman named Cindy," he said. "She was my high school sweetheart."

"What happened to her?"

"Cindy died of cancer."

"Sorry. It sucks to lose people."

"Yes, it does."

"What about that woman who was in the house this morning?"

"Maggie's my police partner," Stride explained.

"There's nobody else? How about that woman whose clothes you gave me? Serena."

Stride realized that Cat didn't miss much. "Serena and I aren't together right now."

"That's sad."

"It is what it is," he said.

Cat pushed off her knees and kissed him on the cheek. Her breath smelled of peppermint. He saw a small birthmark on her forehead, like a dimple. When she stared at him, he recognized her eyes from long ago, when she was a child, and it took him back to those days.

Bad days.

"You're looking at me funny," she said. "What is it? What do you see?"

"You look like your mother," he said.

It was January. Insanely cold—twenty degrees below zero. Stride felt the wind chewing like maggots at his face. Beside him, Michaela appeared unaffected. He wore a wool cap pulled down over his ears, but she wore no hat, and her straight black hair blew loosely into a bird's nest around her cheeks.

"He's back," Michaela told him. "Marty snuck into Catalina's bedroom last night after I was asleep. She won't say anything to me about it, but I know he was here."

Stride stared at the girl playing in the winter yard. She was bundled up in a white down coat that was so thick she could barely move her arms, and her pink scarf flew behind her as she chased a smattering of dead leaves. A stand of evergreens towered over her, and behind the trees, the red and green lights of antenna towers flashed like sentinels. He smelled smoke. Someone had built a wood fire. Below the porch, he spotted the tracks of deer and rabbits crinkling the fresh snow.

"Did you talk to her about it?" he asked.

Michaela's warm eyes never left her child. "All she does is giggle and say it's a secret. She doesn't understand. Marty brings her gifts and she hides them from me. What can I do? He's her father, and she still loves him."

"The protective order says he can't come near either of you," Stride said. "If he violates again, we can get him back behind bars."

"Don't you think he knows that?" Michaela asked. "He's careful. He's smart."

"If you see him, you call me."

"I never see him, but I know he's been here."

She didn't show fear, but he knew she was afraid. In the years Marty Gamble had spent in Michaela's life, he'd beaten her savagely on multiple occasions. The last incident had cost him a third-degree assault conviction, with a sentence of almost two years, but he'd spent only forty-five days behind bars before his release on probation. The dirty secret of criminal prosecutions was that it was hard to spend any real time in prison without killing someone or using a gun.

"You know what I'm going to tell you," Stride said. He'd encouraged her over and over to leave town. Run somewhere far away. Hide.

"Yes, and you know how I feel about it, Jonathan. I've worked like hell to make a life for me and Catalina these past six years. To have a home. I won't give it up because of him."

Stride wished she weren't so stubborn, but he knew how she felt. His own cottage on the Point, with Cindy, was a hundred-year-old matchbox, and nothing ever worked. The winter wind sailed through the cracks. The roof leaked. Mice ran underneath the pilings and gnawed through the walls. Even so, they wouldn't have lived anywhere else. Michaela felt the same way. She'd scraped together a down payment on a house that was barely larger than a trailer, in a section of the city known as the Antenna Farm. It was heavily wooded, with dirt roads, on the peak of a hill only blocks from the downtown streets. Crossing into the Antenna Farm was like driving into the rural badlands. There was no money there. Michaela and Cat slept in two tiny bedrooms and shared a single bathroom and shower. It didn't look like a dream, but for Michaela, that was exactly what it was. Her dream. Her escape.

Leaving would have been as bad as dying.

She put a cold hand on his face. She wasn't even wearing gloves. "You look tired, Jonathan. I haven't heard from you in weeks. I've been worried. Are you all right?"

"It's the long hours," he said. "Maggie and I have been working a home invasion case since before Christmas. We finally found the gun that killed the wife and recovered the stolen jewelry. It was an Asian gang member from the Cities. We got him off the streets for good. I'm sorry I've been out of touch, but I've been thinking about you."

"So have I. I saw Dr. Steve last week. I'm afraid I prattled on about you."

"I told Cindy that I was seeing you tonight. She said that you and Catalina should come for dinner soon."

Michaela smiled. "I'd like that. I would love to meet the woman who stole your heart."

When he said nothing, a cloud passed over Michaela's face, as if she realized she'd said the wrong thing. She covered her mouth with her hand. "I'm so sorry," she went on. "I didn't mean anything. Did you tell her that I . . . ?"

"No, of course not."

"Thank you. I'm embarrassed."

"You shouldn't be."

Michaela shivered in the cold for the first time. *"Catalina!"* she called from the porch. *"Come now, let's go inside."*

The girl pretended she didn't hear her mother calling. She fell on her back, making a snow angel. Her cheeks were pink and wet.

"Catalina!" Michaela called again testily. She shook her head. *"That child,"* she said to Stride.

"As stubborn as her mother," he replied.

Michaela laughed, and it made Stride wish that she laughed more often. He liked to see the sadness lift from her face, even briefly. She wasn't classically beautiful, but he found it impossible not to stare at her. She had dark chocolate eyes. Her nose was rounded and small. For her young age—she was only twenty-six—she already carried the weight of her past, like a smoke ring that never cleared. He could see the lingering effects of the ferocious beatings she'd endured. The scar on her forehead. The dent in her jaw where it had been broken. The wince of pain tightening her lips when she moved.

Her laughter melted, and she gripped the wobbly wooden railing of the porch. *"Marty is convinced you and I are having an affair,"* she said. *"I talked to his cousin Bill."*

"What did you tell him?"

"I told him no, of course, but Marty won't believe anything I say. Sooner or later, he'll get drunk and come back for me. You know that."

"If it would be better, I don't have to come here myself. I could send someone else to check in on you."

"It wouldn't matter. He thinks he owns me. Besides, I look forward to seeing you. So does Catalina."

"She's a sweetheart."

Michaela beamed, watching her child in the snow. The girl was now dancing like a ballerina around the outline of her angel. *"Sometimes I can't believe God gave her to me after all my mistakes. I led such a stupid life after I lost my parents. All the parties, all the drugs, all the bad boys. Back then, I thought I deserved the things that Marty did to me."*

"You didn't."

"Girls can be blind, Jonathan. I loved him. He was tough and hard. That was what I thought I wanted. When we had Catalina, I hoped he would grow up, and I guess he did, a little. He's good to her. It's me that he hates."

Stride said nothing. He saw no goodness at all in Marty Gamble. The man's chiseled face was emblazoned on his brain: a tattooed skinhead skull, square chin, thin, flattened nose. His eyes were blue marbles. He had scars on his knuckles. He wasn't tall, but he was buff from lifting weights and boxing at the Y. When he was drunk, his temper was like rocket fuel.

"Dory tells me I'm a fool," Michaela went on. "She knew he was a monster from the beginning. She would scream at him to stay away from me, and Marty just laughed at her. It's pretty sad when your drug-addict little sister has better judgment in men than you do. I wish I'd listened."

"This isn't your fault."

"Oh, some of it is my fault. We make our choices, and Marty was my choice. I have to live with that." Her face grew worried, and she added, "Dory sounded frantic when I talked to her yesterday. Worse than usual. I think Marty went to see her. He's probably not stupid enough to harm her, but I'm worried."

"I'll have Maggie talk to her."

"Thank you."

Michaela took his arm. It was a simple, warm gesture, but her closeness made him draw back. She knew she'd crossed a line, but before she could remove her hand, her fingers tightened into a vise around his coat. Her whole body stiffened like a wire.

"Jonathan," she said sharply.

He followed her eyes to the road. At the end of her rural lot, he saw the twin gleam of headlights in the darkness. The car lights shot toward the house, illuminating the two of them like escaped prisoners. Catalina, in the snow below the porch, stared curiously at the bright eyes.

"Get inside," Stride told Michaela.

Michaela ran down the porch steps and scooped the little girl into her arms. Catalina squealed in protest, but Michaela carried her inside, slamming the door of the little house behind her. Stride was alone. He marched down the long driveway, shielding his eyes. He drew his gun into his hand. Whoever was in the car let Stride get within twenty yards before lurching backward between the trees. The wheels roared and spun on the dirt. The driver leaned into the horn, blaring noise through the quiet night like a victory wail. By the time Stride bolted into the middle of the snow-rutted road, the car had disappeared. Even the taillights were gone.

He stood there, holding his gun, his other fist clenched, powerless.

When he returned to the house, Michaela stood on the porch again, blocking the door. Catalina was inside.

"It was him," she said.

"I couldn't see the car."

"It was him," she repeated.

He came close to her. Too close. "I really wish you'd leave town for a while, Michaela."

"And lose my job?" she said. "Lose my house? I won't let him make me run. You'll protect me, Jonathan. I have faith in you."

He felt her trust. Her faith was like an embrace. She believed in him.

Two days later, he stared down at her dead body, riddled with stab wounds, her blood like a lake. Marty's body lay sprawled beside her, a gun in his hand, with his bone and brains shot across the hardwood floor of the matchbox bedroom.

11

"Do you remember Marty Gamble?" Maggie asked.

Ken McCarty, who was naked on top of her, paused in his thrusting. His face screwed up like a dried apple and she felt him wither inside her. "Wow, you really pick odd times to talk about work," he said.

Maggie wrapped her legs around his backside and pulled him deeper. "You're right. Continue."

Ken launched into his rhythm with renewed vigor. His face reddened with effort as he shook the bed frame, but the more he labored, the more he shrank, until she couldn't even feel him between her thighs. Finally, in frustration, he withdrew and flopped over on his back beside her. His skin was damp with sweat. "Sorry."

"No biggie," Maggie said.

"Thanks for reminding me."

"Oops," she giggled. "That's not what I meant." She turned over on her side and reached between his legs to caress him. "Want me to work my magic?"

Her fingers kneaded and twisted as if she were working on bread dough, but the dough failed to rise.

"I better take a rain check," Ken said. "Either that or I need some blue pills. That would be a first."

"My fault."

"Don't worry about it. I like it better at night anyway. Hey, I caught a Bree Olson video on pay-per-view last week. There's a hot position I'd love to try. You game?"

"Always."

He kissed her, and they tongued back and forth. His hands roamed her body. "God, you're hot," he said.

"Even for an older woman?"

"Twentysomethings got nothing on you, babe."

Maggie grinned. She knew that Ken had had his share of younger girls over the years, and he probably still did. They'd only hooked up a couple of times. Even so, she was oddly pleased to think that he was watching porn when he wasn't with her, rather than bringing home a girl from a Dinkytown bar.

She also knew that if she did anything well, other than her job, it was sex. She was open to anything and always had been. Sex didn't really mean much to her, so she didn't care about crossing lines. She'd never put sex and love in the same equation, not until she'd finally slept with Stride, and that had been a huge mistake, right up there with the McDonald's McLean burger. A relationship with Ken, if it went that far, was safer. Wild sex. Lots of time apart. No pressure. The two hours between Duluth and Minneapolis felt like the right distance.

Ken rolled his naked body out of bed and pulled on his tighty-whities. He wasn't tall, but everyone was tall to Maggie. He had a sandy crew cut and the tough-as-nails bulky physique of a carb-loaded cop. His blond goatee was neatly trimmed, and he had an easy grin. He still had a young, carefree style, which she liked. He was thirty-four, but he could have been twenty-four, an adult who was happy to stay a kid.

He wandered to the window in his underwear. Maggie had a condominium on Superior Street above the Sheraton Hotel, with a million-dollar view. Most of the other owners around her were rich doctors from St. Mary's and St. Luke's, who had mansions in the Cit-ies and used the condos as their home base when they breezed into town to do surgery. Maggie was the only cop in the building. She'd inherited money after her entrepreneur husband was murdered, and she didn't need to work anymore. However, she couldn't imagine living like a socialite, getting her nails done and pretending to care about the Symphony Ball. She was a cop and would always be a cop. It also meant she kept working with Stride.

"So do you?" she asked.

"Do I what?"

"Remember Marty Gamble."

Ken turned around and scratched his beard. "Wasn't he the skinhead who stabbed his wife and then blew his head off?"

"That's him."

"That was a long time ago. He was a brutal son of a bitch. We all knew him. Why, what's going on?"

She explained about Cat and Stride. "I think he's taking on more than he should. I don't trust this girl."

"Gamble's dead. What does this have to do with his daughter?"

"The girl's obsessed with knives," she said. "Just like Daddy."

"You think she's violent?"

"I don't know, but the whole thing feels wrong to me."

Ken wandered back to the bed. He sat down and played with her nipple, and she started to get horny. It made her think about peeling off his tighty-whities and trying again.

"If your instincts say something's wrong, then something's probably wrong," he said. "Trust your gut."

"Thanks."

Before she could pounce on him and straddle his groin, he bounced off the bed. "So what should we do this afternoon? You want to go down and hit the casino? I like the idea of a rich girlfriend staking me at blackjack. I can go for this whole boy-toy thing."

"Listen, about this afternoon," she said.

Ken groaned with displeasure. "Oh, shit, tell me you're not busy, Maggie. It's Saturday. It's play day."

"You surprised me. I'm behind on my paperwork. I've got to go into the office for a few hours."

"How many hours?" he asked.

"Three, max, I promise. Four at the outside. Okay? We can hook up tonight."

"Fine, I'll go to the casino and spend my own money. Nickel slots and free Mountain Dew. Are you happy?"

"You want some cash?"

Ken laughed. "Please, I am an old-fashioned chauvinist male. I refuse to sponge off a woman unless she is physically with me."

"Suit yourself," she said.

She came up and pressed her body against him. She worked her hands inside his underwear and squeezed his cheeks like she was testing melons at the farmers' market. "You going to give me any hints about this position you want to try? Because chances are I've tried it."

"Well then, you can be the teacher, and I can be the naughty student."

She slapped his ass and pulled out her hands. "What do you want for dinner? How about T-bones right here? Au gratins, cabernet, candlelight."

"Now you're talking."

She sat down on the bed and pulled on her black socks. He watched her with hungry eyes, and she liked the fact that he didn't hide his desire for her.

"There's nothing sexier than a woman wearing nothing but socks," he said.

"Funny."

"No, it's true. Besides, socks keep my shoulders warm."

She giggled. She didn't giggle very often, but she found herself doing it a lot with Ken. Maybe it was true that dating a younger man was the secret to the fountain of youth. Her lips turned upward, and her white teeth beamed.

"That's what I like to see," he said. "That smile."

"Sorry. I've been distracted this morning."

"I could tell."

"It's this thing with Stride," she said.

Ken frowned, and Maggie knew she'd put her foot in her mouth by mentioning Stride's name. They were new lovers, but they were old friends. It was hard to keep secrets from someone who knew you well. She'd been the one to hire him away from his job as a UMD campus cop; she'd trained him, supervised him, gone on calls with him, and complained to him. When he'd transferred to the Minneapolis police four years earlier, she'd been disappointed, because she liked spilling her guts to Ken. There had always been a hint of sexual tension between them, but it had never amounted to anything until now. They both knew why.

"It's always about Stride, isn't it?" he asked. "Nothing ever changes with you."

"That's not what this is."

"Yeah?" He wasn't convinced.

"Really, it's not. Not anymore."

"Sure."

She couldn't pretend that she'd never had feelings for Stride. It was an open secret in the department, and she'd shared a lot—probably too much—with Ken when he'd worked with her in Duluth. However, she hadn't told him about her short-lived affair with Stride over the winter. No one knew about that.

No one except Serena.

"Does Stride know about us?" Ken asked.

"I told him this morning."

"What did he say?"

"He asked who you were. He didn't remember you."

Ken looked crestfallen, but then his eyes narrowed as he studied Maggie's face and realized she was joking. "You lying bitch."

She laughed. "Sorry. He gave us his blessing. He said we were two crazy kids, and he said to make sure we were using protection."

"Right."

Maggie continued getting dressed. She squeezed herself into tight jeans and let him admire her, topless, before reaching for a T-shirt. Not that there was much to admire upstairs. Her breasts weren't exactly mountains. She slipped her shirt over her head and tucked it in. Her hair was mussed, and she blew her bangs out of her eyes. Ken came over and fondled her bowl haircut.

"Red, huh? I can't picture it."

"Where did you hear about that?" she asked.

"I talked to Guppo. He said it was a sight to behold."

"I bet he did. He told me I looked like a felt-tip marker. Guess I'll stick with black."

"Oh, I don't know. Red's sexy. You must have been hot."

"Thank you." She kissed him, but then her eyes widened in horror. "Holy crap! You didn't tell Guppo about us, did you?"

"Hey, I was tempted, but no. I think he probably guessed, though. I can't keep it off my face when I'm having sex."

"You can't keep it off my face," Maggie replied, winking. She studied him in his underwear and added, "I don't know exactly what we're doing here, but I kinda like it."

"Me too. I had a crush on you in the old days, you know."

"So why did you never make a move on me?"

"Are you kidding? Back then, you scared the shit out of me. You and your Terminator sunglasses and your snarky mouth. I figured you must be some kind of dominatrix in bed."

"And now?"

"Now I'm into that," he said.

She strapped herself into her boots, which really did look like something a dominatrix would wear. She grabbed sunglasses from her nightstand and slid them over her face with both hands.

"Ah'll be back," she rumbled.

"Just like Arnold," he said.

She headed for the door, but before she could leave, he called after her. "Hey, Maggie?"

"Yeah?"

"You want to tell me where you're really going?"

She took off her sunglasses and acted surprised, but he'd caught her. "What do you mean?"

"Maggie Bei never got behind on paperwork in her life," Ken replied coolly. "What are you up to?"

He was a cop, and you can't fool a cop.

"Okay, okay, I want to dig around into this girl a little bit more. She hangs out at the shelter downtown. I'm meeting Brooke Hahne to see what she can tell me."

"Sounds like I better not count on steaks and sex tonight."

"It depends on what I find. It's probably nothing."

"You could have told me the truth. Why is this so important to you?"

Maggie frowned. It bothered her to say what she was really thinking. "Forty-one times. That's what I keep thinking about. That's what scares me."

Ken's face scrunched up in confusion. "What?"

"Forty-one times. The medical examiner counted the stab wounds during the autopsy of Michaela Mateo. I remember the number. Marty Gamble stabbed his ex-wife forty-one times while he was killing her."

"It was horrible, but what's your point?"

"My point is, this girl heard the whole thing. She hid under the porch, listening to her father stab her mother, listening to her mother screaming, listening to her father when he took a gun and blew his own head off. And now that same girl is staying *in Stride's house.* I don't like it." She put her sunglasses back on and shook her head. "Forty-one times. What does that do to a kid?"

12

Stride sat with Cat's legal guardians, William and Sophie Green, in a tiny kitchen decorated with vinyl wallpaper that was printed with daisies. The wallpaper had bubbles at the seams. The closed-in air of the room smelled like cigarette smoke and curdled cream. He saw a neon NASCAR clock, with a picture of Dale Earnhardt, hanging over the refrigerator, but it had stopped, and it still showed the time as 9:07. A religious calendar, with an illustration of Jesus spreading his arms on a cliff top, was opened to February, not April.

"Is that your Coupe de Ville in the driveway?" Stride asked William Green.

Green swigged a can of Budweiser and wiped his mouth. He looked surprised by the question. "Yeah. It's an '84. I've been overhauling it for months. Scrounging for parts."

"You're a car guy, huh?"

"That's right. I fix 'em up and sell 'em. It's a hobby."

"You go to the auto show in Minneapolis?"

Green shot an uncomfortable glance at his wife, Sophie, who stared at the kitchen table. "Most years, sure," he said.

"That was a month ago, right?" Stride asked. "Were you there?"

"Yeah, I was. So what?"

The man's dark eyes flamed with anger. His wife looked oblivious to the undercurrent in the conversation, but Stride wanted Green to know that he was aware of the man's arrest for solicitation the previous month.

"What is this about?" Sophie asked in a thin voice.

She had wispy auburn hair and a plain face with overdone makeup. She wore a floral dress suitable for church and had a cross on a slim chain around her neck. A purplish bruise peeked out from the half sleeve on her upper arm.

"I'm trying to find out exactly what was going on that weekend," Stride explained. "Cat says someone chased her outside the house on Saturday night."

"Chased her? Who?"

"I don't know yet. Do you remember seeing any strangers in the neighborhood in the last few weeks?"

Sophie shook her head. "No."

"Were you and Cat the only ones in the house while your husband was away?"

William Green put down his can of beer. "What kind of question is that?"

"I want to know if anyone else was around who might be a witness," Stride said.

"It was the just the two of us," Sophie replied, "but by Sunday morning, Cat was gone. I wanted to take her with me to church, but her room was empty."

"Weren't you concerned?"

"I—I called her cell phone. She said she was staying with a friend. She didn't say anything to me about someone stalking her."

Sophie's husband sat down and laid his burly forearms on the table. He was heavy, with a round face blooming with thick blood vessels and curly brown hair tied into a ponytail. He had a fat nose with a crooked bridge, as if it had been badly broken. He wore a Twins T-shirt and dirty sweatpants smeared with oil. Stride guessed that Green was about forty years old. He knew that the man was Marty Gamble's cousin, but there was little family resemblance. Marty was lean and mean; Bill Green was lumpy and shifty.

"Look, Kitty Kat loves to tell stories," he said. "Most of the time, it's all in her head."

"You think she's lying?" Stride asked.

Green grabbed a second can of beer from the table and popped it open. "I'm saying, you can't trust what that girl tells you. It's probably the drugs."

"You knew she was using?"

Sophie's pale lips dipped into a frown. Her voice was hard to hear. "She said she stopped, but it's hard to know if that's true when she runs away so often. We don't always know where she is or what she's doing."

"Did you talk to anyone about her?"

"Oh, yes, of course. I talked to my minister. I talked to the school. I talked to her Aunt Dory and to Ms. Hahne at the shelter downtown. I even thought about calling the police, but I didn't want to get her into trouble."

"Why does she run?"

William Green leaned forward with a beefy hand over the top of his beer can. "You know what she went through with her parents. She's messed up. Is that so hard to figure out?"

"Her teen years have been very hard," Sophie added. "She's a loner. She doesn't have many friends. She's had nightmares as far back as I can remember. As she's gotten older, it's been getting worse."

"Did you get any psychological help for her?"

"Ms. Hahne said she would have a counselor at the center talk to Cat," Sophie said.

A counselor at the center.

Stride hesitated. Like an alarm going off, he remembered a name and a darkly handsome face from a police report out of Minneapolis several months earlier. He didn't like coincidences.

"Do you know if she did talk to a counselor?" he asked. "Did Cat tell you she was seeing anyone?"

"No."

"Did she happen to mention a man named Vincent Roslak?" he asked. "Or did Ms. Hahne talk about Cat seeing Roslak?"

"No, she didn't. Why?"

"It's probably nothing," Stride replied. "I just need to cover all the bases."

Cat and Roslak. Maybe it really was nothing. He didn't want to put the two of them together in the same space of time, because it led him down a dark road. Roslak was a counselor who had volunteered at The Praying Hands Shelter, before he lost his license and fled the city. He was charming. Seductive. Immoral.

He was also dead.

Murdered.

"You think all of this is our fault, don't you?" Green demanded angrily, interrupting his thoughts. "Hey, listen, that girl had nobody. If it wasn't for us, she would have been in foster care, bouncing around like a Mexican jumping bean. We gave her a home, and it cost us, let me tell you. It's not like the state gave us any dough, and it's not like Marty ever had any money."

"So why did you take her in?" Stride asked.

"She was family," Sophie told him. "Dory was in no shape to take her, so that left us. Besides, Bill and I always wanted kids, but we couldn't have children of our own. Bill has a low sperm count."

William Green exploded. "Fuck, Sophie! Do you have to tell everybody who walks in the goddamned door about my swimmers? Why don't you take out an ad in the fucking newspaper?"

The man uncoiled like a spring and his fingers hardened into fists. Stride thought that if he hadn't been there, Green would have taken out his anger on his wife's face. Instead, the man leaped to his feet, grabbed his beer, and stomped out of the kitchen. Stride heard the front door open and then slam so hard that the walls shook.

"I'm sorry," Sophie murmured. "I shouldn't have said anything. Bill is sensitive about that."

"Mrs. Green, may I ask where you got that bruise on your arm?" Stride asked.

"What?"

"Did your husband do that to you?"

Her eyes widened and she touched her arm tenderly. "No, no, I slipped on the ice."

"If he's violent to you, Mrs. Green, you can get help."

"Oh, no. No, I'm sorry if I gave you that impression."

"Does he ever hit Cat?"

"Cat? No, of course not. Bill loves Cat. You heard him, he calls her his little Kitty Kat."

Stride didn't think he was going to get an honest answer from her. He tried to keep his anger focused where it belonged—on William Green, not on the wife he'd intimidated into silence. He'd been in too many homes like this one to believe her denial. Maybe she was lying to protect her husband. Maybe she really didn't know. Or maybe she was trying to convince herself, because the truth was too awful. It didn't matter. He was as certain as he could be, watching the family dynamics, that William Green had been physically abusing Cat for years.

That was what she'd been running from. That was where it had started.

"I'll let myself out," he said.

He felt disembodied, as if he could see himself and watch what he was doing. Coldness descended on him. His muscles tensed into knots. He stepped outside into the sweet air and took a deep breath, but it failed to defuse his rage. He descended from the porch and saw the propped-open hood of the Coupe de Ville and heard the clamor of tools. He stepped inside the garage. The space was dimly lit under a curly fluorescent bulb. A static-filled FM station played Poison from a boom box.

William Green looked around the hood angrily. "What the—?"

The man blanched when he saw Stride. His hands were greasy, and he wiped them on an old towel. "What do you want?"

"I have a message for you, Mr. Green."

"What? What message?"

Stride came up to him, close enough to smell beer and smoke on the man's breath. Green stumbled backward until he bumped against the pegboard on the rear wall of the garage. Stride studied the tools and removed a hacksaw from its hook and held it in his hand, running a finger over the jagged teeth of the blade. When he was angry, Stride channeled his rage into the calmness of his voice. He spoke as calmly as he ever had in his life.

"Let me explain something to you, Mr. Green. If you ever lay a finger on Cat again, I'll be back here. If you ever even *think* about touching her or your wife again, you better see my face in your head, because I will be back here. I will leave my badge at home, and I will come visit you in the night. Do you understand me?"

"Hey, listen, I don't know what—"

"*Do you understand me?*"

Green didn't take his eyes off the saw. "Yeah. Fuck, yeah."

Stride let the saw drop from his hand and clatter to the ground. He turned around and walked through the garage and stood in the driveway until the roaring in his head subsided. When he could breathe again, he headed for the street. He realized that Cat was right and he was wrong. It would have been a mistake to bring her back here. She was better off with Kim Dehne, as far away from this house as possible. When he saw Cat, he wanted to tell her that, for the first time in a long time, things were going to be all right. He was never going to let William Green get near her again.

He looked up at Cat's bedroom window on the side of the house. It was twelve feet from the sash to the ground, but she said she could jump it, particularly during the winter, when the snow cushioned her landing. That was her escape route. She'd used it dozens of times.

One time, three weeks ago, someone had been waiting for her.

Stride shoved his hands in his pockets and walked to the corner, where he sat on a yellow fire hydrant. He stared at the weedy cracks in the pavement and at the slope leading up toward the railroad tracks. The street looked empty, but if anyone wanted to watch Cat, there were plenty of places to hide. The shaggy trees. The dead-end road on the other side of Sixty-Second Avenue. The foreclosed rambler with the broken windows.

He noticed a stop sign that had been defaced by graffiti. Someone had painted the word *me* in drippy green letters, so now the sign said: STOP ME. The paint looked fresh. The message felt like a warning: *Stop me, stop me, stop me, stop me.*

He didn't like it.

Stride got back into his Expedition. When he turned on the engine, warm air blew into his face. He was running out of time and daylight. He needed to find Curt Dickes and the other teenage run-away, Brandy. One of them might be able to help him figure out who was hunting Cat. And why.

He also couldn't get another name out of his head.

Vincent Roslak.

13

Brooke Hahne was late.

Maggie stood outside Sammy's Pizza downtown, across the street from The Praying Hands. Runaways, drug addicts, prostitutes, and abused teens all wound up at the shelter's door. Some kids needed medical help. Some needed tips on jobs. Some simply needed a hot meal and a safe place to sleep.

The street corner opposite The Praying Hands was deserted on Saturday afternoon. Usually, a dozen teens hung out there, but everyone recognized Maggie's yellow Avalanche in the central Hillside area, and everyone knew she was a cop. When she showed up, the teens melted away like ice cream on an August sidewalk.

Inside the pizza joint, a cook in a greasy apron waved through the store window. She was a regular at Sammy's. So was Stride. The restaurant had served as the weekly hangout for her, Stride, and Serena; it was the place where they talked about open cases over garlic bread and sausage pizza. They hadn't done that since the breakup. When she ate Sammy's pizza now, it was usually a late-night delivery to her condo. Alone. With a beer.

Serena.

Maggie hadn't seen Serena Dial in months, since before the long winter. They weren't friends anymore. Serena had moved out of Stride's cottage in November and joined the sheriff's department in the lake town of Grand Rapids an hour away. She was a name on Itasca County bulletins now. When updates about the Margot Huizenfelt case came up at the morning meeting, Serena was the contact. Other than that, she was a ghost who never showed up in Duluth. Maggie missed her, but she had no one to blame for the split but herself.

Her affair with Stride had begun after his near-death fall from the Blatnik Bridge, which had triggered debilitating flashbacks that left him emotionally numb. Like strangers, Stride and Serena had blocked each other out, unable to talk about the rift between them. Maggie had found Stride at his lowest ebb, on the floor of his cottage, cut and bleeding, dazed and suicidal. She'd cleaned him up. She'd put her arms around him. She'd listened to him talk about feeling dead inside. When he reached for her, not as a friend but as a lover, she'd reached back.

A mistake.

Her instincts had told her to run, but she stayed. They kissed. They made love. It should have been one time, it should have been their secret, but those kinds of secrets had a way of getting out. Stride couldn't hide the truth from Serena. It was in his face. When he told her, the fissures in all of their relationships split open like cracks in the earth. There was no going back to the way they were.

Maggie climbed the hill past the restaurant, with the fire escapes of the old brick building on her left. She crossed the street through a cloud of steam belching from the sewers. Near the next corner, at Second Street, she stopped where Cat had told Stride that a car tried to run her down. She noticed a parking meter with a bent frame, as if a car had struck it. It could have happened the way Cat said, with a vehicle weaving on and off the sidewalk as part of a hit-and-run. Or the meter could have been damaged like that for months. She'd banged up a few meters herself over the years.

Maggie spotted a white Kia Rio parallel parking near Sammy's. She recognized the car and saw Brooke Hahne get out and head toward

The Praying Hands. Brooke, who probably made less money than a first-year teacher, was dressed in an above-the-knee black skirt and a burgundy blouse with gold buttons. Everything she wore was sec-ondhand, but she made thrift-shop specials look good. At thirty, she was cheerleader pretty, with long, straight blonde hair. Her high heels made her nearly six feet tall. She was as skinny as a praying mantis, which was what Duluth politicians often called her. She had a razor tongue about city budget cuts.

Brooke stopped and turned when Maggie called her name. They met on the street.

"Sorry I'm late," Brooke said. "I had a donor meeting in Grand Marais."

"Get the gift?"

"Oh, sure."

People rarely said no to Brooke. She was relentless about fundrais-ing. She was sexy, too, which was a plus with middle-aged men who had money to burn.

Maggie had known Brooke since she'd graduated from UMD. She'd started at the front desk of The Praying Hands, doing intake for kids walking in the door, and six years later she'd taken over as the director. She knew every kid by name, and she knew their stories. The shelter was her crusade.

Brooke nodded at Maggie's Avalanche, which was parked in front of Sammy's. "Couldn't you get a Corolla or something, babe? Every time you come down here, you scare the kids."

"Little cop, big truck," Maggie said.

"I think you're overcompensating."

"You're not the first to say so."

Brooke led her across the street to the shelter, where conversations froze as the two of them walked inside. No one made eye contact with Maggie. Runaway teens shared an instinctive guilt, even if they weren't doing anything wrong. When you saw a cop, you didn't invite attention.

Maggie followed Brooke into a stairwell that smelled of vomit. They took the stairs to her second-floor office. The two windows looking toward the street were dirty and cracked, and a loud fan kept air moving, even during the winter. Brooke sat down behind her battered oak desk and casually rolled up a months-old *People* magazine to swat a cockroach on the window ledge.

"So how are you, Maggie?" Brooke asked, dumping the dead bug in her wastebasket. "How are the new offices? Must be nice, right? Flat-screen TVs, sushi in the cafeteria, personal masseur on call."

"Ha ha," Maggie said.

The Duluth police had been headquartered in the city hall building for as long as Maggie had been on the force, but they'd recently moved to a new facility that they shared with the Saint Louis County authorities. The modern building was a step up from their downtown space, but it was in the flatlands near the airport, far from the center of town.

"I still don't know how K-2 got the council to spend the money," Brooke said. "When I'm looking for a grant, they always tell me the city's broke."

"Well, Stride beat a rat to death in the men's room with a baton. When he dropped it on the chief's desk, they got serious about a new building."

"We've got plenty of rats around here," Brooke said.

"Yeah, I know. Are you keeping your head above water?"

Brooke folded her hands together. Her red fingernails were long and neat. She looked elegantly out of place against a backdrop of posters on meth, STDs, and family planning. "This isn't Hazelden," she said. "We don't have a lineup of wealthy celebs handing us money. We're lucky to get a donation here and there and a few bucks from Medicaid."

"That's recession economics. Demand goes up, funding goes down."

"Well, God forbid we should ask any of our millionaire CEOs to drop an extra dollar in the tax bucket," she said sourly.

"Don't you hate rich people?" Maggie asked, winking.

"Hey, you're my favorite rich person and you know it. I just wish you'd let us put your name on something. You give twice as much as that son of a bitch Lowball Lenny, and I've got to suck up to him at every council meeting and invite him to donor dinners to meet the kids. What a hypocrite."

"I hear you."

"Sorry. I get frustrated sometimes. I see kids who have nothing, and I can barely scrape together enough dollars to help them without getting on my knees for these rich bastards." She plastered a smile on her face. "Anyway, I'm grateful for people like you. What can I do for you, Maggie?"

"It's about that girl I mentioned on the phone. Catalina Mateo."

Brooke nodded. "Okay. What's going on?"

"She says someone is trying to kill her," Maggie said.

"Is this for real?" Brooke asked, with a dubious furrow in her brow. "I mean, you know how it is with these girls. You can't always take what they say at face value."

"Exactly. That's what worries me. You know all about Cat's family background, right? You know what happened to her parents?"

"Of course. It's awful what she went through. Unfortunately, awful is the ticket of admission around here."

"What can you tell me about her?"

Brooke rocked back in her chair and fiddled with a ballpoint pen. "Look, Maggie, I want to help, but I can't talk about what's going on with any of these girls without their permission. They have legal rights. I won't put them in jeopardy."

"I realize that but I'm not trying to bust Cat for anything. Stride's got a signed release from her, too. If you need it, I can fax it over here."

Brooke looked uncomfortable. "Fine. Okay. I'll tell you what I can, but that's not much."

"How long have you known her?"

"About two years. Her aunt, Dory, was one of my best friends at UMD before she dropped out. Dory brought Cat to the shelter when she started running away. Cat sleeps here off and on, but it's been a couple weeks now since I've seen her. If something's going on, I haven't heard about it."

"She says someone almost ran her down a block away."

"Here?" Brooke asked. "That's news to me."

"It happened in the middle of the night."

"Maybe so, but stories like that get around."

Maggie leaned across the desk and lowered her voice. "I'll be honest with you, Brooke. Something about this girl bothers me. I want to get inside her head. Is she paranoid, or do you think it's something more than that?"

Brooke frowned. "It's hard to be sure. Most of the kids who come here, they're on the streets for a reason. Their problems are intractable. You're talking about severe abuse and emotional dysfunction. This is life or death every day, it's not 'my mommy didn't love me.' Next thing you know, they're deep into prostitution and drugs."

"I know that."

"It's funny, I remember writing a paper in college about legalizing prostitution. Make it legal and safe and regulate the hell out of it. I was pretty self-righteous. If a woman wants to use her body as a business, why should the government care? I figured, no harm, no foul, right?"

"A lot of cops feel that way," Maggie said.

"Yes, believe me, I know they do. Cops look the other way all the time. Everybody does. Unfortunately, you can dress it up any way you like, but it's still abuse. I don't care whether it's fifty dollars in some doorway or a thousand dollars in a Minneapolis hotel room. These girls are being permanently damaged. It messes with their heads forever. I wish I'd known that back in school."

Maggie heard the emotion in her voice. "I'm on your side, Brooke, but what does this have to do with Cat? Is she one of the really messed-up ones?"

"Well, there's obviously ugly stuff in her head."

"That doesn't help me."

"I'm sorry, but I don't really know anything more."

"Come on, Brooke. I know you. You're not telling me everything. What's going on?"

Brooke screwed up her pretty mouth, as if she were chewing on sour candy. "It's a suspicion, nothing more. I can't prove it. Besides, I don't like to drag up old ghosts."

"Ghosts?"

"Vincent Roslak," Brooke said.

Maggie frowned and put the pieces together. "The psychologist who was murdered in Minneapolis? What does he have to do with this? I remember he had a connection to the shelter."

"Roslak was a psych volunteer," Brooke acknowledged. "Honestly, at the time, we were thrilled to have him. We needed a counselor and he had great credentials. We can deal with the physical needs these kids have, but if we ignore their mental and emotional problems, we're never going to make any real difference in their lives."

"I saw his photo," Maggie said. "He had more than credentials."

Brooke smiled. "Yeah, he was easy on the eyes, too. We didn't have to twist any arms to get the girls to see him. Unfortunately, he was one of those shrinks who likes to counsel with his cock."

"How did you find out what he was doing?" Maggie asked.

"Steve Garske got suspicious. He talked to several of the girls when he was doing their physicals. Three of them admitted that they were having sex with Roslak. He was a smooth operator, I'll give him that. These were tough street girls and they were gaga for him. That was the last time I let him in the door."

"I never saw a police report about it," Maggie said.

"No, the girls didn't want to get him in trouble. No way they would have admitted anything to the police. Steve worked with the licensing board. Roslak's license got yanked, and he moved to Minneapolis."

"So what are you saying?" Maggie asked. "Do you think Roslak was sleeping with Cat?"

"She wouldn't admit anything to me or Steve, but Roslak saw her several times. I know that."

Maggie frowned. She didn't say anything, but Brooke could read the tension in her face.

"Hey, I know what you're thinking," Brooke said, "but Roslak was murdered in Minneapolis. He slept with a lot of women. He probably left a trail of jealous husbands, too. You'd have to take a number to get in line with everyone who wanted him dead."

"Maybe so, but there are things about the case that weren't in the paper," Maggie said. "The Minneapolis cops didn't release all of the details."

"What details?"

"Roslak's death was pretty ugly," Maggie told her. "He was killed with a knife. Just like Michaela. Somebody stabbed him, like, fifty times."

14

Talk to me, Cat. Tell me what you see. I can help you, but you have to let me get close to you. Will you do that?

"Cat?"

And then again: "Cat?"

It was Kim Dehne, with a quizzical smile on her face.

Cat looked up, startled, and realized that she'd become hypnotized by the thunder of the falls. The two of them stood on a stone bridge over the Lester River, which cascaded furiously toward the lake, its water muddy brown. Slick black boulders, dotted green with lichen, lined the banks.

"Oh, sorry," Cat said. She had to raise her voice to be heard over the roar of the water.

"You looked far away," Kim said. "Off on another planet."

"Just thinking."

Kim picked up a fallen oak branch about two feet long and dropped it off the bridge. The sucking power of the river grabbed the stick and fired it through the rapids, like a circus performer hurling a knife. "Scary, huh? I hate it when we lose kids in there. Seems like every year some ten-year-old gets too close, and the current takes them like *that*." She snapped her fingers.

"Yeah." Cat shivered.

"Sometimes it's days before they find them. Some boater out on the lake fishes them out. Poor kids. You always think you're invincible at that age, you know?"

"Sure." Cat didn't think she'd ever felt invincible.

Kim tugged on her arm. "Come on, let's grab a bench in the park. I want a cookie."

"Okay."

They wandered off the bridge toward the wet grass of the riverside park. Kim Dehne was twenty-eight, but with her squeaky voice she didn't sound much older than Cat. She had a talky, perky way about her, but Cat liked it. Kim smiled a lot. She laughed a lot. That was cool. Kim wasn't much taller than Cat, but she was heavyset, a well-fed Norwegian with curly blonde hair, blue eyes, and fair skin. She had big hands; her tiny diamond ring looked squeezed on her finger. She wore an untucked orange sweater over black jeans.

"Sorry you're stuck babysitting," Cat said.

"Hey, I owe Stride. He helps me and Bob find house-sitting gigs. Anyway, I like having some company. Bob's with his folks this weekend. I didn't have anything to do except work and eat."

They crossed into the park through a stand of towering evergreen trees. Twenty yards away, Cat spotted a deer on the dirt trail. It was a doe with a small physique, still no more than a baby. The deer studied them, wary but uninterested. Cat didn't move, and she took Kim's elbow, holding her back. They waited as the animal sniffed its way toward the trees and disappeared. Something about the sight of the deer made her place her palms gently on her stomach. Kim noticed the gesture.

"You're preggers, right?" she asked.

Cat was surprised. "Did Stride tell you?"

"No, but I can tell. A woman can always tell."

Cat waited for the lecture but didn't get it. "Do you have kids?" she asked.

"Nope. Not yet."

"Do you want them?"

"Someday? Yeah, absolutely. Gotta make some money first. Bob says he wants three, but that sounds like a lot to me."

"It would be nice to have brothers and sisters," Cat said. "I always wanted a sister. What about you?"

Kim shook her head. "No, I'm a one-and-out, like you. Bob's got six siblings, three boys, three girls. Holidays are crazy, but I sort of like it."

They sat down on one of the lonely park benches. The seat was damp and Cat squirmed in her jeans. The wind made the woody tree branches sound as if they were whispering to each other. *That's her. That's the girl.*

Kim opened a plastic bag and took out two peanut butter cookies. She offered one to Cat, who shook her head. Kim shrugged and popped a cookie in her mouth.

"How long have you and Bob been married?" Cat asked.

"Almost two years," Kim said. As she chewed, she worked peanut butter out of her teeth with her tongue.

"Does he do computer stuff, too?"

"No, he's a teacher. High school science."

"Denfeld or East?" Cat asked.

"Denfeld." Kim grinned. "And yeah, you had him for freshman biology. I asked. He remembers you."

Cat nodded. "Mr. Dehne. Sure, I remember him. He was nice. I suppose he said I was pretty stupid."

"In fact, he told me you were pretty smart. He was pissed off that you missed so many classes and he said he hopes you try again. Sounds like you had a knack for the science stuff. Me, I can't cut up frogs. Sorry, won't do it."

Cat smiled. "It's hard to think about school now, what with the baby coming."

Kim ate the other cookie in two bites. She picked crumbs from the side of her mouth. "You want to help your baby? Get your butt back to Denfeld."

Cat didn't know what to say. Kim didn't push her or scold her; she just said what she thought and moved on. The young computer programmer sucked in a chestful of sweet, cold air, flaring her nostrils. She hummed as she sat on the bench, and Cat recognized the tune. It was a Rascal Flatts song about fathers and daughters that always left a hole in her heart. Everyone told her that her father was a monster and a murderer. She knew that was true, but she missed him anyway. She wrapped her fingers around the ring he'd given her, dangling on the chain around her neck. *This way you'll always know I love you.*

"I'm a big country fan," Kim said, breaking off the song in mid-hum. "Bob and I never miss the festivals. You a Toby Keith fan?"

"I guess. He's okay."

"Just okay? Me, I love the Tobester. Kick-ass country. None of this Taylor Swift crap. That girl is too tall and too skinny. Who's your fave?"

Cat actually liked Taylor Swift a lot, but she wasn't going to say so. "I don't know. Sara Evans?"

"Yeah, same with Stride," Kim said. "He's sweet on Sara, too. He talks about what a great voice she has. Personally, I think it's that ass of hers, but what do I know?"

Cat laughed. It was funny to think of Stride with a crush on a singer. She thought about where he was right now and who he was talking to. People like the Greens. People like Curt Dickes. She wondered if he'd still want her around when he learned about the life she'd been living.

Her feelings for him were all mixed up. She'd been without a real father for so long that she had no idea what it felt like to have someone take care of her. To keep her safe. She barely knew Stride, but she'd dreamed about a father like him for years. He was a man, too, and she knew all about what men wanted. She could never have him that way, because he wasn't like the others. To him, she would always be a child, and she didn't know how she felt about that. Part of her wanted to fall asleep in his lap like she was a little girl again. Part of her wanted to seduce him.

Her mixed emotions showed on her face. When she looked up, Kim was staring at her again.

"Your brain taking another rocket ship to Mars?" she asked.

"I guess I have a lot to think about."

"Yeah, I hear you. Sorry, sensitivity's not really my thing. Stride told me about your mom and what happened. Wow, must have been awful. Makes me glad to have parents who are relatively normal. Seems like not a lot of people can say that. Now, my in-laws? Don't get me started."

Cat said nothing. She didn't want to think about her parents; she didn't want to remember them now. She was relieved when Kim changed the subject.

"Hey, Stride said to take you to dinner wherever you want. His treat. What sounds good?"

"I'm not really hungry."

"How about Black Woods? You been there before? I love that barbecue-glazed meat loaf. Yum."

"Sure, whatever."

"Fabuloso." Kim reached over and poked her in the shoulder with a thick finger. "Listen, I'm not trying to pry or anything, but sometimes it helps to talk to someone about things. You know, if you've got bad things in your past, it's good to let them out."

"I don't really feel like talking."

"I don't mean to me! Wow, no. I talk to computers mostly, because they don't talk back. You should talk to someone who knows how to poke around upstairs."

"Like a shrink?" Cat asked.

"Yeah, like a shrink. Lots of people do it. I've done it. It really hit me hard back in school when I had a girlfriend who committed suicide. I spent a year on the couch. It helped."

Cat heard a roaring in her ears, louder than the river. She was a locked room, and she felt Kim jiggling the handle, trying to open the door.

"You ever done it?" Kim asked, not letting go. "Talked to a shrink?"

Cat could see Vincent's face. She could feel his warmth, his arms around her, his kiss. She wanted to forget that she had ever met him. She wanted to erase him from her memory. She wished she had never fallen in love with him.

She couldn't afford to let anyone inside her head or her heart. Not again. Not after what had happened.

"No," she said. "I've never seen a shrink. Not ever."

15

"Why do you carry a knife, Cat?"

"*It makes me feel strong.*"

"Your father carried a knife. Was he strong?"

"*Yes.*"

"Did he love you?"

"*Yes.*"

"And yet he did a terrible thing."

"*Yes, he did.*"

"He killed your mother, and then he killed himself."

"*That's what people say.*"

"You don't believe it? You were there."

"*I—I don't know.*"

"You still dream about it."

"*Yes.*"

"What is it that bothers you most?"

"*I don't understand.*"

"Well, does it bother you that your father killed your mother? Or that he left you alone by killing himself, too?"

"*I—*"

"Do you think he would have killed you, too? If he'd found you?"

"*I—I don't. . .*"

"What is it, Cat? Talk to me."

"*It's hot in here.*"

"Do you think your father planned to kill you, too?"

"*Sometimes I wish he had.*"

"Why?"

"*Look at my life. Look at what I do.*"

"Are you ashamed of what you do?"

"*Yes.*"

"How many men have you had sex with?"

"*Um, I think, maybe twenty. Or more. I don't count.*"

"For money."

"*Yes.*"

"All of these men were older than you."

"*Yes.*"

"Were some of them as old as your father?"

"*Yes.*"

"Did you hate them?"

"*I suppose so.*"

"Did you want to kill them?"

"*Sometimes.*"

"Why didn't you? You had the knife."

"*I—I thought about. . .*"

"You thought about it? You thought about murdering them."

"*Yes.*"

"It would have felt good."

"*Yes.*"

"Is sex a violent act for you?"

"*I don't know. I guess.*"

"Are there any sexual acts you won't do?"

"*No.*"

"None at all?"

"*No.*"

"Do you think you could kill someone?"

"*I don't know.*"

"If you carry a knife, you must think you could use it."

"*Please. It's hot in here.*"

"I'll open a window."

16

Stride found Curt Dickes in Canal Park, steps away from the steel lift bridge that towered over the harbor. Behind him, angry lake waves hit the rocks and blew up in clouds of spray over the boardwalk. There was no sun, but Dickes wore metallic sunglasses. He was dressed in a black wool coat that draped to his ankles, and the wind swooped his coat behind him like a cape. Underneath, he wore a lavender silk shirt and pleated tan pants that ballooned at his skinny waist. A square-bottomed tie blew over his shoulder. His shoes were black sneakers.

When Dickes saw Stride, half of his face folded upward into a cocky smile. "Hey, Lieutenant Stride. I don't usually get to see the big guy anymore. Most of the time it's Sergeant Guppo or one of the other boys in uniform."

"Hello, Curt," Stride said. "Nice outfit."

"It's trendy, huh?"

"Sure. Pretty nice ride you've got there, too."

Dickes stood next to a showroom-new red Ford Fusion in the parking lot. "It's sweet, isn't it? Plus, I'm saving the planet. Very cool."

"Yeah, you're a regular Al Gore, Curt."

Stride noticed an advertisement on the vehicle plates from Low-ball Lenny's huge Ford showroom on Miller Hill. He didn't like the coincidence of Curt Dickes showing up in a car he couldn't afford, the day after Leonard Keck's party aboard the *Charles Frederick*.

"So where'd you get the money for the car?" he asked. "You're a janitor, aren't you? You throw sawdust on puke."

"In my day job, sure, but I'm also an entrepreneur."

"Oh, yes? Doing what?"

Dickes used his index finger like a comb to smooth his black, greased hair, which barely moved in the ferocious wind. The breeze off the entire lake, however, wasn't enough to overpower Dickes's Monsieur Musk cologne, which oozed from his skin like burnt incense. The twenty-five-year-old dug in his coat pocket and extracted a business card and handed it to Stride.

"Entertainment Advisor?" Stride asked, reading the title. He shook his head and laughed.

"That's me."

"I hear you're a pimp now," Stride said.

Dickes slapped a hand over his heart in mock dismay. "Tourists have lots of entertainment needs. I do what I can."

Stride looked the kid up and down. He'd probably arrested him twenty times over the years. Curt Dickes had a radar for scams and an addiction to cash, which usually didn't last long in his pocket. "Look, I've known you for a long time, Curt. You're not a bad kid, but there's a big difference between selling fake Yanni tickets outside the DECC and getting in the middle of prostitution and drugs. That can go bad for you in a lot of ways. If someone gets hurt or killed, you could be staring at real time."

"Thanks for the warning, Lieutenant, but I've got friends looking out for me now."

Stride ran a hand over the car's spoiler. "Friends like Lowball Lenny? Did he give you the car?"

"It's more like an extended test drive," Dickes said. "You know Lenny, he takes care of people."

"Yes, he does."

Stride had bought a Ford Bronco himself from Lenny years earlier. It was his first Ford; he'd driven a Chevy Blazer until then. Lenny insisted on selling him the new truck at cost, as appreciation for Stride's work in putting away the burglar who'd shot Lenny's wife. Lenny was also a candidate for city council at the time, and it made good headlines to play nice with the police. Since then, their relationship had soured. As a politician, and a good friend of the chief, Lenny liked to throw his weight around, and Stride didn't like backseat drivers on his investigations.

"I know about Lenny's party on the boat, Curt. Somebody saw you arrive with the girls."

Dickes shrugged. "So what?"

"I talked to one of them. You gave her money."

"I hired girls to dress up a party. That's not a crime."

"Not to have sex?"

"Hey, what they do with the guys is their business, not mine. Come on, Lieutenant, who are we kidding? This is a college town. Tuition keeps going up. A sophomore at UMD can work thirty hours a week toasting sandwiches at Quiznos or she can spend a couple hours with a bored convention rat and make twice the dough. Your own cops know these girls need the money. Most of the time, they look the other way."

"I'm not interested in the college girls. I'm talking about a street girl. Her name's Catalina Mateo."

"Sure, I know Cat. Men will pay big for a face like hers."

"She's sixteen."

For the first time, Dickes paled. "Fuck, no, no way! She had a license, it said eighteen."

Stride shook his head. "Sixteen."

"Hey, I don't mess around with kids."

"Like I said, this is the kind of business that can get you into real trouble. Tell me about Cat."

"Not much to tell, man. She comes and goes. Sometimes I don't see her for weeks. When she needs cash, I hook her up."

"She thinks someone is coming after her. You hear anything about that?"

"She told me about a car almost running her down near the shelter. That's all I know. I figured it was some drunk."

"Did you set her up with any creepy guys? Stalker types?"

Dickes shook his head. "Nobody worse than anybody else. Come on, the guys up here are mostly bald Swedes on business trips, not serial killers. Besides, if some john got obsessed with her, I figure he'd come to me to find her again. Nobody did."

"No one asked for her by name?"

"Nope."

"Do you have a list of guys you set her up with?"

Dickes groaned. "What, do I look like I take American Express? It's not like I check IDs."

"What about parties? Could Cat have seen something that she wasn't supposed to see?"

"I don't see how, man. Most of the time, it's bachelor parties and high school reunions."

"Okay, tell me about Lenny's party. Someone *knew* Cat was going to be there. He waited for her outside. How would anyone know about that?"

"I put the word out," Dickes told him. "Girls talk. Lots of people probably had the lowdown. It was all over town."

"Cat also says someone was asking around about her a few weeks ago," Stride said. "Did you hear anything about that?"

"Nah, that's news to me. Who told her that?"

"One of the street girls named Brandy."

Dickes whistled. "Whoa, Brandy, she's a trip. You don't mess with Brandy. With those eyes of hers, she's like an alien. Like something out of Area 51. She scares the shit out of me. I count her money twice, because you don't want Brandy thinking you're trying to rip her off."

"Brandy told Cat someone was trying to find her. This was down near the graffiti graveyard under the freeway."

"Yeah, if I was looking for a street girl, I'd check there."

"But you don't know who it could be?" Stride asked.

"I don't."

"Have any of the girls talked about someone hassling them?"

"Nothing they couldn't handle. If anyone was causing problems, I'd hear about it."

Stride frowned. He wasn't finding any answers. "Where does Brandy hang out?"

"Brandy goes wherever there's money. It's Saturday, so she'll probably be cruising around here this evening. There's always business on the weekends no matter what time of year it is."

"What about right now?"

"Now? Who knows? It's daylight, man, that's when the vampires stay inside. Your guess is as good as mine."

"So make a guess," Stride said.

Dickes shoved his hands into his coat pockets. "Okay, but you did *not* hear about this from me. If the girls find out I'm rousting their hiding places, it's bad for business."

Stride waited.

"Check over at Central High," Dickes went on. "Ever since they closed the school, some of the smart ones have figured out how to get inside and treat the place like a motel for hookups. Brandy's definitely one of the smart ones."

The old high school had one of the prime locations in the city, with sweeping views down the hillside to the lake. Stride parked near the entrance to the brick building. The school was vacant, a victim of shrinking enrollment, but there were still torn posters for the Trojans taped to the windows, as if classes were in session and students would walk through the doors. He couldn't visit this building without seeing ghosts in the hallway from his teenage years.

This was his school. He and Cindy had both gone here.

Stride got out of his truck and breathed in the cold afternoon air. It was almost dusk. He began a slow walk around the perimeter of the building. The area was oddly desolate, like an abandoned town. The parking lots were empty. So were the athletic fields. At the school windows, he squinted and saw deserted corridors and overturned chairs, their metal legs jutting up like a field of nails. Each classroom carried an imaginary echo of voices, but the echoes wouldn't last. Soon enough, the building would be torn down, replaced by more soulless condos. Sometimes he wondered if he would recognize the city in a few years.

When he cupped his hands on the glass at one window, he saw a shadow move. It was there and gone, as swift as a spirit. It could have been someone inside, or it could have been a trick of the light. He stayed at the window, watching, but he finally decided that he couldn't trust his eyes.

He continued to the rear of the school. A separate building for the physical plant was built in front of a large inset in the school walls. The plant facility created a U-shaped concrete passageway that was partly hidden from view. When he checked the passage, he found evidence of habitation. Musty blankets. Old food wrappers crackling as they blew in the wind. Broken glass. Someone had been urinating against the wall. When he peered through the rear windows, he saw debris inside. Curt Dickes was right; people had been coming and going, using the school as a refuge.

He followed the school walls and found a door tucked in a shadowy nook that gave way when he pulled on it. When the door opened, an old school desk tumbled onto the cement with a crash. He swore. Someone had rigged the desk as a primitive alarm, and if anyone was inside, they knew he was here. Meanwhile, the real security system had been disconnected. His arrival didn't trigger any sirens.

Stride found himself in a corridor lined with tall red lockers. It had a shut-in smell of dust and dampness. The air was cold; the furnace had been set just high enough to keep the pipes from freezing. The corridor was dark, like a tunnel. He could see only a splash of light at the far end, where the corridor opened into the school cafeteria. The dim glow made the handles on the lockers gleam like a trail of silver. He made his way down the hallway.

One of the lockers was cracked open. He nudged the metal door with his finger and found a winter coat hung on the hook, a bottle of water, and a pack of cigarettes on the locker shelf. He saw a worn leather wallet, too, and when he opened it, he spotted a driver's license with a photo of a man named Alton Koren. Stride remembered the name from a report of a vehicle break-in several days earlier. The wallet itself had been stripped; the money and credit cards were gone.

He spotted a second wallet on the floor of the locker. He squatted to retrieve it, but as he did, a door banged behind him. He glanced back and saw a girl burst from inside one of the classrooms. She screamed like a banshee, swinging the forked head of a crowbar toward his skull. Twisting, he shunted away and heard the whoosh of the heavy steel sail past his ear. The hook missed his head, but the rod landed on the meat of his shoulder and drove him to the floor. The crowbar clattered to the ground beside him, and the girl leaped over his body, but he landed a grip on her ankle, making her trip and fall. As she scrambled to get up, he grabbed a belt loop on her jeans and dragged her toward him.

She squirmed like a cat wriggling to get free. Shouting, flailing, she hammered his shoulder, and one of her sharp nails scratched his face. He yanked her up, keeping a tight lock on her arm, and marched her down the corridor to the bright, open space of the cafeteria. A wall of picture windows looked out toward the lake. The room was filled with dozens of round tables topped with plastic chairs. He overturned one chair and forced the girl into it. When she scrambled to her feet, he pushed her back down.

"Who the hell are you?" she snarled.

"My name's Stride. I'm with the Duluth police."

"What do you want?"

"Are you Brandy?"

"Go to hell. I don't have to tell you who I am."

He grabbed another chair and sat in front of her with their knees almost touching. He knew she was Brandy. Cat and Curt Dickes had both mentioned the girl's eyes, and they were her most distinctive feature, huge and blue. They were nakedly sexual eyes, and tough, like a tiger that wanted to eat you. She should have been pretty, but life and want had gnawed at her face like an attack of bedbugs. She wore a dirty yellow tank top over her jeans. She had tattoos covering most of her arms, and her long hair was streaked with blue and purple, with a racetrack shaved over her right ear. She was feral, and she didn't like being caged.

"I just want to talk," Stride said.

"I said, I don't have to tell you a fucking thing!"

"No, you don't, but you've got a choice to make. I can take you in for trespassing and possession of stolen property, which are misdemeanors, or I can add on first-degree assault of a police officer. That's a minimum of ten years, no parole."

"You don't scare me," she insisted.

"If I don't, I should. What's it going to be, Brandy?"

Her eyes never left his face, and her stare was so direct it unnerved him. Calculations spun in her mind, as obvious as reels on a slot machine. Her features softened. Her lips nudged into a smile, as if she could flirt him into submission.

"What do you want to know?" she asked.

"Tell me about Cat Mateo," he said.

"Cat? She's a pretty little kitty. What about her?"

"I understand you like to beat her up."

"Sometimes."

"Why?" he asked.

"Why not? If you're going to join the circus, you better expect to step in some elephant shit."

"You told Cat that someone was asking around about her. Is that true?"

"I don't know, is it? Maybe it is, maybe it isn't. She's fun to mess with. So paranoid. Always thinking somebody's after her. Maybe it's because of how Mommy died." Brandy made a fist, as if she were holding the knife, and stabbed the air.

"Is it true, or did you make it up?" he repeated.

"If I tell you, will you let me go?" She grinned.

"No."

Brandy pulled her tank top down, squeezing it against her breasts. Her nipples protruded like bottle caps. "You sure? I'll give you a freebie."

"If you tell me, I'll forget about the assault charge."

She pouted. "Yeah, okay, fine. It's true. Somebody was looking for Cat."

"When was this?"

"I don't know. A month ago?"

"What did he look like?"

Brandy wagged a finger at him. Her silver nails were filed into points, like talons. "Not a guy."

"It was a woman?" Stride asked, surprised.

"That's right."

"Who was she?"

"Who knows? I was in a sleeping bag with a guy in the graffiti graveyard. I heard some chick asking about Cat on the other side of the embankment."

"What did she say?"

"Just that she wanted to find her. It sounded like they knew each other. She said she'd found her there before."

"In the graffiti graveyard?"

"Yeah."

"Did you ever see this woman again?" he asked.

"Nope."

"You said it was a month ago. Do you remember exactly when?"

"The guy I was with, he was wearing a Jason Aldean T-shirt. Wasn't there a concert or something?"

Stride nodded. "There was."

"See? That's worth a free pass. Now let me go."

"Cat thinks someone is trying to kill her," Stride went on. "Do you have any idea who that might be? Or why someone would want to hurt her?"

Brandy's bony shoulders shrugged. "Doesn't sound real to me. Sounds like one of her dreams."

"Dreams? What do you mean?"

"Cat goes crazy at night. It's like howling at the moon, you know? She wakes up screaming. Fucking annoying if you're close by. It's all death and blood and knives." Brandy leaned forward, taking him by surprise, and shrieked in his face. "*I'll kill you, I'll kill you, I'll kill you, I'll kill you, I'll kill you!*"

She sat back, bubbling with laughter. Her tiger eyes danced. "See? Fucking annoying."

"Cat dreams about someone trying to kill her?"

"No, man, it's the other way around."

"What do you mean?"

Brandy made the stabbing motion with her fist again. "I think the sweet little bitch dreams about *killing somebody*."

Her words hit him in the face, and he took his eyes off the girl, just for a moment. That was all she needed.

Brandy lowered her head and charged like a ram. She collided with his injured shoulder and butted him backward over the chair. The pain froze his muscles and left him immobile. By the time he recovered, Brandy was halfway across the cafeteria, and he was too far away to catch her. He watched her bolt through the door out of the school with a rebel yell. She jumped the balcony, tore across the wide lawn with her hair flying behind her, and disappeared down the slope leading to the city.

17

He parked near the beach after nightfall.

The black Charger was nearly invisible under the cloud-swept sky. There was no moon to make the lake glisten. The rain would come soon. He stayed off the main street of the Point, tramping through the dunes that led down to the water. As he made his approach, he listened to the swoosh of the waves, rhythmic, like a heartbeat.

The sand slowed his pace, but he was in no hurry. The ridge of dunes, mostly covered by twisted trees, blocked everything but the lights from a few higher-floor windows. The beach itself was empty. It was too cold for secret lovers and too wet for the exercise freaks.

He closed in on the house from the south.

It was one of the new mansions for the new rich. Lots on the Point were narrow, so people built up, sometimes three or four stories. Big decks. Glass everywhere. If you had the money, you could build whatever you wanted. A million dollars. Two million dollars. Play money.

He recognized the weather vane on the roof, shaped like a lighthouse. He'd scouted the place in the daylight. With a quick glance up and down the beach, he made his way over the ridge and followed the grassy trail to the back of the house, where the steps of the deck were anchored on concrete footings that had been swept over by blowing sand. He could see the curving driveway. Empty. Lights glowed on the first floor but there was no movement behind the windows.

They weren't home yet. That was good.

He remembered another house. Another night. The number of the alarm code stuck in his head: 1789. Weird, the things you couldn't get out of your brain.

He stayed in the shadows at the base of the deck and slid out his phone. He made the call. "It's me."

There was silence on the other end. Finally: "I know."

"I'm at the house," he said.

"Okay. Fine. Just get it over with."

"You better be right. You're sure this is the place?"

"That's what I was told."

"I'll call you when it's done."

"Then it's over. Right?"

"Then it's over." *Except for you.*

"Thank God."

"I have to go."

More silence. Then: "She's not alone, you know."

"I know. You told me."

"So how will you . . . Jesus."

"Don't worry about it."

"There has to be another way."

"There isn't. This is the best way. Trust me, there won't be any more questions. She'll disappear. Tomorrow she'll be gone and no one will ever see her again."

"How will you . . . ?"

"Do you really want to know?"

"A gun?"

"I think it's better to use a knife," he said. "That's more appropriate, don't you think?"

18

The bag of ice numbed Stride's shoulder. He sipped a can of Coke and studied the pages in the weekly Compstat reports, which detailed calls for police services in Duluth. Vehicle break-ins and thefts. Burglaries. Domestic assault. Drugs. He was looking for connections to Cat among the reported crimes, but so far he hadn't found one.

He sat in his office in the new police headquarters building. It was Saturday night, almost nine o'clock. The oversized windows looking out on the forest were dark. Most of the lights in the department were turned off, but he heard footsteps in the building hallway and recognized the cadence. Police Chief Kyle Kinnick had a peculiar open-toed walk, and his old brown shoes were worn down to the nails, making him sound like a tap dancer.

K-2 appeared in Stride's doorway. He was short and skinny, with a bad comb-over and ears like two cabbage leaves.

"Evening, Jon."

"Evening, sir."

"How's the shoulder?"

"If Harrison Ford is still looking for a one-armed man, that's me," Stride said.

K-2 laughed, which sounded more like a snort, and sat down in Stride's guest chair. He wore his dress uniform, which was unusual. Most of the time K-2 looked like a CEO in his business suit, with his tie perfectly knotted. The chief was nearly sixty years old. He'd led the department for five years and served as the deputy chief before that for as many years as Stride had been on the force. Generally, they got along well together. Stride hated politics, and K-2 ran interference for him. The chief defended Stride and his team like a pit bull at every city forum, but inside the office, K-2 wasn't patient about getting results and had a sharp tongue when things went wrong. Stride had earned a long leash over the years, but at the end of that leash was a choke chain.

"You getting careless, Jon?" K-2 asked. His voice had a reedy quality, like a badly played flute. "Or just old? It's not like you to get run over by an eighteen-year-old hooker."

"Yeah, she rolled me," Stride admitted.

"What's the girl's name?"

"Brandy Eastman."

"You get her yet?"

"No, she's probably holed up somewhere, hiding out."

"You want to tell me why my lieutenant is busting teenage trespassers at the high school on a Saturday afternoon? Seems to me we have patrol officers to handle calls like that."

"I got a tip that Brandy was there," Stride explained. "She had some information I wanted."

"Uh-huh."

K-2 looked around the office, which smelled of fresh paint. Stride still had moving boxes on the floor that he hadn't unpacked. The chief's eyes lingered on the photograph of Stride's late wife, Cindy, on the bureau. The two of them had been close friends.

"So how do you like the new digs?" K-2 asked. "No rats here, huh?"

"No rats," Stride agreed. "I do miss downtown, though."

"Oh, hell, a few extra miles between us and the mayor is a good thing."

Stride smiled. K-2 didn't usually bother with small talk. When he did, he was working toward a subject that Stride wasn't going to like.

In this case, Stride had no trouble figuring out what was on the chief's mind. Word of his visit to the *Charles Frederick* had made its way back to Lowball Lenny.

"So what's up, Chief?" Stride asked.

K-2 scratched his big ears with his palms. "I was at a Realtors' cocktail party this evening. Half the council was there. Leonard Keck pulled me aside. He wasn't too happy with you."

"I'm sorry to hear it."

"I guess he did a little shindig for his top salesmen on the *Frederick*, and you paid them a visit this morning. Sounds like some of his boys didn't like your tone."

Stride shrugged. "I don't lose a lot of sleep worrying about what car dealers think of my tone."

"Oh, come on, Jon, you know it's not that simple. What the hell were you up to?"

"They brought prostitutes to the party. At least one of them was underage."

"You can prove that?" K-2 asked, frowning.

"If I push hard enough, I think so. I take it you're not anxious for me to push."

"Was Lenny there?"

"He was at the party, but the story is he left before the girls arrived. Meanwhile, I've got a pimp driving around town today in a brand-new Leonard Keck Ford Fusion."

To his credit, K-2 didn't look happy. "Okay, you're right, that smells funny. However, you know as well as I do that if we run with it, this will turn into an ugly pissing match with a bunch of lawyers. After we dink around for months, we still won't get any charges to stick. All we'll do is churn up a lot of media gossip, and we'll make an enemy out of someone who can make our lives miserable."

"I know that," Stride said.

"I'll talk to Lenny. I'll tell him to cool it. Okay? Meanwhile, you need to give me a heads-up before you start messing around with the people who pay our salaries. That understood?"

"I don't like politicians who think they're untouchable."

"What politician doesn't think that? You may not like the game, Jon, but one of us has to play it. I know you think Lenny gets away with crap because we go fishing together, and maybe he does. That's life. Get over it. Besides, cut the man a little slack. When Cindy died, Lenny was on the phone every day to see how you were doing. He knew what you were going through."

"I realize that. I'm grateful."

"Good. Glad we had this talk. Now let's get back to you. You want to fill me in on what you're really doing? I hear you have a young houseguest."

"You hear?"

"I corralled Maggie. She always knows what you're up to. She didn't want to rat you out, but I didn't give her a choice. Besides, she's not a big fan of this girl staying with you."

"That's not her call. Or yours, sir. This is personal."

K-2 leaned his elbows on Stride's desk. "Personal? You think so? It's personal until I read a headline about my lieutenant providing a bed for a sixteen-year-old prostitute. How's that sound to you? Jesus, Jon, do you want to answer those kinds of questions?"

"It's complicated," Stride said.

"Yeah, I know all about who this girl is and who her mother was. That doesn't change anything."

"It does to me."

"You think I don't remember Michaela Mateo? Of course I do. Beautiful woman. Hell of a tragic case. You can feel bad about it if you want, but you didn't screw anything up. The fact is, sometimes bad boys do bad things. You can't always be there to stop it."

"I'm not going to let Michaela's daughter wind up like her mother," Stride said. "She's in danger."

"Is she? Someone's out there stalking some little street girl? The whole thing sounds like a bad drug fantasy to me. Last fall, my neighbor called because her teenage son was out back with a shotgun. He said a freaking *polar bear* was attacking the family dog. Kid was doped out on bath salts."

"I don't think this is a drug case."

"Well, I wouldn't bet the farm on it. If she's messed up or abused, the best thing you can do is to get her out of your house and into the hands of county child protection services."

"I want to make sure she's safe before I simply hand her over to the county," Stride said. "Before this girl Brandy ran, she confirmed that someone was looking for Cat in the graffiti graveyard. That's my first corroboration that something more is going on here."

"Corroboration? Another teenage hooker? A girl who attacked you? She was just telling you what you wanted to hear."

"I don't think so. I have a bad feeling about this."

The chief sighed. "Look, Jon, you're a good man, but you've had a bad year. We both know it. I'm not saying this to be a son of a bitch, but I'm not sure you can trust your gut right now."

"Maybe not, but that's all I can do," Stride said.

K-2 stood up. "Fair enough. I learned a long time ago that it doesn't do me any good to try to get a stubborn idea out of your head. All I'm saying is, you're a cop, and I don't see any crime here. I just see a smart girl who's figured out how to get you under her thumb. Think about that, okay? There's *no crime*."

"Didn't I leave a light on?" Kim asked Cat as they pulled into the driveway. The lakeside house on the Point was so dark that it was nearly invisible. Not a single light shone inside.

"It was still light outside when we left," Cat said. "Maybe you forgot."

The young computer programmer nodded, but she squinted at the house and chewed her lip. "Yeah, I guess you're right."

She parked the Hyundai and they both got out. Cat followed Kim inside the house, which boasted high ceilings and plush carpet that made her want to go barefoot. There were delicate glass sculptures everywhere that looked as if they would shatter if you touched them. Immediately inside the foyer, a tight staircase with a wrought-iron railing wound like a corkscrew to the upstairs bedrooms. The rear wall of the staircase had tall windows looking out to the beach.

"I can't get over what a cool place this is," Cat said.

Kim laughed. "Yeah, it makes me and Bob feel rich."

"When do the owners get back?"

"Next month sometime. That's when we go back to our apartment in West Duluth. Kind of like Cinderella's coach turning into a pumpkin, you know?"

"Nothing good lasts, huh?"

"Not some things," Kim agreed. She kicked off her sneakers; she was wearing thick black socks. "I'm going to make some coffee. You want anything? Pop or something?"

"No, I'm fine."

"I'm stuffed," Kim said. "Man, that meat loaf is good."

The kitchen smelled of fresh cookies. It gleamed with stainless steel appliances, and the countertops were black granite. Kim pulled a plastic jug of coffee from inside one of the cabinets and filled the carafe from the coffeemaker under the faucet at the kitchen island. As she did, she popped a peanut butter cookie into her mouth from the cooling rack.

"I thought you were stuffed," Cat said, smiling.

"Dinner stuffed, not cookie stuffed."

Cat stared through the kitchen's bay window. The lake was out there, but she couldn't see anything except her own reflection in the glass. When she leaned closer, she could barely make out the wooden floor of the deck, which was dusted with sand.

The coffee machine hissed and belched. Kim removed the glass pot, and a few drips sizzled as they fell. She poured coffee into a ceramic mug and replaced the pot, then took a sip and licked her lips. "I work at night a lot, so I got used to caffeine in the evenings. Bob has to grade papers and stuff, so we sit around and do our thing. I'd rather work than watch *Real Housewives of Beverly Hills*. 'Cause let me tell you, there's nothing real about those chicks."

Cat laughed.

Kim took another swallow of coffee, but then she put down her mug on the stone countertop. "Did you hear that?" she asked.

"What?"

"I thought I heard something upstairs," she said.

Cat shook her head. "I didn't hear anything."

Kim's head swung toward the ceiling. She wandered into the hallway, eating another cookie. Her feet made imprints on the deep carpet. She stayed there, listening, as if there were rats overhead, scurrying between the floors. Cat hated rats.

"What's wrong?" she asked.

"Sometimes Bob forgets to close the window and the wind blows stuff over. If anything's broken, I'll kill him."

"Maybe we should call Stride."

"I'm sure it's nothing," Kim said.

She finished the cookie, licked her lips, and marched toward the foyer. Her footfalls made a heavy thud as she jogged upstairs. Cat backed up into a corner of the kitchen with an odd sense of dread. Ice from the automatic machine dropped in the freezer, startling her. The coffeemaker kept spluttering. She eyed the door on her right, which led outside to the cedar deck, with steps down to the thin strip of beach. When she looked outside again, she thought she saw footprints in the sand.

"Kim?" she called.

There was no answer from upstairs.

On the kitchen island, steam rose from Kim's mug like a smoke signal. Near the sink she spotted an expensive block of knives with shiny black handles jutting from the slits in the wood. The largest knife was gone. The wide slash in the wood was empty. Cat thought to herself: *Did I steal it and not remember?* She reached into her boot, but she had nothing hidden there. The comforting feel of a blade near her fingers was missing.

She slid one of the other knives out of the wooden block and into her hand.

"Kim?" she called again.

Kim didn't reply.

Cat tiptoed down the hallway. When she reached the foyer, she stared up through the twisted iron railing of the staircase at the hallway on the second floor. She saw doors and paintings and the black windows. No one was there.

"Kim," she said again, but she whispered this time.

Noise groaned from above her. The floorboards wailed, as if a nail were being pounded into a hand. Cat jumped. She wanted to close her eyes but she kept them open, staring. She listened, and in her brain, she heard a voice. It was her mother's voice, talking in her ear as she held her.

"*Hide under the porch,*" her mother told her. "*Hide under the porch, and do not come out, no matter what you hear, no matter who it is, no matter who calls you, do not come out, do not come out.*"

That was what Cat did that terrible night. No matter how loud the screams got, she hid, and she didn't come out.

Now, as she waited for Kim, she heard another scream, loud and long and desperate. She knew that scream. It was the sound a person made when a knife violated their body over and over and over. The sound of agony. The sound of death. This wasn't an echo; this wasn't a warning from her mother's soul.

This was real. This was happening over her head.

Kim's ragged voice cried from above her, as if from heaven.

"*Cat, run!*"

19

"Sorry, boss," Maggie said.

Stride saw his partner's pixie-like silhouette in the doorway. He'd just turned out the office light and slipped on his leather jacket to go home. He leaned back, propping himself against his desk. Maggie joined him in the shadows and pulled herself up to sit beside him.

"Sorry for what?" he asked, but it didn't matter what she said. They were both sorry for things that had gone wrong between them.

"K-2. I told him more than he needed to know."

"Forget it."

Stride didn't bother turning on the light. It felt normal to be with her in the dark. Throughout the winter mornings, before sunrise, they'd talked in bed. That was when they'd made love, too, as if it were better not to see the other's eyes too clearly.

"We need to talk," Maggie said.

"About what?"

"Cat."

He knew something was wrong. He could hear it in her voice.

"It's Saturday night, Mags. Why are you here? Shouldn't you be doing something with Ken McCarty?"

"I should," she said. "He's pissed at me, but he's a cop. I told him I found some things that bothered me and he offered to go back to Minneapolis and do some digging."

"Digging into what?" Stride asked.

"Vincent Roslak."

Stride frowned at the name. "Why him?"

"You know why."

"Okay, sure," he acknowledged. "Roslak had a connection to the shelter, and he was stabbed to death."

Maggie didn't reply right away. He felt her awkwardness, as if she suddenly had to be careful with her words. "I checked with Brooke at The Praying Hands. Cat saw Roslak multiple times last year."

Stride pushed himself off the desk and wandered to the window that looked out on the woods. His shoulder throbbed. He wished he were more surprised to hear the truth. "So exactly what do you want Ken to do in Minneapolis?"

"I want him to talk to the detective who's handling the case down there. I'm betting they never interviewed Cat, and they should."

"There's no evidence that Cat was involved."

"Maybe that's because nobody looked at her," Maggie said. "Fifty stab wounds? That sounds pretty familiar, doesn't it?"

"That was Marty Gamble."

"Yeah, and Marty's daughter seems pretty fond of knives."

Stride kept staring out the window. They'd both been briefed by the Minneapolis cops about Roslak's murder. He pawed through the facts in his mind. "Roslak was killed last summer, right?"

"Eight months ago. July third." Maggie always remembered details.

"He left Duluth four months before his death. Closed his office, sold his house, rented a cheap apartment down in the Cities. The boys in Minneapolis don't think he ever came back. He had no credit card receipts here in town. He severed his Duluth connections long before he was killed. If you're a woman up here, why would you wait so long before going after him?"

"I don't know. I hope there's no connection at all."

Stride sat down at his desk. He booted up his computer and the monitor cast a ghostly glow in the dark room. He tapped the keyboard and brought up a photo of Vincent Roslak from the *Star Tribune* report on his murder. The psychologist was young, only thirty-four years old when he was killed. He had jet-black hair, short on the sides and curly and gelled on top. He had a lean, narrow face, with long sideburns and a dark beard line. His eyes were cool blue, wolfish and smart. He had what Stride considered a snake charmer's smile: utterly false and oddly irresistible.

"So this is what women go for?" Stride said.

"I hate to tell you, but yeah."

"A lot of his patients wanted to keep seeing him, even after he lost his license and left town."

"Maybe some did," Maggie replied. She added after a pause, "Maybe Cat did."

Stride shut off the screen, enveloping the office in darkness again. "She's not a killer, Mags."

"You may be right, but we should find out what's going on in that pretty little head of hers. It may not be so pretty."

"Okay. Do what you have to do, but step lightly." He got out of his chair and realized how tired he was. He ran his hands back through his hair and then shoved them in the pockets of his leather jacket. "It's late. I'm going home. I need to get my shoulder into a hot shower."

"You want company?" Maggie asked with a smile. As quickly as it came, her smile vanished. "Sorry, I'm kidding, that was a joke. A bad joke. I don't know why that came out of my mouth."

"Do you want to come home with me?" he asked. "To talk to Cat, I mean."

Maggie hopped down from his desk. Her bangs fell across her eyes. "No, I better not."

He wondered if she thought nature would take its course. Wine. Jokes. A fire in the fireplace. Falling into bed again, making the same mistake again. Ken was gone, and Maggie was lonely. If he admitted it to himself, he was lonely, too.

She saw him wince as he moved his arm.

"Is it fractured?" she asked.

"I don't think so. It just hurts like hell."

"You're lucky that girl didn't kill you."

Stride shrugged. "Brandy's a whack job, but I think she was telling the truth. A woman was trying to find Cat, and I'd like to know why."

"Do you think Cat knows who it is?"

"Maybe. Brandy said this woman had found Cat once before. I also want to know if Cat remembers anything unusual happening in the days before the Jason Aldean concert at the DECC. That's when this woman showed up looking for her."

"Jason Aldean? It was that weekend?"

"Yeah. It was a great show. I went with Guppo. Steve had tickets that he couldn't use."

Maggie sucked her lower lip into a frown.

"What?" Stride asked. "Are you going to give me another lecture about country music? We can't all be Aerosmith fans."

"No, no, don't you remember? I'm thinking about that reporter from Grand Rapids, Margot Huizenfelt. She disappeared the very next day, on Sunday. It was that same weekend."

"Can you think of anything that might link Margot to Cat?"

"Well, according to the background bio, Margot wrote a book called *Lost Life* that was all about teenage prostitution in the Midwest. And now we've got a mysterious woman trying to track down a teenage prostitute? That's worth a closer look."

"What was Huizenfelt working on before she disappeared?" Stride asked.

Maggie shook her head. "Nobody knows. Her notes, her laptop, everything was gone. Somebody wanted to cover it up."

"Okay, I'll talk to Cat," he said.

"There's somebody else you need to talk to, boss."

Stride knew who she meant.

Serena.

The Margot Huizenfelt disappearance was Serena's case.

"You're right," he said. "I'll call her."

"Lucky you." Her voice was curt.

"Mags."

She said nothing. They'd both put their hands on a hot stove.

He knew she'd just seen something in his eyes that was missing when he looked at her. She'd wanted him to be wildly in love when they were together, but it just wasn't in his heart. Not when he was in love with someone else.

She turned and stalked for the doorway but stopped as Stride's office phone started ringing, like an alarm bell between them. It was Saturday night. The phone rarely rang. He didn't recognize the caller ID, but he picked it up, half-expecting to hear Serena's voice. There had always been a kind of sixth sense between them.

"Stride," he said.

"It's me, it's me, oh God!"

"*Cat?*"

The girl's voice was choked with panic. "Help me!"

"Cat, what's going on? Where's Kim?"

"She told me to run—I know it was him—he was there!"

"Cat, tell me what's happening. Are you still at the house?"

"No, no, no, I had to get out of there. I ran. Please help me!"

"I'll help you, just tell me where you are."

"I'm—I'm on the beach. On the Point."

"Stay there. Don't move."

"No!" Cat hissed into the phone, barely louder than a whisper. "No, I can't stay. I have to go. I'm sorry, I'm so sorry. *He's coming!*"

20

Cat pushed the phone back into the hands of the ten-year-old girl, whose damp round face peered curiously at her through the flaps of the bubble-shaped tent. The tent was pitched high on the beach, above the lake's crashing waves. Raindrops slipped down the nylon like tears.

"Are you okay?" the girl asked.

Cat felt as if death were following her like a dog that wouldn't go away. "Go inside," she told the girl. "Right now."

"But Mom and Dad said I could sleep out here tonight. We're going camping in Canada next week."

"*Go inside!*"

The frightened girl scampered with her sleeping bag and pillow into the long grass and disappeared. Alone, Cat slogged through the heavy sand to the wet fringe of the beach, which was packed down like brown sugar. Rain spat on her face. White waves thundered from the lake and shocked her ankles in a swirling bath. The gauzy lights of the city tracked the hillside to the north. Behind her, everything was dark on the finger of the Point, but then she saw a flashlight beam whip like a laser from the water to the sand.

He was two hundred yards away. He'd found her.

She kicked through the water, dodging the bleached driftwood that littered the beach. Above the surf line, she labored frantically through humps of sand toward the city. The lift bridge over the ship canal towered like a giant barely half a block away, and spotlights on the piers made the web of steel shimmer. The rain intensified, falling in streaks through the light and blinding her eyes. Where the beach ended, she vaulted a low concrete wall into a small square of dead grass beside the bridge, and she lost her footing, spilling into the mud. Righting herself, she slid like an awkward dancer toward the bridge deck stretching across the water. Two hundred feet of interlocking steel looked down on her.

She was alone, but when she stared back down the Point, headlights flashed to life on the street. A car engine roared. His car.

She charged across the bridge with the wind assaulting her face. Below her, choppy lake water rose and sank in troughs between the piers. She couldn't run fast enough to escape him, but as she neared the city side a deafening alarm clanged in her ear, and she jumped. She saw an ore freighter well beyond the piers, gleaming like an electric centipede as it steered for the harbor. A voice boomed over her head, and it could have been the voice of God.

The bridge was going up.

He wasn't going to make it across.

She skidded off the bridge onto the sidewalk on the town side. The bell clamored, warning everyone away. She looked across to the Point side and saw his headlights trapped there, but her relief died in her chest. As she watched, helpless, the car shot onto the bridge deck just before the barriers fell.

With a scream, Cat dove toward the pier. She half-ran, half-fell through the slick grass to the walkway bordering the canal. Waves jostled against the concrete, sending spray over the low wall into huge puddles. The standing water mirrored the streetlights. She splashed through the water and ducked under the bridge. The wheels of the car whined on the honeycombed metal only inches above her head.

The car cleared the bridge and hit the wet street, but she didn't hear the squeal of its brakes. It didn't stop; it kept going, traveling deeper into Canal Park, farther away from her.

Cat hesitated, but she didn't stop running. She sprinted to the end of the pier and turned the corner at the brick wall of the old Paulucci factory, which led her into an empty parking lot. She listened for a car engine; she watched for lights. She saw no one. Walking briskly now, she hugged the railing overlooking the water. The narrow channel led toward the big ore boat, the *Charles Frederick*. She reached a pedestrian bridge and jogged to the other side, which left her in front of the sprawling DECC complex. She stayed in the shadows of the convention center and made her way toward the south end of Harbor Drive.

She felt the burn of eyes from somewhere. He was still out there.

Cat reached the southeast corner of the DECC. The open harbor was on her left. The Great Lakes Aquarium was immediately across the street. She bit her lip and shivered in the cold. Her feet were soaked inside her boots. The road in front of her led toward the north–south overpasses of Interstate 35. Hidden under the freeway roadbeds was the graffiti graveyard, but to make it there she would have to cross a quarter mile in the open, fully exposed. Anyone who was watching would see her.

She saw the blinking lights of the Antenna Farm high above the city, and it made her think of home. Her real home. It felt far away. She inched along the DECC's south wall and checked each door. There were so many doors in the huge complex that at least one door was usually open on any given night. Inside, it was a maze of dark rooms and corridors in which she could hide.

She reached the next corner, which faced north toward downtown. Near the DECC's parking ramp, a long skywalk led all the way from the entertainment complex over the freeway into the heart of the city. She raced for the main entrance, which was a row of nearly twenty glass doors. She tried each door, one after another, but they were all locked.

Until the eighteenth door. The eighteenth door was open. Cat slipped inside out of the wet night.

She'd never been here, and she could barely see in front of her. She made her way past the lobby and found herself in a long, lightless hallway lined with doors. She opened each one but saw only empty meeting rooms with barren walls. She could tuck herself into a corner of one of the rooms, but there was nowhere to escape if he found her.

Cat held her breath.

Somewhere in the building, another door opened and closed. The sound was hollow; she didn't know if it was ahead of her or behind her. All she knew was that she wasn't alone anymore.

Moving faster, she pushed through swinging doors into a catering facility, which was an obstacle course of shelves stacked with glassware and pots. Her arm brushed against something cool and metallic, and she panicked, lurching away. As she did, she collided with a wheeled cart, sending a column of stainless steel plate covers toppling to the floor. The clatter was ungodly loud. She bolted from the kitchen, found herself in another hallway, and ran again, spilling through double doors.

The world opened up around her.

She was on the performance floor of a large arena. The floor under her feet was varnished smooth and went on like a football field from one end to the other. Above the arena walls, dozens of steep rows of bleacher seats climbed for the ceiling. She wandered into the center of the floor, hearing the click of her heels. There was no light anywhere except the glow of emergency exit signs dotting the doorways. Crowds could have been in the seats, watching her, and she wouldn't have seen them. She could feel them anyway, frowning at her, judging her.

She didn't know where to go or what to do. She'd run as far as she could run. She sank to the floor and wished for everything to be over. Her mother was dead. Her father had killed her. She wanted to join them. If she could go back, she would slither out from under the porch and tramp through the packed snow to confront him. *Here I am. Kill me, too.*

Tears fell. Rivers of tears. Her chest heaved silently. She closed her eyes. It was just like it was in her dreams, with the disconnected voices.

Marty, no! Please! Think of Cat. Don't do this!

Fucking whore!

Don't do this, oh God, stop, stop, stop, no, no, no!

I'll kill you I'll kill you I'll kill you I'll kill you.

Where's the girl?

Cat's eyes flew open. She couldn't breathe.

Where's the girl? Where's the girl?

She clapped her hands over her ears, but the gun went off in her brain, the way it had all those years ago. One loud bang, louder than the screams, and then an awful silence. A silence in which nothing would be the same, nothing good would ever come again.

Cat? Where are you, Cat? I'll protect you.

In the empty arena, Cat scrambled to her feet. She wiped away her tears. Beyond the doors, where she'd come from, someone kicked one of the metal lids strewn across the commissary floor, and the jangling noise rippled through the wall like a warning. He was coming for her.

She could make out square columns underneath the bleachers and she took cover behind one of them. Her breathing sounded loud. Her wet hair dripped on the floor, and she could hear the splashes. She squatted and reached inside her boot; the knife she'd taken was still there. She drew it out into her hand and clutched it in front of her chest.

Cat? Where are you, Cat?

"I'm right here," she whispered.

Stride didn't want to count the stab wounds; there were too many. Each one made a red river, flooding the ivory carpet beneath Kim Dehne. Mercifully, her eyes were closed. Her face was at peace, as if, after all the pain, she'd finally lost consciousness as the blood drained from her body. She'd slept before she died.

She looked like Michaela.

"This is my fault," he murmured.

Maggie overheard. "That's bullshit."

"I should have had a cop stay with Cat. Not a civilian like Kim. She didn't stand a chance."

"Get a cop to babysit a sixteen-year-old girl? Come on. You heard K-2. There was no crime."

"Well, there's a crime now," Stride said.

He retreated down the hallway and took the winding staircase. In the foyer, he headed outside, where the damp chill got inside his bones. Maggie followed. The night was alive with the lights of squad cars. The crime scene team came and went from their van. He leaned against the light post in the front yard.

"Did you find a cell number for Bob Dehne?" he asked.

"I did. You want me to make the call?"

"No, I should do it."

"Any luck finding Cat?" Maggie asked.

"Not yet."

It had been two hours. They'd started the search on the Point, and then they'd widened the circle to Canal Park and the areas bordering the harbor. Bayfront Park. The railroad tracks and the shipyards. The graffiti graveyard. Lake Place, where the homeless slept. Cat had vanished.

"So?" Stride asked, nodding at the house. "Have you figured out how it went down?"

"We're still piecing it together," Maggie told him. "We don't have the murder weapon or much of anything else. We got a call from a family whose daughter saw Cat on the beach, but the girl couldn't really tell us anything."

"Talk to the neighbors near my place," Stride said. "This guy may have been watching my house."

"You think he knew that Cat was with you?"

He nodded. "Curt Dickes knew. The Greens knew. So did Brandy."

Maggie's face twisted into an uncomfortable position. "Not to piss you off, but are we absolutely sure a third party was involved?"

"You mean, maybe Cat stabbed Kim and then ran?"

"So far, the crime scene guys can't prove someone else was there."

"Someone was there," Stride told her flatly. "I went up in the lift bridge. Their cameras have Cat on tape, running across the bridge, and then a car coming after her off the Point. Looks like a black Charger."

"You're certain the car was chasing her?"

"We got the plate, and the registration doesn't match the vehicle. We've also got a report on a black Charger stolen from a casino parking lot in Hinckley a month ago. Does that sound like a coincidence to you?"

"No, it doesn't. Sorry. I'm not trying to be a bitch about this."

Stride shrugged. "I put an ATL on the vehicle."

Maggie said nothing. She looked as if she wanted an argument, but he was too exhausted to find anything else to say. "Do you have that cell number?" he asked her. "I need to get hold of Kim's husband."

"Yeah."

She handed him a piece of paper. He took it without saying anything more and headed for his Expedition, which was parked across the street. He felt her eyes watching him go. Inside, in the silence of his truck, he made the call, but there was no answer. It was almost a relief, but all it did was postpone the tragedy. He left a message asking Bob Dehne to call him immediately.

Stride leaned his head back. He closed his eyes for only a second, but in that second weariness won out and he slept. His dreams were violent, but they fled when he awoke to someone banging on the truck window. He shook himself and realized he'd been asleep for nearly an hour.

It was Maggie. He opened the door and she stood in the rain, her golden face drained of color, her hair wet and stringy.

"Guppo just called," she told him. "He's at the DECC. They found the body of a teenage girl."

PART TWO
LOST LIFE

21

Serena Dial couldn't sleep.

Her eyes stared into the bedroom shadows. Outside, oak tree branches scratched like fingers on the wire screen, as if they wanted to creep inside and crawl into bed beside her. Spatters of mist blew through the open window onto her skin, stroking her bare breasts like the touch of a lover. The sensation unnerved her, but she'd grown addicted to fresh air, even on the bitterest nights. That was Stride's influence. She was a desert girl, but he'd taught her to love the cold.

"It's me."

She heard his voice again. She'd spent an hour replaying his message in her head. Finally, when sleep continued to elude her, she got out of bed in frustration and decided to go downstairs to the kitchen.

Tea would help.

Serena didn't turn on a lamp. The skylight above her head allowed her to see in the dark. She slipped a T-shirt over her torso; the fabric was cool. She poked her feet into sandals but left her long legs bare. Outside the bedroom, she tiptoed on the hardwood floor so as not to awaken her roommate, Valerie, who slept in the master bedroom with her daughter. When she passed their door, she heard Valerie's little girl, Callie, humming a lullaby in her sleep. It made Serena smile.

Downstairs, she opened a window and started an electric kettle. When it boiled, she filled a mug and sat at the breakfast table, dipping a tea bag in and out of the water like a seesaw. The porch bloomed with the aroma of raspberry. She stared toward the lush woodlands of Pokegama Lake beyond the wall of windows, but she could see only her own reflection staring back at herself. Long, thick black hair, in need of a wash. Fair skin, winter white, not the burnt tan she wore in Las Vegas. A flash of emerald in her eyes.

She was distracted. When she sipped the tea, she burnt her lip. She reached to the kitchen counter behind her and pushed the button on the answering machine. This was the tenth time she'd played it.

"*It's me,*" Stride said.

A long silence followed. It was the silence of being apart. Five months of lonely separation. The real message, from him to her, was in that clumsy pause. It said everything; it got under her skin; it made love to her. The rest was work.

"*Listen, I have a case that just got ugly. A street girl named Catalina Mateo is involved, and we think there's a possibility that Margot Huizenfelt was looking for Cat the day before she disappeared. Nothing definite, but the timing is suspicious. Cat is—well, her mother was someone I knew. Anyway, we should talk.*"

That was all.

She didn't expect him to say anything about the two of them. He'd apologized long ago. He'd said he loved her, and she'd said she loved him, but their idea of love was to live behind walls, locking away their pain from each other. She wouldn't live like that anymore. She'd worked too hard to face her demons.

Serena propped her feet on a chair. She was tall, nearly six feet, mostly legs. In the past five months she'd run four times a week with Valerie, and she'd lost fifteen pounds, making herself as svelte and strong as she'd felt in years. She was nearly forty, but she looked and felt younger. When she'd first arrived in Duluth, she had brought her Sin City glamour with her. She liked the hunger she saw in Stride's eyes; she liked the stares on the gray Duluth streets. Since then, she'd tried to fit in, which meant not standing out. She dressed down. She wore less makeup. She didn't fight the scale.

This winter, she'd changed all that. With Valerie's help she became more of who she was again. Glamorous. Sexy. She liked what she saw in the mirror now.

Except for the scars. White, jagged, tough, ugly scars. She'd had to make peace with them. When she touched her legs, she remembered the fire two years ago, and she remembered the agony of recovery. The scars went back much further, though. She carried invisible scars all the way to her teenage years, and she wore them inside and out. So did Stride.

Now she would have to see him again. She had known this moment would come sooner or later. It was inevitable. He would call her, and when he did, he would use the job as a pretext to see her. They were on a collision course with each other, and the only question was what would happen when they met. How he would react. How she would feel. She knew through the grapevine that his relationship with Maggie had crashed and burnt almost as soon as it started, but that was no surprise. She took no pleasure in it.

Well, maybe a little pleasure. She was human.

She'd forgiven Stride for crossing the line, but it wasn't about that for her anymore. It was about whether they were better together or apart. She missed him, she loved him, but she didn't know if she could live with him again.

Serena played the message from Stride one more time, and this time she thought: *Margot Huizenfelt.*

One month ago, Margot vanished, leaving behind a brand-new SUV on a dirt road by the banks of the Swan River. There was nothing accidental about her disappearance. Someone had rifled her garage apartment at her parents' home in Grand Rapids, taking any notes or clues that might have explained why she'd been abducted. As a liberal blogger, Margot saw conspiracies everywhere, but this time she'd been right to be paranoid. Someone had come after her.

Margot was forty-five years old, middle-height and heavy, with a mannish look. She kept a chopped haircut covered under a Twins baseball cap, and she lived in sweatshirts, jeans, and trail boots. Serena had investigated her love life and found nothing. No one remembered seeing her involved romantically with anyone, male or female. She had one brother, who lived in Anchorage. Her parents spent seven months of the year in Coral Gables while Margot looked after their Minnesota home. As far as Serena could tell, Margot spent most of her time hiking in the state parks and writing her freelance stories.

She had a quirky eye for journalism. Sometimes she spent weeks on the rural highways, writing about ethanol plants, small-town religion, and farm suicides. Sometimes she haunted city streets, digging up stories about violence and homelessness. She had a hatred for politicians and powerful men that showed up in her writing like a giant flag flying on the lawn. Serena had read a banker's box full of articles and blog posts going back fifteen years, as well as her book, *Lost Life*, which was a compilation of vignettes on girls who had fallen off the grid. For a loner who wasn't particularly likable, Margot showed a surprising tenderness for the damaged lives these girls led.

A street girl named Catalina Mateo is involved.

Serena took her tea and padded in her sandals to the far end of the house, where she'd taken over a small den as her home office. The room was a shrine to Margot Huizenfelt now. Photos. Phone records. Credit card receipts. Magazine clips and printouts from her Web site. None of that effort in recreating Margot's life had brought Serena any closer to finding her.

She was under no illusions. It had been a month. Margot was dead. Maybe with the spring thaw they would find her body, or maybe they wouldn't. There were too many miles of wilderness in northern Minnesota and too many scavengers. She could smile for Margot's parents and tell them to keep hope, but everyone knew the truth. Their daughter wasn't coming home.

From under the desk, Serena slid out a box that contained copies of Margot's writings. The reference to Cat Mateo struck a chord in her memory, not because of the name, but because of the story. She knew about Stride and Michaela. It had come up once when they were driving through the dirt roads of the Antenna Farm and Stride had stopped near a run-down bungalow. He hadn't said much, even when she pressed him. *I knew the woman who lived here. She was killed*. Instead, it was Maggie who'd told her the whole story, confirming what Serena had already suspected when she looked in Stride's eyes. Losing Michaela had been one of the most devastating moments of his life. More than that, his relationship with her obviously went deeper than he'd ever admitted.

She pawed through the copies. It took her fifteen minutes to find the essay she remembered. The article had appeared three months earlier in a Duluth e-zine. There was no photo accompanying the story, which wasn't uncommon. Most of the girls didn't want their faces showing up online or in print. Margot had used an alias, calling the girl Tina. She described her:

> You know how sometimes you find a quartz on the beach amid all that muddy sand? That's Tina. She's a shiny quartz, huddled against a wall that's wild with spray paint. Pretty. No, make that gorgeous. Prom queen gorgeous.
>
> You want her? You can have her. Fifty bucks, and guess where she'll put *la boca*. You like? She's sixteen.

Serena winced at Margot's directness, but that was something she'd come to like about the woman's writing. Margot didn't sugarcoat. She told it as it was. Further down the page, Serena saw the passage she remembered:

> Tina loves her father. Daughters like to tell stories on their fathers. She wears a ring he gave her on a chain around her neck. Sweet. It's gaudy paste, but she won't let you near it because you might try to steal it. If you try, watch out, because Tina is quick with a knife. Daddy taught her well.
>
> Thing is, Daddy's dead. He stabbed her mother a few dozen times, and when he saw what he had done, he blew a hole in his head. Tina? She was hiding. Heard the whole thing. Dad murdering Mom. Dad committing suicide. You and me, we might skip Father's Day after something like that, but not Tina. She says he's still looking out for her. He still talks to her sometimes, like a guardian angel.
>
> I really hope she's wrong about that.

Even with a fake name, the girl named Tina was clearly Catalina Mateo. There weren't two girls with her story in Duluth. Anyone who knew her would make the connection. Three months ago, on one of her hikes through the seamy belly of the city, down near the graffiti graveyard, Margot Huizenfelt found Cat Mateo and made her the latest lost girl in her series of profiles.

If Stride was right, Margot came back to Duluth a month ago to find Cat again.

Then she vanished.

Why?

22

"This has to stop."

"It stops when we're safe," he replied. "Don't you get that?"

He heard ragged breathing on the phone. Angry breathing. It was starting to worry him.

"You said it would be over by now."

"It was. It should have been over ten years ago, but loose ends have a way of unraveling. Don't blame me. I'm cleaning up the mess."

"Not like this. Two more people killed? What kind of monster are you?"

"You called me. Remember? I'm handling this, which is just what you wanted. You were the one panicking. You said we had to do something. You said it was all going to come out."

"Maybe it's better if it does. I can't take it anymore."

"No, it's *not* better. I don't want to hear you talking like that. We are going to take this genie by the throat and cram him back into his bottle. We do whatever it takes. You got that?"

Silence.

"*You got that?*" he demanded.

"Yeah, I understand." Then: "I wish I'd never met you."

"Real nice. I saved your ass and that's all you can say to me?"

"I can't believe I let this happen. I wish I'd just—"

"What?" he asked. "You wish you'd gone to prison? Don't waste time on fairy tales. It's too late for that. If you see the inside of a jail cell now, it's for the rest of your life. Remember that."

"We can't stop this. The police are getting close. What happens if they make the connection?"

"They won't."

"That's what you said before. Now we have more blood on our hands. This is driving me crazy. I can't live with it."

He took the menace out of his voice. He needed to be calm now. Reassuring. "You have to be patient for a little while longer. Soon we'll be free, and we'll never have to see each other again. That's what you want, isn't it? To forget me? To walk away from what happened?"

"That's what I want."

"So do I. Don't worry. No one is going to make the connection, and even if they do, they're never going to tie anything back to us. Not anymore."

"I'm not so sure."

"Let me take care of it. All you have to do is keep an ear to the ground, and if you hear anything, you let me know right away. Okay?"

The reply was long in coming. Too long. "Okay."

"I'll be in touch."

He hung up the phone.

He didn't like what he heard. He'd spent his whole life reading people, and he knew when they were about to crack. This was going to be a problem.

23

Stride recognized the tattoos on the girl's skin and the rainbow streaks in her hair. He also remembered her frozen eyes, which were wide open and as crazy-wild in death as they'd been in her short life. Even now, she looked ready to leap to her feet and run away with a wild laugh. He hated to feel relief at any victim of a crime, but his heart felt so light that it climbed into his throat.

The dead girl on the floor of the DECC was not Cat. It was Brandy Eastman.

She lay outside the doors of the arena commissary, her head propped at an obscene angle against the wall. Her forehead was split in two, the result of a blow from a fourteen-inch pipe wrench that sat in the lake of blood underneath her skull. Nearby, outside the reach of her hands, he saw a knife, with a handle that matched the expensive Victorinox set in the house where Kim Dehne had been killed. The knife showed no evidence of blood.

"Is this the girl who attacked you?" Maggie asked.

"That's her."

"Looks like she planned to hide here for the weekend. Guppo found some provisions in a banquet room on the other side of the kitchen. Blanket, cigarettes, Red Bull, candy, empty BK Whopper wrapper."

"Are we absolutely sure the Whopper wrapper was empty when he found it?" Stride asked.

Maggie grinned. Sergeant Guppo had a waistline the size of a snow tire. "So he claims."

"Anything else?"

"Yeah, paraphernalia from The Last Place on Earth."

Stride frowned with disgust. The Last Place on Earth was a downtown Duluth head shop with the resilience of a radiated cockroach. The police and the city council had tried without success to shut it down for years, and all the while the store rang up millions in sales. The owner liked to boast that urine cleaners for drug tests had bought him a vacation home in Mexico.

"So what do you think happened?" Stride asked.

"It looks like Brandy came through the doors and got surprised. Someone brained her, and the blow drove her backward against the wall."

"Hard to surprise that girl."

Maggie shrugged. "The lights were off. She would have been practically blind. She never knew what hit her."

"Evidence?"

"Not much. We'll run tests on the wrench, but I don't think the murderer brought it from outside. We found tools near one of the truck entries."

Stride gestured at the floor. "What about the knife?"

"It's definitely from the house where we found Kim Dehne. The butcher knife that killed her is still missing, but somebody took this blade from the same set."

"Is it possible that Brandy killed Kim?" Stride asked. "She was crazy enough, and she had the strength, particularly if she was drugged up."

Maggie shook her head. "It looks like Brandy was already holed up here at the DECC. She probably heard someone inside the building and went to check it out, and *pow*."

"Is there any sign of Cat?" Stride asked.

"She was here."

"Are you sure?"

"One of the patrol officers spotted a girl running through the sky-walk toward downtown. By the time we got somebody to the other end, the girl was gone, but the description matched Cat. That's what led Guppo to launch a search inside the DECC, and we found Brandy. Oh, and there's evidence of a fight inside the arena. We found blood and torn clothing."

"Show me," Stride said.

Maggie led him into the cavernous arena, which was now bright under the overhead floodlights. Police officers moved back and forth through the bleachers, and a section at the far end of the arena was taped off. Stride walked to the scene and saw the markings of blood on the floor near a support column and a striped sleeve from a girl's top. He recognized the clothing; he'd bought it for Cat yesterday at Target.

"Yeah, she was here," he confirmed.

"We found blood on Brandy's knuckles, which doesn't look related to her death. She hit someone."

"So she and Cat struggled, and Brandy took the knife." Stride squinted at the lights. "If it was dark in here, whoever was waiting in the commissary may have thought Brandy was Cat. He heard the girl coming back and hit her with the wrench. Then he realized he killed the wrong girl."

"Maybe," Maggie said. "Or Cat killed Brandy and took off."

Stride shrugged. "If Brandy came after Cat in the arena, I don't see Cat going back for more. Plus, there's no way Cat's got the upper body strength to wield a wrench with the force necessary to split open someone's skull."

"You're probably right," Maggie agreed.

His phone buzzed and he yanked it out of his pocket. He saw the name on the caller ID.

Dory Mateo.

"Dory," he said. "It's Stride. What's up?"

"You better get to the Seaway right now," she told him. "Cat showed up in my room overnight. Someone beat her up."

Stride couldn't count the number of times he'd climbed the stairs to the second floor of the Seaway Hotel in his career. The flophouse on the south end of Superior Street, steps away from Curly's Bar, was ground zero for trouble. Fights. Stabbings. Hookers on their knees in the doorways. Drunks that needed transport to rehab. The joke among the police was that the place could never burn because of the urine and vomit permanently soaked into its carpets.

Dory's room was at the end of the hallway, overlooking the back alley. Her door was open, and he found her on the twin bed with her hands on her knees. The room was barely six feet by ten feet and was furnished with nothing but a bed, a warped dresser, and a sink. The bathrooms were communal. The room was lit by a single bare bulb with a string cord. He smelled smoke, and he saw an ashtray on the window ledge.

He walked inside and closed the door behind him. "Where's Cat?"

Dory stared at the floor, her shoulders slumped. Her bleached blonde hair was flat and unwashed. "Taking a bath."

"How is she?"

"Cuts and bruises."

"Did she say what happened?"

"No. I woke up and she was sleeping on the floor. I could see she was hurt. I let her rest for a while, and then I put her in the bathroom and called you."

He looked out the window. It was still dark outside. He noticed a pile of clothes crumpled on the floor. "Are these Cat's clothes?"

"Yeah."

"I need to take them with me. Do you have anything else she can wear?"

"Sure. Why do you need them?"

"Evidence. Two people were killed tonight."

Dory finally looked up. Her eyes were bloodshot. Mucus dripped from her nose. "Don't tell me Cat did it."

"I hope not." He slid a pen from his pocket and pushed around the clothes on the floor. He didn't see any bloodstains. That was good. When he looked at Dory, he didn't like what he saw in her face. Her skin was gray. "Are you okay?"

"Bad night," she said.

"Do you want me to get you some help?"

"No."

Stride sat down on the bed next to her. "I need to ask you some questions about Cat."

"Whatever. Go ahead."

"Do you recognize the name Margot Huizenfelt?"

"Margot? Sure."

"Did Cat ever talk about her? Do you know if they knew each other?"

"Margot talked to Cat for one of her stories. I set it up."

"You did?"

"Yeah, she was willing to pay for an interview. Cat needed the money. It was months ago."

"How do you know Margot?" Stride asked.

"She knows lots of girls like me. What's the big deal?"

"Margot's missing," Stride said. "She disappeared a month ago."

Dory looked shaken, as if he'd slapped her out of a coma. "*Missing?*"

"Someone took her."

"I didn't know. Jesus."

"Did you ever see the story?"

"What?" Dory's eyes were vacant and distracted.

"The story Margot wrote about Cat."

"No, I didn't. How would I? Why are you asking me about this?"

"Margot may have been looking for Cat before she disappeared. Did she come to see you?"

"Me? No, of course not. Why?"

"To find Cat," Stride said.

He watched Dory physically shutting down, drawing away from him. Her eyes shot toward the door. "I never saw her."

"Are you sure?"

"I said no!" Dory exploded. "I don't know anything!"

He held up his hands to calm her. "Okay."

"Leave me alone!"

"I'm not trying to upset you, Dory. I'm trying to help Cat."

"If you want to help her, get her the hell away from me. I don't want her in a place like this."

"I will. I just need to know a little more from you first. What can you tell me about Cat and Vincent Roslak? He's a shrink."

Dory rubbed her fingers together, as if she needed a cigarette. She stared at the ceiling. "Yeah, I know who he is."

"Cat saw him at the shelter. Roslak was sleeping with some of the girls there. Do you know if he slept with Cat?"

"How would I know? Cat doesn't talk about bad shit."

"Roslak's dead."

"I remember. So?"

"He was stabbed to death."

Dory paled. "So what? He was a bastard to lots of people, right? Sometimes bastards get payback. Cat carries a knife, but that's just for show. She'd never use it. She knows what knives do, you know?"

"Yesterday she assaulted a man."

"On the ship? Yeah, she told me. The pervert wanted to butt-fuck her, for God's sake."

Dory stalked to the window and pushed it open with a bang. There was no screen. She slid down the wall of the bedroom and sat on the floor. She pulled a pack of cigarettes from her pocket, lit one, and blew the smoke out into the darkness. She wrapped her arms around her knees.

"Men," she said. "They're all fuckers. Look at Marty Gamble."

"I know."

"Cat won't let me say things like that. She still loves the son of a bitch."

"He was her father."

"Some father. What an asshole. I guess I can't talk, huh? I'm no prize, either. Back then, I would do anything for money to stay high. If Cat knew the things I did, she'd hate me."

"What did you do?"

Dory sucked on the cigarette. "It doesn't matter."

"I said I can get you help."

"I don't want your help. I don't care about me. I want to help Cat, but all I do is make it worse. Michaela must look down at me and spit."

"You *do* help me, Dory."

Stride's eyes swung to the doorway, where Cat stood in a fraying terry robe. Her cheek had a fierce bruise. She had a long scratch on her neck that glowed red from the hot water. She slipped inside and shut the door and got down on her knees beside her aunt.

"You help me all the time," Cat said. "I'd be lost without you. You've always protected me."

Dory flicked the cigarette out the window and shook her head. Like a dam breaking, she began to bawl. Her body wilted and she sank into Cat's arms. Cat held her, letting Dory cry herself out in terrible sobs. Stride began to understand why, as young as she was, she wanted a child of her own.

Cat stared at him, and her sad, beautiful eyes suddenly looked older. "I'm sorry for running away. I didn't hurt anyone. I swear."

He studied her face, and all he could do was rely on what it told him. "I know you didn't," he said.

24

"Is Kim dead?" Cat asked.

They sat on a green bench at the end of the Point. Calm waters from Superior Bay lapped at a strip of sand at their feet. It was finally light outside, but the morning was grim. This place on the harbor was like sacred ground for Stride. He had stopped and sat on this same bench at every crossroad in his life. It was the first place he had gone after Cindy died, in order to cry in private, away from the memories in their home. It was the first place he'd gone after Serena left.

"Yes, she's dead."

Cat's eyes closed. "I should have stayed."

"Then you'd be dead, too."

"Was she—stabbed? Is that what he did?"

"Yes."

"I saw that a knife was missing." Cat hugged herself and shivered. "Did you take another one?"

"Yes, but I lost it at the DECC."

Stride nodded. "Do you have any idea who did this?"

"No. I'm really sorry. Why is this happening to me?"

"That's what we need to find out," Stride said. "Tell me about last night."

Cat took a deep breath. Her fists clenched. "Kim heard something upstairs and she went to check it out. The next thing I knew, she was screaming. It was just like—it was just like with my mother, you know? When I was a kid. Kim yelled at me to run, so I did. I grabbed a knife and I ran. I didn't get far before I saw him coming after me."

"You saw him?"

"No, I only saw a flashlight on the beach. I made it to the bridge and he followed me into the city. When I got inside the DECC, I thought I could hide there, but I heard someone coming. I figured it was him, but it was Brandy."

"What did she want?"

"Money. Food. Whatever I had. I told her I didn't have anything, and she went crazy and started punching me. I think she was high. I dropped the knife, and I got out of there. I found my way to the skywalk and headed for downtown. From there, I walked all the way to the Seaway. That's it."

"Did you see or hear anyone else inside the DECC?"

"Just Brandy."

"Brandy's dead," he told her.

"*What?*"

"Someone hit her with a wrench."

Cat leaped to her feet. "It wasn't me!"

"If it was self-defense, you can tell me the truth," Stride said. "Or if you thought it was the man chasing you, I need to know that. Even if you're scared, you can't lie to me about this, Cat."

"I'm not lying! I didn't do it!"

Stride took her hand and made her sit down again. "Okay, I'm sorry. I needed to ask."

"Brandy came after *me*, not the other way around," she insisted, kicking the sand.

"Okay."

"There's somebody out there who wants me dead. That's all I know."

"We'll find him, but I need your help."

"Anything. I just want to make this stop."

"I need to ask you about Vincent Roslak," he said.

Cat flinched. "Vincent doesn't have anything to do with this."

"You know who he is, right? You saw him for counseling?"

"A few times. What difference does that make?"

"Vincent Roslak was stabbed to death eight months ago. Last night, Kim Dehne was stabbed to death, too."

"There's no connection," Cat said.

"There *is* a connection. You. Somehow, this may be the link that explains why someone is coming after you."

"No, no, no, it can't be. Vincent moved away. I never saw him again. You're wrong."

"Did you sleep with him?"

Cat wiped her eyes, which were moist. "Don't make it dirty. He cared about me." Her voice hardened. "Then he went away and that was the end of it."

Stride put an arm around her shoulders, but she tensed at his touch. "Listen to me, Cat. Roslak abused the trust that his patients put in him. We don't know how far it went. If you told him things about other people, he may not have kept it confidential. Or maybe someone was afraid about what you might tell him, and that's what got him killed. Maybe that's why you're in danger."

Cat sniffled. "I told him stuff from my past. That's all. Years ago. My parents."

"What else? You were on the street, Cat. You saw things, you did things, that people like to keep in the shadows."

"I know, but I can't think of anything like that."

"What about men you slept with?" Stride asked.

"It's not like I know their names. They come, they go, you know what I mean?"

She laced her fingers with his and held on tight. He could almost feel her wishing and praying that the past was behind her. She was young. It would be a while before she learned that the past never went away.

"I don't want to talk about Vincent anymore," she said. "Please."

"Okay, but there's someone else I need to ask you about."

"Who?" Her voice was soft and fragile.

"Margot Huizenfelt."

"I don't know who that is," Cat said.

"She's a reporter. Dory says she sent Margot to you. She's missing."

"Oh, her," Cat said. "Yeah, a few months ago, a woman found me under the overpass. She said she was a reporter. She mentioned Dory. She offered to buy me lunch. It was winter, so a hot lunch sounded good."

"What did she look like?" he asked.

"Heavy. Butch."

"That sounds like Margot."

"You say she's missing? Is it because of me?"

"I don't know yet, but she may have been the person who was looking for you in the graffiti graveyard. What did the two of you talk about?"

"She asked me lots of questions. How I got there. The life I led. My parents. Eventually, she said she wanted to write a story about me. She gave me a hundred bucks, so I said sure."

"Did you ever see the article?"

Cat shook her head.

"What else did you tell her?"

"Oh, you know, why I was on the street, what my days were like. She asked where I slept, how I got money and food, what I thought about men and life and all sorts of crazy things. I felt like I was on a reality show or something."

"Did you give her your name?"

"Yeah, but she promised she wouldn't use it."

"Did Vincent Roslak come up?"

Cat shook her head. "No. I didn't talk about him."

"Anyone else? Any names?"

"I didn't mention anybody. She wanted to know how I got hooked up with people. You know, did I have a pimp or something. I just said there was a guy in Canal Park who was connected."

Stride didn't think it would have taken Margot long to home in on Curt Dickes.

"She said I was pretty and that guys must really like me," Cat went on. "She wanted to know if I ever did guys who paid better than others. Rich guys. High roller types, you know?"

"Did you?"

"Yeah, a couple times Curt got me dates for twice what I usually make. One time, like a year ago, I even got a fancy dress and a limo ride out of the thing. That was cool."

"Where did the limo take you?" Stride asked.

"Some resort on the north shore. There was a guy waiting in one of the rooms. He had bucks."

"Do you know who it was? Did you recognize him? Or did you get a name?"

"No, we just did it. Ten minutes, like most guys, and I was out of there. Nice tip, too, like I was a waitress or something."

"What did he look like?"

Cat shrugged. "I don't look at their faces."

"Do you remember the resort?"

"No. I guess we drove for at least an hour. I don't remember where it was, except it was right on the lake."

"You told Margot all of this?"

"Yeah, I told her the story."

Stride smiled at the girl. "Thank you, Cat."

"You think it's important?"

"I think if I were a reporter, I'd have turned over rocks to find out who that guy was," Stride said. "I'm betting he's not the kind of man who would want Margot tracking him down."

25

Steve Garske peeled off his gloves and flopped down on the sofa next to Stride. His legs jutted out like stilts. He rubbed his hands through his blond hair, leaving it with wings, and he blinked as if he were not entirely awake. He grabbed a mug of cold coffee from the end table and slugged it down.

"It's too early to be conscious on a Sunday morning," he said, glancing at Stride, whose own face was dead with exhaustion. "I know, I know, I get no sympathy from you."

"None," Stride said. "Did you have a gig with the band last night?"

"No, just my usual insomnia. I'm still on island time. I had late rounds at St. Luke's, too. Anyway, Cat's fine. I cleaned the cuts with antiseptic, and I'm going to put her on a round of antibiotics just to be on the safe side." He added, "How's the shoulder, O brave warrior?"

"Hurts, but it's getting better."

"We should x-ray it. Swing by tomorrow while you're out and we'll take a picture. In the meantime, ice it."

"Will do. How about her baby? Are there any risks from the fight?"

Steve shook his head. "I don't think so. There's no sign of abdominal injury. Cat says she wasn't kicked or punched there. The baby should be fine. Even so, I want her in soon for a full checkup."

"Sure."

Steve studied Stride's living room. He ran his index finger along the wood of the end table and held it up to examine. He shook his head. "I'm going to get you a Swiffer. Have you dusted this place since Serena left?"

"I don't think of it as dust. I think of it as skin cells I might need again someday."

"Uh-huh. It's the brain cells I worry about."

"You should be worried," Stride replied with a smile. "Is Cat on the porch?"

"Yeah, she's working on that puzzle you've had sitting there all winter. You mind telling me why a man who lives in Duluth buys a jigsaw puzzle with a photo of the lift bridge? Couldn't you find a picture of the Pyramids, or Hawaii, or something like that?"

"It was a gift."

"A gift? You need better friends."

Stride chuckled. "This one came from a little girl, actually."

"I forgot, cops get gifts from grateful members of the public. Wish I could say the same. It's not like my patients send me fruit baskets. 'Hey, Steve, thanks for the Pap smear.'"

"I'll remember that after my colonoscopy."

"You do that. I want some kind of tropical fruit-of-the-month club thing. Make it something with mangoes."

"Got it."

"Sounds like you had a rough night," Steve said.

Stride nodded. "The media's all over the county attorney this morning. We're not releasing much. I'm trying to keep Cat out of it for the time being. She couldn't handle a media circus."

"Any leads?"

"There's a stolen car that we haven't found yet. A black Charger. Other than that, our only lead is Cat. I need to keep her safe."

"She trusts you," Steve said. "Must take after her mother. There was a little bit of a crush there, right?"

"Michaela and I were friends," Stride said. "That's all."

Steve gave him a sideways glance, and Stride wasn't sure if his friend believed him. The room was dimly lit, and they were both in shadow. He glanced at the kitchen to make sure the girl hadn't come inside from the rear porch. "Tell me something. When you saw Cat last year, did you talk to her about Vincent Roslak?"

"I did. Sorry, I should have mentioned it. Brooke called last night and said that Maggie had been around, asking questions."

"So tell me now."

Steve stood up from the leather sofa and winced as he rubbed his lower back, which was a perennial source of pain. He'd suffered a mean tackle on the football field in college. "Hang on, I need more caffeine for this. There anything left in the pot?"

"Always."

The doctor took his mug into Stride's kitchen, poured the remnants down the sink, and refilled it. He disappeared through the back door toward the cottage's screened porch and Stride heard the muffled hum of voices and his friend's easy laughter. Steve returned to the living room and sat down on the sofa, balancing his coffee mug in his lap.

"Cat's already two-thirds of the way through that puzzle," he said.

"Everybody says she's smart," Stride said.

"We should run some tests and see just how smart. There's something special there. Anyway, Roslak. Some guys, they smile, and you know they're trying to pull one over on you. He looked the part, he dressed the part, he said the right things, but you know how it is. You meet a guy, you decide in five minutes if he's solid or not solid. Roslak wasn't solid."

"How did you find out what he was doing?"

"I got a tip at my clinic. One of my regular patients said he was sure his wife was sleeping with her shrink. He asked me if I knew the guy and whether I'd heard any dirt about him. It was Roslak."

"What did you do?" Stride asked.

"At first, nothing. I wasn't going to risk the guy's career over innuendo, even if it was someone I didn't particularly like. Besides, husbands always think their wives are screwing the shrink."

"But?"

"But I kept my eyes open. I saw one of the street girls for a physical, and I asked her some leading questions to see if she volunteered anything. She clammed up instead. Wouldn't talk about Roslak. I got the same treatment from the next girl. Didn't seem to matter what he did. The girls wanted to protect him."

"So how did you crack the wall of silence?"

"I saw some of the girls immediately after therapy. There was evidence of sexual activity. Two of them finally admitted it to me. The details were pretty extreme, but the girls refused to go to the police. Instead, I worked with a friend on the state licensing board, and they basically gave Roslak a choice. Give up his license and get out of Duluth, or they'd pursue civil and criminal action against him."

"Did Roslak know you were the one who turned him in?" Stride asked.

"Oh, yeah, he knew. He didn't take it well. He stopped by my house one evening, and it almost came to blows. I thought about calling you for a little backup, but I figured I could handle myself. In the end he left without a fight, which was what he did over his license, too. I was surprised he gave up as easily as he did, but of course we later discovered that he was sleeping with a lot of his paying patients, too. He knew it would all come out."

"What about Cat?"

"She denied a relationship with him."

"Do you believe her?"

Steve frowned. "No."

"Roslak left town a year ago," Stride said, "and Cat claims she never saw him again. Four months later, someone murdered him in Minneapolis."

"Do you think there's a connection?"

"I would have said no, but after last night I'm not so sure. Now I'm wondering if Cat told Roslak something that got him killed. I think she told Margot Huizenfelt the same thing and that's why she was grabbed."

Steve's eyebrows arched in surprise at the reporter's name. "Cat knew Margot?"

"She interviewed Cat a few months ago."

"So what the hell does Cat know that's worth killing over?"

"We're talking about an underage street girl. That's lethal exposure for any man who touches her. Particularly if he's got a wife or a public job. Margot was pushing Cat about whether she'd slept with any men with money."

Steve said nothing but Stride could read his friend's face. Something was wrong.

"You look like you know something," Stride said. "What's up?"

"I'm not sure I can say anything," Steve replied. "Patient confidentiality."

Stride waited.

"Obviously, I can't name names," Steve went on.

"Obviously."

"The thing is, I've noticed an odd trend at the clinic."

"Odd? How so?"

"STDs," Steve said. "They've been showing up in places I wouldn't expect. Like some very well-off husbands and wives. Normally I might see one case every now and then, but this is multiple cases in a short period of time. One of the men admitted that he'd had sex with a girl at UMD. Not his wife, needless to say, and she wasn't screwing him out of the goodness of her heart. She was a paid escort, looking for tuition money."

"You think she saw some of your other patients?" Stride asked.

"No, I think it's more than that. This isn't about one girl. It feels organized to me. I think there may be an upscale prostitution ring operating in the city."

Five minutes after Steve left, Stride heard a knock at the front door of the cottage. He noticed Steve's coat slung over a dining room chair and assumed that his friend had come back to retrieve it.

Stride swung open the door, ready with a joke. When he did, he saw that it wasn't Steve standing on his front porch. The smile on his face bled away, and his mind went blank. The two of them stared at each other in silence, like old friends, like old lovers, which was what they were. He didn't know what to do, now that the moment was here, now that they were together again. Gather her into his arms. Kiss her. Or try to pretend he didn't still love her.

Finally, she spoke first.

"Hello, Jonny."

26

Serena first came into his life at the Duluth airport as she walked off the plane from Las Vegas, dressed like a model. Baby blue leather pants, honey sunglasses, a form-fitting white T-shirt, and a black rain-coat so long it almost swept the floor. She wasn't like anyone he'd ever met. His first wife, Cindy, had been small and fiery, a sprite who wore every emotion on her sleeve. Serena was as tall as Stride in her sky-high heels, and her attitude was cool and wary. She was as curvy as a showgirl, with a razor-sharp wit, but she wore a sign warning away strangers from trespassing.

Don't come inside. Stay away.

He wore a sign like that himself. His own sign, with Cindy's name on it, was about grief and loss. Serena's was about a childhood wrecked by abuse. They were both damaged, both alike, for better or worse. Two half souls.

In their first days together they worked a cold case from Duluth to Las Vegas, and along the way their attraction spilled over into sex. They fell in love. He was married then—a second marriage, a bad marriage. He and a teacher named Andrea had pretended to be in love, but when he met Serena, he realized that his marriage was a sham. When it fell apart, he moved to Las Vegas to be with Serena, but he was a fish

out of water among the barren mountains and casinos. There was only
one place Stride could live, and that was in Duluth, in the shadow of
the lake, under the dark cover of the bitter winters.

He came home, and Serena came with him. Neither one of them
really thought it would work. You couldn't take a girl who grew up
in the desert, like a saguaro, and expect her to thrive in the frozen
north. They were both wrong. Serena had no roots here, but slowly,
with each season, she came to feel at home in Minnesota. He'd always
taken the idea of home for granted, because every street in Duluth was
the sum of its memories for him. Not for Serena. To her, home meant
tearing down the past and starting over.

That was what they tried to do on the Point. They ate breakfast on
Sunday mornings at Amazing Grace. They made love in the middle of
the night, breathlessly, invisibly. They listened to the waves of Superior on the other side of the dune. They were as close and connected
as two people could be, but sometimes it was like they lived apart,
behind the walls they'd built. He'd feel her pushing him away when
she felt vulnerable. He would do the same thing.

Don't come inside. Stay away.

For him, Michaela was one of those walls. He'd never mentioned
her to Serena; he'd never even breathed her name. Michaela, who still
haunted him. Michaela, who had been the only woman in his married life to make him wonder, even for a day, whether he could love
someone other than Cindy. Michaela, whose death had made him feel
every stab wound as if it had gone into his own body.

He stared at Serena in the doorway, and his first thought was: *Why
did I keep Michaela a secret from you?*

"You look great," he said, and she did.

She'd lost weight. Her stomach was flat and hard. Her arms looked
strong. She wore a black turtleneck that hugged her skin and accentu-
ated the swell of her full breasts. Her jeans made her legs look long
and sleek. Standing atop sharp heels, she was eye to eye with him.

"So do you," she said.

He invited her inside. It felt odd, because she didn't need an invitation. She'd lived here for years. She would wander through the back

door, kick off her heels, and drop grocery bags on the counter. She would join him in the living room from the shower, trailing steam, working a brush through her damp hair. The most natural thing in the world was for the two of them to be here together, but they both felt awkward.

"I heard about Kim Dehne," she told him. "Did you talk to Bob?"

"I finally reached him."

"They were a sweet couple. It's an awful thing." She added, "The girl you found in the DECC—it wasn't Cat Mateo, right?"

"Cat's fine," Stride said. "She's on the porch out back."

"I got your message, and you were right. Margot knew her. I found an article she wrote, and it's obviously about Catalina." Serena pulled a folded piece of paper from her back pocket and handed it to him.

As he read the article, Serena made a tour of the living room. Her eyes flitted to the walls and the furniture, and he knew she was noticing that he'd changed nothing since she left. Maggie had come and gone from the house without leaving fingerprints. Serena stopped near the attic stairs. Each wooden stair was narrower than the one above it, and at the top were two closed doors. They had talked about finishing the attic, but they had never made plans for how to use the space, so it was still a mess of spiderwebs and sharp nails jutting from the roof beams.

"Steve says I need to dust," he told her.

"Yeah, it could use a wipe-down, Jonny. I suppose you're not home a lot."

"You know how it goes."

"I do."

He finished the article and knew that Serena was right. Margot was writing about Cat. She'd done a beautiful job of capturing the girl's broken life and of making her human rather than a shadowy other who hangs out in doorways. See this girl? She could be your daughter.

He also noticed that Margot made no reference to Cat taking a limo ride up the north shore to service a wealthy man at a vacation resort. He'd read Margot's writings before, and she loved that kind of savage detail, particularly if it exposed the intersection of heartlessness and power. A sixteen-year-old girl with a rich lawyer or banker? The only way Margot would have skipped that anecdote was if she omitted it deliberately in order to investigate further. She was a reporter, and reporters knew the smell of scandal.

He looked up. Serena was staring at him.

"So do you want to bring me up to date?" she said.

She kept their reunion on safe ground. Talk about work. Talk about the case. Don't talk about each other. He gave her a summary of the events of the weekend. Cat's story, his suspicions about Vincent Roslak and William Green, the clue from Brandy that led to Margot, the vicious murders overnight. He also mentioned Steve's speculation about hookers with wealthy clients.

"Did you find any hints in your investigation that Margot could have been looking into upscale prostitution?" he asked.

"I can't be sure, but it's definitely possible. Based on her phone records and credit card info, she met with a lot of one-percenters around the northland in the weeks before she disappeared. Nobody volunteered anything about escorts, but it's not like they would. I can get a list of names and photos of the people Margot saw. Maybe Cat will recognize one of them."

"Margot may have been thinking the same thing," Stride suggested. "That would explain why she was trying to find Cat again."

"And why someone would be desperate to get rid of both of them," Serena said. "I want to find out exactly who Margot talked to that last weekend. We know she was in Duluth trying to find Cat, but nobody breathed a word about it to the police after she disappeared. That sounds like somebody didn't want us to connect the dots."

"I know where I would have started if I were Margot," Stride said. "Cat's guardians. William and Sophie Green."

"Yeah, me too."

They both turned toward the kitchen as a young voice shouted from the porch.

"I finished the puzzle!" Cat announced.

She slid into the great space in her socks with a girlish excitement that made her seem younger than she was. "That was a really easy one—" she began, but she skidded to a stop as she saw Serena standing by the stairs to the attic. "Oh!"

"Hi, Cat," Serena said.

Cat's eyes flicked between the two of them. "Who are you?"

"My name's Serena."

Cat studied her with curious interest, as if she were a model on a runway. "Wow, you're like really gorgeous."

Serena laughed. He'd missed her laughter. "I was about to tell you the same thing."

Cat blushed in embarrassment, but Stride could tell she was pleased by the compliment.

"You used to live here, right?" Cat said. "Mr. Stride let me wear one of your shirts."

"*Mr.* Stride," Serena said, with amused eyes. "I bet he'd be okay if you called him Stride. Most people do. And yes, you're right, I used to live here."

"But you don't anymore?" Cat asked.

"No, I don't."

"Serena works for the sheriff's department in Itasca County," Stride interjected quickly. "She's investigating the disappearance of that reporter you met. Margot Huizenfelt."

"Oh, okay." Cat's mouth twitched with concern. "Is she dead?"

"I hope not," Serena said.

"Do you know why she was looking for me?"

"No, but Jonny and I are going to find out."

The name slipped easily from her lips. *Jonny.* She'd always called him that. Just like Cindy did. Cat didn't miss the familiarity in her voice or the fact that they stood on opposite sides of the room, like nervous boxers. For a young girl, she didn't miss much.

"People are dying, and it's my fault," Cat said.

"It's not," Stride told her.

"He's right, Cat," Serena added. "Don't blame yourself."

"I ran away. If I'd stayed home with the Greens, none of this would have happened."

Serena sat down on the attic steps. She leaned forward with her elbows on her knees. "We don't know if that's true, and from what Jonny tells me, you didn't have much of a choice about running away. You were being hurt, right? It's okay to say so."

"Yeah, Mr. Green would hit me sometimes. A lot of times, I guess. I probably deserved it."

"You didn't. No child deserves it."

"I could have done something. I could have said something."

"That's not always how it works," Serena said. "It's nice if you can, but sometimes you can't. I get it."

Cat shrugged. "You're strong. Someone like you would have just kicked him in the balls."

Stride watched Serena and saw the hardness in her face come and go. The memory. The pain. He wondered what she would say, if she would say anything at all. Back then, she would have kept her past hidden; she would never have shared it with a stranger.

"I wish I had," Serena told Cat softly, "but I ran away, too."

Cat's head cocked in confusion. "What do you mean?"

Serena said nothing, but she held Cat's stare across the room, girl to girl, woman to woman. Eventually, Cat understood. "You?" she asked.

"Me," Serena said. "Not just physical abuse. There was more. Bad stuff."

"How old?"

"Your age. Sixteen."

Cat's brown eyes welled with tears. She stuck a finger in her mouth and chewed a nail.

"I don't talk about it a lot," Serena went on, "but I live with it now. You will, too."

Cat swallowed hard. Her hair fell across her face. She danced on her feet, and without saying a word, she turned and ran through the kitchen. Serena winced, as if she'd breathed on a house of cards and made it fall. He heard her swear at herself under her breath.

Stride followed Cat and found her on the musty sofa on the rear porch. He sat down next to her. The young girl stared at the completed puzzle of the lift bridge, its pieces knitted together. She continued to chew a nail. One tear made a glossy line on her cheek.

"You okay?" he asked.

Cat shrugged her shoulders.

"You don't have to deal with any of this alone," he said. "Serena knows what it's like. She can help. So can I."

Cat still said nothing. Her stare was blank. He felt her pushing him away.

"Serena and I have to go out for a while," he told her. "I have a police officer coming to stay with you while we're gone. We won't leave until he gets here."

Stride stood up, and Cat turned and threw her arms around his waist. He didn't move. She clung to him silently, and when she finally let go, she wiped her face and ducked her chin into her neck. He reached out and stroked her hair.

"Hey, Stride?" Cat murmured, as he turned to leave.

He stared down at her. "What is it?"

"I like her."

27

They drove in Stride's Expedition. Neither one of them spoke.

As he came out of the S-curve on the Point near the canal, he spotted an ore boat in the harbor heading toward the lake. The lift bridge was already closed. Five cars waited in line, and he pulled in behind them and shut off the engine. The radio, which had been playing a Patty Loveless bluegrass song, went quiet.

He opened the driver's door and cold air blew inside. There was no rain, but the streets and sidewalks were wet.

"I'm not sure what to say to you," he admitted.

"You don't have to say anything, Jonny."

Across the short space of the truck, he could smell her perfume. Her fragrance hadn't changed. She wore the emerald earrings he'd given her.

"That was sweet of Valerie and Callie to send me that jigsaw puzzle for Christmas," he said. "Are you still living with them?"

"I am."

"I'm glad you stayed close by."

Serena looked out the window. "I went back to Las Vegas for a week in January. I wanted to see if there was anything still there for me."

"Was there?"

"My old partner, Cordy, he said they wanted me back on metro. All I had to do was say yes."

"What did you tell him?"

Serena didn't answer. She turned and stared at him. It had been a long time since he watched her green eyes. "I stayed with Claire while I was there," she added.

"Okay."

Stride remembered Claire. In the short time he'd spent with Serena in Las Vegas, they had become enmeshed in a case involving a serial killer and an old-line mob family. Claire, whose father ran one of the city's largest casinos, became a target, and Serena had been the cop assigned to protect her. Along the way, Claire fell in love with her. The relationship had awakened confused sexual feelings in Serena, and Stride had thought he might lose her.

"Claire asked me to take a job as head of security at her new casino," Serena said. She gave a little ironic smile. "And live with her, of course. She has a mansion in Lake Las Vegas. Really nice."

"So what did you decide?"

"I told them both no," she said.

"Why?"

Serena shook her head without explaining. "Your turn, Jonny. Tell me about you."

The superstructure of the ore boat glided like a graceful giant under the span of the lift bridge. "I'm sure you heard that my relationship with Maggie went nowhere," he said.

"I did."

"She said she was tired of living with a ghost, and she didn't mean Cindy. She knew I still loved you."

"I guess I should say I'm sorry."

"That's the last thing you should say. I'm the one who's sorry."

Serena brushed a strand of black hair from her eyes. "You said you were sorry months ago. I said I forgave you. I nearly fell in love with Claire a few years ago, and you forgave me. We're not perfect. I don't expect us to be. As angry as I was, I never doubted that you were still in love with me."

"But?"

"But it's not about that anymore."

"Then what is it about?"

"I won't be in love with a stranger, Jonny."

"I'm not sure that's fair," he said.

Serena took a breath before she went on, as if she wanted to get each word exactly right. "Maybe not, but it felt that way last fall. You were a million miles away from me, and I couldn't reach you. I know we were both at fault. I know I closed myself off, too, but that's over. I'm done running from my past. No shame. No apologies. This is me." Her voice rose, and it quivered as she talked louder. "I came back from Las Vegas for one reason. Not for a job. Not for a home. I came back because I still love you. But that's not enough, not when I don't know if you'll shut me out again the next time things get bad. If you still want me, if you really want me, then you're going to have to come get me, and you better be prepared to let me inside. All the way. No more secrets."

He'd never seen this side of her. She'd always been tough, but toughness meant stringing up barbed wire around her soul. This was different. Now she was holding out a hand for him to join her, and he didn't know how to take the first step.

Someone hit the horn behind them.

He looked up and saw that the bridge was back down, and the traffic in front of him had cleared. He drove into Duluth.

Twenty miles south of the city, near the exit to the Black Bear Casino, traffic stalled as orange pylons blocked the right lane. Stride put an emergency light on the hood of his truck and steered onto the gravel shoulder. He drove a half mile and stopped near a paving truck where a band of highway workers jackhammered the asphalt. One of the men, fat and round, with a ponytail dangling from his hard hat, was William Green.

Drizzle spattered the windshield. Stride removed his gun from the holster inside his jacket and locked it inside his glove compartment.

"What are you doing?" Serena asked.

"I'd prefer not to shoot him," he said.

"Good thinking."

They got out of the truck. Six feet away, on the other side of the ribbon of cones, traffic whipped by with a surge of air pressure. The noise was deafening, and the ground shook under their feet.

Green saw them, and Stride crooked his finger, beckoning the man closer. The highway worker made a slashing motion across his throat to the other men, and the jackhammer went silent. He marched closer, only inches from the speeding cars. When he reached Stride, he took off his hat and wiped his sweaty brow.

"What do you want?" he said. "I'm busy. Frost heaves blew out the lane overnight. We need to patch it up."

"This won't take long," Stride said.

He introduced Serena, and Green checked out her body with a quick glance. So did the other workers behind him. He thought they would have wolf-whistled if she hadn't been a cop.

"Where were you last night, Mr. Green?" Stride said.

"Home."

"Doing what?"

"Watching the Wolves and the Heat. Drinking beer. Why?"

"Was your wife with you?"

"No, we had a fight after you left. She stayed at her sister's in Cloquet."

"Did you talk to anyone? See anyone?"

"Just LeBron."

An SUV passed, close enough to clip one of the traffic cones and send it spiraling into the air. It flew close to Green's head, but the man didn't flinch. He gestured at one of the workers to retrieve it, and he shoved his hands into his baggy pockets. Behind them, other cars braked as the cone rolled into the lane.

"You ought to give that son of a bitch a ticket," he told Stride. "Do something useful instead of leaning on me."

"I'm just getting started."

"What does that mean?" Green asked. "What is this about?"

"It means we talked to Cat about you."

"Yeah? So?"

"She says you liked to beat her up."

Green wiped rain from his nose, leaving a smear of dirt on his face. "Whatever she told you, it's not true. I never laid a hand on her."

Stride tried to calm himself, but the thumping vibration and rush of air with each speeding car fed his adrenaline. "Remember what I told you yesterday, Mr. Green? I made you a promise."

"Yeah, I remember."

"I'll be watching you," Stride told him.

"I bet you will."

Serena physically stepped between the two men. "I have some questions for you, Mr. Green. It's about Margot Huizenfelt."

"Who?"

"She's a reporter. She's missing."

"Huizenfelt. Yeah. Okay, sure, I saw it on TV. What about her?"

"The day before she disappeared, she was looking for Cat. Did she talk to you?"

Green didn't answer immediately. The dust of crushed rock blew in their faces. "I don't remember."

Serena and Stride exchanged a glance. She rubbed dust off her skin. The passing cars felt huge and dangerous.

"Maybe your neighbors remember her, Mr. Green," she said. "We could talk to all of them. We could ask them about you and Cat, too. Or how about your coworkers over there? Most of them are parents. I wonder what they'd think if they knew you liked to take out your anger on a teenage girl."

Green glanced nervously over his shoulder. "Shit, all right," he hissed. "It's no big deal. This reporter came to the house on a Saturday afternoon. She asked me how she could find Cat. I didn't know where the hell she was, and that's what I told her."

"Margot wrote an article about Cat a few months ago. Did she talk to you back then?"

"She tried. I told her to get lost."

"What time did she show up at your house on that Saturday?"

Green shrugged. "I don't know. Four, five, something like that. Sophie was going to be back any minute, and I wanted that bitch out of there before she got home. I told her if she wanted to find Cat, she should try the usual places. The shelter. The graffiti graveyard. Lake Place Park. Wherever the runaways hang out."

"Did she say why she wanted to find her?"

"No."

"She must have said something," Serena insisted.

"She wanted to know about Cat and her parents. What did I know about Michaela and Marty. Shit like that."

"What did you tell her?"

"I told her Marty was a son of a bitch! What the hell else would I say? Whenever he was drunk, he beat the shit out of whoever was closest to him. Usually, that was me." Green pointed at a two-inch white scar high on his forehead. "He gave me that one in December that last winter. I've got more."

"Anything else?" Serena asked. "Did Margot want to know about anyone else?"

"Yeah, she asked about Dory," Green replied. "She wasn't just looking for Cat. She was trying to find Dory, too."

28

Brooke Hahne sat in the basement café known as Amazing Grace. It was a college hangout, but Brooke came here several times a week. Sometimes she kept an eye open for kids who needed help. Sometimes she hid in a corner and nursed a chai latte as she wrote grant proposals for The Praying Hands. Sometimes, like tonight, she came for the band.

Steve Garske's band was called Doc of the Bay. That was cute.

Steve was no Brad Paisley on the guitar, but he could lay down a good riff on songs like "One More Last Chance." He had a mellow voice that made for a good cover of Vince Gill, who was one of Brooke's favorites. She liked the old-style, twangy country music. Prison songs. Raspy, bourbon-soaked voices. Lots of steel. She was probably the only George Jones fan who had just turned thirty.

Onstage, Steve's fingers flew like a pro. She saw a sheen of sweat on his brow under the hot lights. As he wrapped up his solo, the crammed café erupted in applause, and he bowed with a shy grin, pushing back his blond hair. Brooke toasted him with her latte. Steve winked at her.

She examined the crowd squeezed around the handful of weathered wooden tables. Most of them were under twenty-five, except for a handful of aging ex-hippies in hemp sweaters. She had a tiny circular table to herself, but a dozen people stood over her. When the music stopped, a college kid squatted next to her. He couldn't have been more than nineteen. He was cute and gangly, with a shaggy haircut that went out with the Monkees, and he didn't even look old enough to shave. College boys had no sense of a woman's age.

"Hey, you alone?" he asked.

"I'm waiting for someone," Brooke said.

"Well, how about I wait with you?"

Brooke rolled her eyes. Tall, skinny, fit blondes drew boys like mosquitoes. Usually, they wilted away with a simple brush-off that dented their egos. Others, the cocky ones, needed a firmer rejection.

"I'm involved," she said.

"Yeah? With who?"

She gestured at Steve Garske, who gulped bottled water onstage as they geared up for the second set. "Him. The singer."

The boy's hair almost dangled in Brooke's drink. "He's like a million years old."

"What can I say? I'm a groupie."

"What's he got that I ain't got?"

Brooke cupped her hands by his ear. The kid's face scrunched up with disbelief. "No way," he said.

Brooke took her index fingers and slowly spread them apart.

"Holy shit," the kid said. He left her alone and she saw him talking frantically to three of his buddies.

Brooke smiled to herself. The truth was that she was dating no one, but an imaginary boyfriend spared her an evening of come-ons. Poor Steve. She couldn't remember him dating a soul in the years she'd known him. He always claimed to be too busy for sex, between his medical practice and his band. After tonight, he'd probably wonder why women were clamoring for his attention.

She liked Steve. The fact that he was as asexual as she was made her feel comfortable around him. He'd never made a salacious comment of any kind about her, and that was rare. Most men, married or unmarried, didn't wait five minutes to comment on her looks.

Donors to the shelter were the worst. With other men, she simply shot them down, but with donors, she had to play the game, as dirty as it made her feel.

Brooke hadn't slept with a man in five years. Her last relationship, with an intellectual property attorney from Minneapolis, had ended after their first night together. She didn't blame him. She was frozen in bed, not even mustering a pretense of excitement. To her, sex was a chore. Since then, she'd routinely turned down dates, because she was tired of faking interest. She wasn't gay, but she loathed men. Rich or poor, young or old, handsome or ugly, they were all the same. Abusers. Manipulators. Predators.

Her cell phone vibrated on the table. She picked it up and read the incoming text.

I'm outside.

Brooke drained the last drops of her latte and stood up. Her table was immediately swarmed. She climbed onto the stage and marched in her black heels up to Steve, who was draped over a wooden chair that was too small for him. His face was flushed, and he laughed as he chatted with his bandmates. She bent down and practically had to shout.

"I have to go. I'm meeting someone."

Steve wiped his forehead with his sleeve. "You're going to miss 'House of Gold' if you bug out."

"My favorite."

"I know."

"Rain check for the next gig," Brooke said. She didn't think she could hear the song tonight anyway. It always made her cry.

When she turned away, Steve tugged on the sleeve of her blouse. He eyed the front row of women in the crowd, who were giggling to each other and sneaking glances at him. "Hey, is it just me, or are the gals looking at me funny?"

Brooke smiled. "It's just you."

She left the stage and pushed through the mass of bodies in the café. When she reached the door, she broke out into the cool air and climbed the steps to the street. She had a jacket over her arm, and she slipped into it. The lake wind cut through her tapered black slacks. She reached behind her head and bundled her long hair and expertly tied it into a ponytail.

On the other side of the park, near the ship canal, she saw the foggy blur of the lighthouse towers. She crossed Buchanan Street into the crowded parking lot, where the neon sign for Grandma's Saloon glowed behind the cars. Her Kia was parked in the first row.

She saw someone sitting on her bumper.

"Dory," Brooke said. "What are you doing here?"

Dory Mateo scrambled to her feet. She was smoking a cigarette. Under the streetlight, her skin looked white enough to see veins. "Brooke. Hey, how are you?"

"I'm okay. How about you?"

"How do I look?" Dory asked.

"Not too good, sweetheart."

Dory's mouth carved out a faint smile. "Yeah."

"Can I do anything?"

"No, I just need to talk."

Brooke opened the car doors, and Dory crushed her cigarette on the wet ground. They got inside. Dory carried a smell of smoke with her, and Brooke cracked both windows to let in the lake air. Before the dome light went off, she saw the sunken half-moons under Dory's eyes. Dory's fingers shook.

"I'm going to drive you to the hospital," Brooke said.

"No! No doctors."

"Dory, you need help."

"I don't care. It doesn't matter."

Brooke had seen Dory at the bottom of some black holes in her life, but she'd never seen her like this. The two of them went back for years. She'd met Dory in her freshman year at UMD, where they quickly became inseparable. They moved into a crappy studio apartment together, and they shared sob stories about money, men, sex, and families. They vowed to help each other make it in the big bad world, but it didn't work out that way. Dory lasted only one year at UMD before dropping out. She burnt through thousands of dollars on drugs. Watching Dory spiral out of control, Brooke became cynical about what it took to survive in the world.

"How's Cat?" Brooke asked. "Is she okay?"

"She's with the cops. She's safe for now."

Dory fidgeted as they heard a burble of voices from the restaurant behind them. A gang of teenagers rode skateboards back and forth in front of Amazing Grace, and she squinted at them as the rolling wheels shunted and banged.

"Across the street," Dory said. "Is that a man in the alley?"

Brooke studied the shadows. "I don't see anyone. Dory, what's wrong?"

"Margot Huizenfelt disappeared," Dory said. "I think I'm next."

"Next? What are you talking about? What does Margot have to do with you?"

"Margot was trying to find Cat when someone grabbed her. The police think there's a connection."

"What kind of connection? What is this about?"

"I don't know, but two people are dead, and Cat barely got away alive. He's going to come after me, too. I know he is. I'm being punished."

"Punished? Come on, that's crazy. Why do you think that?"

Dory turned, and in the strange shadows of the car Brooke felt as if she could see through Dory's skin to her skull. "I did a terrible thing back then," her friend said. "We both know that. It's like a curse. I can't escape it."

Brooke felt a chill. Dory looked like the devil, staring at her. Her eyes were almost red. "What are you talking about?"

"You know what I did. Remember?"

Brooke closed her eyes in frustration. "Dory, that was ten years ago. We were kids. We all made mistakes. If I could go back and start over, don't you think I'd change my life, too?"

"It's not the same."

"Yes, it is. You can't keep torturing yourself. Whatever's going on now, it has nothing to do with you. Let it go. Please. Just get yourself some help, sweetheart, before it's too late."

"I can't keep the secret anymore. It's like this weight on my chest." Dory leaned forward, clutching the dashboard. "There's a man in that alley. I see him."

"It's your imagination," Brooke told her. "There's no one there."

"No, he's watching us. I know it. He's coming for me."

"Dory, listen to me. You're in bad shape. We both know it. If you want to make up for what you did, turn your life around and get healthy. It won't change anything to start living in the past. You and I are the only people who know what happened back then. Leave it at that."

Dory shook her head. "Someone else knows."

"You said you never told anyone."

"I needed to get it off my chest. I thought it wouldn't matter anymore."

"Dory, you didn't tell Cat, did you?" Brooke asked.

"Cat? No, it would kill her to know. I never wanted her to find out."

"Then who?"

Dory pushed open the car door. Her eyes were fixated on the alley. She was ready to run.

"Margot," Dory said. "I told Margot what I did. Don't you see? It can't be a coincidence. This is my fault. Right after I told her, she disappeared."

29

"Nice place," Serena said, as Stride turned on the light in his office. She eyed the half dozen moving boxes scattered on the floor. "One of these days maybe you'll unpack and stay awhile."

"Someday." He reached for a folder on his desk and flinched in pain.

"Does your shoulder hurt?" she asked.

"Yeah."

"Next time, duck," she said, smiling.

"Thanks."

Serena picked up the photo of Cindy on his credenza. The picture was the only personal item she saw in his office. She studied Cindy's face, noticing the flirty confidence in her eyes and smile. Stride's first wife was cute, but not anyone's idea of beautiful. She had straight dark hair, parted in the middle, and a sharp little V-nose. It was her attitude that made her attractive. Always teasing. Always full of life.

Serena had never met Cindy. She'd been dead for years when Serena first arrived in Duluth. Had they met, she thought that she would have liked Cindy, so it was strange how jealous she felt of her. She'd always imagined that she was competing with Cindy for Stride's heart.

She noticed him watching her. He didn't say anything.

"I'm going to the ladies' room," she told him.

"Okay. I have what I need. We can go back to the Point."

"Thanks."

"You want to hang around before you head home? I could use a drink."

"Maybe I will."

Serena went into the dark hallway of the police headquarters. She saw a sign for the restroom, and she went inside and stood in front of the wide mirror. Her face was dirty from the rain and road spray at the highway site so she ran hot water and washed her skin, removing her makeup at the same time. Her natural face stared back at her. She ran a long nail over the age lines that had crept beside her mouth.

As she stood by the mirror, the bathroom door opened. In the reflection, she saw Maggie Bei.

The small Chinese cop stopped in awkward surprise as she spotted Serena. She reached for the door to leave, but then she shrugged and let it swing shut behind her. She came up to the mirror, standing in front of the twin sink. She washed her hands without looking up at the glass.

"Hi," Maggie said.

"Hi," Serena replied.

Maggie turned off the water and flicked her hands into the bowl. She took a paper towel and dried them. "I figured you'd be coming to town. You working with Stride?"

"Yeah."

"Good." Maggie worked her mouth as if she were chewing gum. She gestured with her thumb at the bathroom door. "So do I need my gun?"

"If I were going to kill you, I'd use my bare hands," Serena said.

"Nice. Okay."

"If you have things to do in here, don't let me stop you."

"Actually, things just sort of squeezed shut on me. Weird."

"Yeah, weird," Serena said.

They stood next to each other in silence. One of them had to leave, but neither one did. Maggie played with her bangs. Serena bent forward toward the mirror and smoothed her eyebrows.

"Black hair again, I see," Serena said.

"Uh-huh."

"I didn't tell you, but the red was awful."

"Thanks."

"So you and Jonny went nowhere. Gee, that's too bad."

"I guess sticking the pins in the Maggie doll worked."

"I guess."

"Do you want to slap me or something?" Maggie asked. "Would that make you feel better?"

"If it would, I'd have already done it."

"Right. Sure. Mind if I tell you something?"

"Go ahead."

"Fuck off, Serena."

Serena straightened up. "Well, that's mature."

"Hey, if you want to torture me, go ahead. I don't care. I already told you that I never meant for anything to happen with Stride, but it happened. I can't change that. I get it that you can forgive him, not me. I don't expect us to be best friends again."

"Good."

"Just don't expect me to walk away. I'm his friend. I'm his partner. I've known him longer than you have. I'm not going anywhere."

"Yeah, I always know where I can find you, Maggie. Right next to Jonny."

"If you think I'd let anything happen between us again, you're crazy."

"Said the spider to the fly."

"I mean it."

"I know you do, and if you think I believe you, *you're* crazy."

Maggie grabbed the door and opened it halfway. "This is getting us nowhere. You know what's too bad? I still like you, Serena. I hope someday we'll be able to get past this."

Serena said nothing.

"One thing," Maggie went on. "If you're working with Stride, do me a favor. Watch his back."

"Meaning what?"

"I don't trust Cat Mateo. She's obsessed with knives, and I think she's becoming obsessed with Stride. I don't like it."

"Jonny can take care of himself."

"Yeah? For all we know, Cat murdered Vincent Roslak. Hell, maybe Margot figured it out and Cat killed her, too. Did you think about that?"

"Come on. This girl's not a serial killer."

"I forgot, you're biased, too," Maggie said. "Stride feels guilty because of Michaela. You feel guilty because of your childhood. What a cute little codependent trio you guys make."

"I've never worn rose-colored glasses about anyone. Except maybe you."

"Fair enough. I deserve that, but I'm not kidding around. I got a call from a friend of mine on the Minneapolis police. Ken McCarty. He did some digging on the Roslak case and he found something about Cat in Roslak's files. A video. He says it's pretty scary stuff."

"Ken McCarty," Serena said. "Is he the latest *friend* you're sleeping with?"

"Where the hell did you hear that?" Maggie demanded. "Did Stride tell you?"

"Guppo knows. You can't keep things from Guppo."

"Fine. I'm sleeping with Ken. So what?"

"Well, you can see why I don't exactly swoon when you cross your heart and swear that you and Jonny are just friends. You seem to make a habit of fucking your friends."

Maggie's fists clenched. "All I'm saying is, you need to be careful about Cat."

"Understood. Is that all you want to say?"

"No, it's not." Maggie dug in her pocket and pulled out a ring of keys. She flipped the keys until she found the one she wanted, and then she pried it off the chain. She held it in front of Serena's face. "See this? It's Stride's key. I've had it for years. Back when Cindy was alive? I had the key. When you two were shacking up? I had the key."

Maggie slapped the key on the bathroom sink in front of Serena.

"Now I don't have it anymore."

Stride and Serena sat on the screened porch at the back of his cottage, with their feet propped on an old plastic cooler. He had a bottle of Miller Lite in his hand. Serena, who didn't drink, sipped mineral water. He felt as if time had gone backward; this was like old times. It was dark and cold, and the lake growled beyond the dunes. In the main part of the house, they heard the buzz of the television. Cat had fallen asleep on the leather sofa in the living room, and they'd left her there.

"Do you think Maggie could be right?" Serena asked, after a long stretch of silence filled with nothing but the rush of the waves.

"About Cat? No, I don't."

"She says Ken McCarty found a video of Cat and Roslak. It's not good."

"I wouldn't trust anything involving Roslak."

He shook his head to stay awake. He found his eyes drifting shut.

"What about the murders? There's still no sign of the stolen Charger?" Serena asked.

"None."

"Maybe the killer knows there's evidence inside. Blood, DNA."

"Or maybe he knows that if we tie the car to Kim's death, Cat's off the hook."

He heard Serena sit up straighter in the darkness. "What do you mean?"

"I mean, why stab Kim Dehne with a knife? There are cleaner, faster, easier ways to kill someone."

"Roslak was killed the same way. This guy could be a psychopath. What's your point?"

"My point is, what if Cat hadn't gotten away?"

"He'd have stabbed her, too."

"I wonder."

"You don't think so?"

"I think we never would have seen Cat again," Stride said. "If we found Kim Dehne stabbed to death, and Cat was nowhere to be found, what would we be thinking right now?"

"We'd be thinking Cat killed her," Serena concluded.

"Exactly. Maybe Roslak and Margot, too."

"But why try to frame Cat? Why not just kill her? He's been after her for weeks. What's changed?"

"Cat came to me," Stride said. "I started listening to her."

Serena took another drink of mineral water, and the plastic bottle crackled. "There's something I don't understand, Jonny. Bill Green said Margot was asking about Cat's parents. Why? What was she looking for?"

"I don't know."

"Was there anything unusual about their deaths?"

"No, it was a straightforward murder-suicide."

"So what did Margot want?"

"Maybe she wanted to get inside Cat's head."

Serena was quiet. "You know, you never told me the truth about you and Michaela," she said finally. "I know she was important to you."

She'd opened the door for him, and all he had to do was walk through it. All he had to do was open up. He wanted to tell her. He wanted to do what she'd done for him and lay himself bare. He wanted to let Michaela into his soul again and share her with Serena, but instead he sat frozen. He didn't say a word, which was the worst thing he could do.

Next to him, Serena stood up, and her demeanor was suddenly like a cool breeze blowing on the porch. He knew she was angry at his silence. "I have to go."

"It's too late to drive back to Grand Rapids. Use one of the other bedrooms."

"I don't mind the drive. Good night, Jonny."

"Serena, wait."

He stood up and took hold of her shoulders and turned her around. He remembered the feel of her body. He could barely see the contours of her face, but he'd memorized them years ago. She was close, but she was distant from him. He'd pushed her away again.

"There are things you don't know," he said. "I have secrets I've never told anyone."

"I know more than you think. You feel guilty. You promised to protect Michaela, and you failed. She was probably half in love with you. Maybe more than half. It's okay. I just wish you'd told me."

"It's not just that. There's something else."

"What is it?"

She waited for him, and he thought: *Tell her.* He could hear Cindy's voice in his head, and she said the same thing. *Tell her.* It was the right time to free himself. It was the right time to admit it. Instead, like a stranger, he said nothing at all.

The moment slipped away from them.

30

Serena found Cat on the front porch in an Adirondack chair. Her legs were pulled up so that her knees were under her chin. Her feet were bare. She stared at the quiet street and the black water of the harbor and took tiny sips from a can of Diet Coke.

"You shouldn't be out here," Serena told her. "It's not safe."

"Are you leaving?"

"Yes."

"Oh. I was hoping you'd stay."

Serena slid down into an empty chair. She still had more than an hour's drive to Grand Rapids, but the girl looked lonely and in need of company. "You couldn't sleep?"

"I woke up, and I started thinking about things. So I came out here."

"What things?"

"I don't know. Everything's messed up."

"It feels that way sometimes."

"For you, too?"

"Me, too."

Cat bit her nails. "I know it's none of my business, but why not stay, huh?"

"I'm not ready yet."

"But you want to."

"Yes," she admitted. "I want to."

"Why did you and Stride break up? You look really good together."

"Things happen, Cat."

"Like what?"

Serena glanced at the girl, who studied her with wide, serious eyes. "I'm not sure he'd want me to tell you."

"Tell me anyway."

"Stride slept with Maggie."

"He *cheated* on you? Stride?" She looked crestfallen.

"It's complicated. I don't really blame him for it. We weren't connecting, and Maggie was there when he needed someone. I haven't always been an angel myself. It's just that he won't tell me things. He won't say anything that makes him vulnerable. It drives me crazy."

"But Maggie?" Cat said, her lip curling. "She's a bitch."

Serena laughed. "She's not, really, but what the hell. She's a bitch."

"She doesn't like me."

"Maggie doesn't like anybody who gets close to Stride if it's not her."

"Stride loves you, not her. I can see that."

"I know."

"But you won't take him back?"

"It's too soon to know what's going to happen between us. We've been apart for months."

"Oh." Cat took another sip of Diet Coke. She shivered as she watched the cars on the Point. "After this is over, what happens to me?"

"We'll make sure you're in good hands."

"Did Stride tell you?" she asked, placing her hands on her stomach.

"About you being pregnant? Yes, he did."

"Do you think I'm too young to have a baby?"

"That's your decision, not mine. Do you think you're too young?"

"Probably, but it's too late for that, isn't it?"

"No. You have options."

"Not good options."

"You're right. I didn't say they were good. Nothing's easy about this."

"Could you ever give up your child?" Cat asked.

Serena said nothing. She felt a tightening in her face.

"I'm sorry," Cat said. "That's too personal. I shouldn't have said anything."

"No, don't be sorry." She took Cat's hand and squeezed it. She was surprised at how easily the words flowed. "I got pregnant at sixteen, too. Just like you."

"Were you scared?"

"Terrified."

Cat squeezed back and didn't let go. "What happened? I mean, how . . ."

"My mother became addicted to cocaine when I was a teenager," Serena said. "We lost our house. My father left us. I was in Phoenix then. We ended up moving into an apartment with her drug dealer. His name was Blue Dog. Brutal son of a bitch. When my mother couldn't pay for drugs, I became the payment."

Cat blinked back tears. "Oh, no."

"When I got pregnant, I didn't know what to do. My girlfriend Deidre took me to the clinic."

Serena opened her mouth and found no more words.

She blamed herself; she had waited too long. She even remembered the name of the procedure. Dilation and evacuation. Not quick. Not painless. It was like punishment for those who couldn't face the truth. There was an antiseptic smell in the room. She could hear the hiss of the pump. Her insides twisted as the doctor cut, scraped, and sucked. She remembered the sound of tissue dripping into an aluminum pan.

And then, two days later, blood. So much blood. She woke up with a pool of her blood in the sheet, the cramping so bad it was like a hot knife cutting her abdomen open. At the hospital, when she was conscious again, they told her she'd almost died. When she got out, she and Deidre left for Las Vegas. She never went home.

"They messed me up inside," she went on. "I can't have kids."

"Serena, I'm so sorry."

"Don't worry. Most days I'm okay with it." She smiled at Cat. "Then there are days when I see a girl's face, like yours, and I wish things were different. Right now, I live with a woman whose child was kidnapped. I helped get her back. I think I love that little girl as much as her mother does."

"You'd make a good mother," Cat said.

"Thank you. That's sweet."

"Can I ask you something?" Cat said. "A favor?"

"Sure."

"I have to go see Dr. Steve this week. You know, for the baby. Would you go with me?"

"Of course, I'll go with you."

"Thanks." Cat played with her hair and added, "You don't have to answer this, but I'd like to know. When you were alone, and you had no money, did you ever—I mean, did you think about . . ."

She stopped. She waited without saying more.

"Did I become a prostitute?" Serena said.

"Yeah."

"Deidre did. She offered to arrange dates for me. Sometimes I look back and wonder why I said no. I worked shit jobs that paid almost nothing. It would have been easier to make money that way, but I think, after what happened with Blue Dog, I just couldn't do it."

"I wish I'd never started. I can't stand the idea of a man touching me like that now. I think I'd kill him."

Serena watched Cat's face, which was suddenly as hard as a mask, filled with violence. Her jaw tightened. The fingers of her right hand curled, as if holding a knife. The girl noticed Serena's stare, and she softened and looked guilty. She knew she'd said the wrong thing.

"Your mother," Cat said, changing the subject. "Is she still alive?"

"Honestly? I don't know."

"Your father?"

"No, he passed away. We never really had a chance to reconcile."

"I miss my parents," Cat said.

"I'm sure you do. I miss what my parents should have been to me. I still need them. That never goes away."

"People think I forgive my dad for what he did. That's not really true. I still talk to him sometimes when I'm lonely. I still wear the ring he gave me. That doesn't mean I forgive him. If he was here right now, I'd scream at him. I just know that, as bad as he was, he loved me more than anything else in his life."

Serena wondered if that was true. "Do you remember that night?"

"I remember it in my dreams sometimes. It goes away when I wake up, but I know it's been there." Cat's eyes glazed over, as if in an instant she went somewhere far away and then came back. Her brow wrinkled in confusion. "It's like an echo. That's all I remember."

"An echo?"

Cat nodded. "I can hear a voice. A man's voice. He's shouting, but I can't make out what he says."

"A man? Your father?"

"I don't know. I just know he scares me. In the dream, he's going to kill me."

31

"Special delivery," Ken McCarty said when Maggie opened the door.

He cradled a Sammy's pizza box in his hands, and the aroma wafted into her condo like an old friend. It was almost midnight, and Maggie was angry, horny, and starving. She took him by the collar and dragged him inside.

"Sausage and pepp?"

"Sausage and pepp." He slid the cardboard box onto her dining room table and held out his hand. "That'll be twenty dollars for the pizza, ma'am. Not including tip, and college boys like me really need tips."

Maggie ran a fingernail down his neck. "Oh, no. Oh, I have no cash. Whatever will we do? Would you take a check?"

"Sorry, ma'am, no checks."

"I'm so embarrassed. Is there anything else I can do?" She undid the first button on his shirt, then the second.

"Do I look like some UMD gigolo trying to pay back my student loans? It's twenty bucks, ma'am."

She scraped her fingernails through his blond chest hair. Her other hand squeezed between his legs. She continued unbuttoning his shirt as she kissed her way down onto her knees. "Are you sure? Isn't there some other way I can pay you?"

When she tugged his zipper down, Ken couldn't keep a straight face. "Okay, okay, you win. The pizza's going to get cold if you keep doing that."

"Cold pizza is the food of the gods. It's like McNuggets. Besides, this isn't going to take long."

She was right. Half an hour later, they sat on opposite sides of her small kitchen table, half-dressed, with open beer bottles in front of them. The pizza was still warm. Maggie began eating the little pepperoni slices before starting in on the pizza itself, which was cut into squares.

"So what's up with the video of Roslak and Cat?" she asked, her mouth full.

"It's creepy stuff."

"Creepy enough that you think she killed him?"

"I don't know. She's screwed up enough that I would say yes. Anyway, you're not going to like it."

"How so?"

"You'll have to watch it and see." Ken popped a square of pizza into his mouth. "You know what we need for dessert? Donuts."

"Sick man."

"I miss House of Donuts."

"Jeez, you and Stride and your donut envy. Steve's the same way. Is this a guy thing?"

"Hey, we used to live on crullers after the bars closed. When they shut down, I barely had a reason to live. That's why I moved to Minneapolis. There was nothing keeping me in a donut-free world."

"What about me?"

Ken rubbed her thigh with his foot. "If you'd greeted me like that in the old days, I never would have left."

"You like it down there?" she asked.

His foot moved up her thigh, close to the mound between her legs. "Down where?"

"Minneapolis, you pervert."

"It's okay. I thought a bigger city would be more exciting, but there's too much racial garbage. The minorities hate us. The left-wing freako politicians are always looking over our shoulder. Everybody thinks they know how to do the job better than we do. Pisses me off."

"There's political crap everywhere," Maggie said.

"Yeah, I know. My dad wants me to move to Florida. He's got a rathole trailer in Tallahassee. Him and me, we'd probably kill each other after a month in the same town. Plus, I hate Florida. All those fucking cockroaches and that fucking humidity. Hurricanes, too. I'm staying in Minnesota for the weather."

Maggie laughed. "So move back here. I could talk to Stride. We could get you on the team again."

She noticed the anxious look on his face, and she backpedaled. "Whoa, not because of me. I just mean, if you don't like it down there, you're not stuck."

"Thanks, I get it," Ken said. "I didn't think I'd miss it the way I do. I guess when you grow up somewhere, you can't get it out of your genes. Anyway, it's a moot point. My mortgage is so far underwater I'd need a scuba tank to see daylight. I ain't going nowhere."

Maggie wondered if that was true or if that was a line to spare her feelings. She'd pushed him too fast. It was way too soon to talk about him moving back to Duluth, even if she had no ulterior motives. If he was happier up here, she wanted him to come back here, with no strings attached. The trouble was, it was hard to say you weren't pulling romantic strings ten minutes after you'd given a man a blow job and washed his hair in the shower.

She said: *Move back up here.*

He heard: *We're a couple now.*

Then again, maybe he was being straight with her. The housing market was on life support, and Ken was still Ken, which meant he'd probably sucked every dollar of equity out of his house to buy toys. She'd lectured him about it when he first joined the force, but Ken never changed. He was still a kid at heart, breezy and impulsive. So was she. Or that was what she told herself. She wasn't getting old, no matter what the calendar said.

"So Serena's in town, huh?" Ken asked, forcing three squares of pizza into his mouth at the same time. "Guppo says she's looking good."

"Serena always looks good," Maggie replied sourly.

Ken had no way of knowing he'd pinned the tail on the wrong donkey. "You two pissing on each other? You mad because she walked out on Stride?"

Maggie shrugged. "Whatever."

"You want to talk about it?"

"The last thing I want to talk about is Serena Dial."

He held up his hands in surrender. "Sorry."

Then, out of nowhere, he added: "So were you ever planning to tell me that you and Stride got it on this winter?"

Maggie slammed her beer on the table. "*Shit shit shit!* Guppo?"

"World's roundest spy."

She pushed her chair back so hard it fell, and she stalked to the window. She slammed a palm against the wall. "I was going to tell you about it."

"Yeah, but you didn't."

"I figured you'd think you were some kind of consolation prize."

"Am I?"

"No. That's not what this is about."

Ken swallowed his pizza and came up behind her. He wore boxers and nothing else. Maggie's shirt was undone. He put his arms around her and fingered her breasts like they were musical instruments.

"I really am sorry," she told him.

"Relax. Fuck me again, and all is forgiven."

Maggie spun around and slapped him hard. He reeled back in surprise, rubbing his face. His smile vanished, and he shook his head. "Guess that wasn't the smartest thing in the world to say."

"Am I a good lay to you? Is that it?"

"Hey, we both seem pretty happy with this arrangement."

Maggie closed her eyes. She was suddenly furious. Furious at Ken, at Stride, at Guppo, at Serena, but mostly at herself. She prided herself on never letting her emotions get in the way of her judgment, but she felt like a fool.

"Let's not do this now," she said.

"Fine with me."

"Maybe we should talk about work."

"Maybe we should."

"Show me the tape," she told him.

"Whatever you say."

Ken slid the unlabeled DVD into the drawer of the Blu-ray player on Maggie's stereo tower. "I spent four hours going through Roslak's files," he told her. "There were hundreds of videos. He taped everything. I don't think it was for any clinical purpose. I think the son of a bitch was just a voyeur."

"You found Cat?"

"Yeah, she was in the pile."

"Why'd they never bring her in for questioning?"

Ken shrugged. "You think the murder of an unlicensed shrink with a rep for screwing patients gets much priority? Around the same time, we had a ten-year-old boy killed in a school bullying incident and an immigrant store owner blown away behind the counter of his shop by two gang members. Guess where the manpower went? It wasn't Vincent Roslak."

"Still, it's been eight months," Maggie said.

"The case has one lead investigator, and he's swamped. We dicked around with a judge about getting access to Roslak's materials at all. Patient privilege, you know? We got permission to do screen captures to sort the videos by face, and we identified a couple hundred people. We've got names for most of them now, but we can't even watch the tapes without consent, which means tracking down each person one at a time. The whole thing is an evidence nightmare."

"What about Cat?"

"With the consent Stride faxed this morning, I was able to pull her videos. Roslak saw her at least five times. I watched all of them. Most of it doesn't tell us much, but the last one—wow. She was hypnotized. He took her on a flashback about the night her parents died."

"She was six then," Maggie said. "Would her memories be accurate?"

"Who knows? He's the shrink, not me."

"Where was this? Duluth or Minneapolis?"

"No way to be sure," Ken told her. "He's got a white sheet as a backdrop. I didn't see anything to identify the location."

"Is it dated?"

"No."

"So what did she say?"

"Take a look," Ken said.

He pushed the play button. The image of Cat Mateo filled the fifty-inch screen. Ken was right; it could have been filmed anywhere. The video showed her and a white backdrop and nothing more. Cat sat on a wooden stool, facing the camera. Her eyes were closed, and her hands were folded in her lap. Her legs were pressed demurely together, like a child in church. She looked serene.

Maggie heard a voice-over behind the camera. The voice dripped with honey and concern. It was Vincent Roslak.

"Are you comfortable, Cat?"

"Yes."

"Relaxed?"

"Yes."

"It feels natural to be here, doesn't it?"

"Yes."

"Good. You trust me, don't you?"

"Of course I trust you, Vincent."

"I would never hurt you."

"No."

"We're going to take a little journey, Cat."

"Okay."

Maggie waved her hand. "Fast-forward. Get to the part you want me to see."

Ken advanced through several scenes. When he stopped, Maggie saw Cat again, but she looked transformed. The peace in her face had vanished. She sat open-eyed, staring into nothingness, her face slack with horror. She clutched the arms of the chair and rocked from side to side. Her voice was the scared voice of a little girl. She wailed at the lens, as if gripped by an unbearable pain, and then she leaped out of the chair and stormed the camera.

"STOP STOP STOP STOP STOP STOP No no no no no no."

Maggie jumped back. "Jesus."

"It gets worse," Ken said.

Cat's voice turned guttural. It was deep and menacing—a man's voice. She shouted at the top of her lungs.

"I'll kill you I'll kill you I'll kill you I'll kill you I'll kill you!"

Maggie listened to the back-and-forth between Cat and Roslak. His relentless questions pushed the girl into the past. She could picture Cat under the porch, cold, scared, and confused. Inches away from her parents as they died. "Roslak was playing with fire," she said. "He could have pushed her over the edge. God knows what she would have done."

"There's more," Ken said. "It's not just that. Listen."

"To what?"

"Listen."

"What's going on, Cat?"

"Oh, no. Oh, no, no, no. He's dead. They're both dead. Oh, God."

"Your father?"

"He killed him."

"What? Who?"

"Sirens."

"Talk to me, Cat."

"I'll protect you."

"Everything's okay. What's my name, Cat?"

"Come out, it's okay."

"My name, Cat. Who am I?"

"Stride. My name is Stride."

Ken stared at her. "You see?"

Maggie stopped the recording and stripped the disc out of the machine. "No, I don't see. What the hell is that supposed to mean? She heard Stride?"

"It's not hard to figure out," Ken said.

"Yeah? Tell me."

"I don't think you want to hear it."

"Shit, Ken, just tell me what you think."

"Cat makes it sound like Stride was there *before* Marty died."

"Are you kidding? No way. She's mixing things up. Or she was acting. That wasn't real."

"It sure looked real to me," Ken said.

"So what are you saying?"

"I'm not saying anything. Cat's the one who said it."

"Marty Gamble killed himself. It was a murder-suicide. Stride sure as hell did not kill him."

"Are you sure?"

Maggie shouted at him. "Of course I am fucking sure! Are you crazy? We're talking about *Stride*."

"Hey, I hear you, but everyone knew he was sweet on Michaela. If he showed up and found her dead? If Marty was drunk or passed out in her blood? What would he have done?"

"No way. This little bitch is either faking it or she's mixing up her memories. That is not what happened."

"You're probably right, but it doesn't look good."

"I don't care how it looks."

"Was he there?" Ken asked.

"What do you mean?"

"Was Stride on the scene?"

"Of course he was there! We were *all* there!"

"When did he arrive?"

Maggie found herself almost hyperventilating. "What?"

"When did Stride arrive at the crime scene?"

"That doesn't mean anything."

"Maggie," Ken murmured. "Come on."

She stared at the dark television. This was wrong. This was a mistake. This wasn't how it happened.

"Okay, yes, Stride was the first responder," she told him. "Michaela called him when she saw Marty's car. He was there before any of us arrived. Just him and the two bodies. And Cat."

32

Stride awoke to the silence of the cottage at three in the morning. He put a hand on the other side of the bed, expecting to touch Serena's skin, but he was alone. She hadn't stayed. He glanced at his Black-Berry on the nightstand and saw the red message light flashing. When he checked his e-mail, he saw a text from Serena, time-stamped only minutes earlier.

The message read: *Did you sleep with Michaela?*

He wasn't ready to answer her. Not yet. Even so, he was comforted to know that she was lying awake, just like him. There had been nights all winter when he stared into the darkness and knew that Serena was doing the same thing in her bed in Grand Rapids. They could still feel each other.

So why was he shutting her out? Why couldn't he face what he'd done?

He heard footsteps across the floor of the living room. A small, attractive silhouette appeared in the doorway of his bedroom. "Cat?"

"Sorry," she murmured. "Did I wake you up?"

"I wasn't sleeping. Are you okay?"

"I had a nightmare."

"Do you want to talk about it?"

Cat didn't say anything, but she slipped across the slanted floor toward him. In the shadows, he could see that she was wearing only a tank top and panties. She stood beside the bed, her thumbs in the elastic waistband. She smelled of the lavender soap that Serena always used, which was still in the shower. Her bare thighs twisted back and forth against the mattress, as if she were spinning on a lazy Susan.

"Do the nightmares happen a lot?" he asked.

"Most nights, yeah. I hate to go to sleep. I try to stay awake until I can't hold my eyes open."

"That was how it was for me after I went off the bridge."

"Did it go away?" she asked.

"Not entirely, but it's not as bad as it was."

"I don't think mine will ever stop."

"What do you dream about?"

"Mostly, it's the same dream. The same night. You know? When it all happened."

"I know."

"Vincent said I keep reliving it because I'm hiding something from back then. He kept pushing me to find out what it was."

"Did you?"

"No. Do you think I'm hiding something? Is there something I don't want to remember?"

"I think anyone who went through an experience like you did would struggle to get past it," Stride said. "It haunted me, too, Cat. It still does."

She laid a hand on his bed. He worried that she would peel down the comforter and try to slide in beside him, and he would have to stop her. He was conscious of the fact that the line between innocence and sexuality had blurred in her mind a long time ago.

"I lied to you," she told him. "I'm sorry."

"About what?"

"Vincent."

"You slept with him?"

"Yes."

"Why lie? It wasn't your fault."

Cat was slow to respond.

"Why are you so sure it's not my fault?" she said finally. "Maybe it was me. Maybe I seduced him."

"You didn't."

"I could have. I'm not a child. Men always think they're seducing women, but usually it's the other way around."

"You still didn't tell me why you lied," Stride said.

"I don't know. I sort of—let him do it to me. I wanted him to have me. I told him to do whatever he wanted."

"That doesn't mean it's your fault. Psychologists have tremendous emotional power over their patients. That's why it's a crime for them to have a sexual relationship with someone in their care. He manipulated you, Cat. It was wrong."

"I loved him," she murmured.

"It felt like love, because he took an interest in you."

"I'd never loved anyone before. I thought he loved me, too. He said he did."

"He used you."

"When he said he was leaving town, and he couldn't see me anymore, I was devastated. I would have done anything to get him back. Anything."

Stride waited. He didn't like what he heard in her voice.

"I was so angry. I felt like he was abandoning me."

"What did you do?"

"I wanted to kill him," she said.

He murmured, "Did you?"

"No, but it's my fault he's dead."

"Why do you say that?"

"Everyone I love dies," Cat said.

He didn't know how to respond or make it better. When he said nothing, Cat went on. "I've been thinking a lot about something Serena told me," she said.

"What's that?"

"You slept with Maggie."

Stride tensed. "Yes, that's true."

"I was upset with you when she told me. I couldn't believe you would do something like that."

"I was upset with myself, too."

"You hurt Serena."

"I know."

"Plus, it's Maggie. Ick."

"That's not fair, Cat. Maggie and I have been friends for years."

"I know. Anyway, I decided I was being too hard on you. You're human. Everybody makes mistakes. It's only sex."

"No, you were right the first time," he said. "It doesn't matter what was going on in my life. I was wrong to let it happen."

"People get too hung up about sex. I don't get it. It doesn't mean anything."

"Yes, it does. I hope you'll discover that someday."

Cat rolled down one inch of her panties, exposing the bone of her hips. "I'd have sex with you if you wanted," she murmured softly.

Stride reached to the nightstand and turned on the light. He threw her a king-sized pillow, which she clutched against her chest, covering herself. Her eyes were wide; she knew she'd made a mistake. She could feel his anger and he made no effort to hide it.

"Listen to me, Cat. I never want to hear you say anything like that to me ever again. Are we clear about that? Never. If it happens again, that's the last night you spend in this house."

"I'm sorry, I'm such an idiot. I don't know why I said that. Now you're going to hate me."

"I don't hate you, but I need to trust you, and you just made it hard for me to do that."

Cat dropped the pillow and ran for the doorway. She stopped there, her back to him, her shoulders rippling as she cried. She turned around and her pretty face was streaked with tears. She stared at the floor, not looking at him. "I won't do it again. I promise."

"That's good," he said.

She yanked her tank top down to hide her stomach, and she crossed her arms over her chest. Her legs were pressed together. Her hair was strewn across her face. "Can I ask you something?"

"What is it?"

"You're not my father, are you?"

He stared at her. "Cat, what are you talking about?"

"I don't know. I just wondered."

"You know I'm not. I didn't even meet your mother until you were four years old."

"Yeah. Okay."

He frowned. "Why on earth would you ask me something like that?"

"I don't know. It's stupid. Everybody said I should have had a better father. There are lots of days when I wish I'd had a father like you." Cat wiped her face. "You did sleep with my mother, though. Didn't you?"

"Catalina is asleep," Michaela whispered. "Finally. That girl never wants to miss a second of life."

"It's almost Christmas. What kid can sleep then?"

"That's true. Thank you for bringing a gift for her. That's sweet. It will be a nice surprise." She closed the door to the girl's bedroom softly, leaving Catalina inside. "Can you stay for a glass of wine?"

"Sure."

"It's not very good," she apologized.

"Don't worry about it."

They returned to the small living room, which was decorated with Christmas crafts that her daughter had made. Cotton-ball Santas. Angels in crayon. A Popsicle-stick crèche. The space smelled of spruce from the twinkling tree in the corner and sugar from freshly made cookies. Strains of holiday music played on the boom box, its volume barely audible. He recognized "It Came Upon a Midnight Clear." The light in the room was dimmed.

She poured two glasses of chardonnay from a box. They clinked a toast and smiled at each other. Her face glowed.

"You look happy," he said.

"Do I? I am happy. I feel safe, and I have you to thank."

"I don't think Marty will bother you again," Stride told her. "Every one of my cops is on the lookout for him. If he so much as jaywalks, I'll make sure his parole is revoked. So hopefully he'll be a good boy."

Michaela shrugged her shoulders. "Nothing lasts with Marty. Sooner or later he gets drunk, and bad things happen. I'm just enjoying the peace for now. It's a good thing."

They stood next to each other by the window that looked out on the woods. She was close to him. When he sipped his wine, it rolled through his head like an ocean wave. He realized she was looking at him, and he looked back. Her face was golden and perfect. Through the shadows, he saw something in her eyes. Love. Need. Desire. It affected him. Her lips parted in a sensual way that asked him to kiss her. Her arms slid around his waist. She got on tiptoes and pressed her lips against his cheek, and then she kissed his lips, too, and her face lingered there. Her perfume intoxicated him. Her mouth was warm and erotic. He kissed her back, but as quickly as it began, he remembered himself and gently pushed her away.

"Michaela," he said.

She looked down at the floor. "No. Say nothing, please."

"I'm sorry, I can't—"

"Of course not. You are married. You have a wonderful wife. I'm ashamed of myself. That was unforgivable."

"If things were different," he said.

"They're not. You don't owe me any kind words. I don't deserve them."

She turned on her heel and marched to the kitchen. He watched her pour her wine in the sink. She made the lights in the room brighter. It made him realize that the moment wasn't spontaneous. She'd planned it and wanted it. This was a seduction. If he'd said yes, they would be making love now.

Their eyes met. She knew what he was thinking, and she hooded her face in humiliation. He couldn't tell her what was in his heart. He couldn't admit how close he'd come to undressing her and laying her down on the floor beneath him.

His phone rang like a warning from the real world. It was Maggie. He answered it and listened and gave a terse reply. When he hung up, he said, "I have to go."

"Of course," Michaela said.

"There's been a burglary in the Congdon Parkway. A woman was shot and killed."

"In the sacred season? That's terrible. Go."

"I feel like I should say something."

"No, you shouldn't. It would be easier if you said nothing." She waved him away.

He nodded at her and left through the front door, and he felt a stab of loneliness on her behalf. Flurries of snow had begun to fall, streaking like stars through the porch light. Inside, the music got louder, playing a piano solo of "Silent Night." He heard Michaela singing the words in a broken voice.

Stride was alone again. Cat was back in the other bedroom.

He picked up his BlackBerry and reread Serena's message. *Did you sleep with Michaela?*

He wondered if she was still awake, like him. This time, he keyed in a reply.

No, I didn't.

He was about to send the message when he added:

It's worse.

33

"Hotcakes and sausage," Steve Garske guessed as he whiffed the air. "Right?"

Maggie looked at him in annoyed frustration. "What?"

"Your breakfast."

"Oh. Yeah, you're right."

"They make those sausages from recycled tires, you know."

"Well, they're still great."

"One of these days I'm going to cure you of your McDonald's addiction. Didn't you see *Super Size Me?*"

Maggie spread the flaps of her long coat and displayed her stick-like physique. "Do I look supersized?"

"No, but you can't be forty and eat like you did at thirty."

"I'm not forty."

"Rounding error," he said with a wink. "For all intents and purposes, you are now middle-aged."

"I didn't come here to talk about my age or my eating habits. And by the way, fuck you, Steve. Can we get back to Cat and this video?"

"Okay, but I'm not a shrink," Steve reminded her. "Why come to me about this?"

Maggie paced in the examining room. It was early, and the clinic in Lakeside wasn't open yet, but she knew Steve arrived before any of his staff to run through patient files ahead of his appointments. He was as reliable and predictable as a Swiss watch. He had his long legs propped on his computer desk, and he followed her with his eyes as she bounced back and forth between the door and the pelvic stirrups mounted on the patient table.

"Because you know Stride," she said. "Because you were there that night. You remember what he was like."

"Sure. I drove him home. He was devastated."

"I've never seen him like that at another crime scene," she said.

She could still see Stride's face. It was one of those moments when she hated having a memory for every detail in her past. She'd arrived, gun drawn, and found him on the sofa, with Cat wrapped in his arms, her face buried in his neck. His eyes were open. She saw fury and helplessness there. He made no attempt to separate himself from his emotions, the way they always did to survive as cops. Every one of the forty-one knife wounds in Michaela had sunk into his own chest.

She left him as she examined the bedroom. Outside, she could hear the sirens and the splash of mud and snow as vehicle after vehicle arrived at the scene. She found Marty propped against the wall, as if he'd been staring at what he'd done when he put the gun to his temple. The gun had fallen from his limp hand, and the room still smelled of burnt powder from the shot. Only inches away, on her back, was Michaela. She lay in her own blood, like a girl floating peacefully on the surface of a lake. She'd worn a white nightgown to bed, and it was now as red as Christmas candy.

There was no mystery about what had happened. Or so she thought.

"Michaela was in love with Stride," Steve said. "I'm sure that made it worse for him."

"Did he tell you that?"

"Stride? He would never say a word about that, but I saw it in Michaela. It was obvious how she felt."

"Do you think it was reciprocated?"

Steve shook his head. "Come on. Jonathan Stride never looked at another woman other than Cindy. Even so, Michaela had a gentleness about her that was very attractive. Plus, she was a mother, and that was a time when Stride and Cindy were trying to have kids without any success. I'm sure his feelings were complicated. He probably felt as much attachment to Cat as he did to Michaela."

"He still does. That's what scares me."

"Well, I wouldn't put much faith in anything Cat told Roslak under hypnosis. It's notoriously unreliable."

Maggie knew that was true, but she didn't like what she saw in Stride's face when he talked about Cat. Guilt. Regret. Anger. "You didn't see this girl. She looked like she was really reliving that night."

"I'll say it again, Maggie. You can't rely on what Cat said in therapy. Obviously, she blocked out everything from that night. Her brain doesn't want to remember it. If a psychologist starts ripping open doors that she wants to keep closed, she may invent things that make the memory safe. Hearing her father kill himself after murdering her mother? Knowing she's utterly alone in the world? That's not something a little girl can process. If she can put someone else in the room, someone she trusts, maybe that's the only way she can handle it."

She shrugged. "I get it. You're probably right."

Steve dropped his feet on the floor with a heavy thud. "What's the alternative? Stride killed Marty? We both know he's incapable of doing anything like that."

"Incapable? I'm not so sure. There's a lot more to Stride than people ever see. I've been there when he was out of control."

Steve eyed her with a stare so direct it made her uncomfortable. "Are we talking about ten years ago, or are we talking about this winter?"

"That has nothing to do with this."

"No? Would you be saying these things if you and he hadn't crossed a line that you wish you could uncross?"

"I'm trying to be objective," Maggie insisted. "Back then, we all thought it was obvious what happened. Marty had a history of violence toward Michaela. He broke in, killed her, and blew his head off. End of story. Nobody was surprised."

"So?"

"So his blood alcohol level was point two four. That's almost catatonic."

"He was able to kill his ex-wife despite being drunk. He certainly could have pulled the trigger on himself."

"I know, but he was slumped against the wall, covered in blood, so drunk he couldn't even stand up. How hard would it have been for someone to take his gun and kill him and make it look like a suicide?"

"Wouldn't your forensics team have found something?"

"Not necessarily. If you don't look for something, chances are you won't find it. Nobody was searching for evidence that this was anything but what it looked like. A murder-suicide."

"That's what it was," Steve said.

"Yeah, I always thought so, too." She said it, but there was no passion in her voice. Steve heard her doubts.

"What are you not telling me?" he asked her.

Maggie leaned her chin on her fist. "I never said anything, but even back then, I wondered. Honestly, that's why I called you to get Stride out of there. I was worried he might—say something. Admit something."

"Why would you think that?"

"The day before Michaela's murder, I went to see Dory," Maggie said. "Stride asked me to visit her. Michaela thought Marty had been harassing her."

"What did she tell you?"

"Not much. She was pretty far gone on drugs. She'd just bought a fresh supply and gone through most of it. She was crying, going on and on about Marty, what a bastard he was, how much she hated him. She said Marty came to see her. He was still obsessed with Michaela."

"Obviously."

"Dory told him to stay away from Michaela because she was having an affair with Stride. She said Stride would kill him if he got close to her."

"Did you tell Stride about this?"

"Sure I did. He said it wasn't true. He said there was no affair."

"Did you believe him?"

"Back then? Yes. Now? I don't know. Anyway, even if they weren't involved, Stride was in the middle of a triangle, whether he liked it or not. When he walked into that bedroom and found Michaela's body, he was going to feel responsible for what happened. The only question is whether Marty was alive or dead when he arrived."

Church bells.

At one point during the session between Cat and Roslak, Stride thought he heard a burst of church bells chiming in the background, and it was jarring to hear something sacred echoing in the midst of something evil. In disgust, he turned off the DVD player in his office. Maggie sat in his guest chair, watching his face. He hadn't watched the video itself, not when it meant seeing Cat completely under this man's control. He'd simply sat in his chair and listened with his eyes closed to Roslak taking the girl apart question by question.

"Vincent Roslak," he murmured. "Now there's a guy who got what was coming to him."

"I think Cat lied to you about their relationship. They sounded like lovers."

Stride nodded. "She told me about it last night."

"What did she say?"

Stride leaned forward on his desk and folded his hands together. "She said she was in love with him. She was devastated when he left town. She said she wanted to kill him. She also said she didn't."

"She's a prime suspect, boss. I'd like to go down there and check out the crime scene in Roslak's apartment for myself."

"What will that accomplish?" Stride asked.

"I'd like to know whether this video was filmed in Duluth or Minneapolis. Cat said she never saw Roslak again after he left town. If that's not true, we have a big problem."

"Cat didn't kill anyone. I'm more concerned with who's trying to kill *her*. And who murdered two other people up here. Did you find the stolen Charger yet?"

"No."

"Well, find it," he snapped. "That's your top priority right now, not a murder that belongs with the Minneapolis cops."

Maggie saluted him sarcastically. "Yes, sir. Should I wave my magic wand? Exactly what do you want me to do, boss? We've got BOLOs out all over the state."

"Sorry. I realize that. We have two murders, and we have *nothing*. I'm frustrated."

"So am I. I'm just not ready to pretend there's no connection between Cat and Roslak's murder, just because a teenage hooker tells you she's innocent."

There was angry fire between them. They could both see it. Their relationship was broken.

"I'm not saying there's no connection," Stride retorted. "I just don't believe that the connection is Cat murdering Roslak. I think it's much more likely that Cat told Roslak something that got him killed. I want to see all the other videos he made with her. Maybe there's something in there that will give us a clue."

"Ken didn't see anything that would help us."

"I don't care what Ken saw. Ken's not on my team anymore. Right now, his only role in this investigation is that he's sleeping with you."

Maggie's face was like stone. "Whatever you want. I'll get the tapes."

Stride stood up and grabbed his leather jacket from a hook near the door. "I'm meeting Serena in Canal Park. We're going to talk to Curt Dickes about the prostitution angle. She thinks that may be what Margot was pursuing. That may be the connection to Cat."

Maggie didn't move.

"Is there something else?" he asked.

She pointed at the television. "You heard what Cat said."

"About what?"

"She mentioned you."

"Right, so what? I was the one who found her under the porch."

"She makes it sound like more than that," Maggie told him. "Like maybe Marty was alive when you got there."

Stride couldn't believe what he was hearing. "What are you saying, Mags?"

"Back then, Dory told me you and Michaela were having an affair."

"I remember. I also remember telling you that we weren't."

Maggie said nothing.

Stride sat down on the end of his desk. He and Maggie had been through ups and downs in the years they'd been together. Arguments. Disagreements. Jokes. Tears. He remembered her early days as a young, stiff, Chinese cop, obsessed with rules and protocol. He remembered her coming out of her cocoon like a wild butterfly. He remembered her standing on his porch, soaking wet, yelling at him that he was making a mistake in his second marriage. He remembered her husband's murder and all the secrets he'd discovered about her sex life that he wished he'd never learned. He remembered the glimmer of doubt in his head that she might have killed her husband over everything he'd made her do.

As close as they were, they still kept secrets from each other. That was the problem. He'd kept it a secret every night he made love to her, when he knew they were making a mistake.

"Do I really need to say it to you, Mags? Do I really need to say the words?"

She looked up at him. Her eyes were bloodshot. She pushed herself out of his chair. "No. You don't. I'm sorry."

Maggie turned for the doorway, but he stopped her. He needed to say the words anyway. He needed her to hear them.

"I did *not* kill Marty Gamble," Stride said. "Would I have shot him if he'd still been alive? I don't know. Maybe I would. But it doesn't matter. He was dead when I arrived on the scene. He killed himself. That's what happened."

34

"Seriously?" Serena said. "She really asked if you killed Marty?"

They sat on a bench on the Canal Park boardwalk, near the lineup of tourist hotels. Choppy lake waves splashed over the rocks. "I don't think she believed it, but the fact that she even brought it up tells me how bad things are."

"That's a woman who does not handle rejection well."

Stride smiled. "What woman does?"

Serena punched him in the arm, but she smiled, too. "I guess I can't really take the high road. I asked if you slept with Michaela."

"I didn't, but she and I were close to each other. Too close. I knew she had feelings for me. I should have kept her at a distance, but I couldn't. Honestly, I didn't want to."

"Did you tell Cindy about it?"

"No, but I'm sure she knew. I suppose she figured that if I'd cheated on her, I would have told her."

"You told me about Maggie," Serena murmured.

"Yes, I did."

"What would Cindy have done?"

"If I'd slept with Michaela? Killed me."

"Sounds like I underreacted," Serena said. "Maybe I should have shot you or something."

"Since I know you're carrying, I'll say no."

"Smart man."

He stared at the lake. He spotted a ship on the horizon, coming closer. "Listen . . . about last night," he said. "There were things I should have told you, and I didn't. I'm sorry for shutting you out again. That was a mistake."

"Tell me now."

He felt her waiting beside him, and he knew what she was waiting for. *It's worse.*

"This isn't about Michaela," he said. "It's about Cat."

Her brow wrinkled in confusion. "Okay."

"When she showed up two nights ago, it was a punch in the chest, seeing what's happened to her these past ten years."

"You couldn't have prevented that, Jonny," she said.

"Yes, I could."

"You're being too hard on yourself. There's nothing else you could have done to protect Michaela."

"It's not that."

"Then what?"

He watched the ship on the lake. Living on the Point, he recognized most of them and knew their names. Even at that distance, he thought the inbound boat was the *Paul Genter.* It was weighted down, its belly deep in the water. He thought about things passing away and disappearing. Cindy was gone. The house they'd shared was gone.

"A few days after Michaela was killed, Cindy woke me up in the middle of the night," he told Serena. "You know we'd been trying to have kids for years. We'd both been tested, and nothing was wrong. She'd been taking fertility drugs. Even so, she couldn't get pregnant. We'd basically given up."

Serena slowly brought a hand to her mouth. She was smart. She knew where this was going.

"Cindy said to me—she said, what if things happen for a reason? Maybe we weren't meant to have kids of our own. Maybe we were meant to rescue someone else's child. She asked me what I would think about the two of us trying to adopt Catalina. Make her a part of our lives."

"What did you say?"

"I said no."

"Why?"

He shook his head. "I don't know. There were lots of reasons. It's one thing to want a child and to have nine months to wrap your head around the idea of your life changing. It's another to have a six-year-old dropped into your lap. I wasn't sure I was ready."

"That doesn't sound like you."

"Cindy said the same thing," he admitted. "She wanted to know the real reason."

"Which was?"

"I just couldn't handle it. I thought that every time I looked in Cat's face, I would see Michaela, and I would remember what happened. It was too fresh. Too raw."

"There's no sin in feeling that way."

"I'm not so sure. Looking back, it feels selfish."

"What did Cindy say?"

"She said she understood, but I don't know if she did. We never talked about it again. I thought about it for months. I began to wish I'd said yes, but by then it was too late. Cat was already with the Greens. That fall, Cindy was diagnosed with cancer. At that point, everything else went out of my head."

He wondered what Serena would say. He didn't want excuses or sympathy. He wanted someone to blame him the way he blamed himself. He'd made a mistake, and that mistake had cost a girl her childhood.

"Saying yes would have turned your lives upside down. You couldn't do that if you weren't sure."

"That doesn't mean I don't regret it."

"Okay, so you regret it. You can't change the past. What are you going to do now?"

He heard the bells of the lift bridge, clanging through the park like a clarion. The *Paul Genter* was lined up on the canal. It was a thousand-foot giant, rust red, moving from the lake to the calm port.

"Now feels like a second chance to make it right," Stride said.

Serena leaned over and kissed him on the cheek. "Well, you know me, Jonny. I'm a believer in second chances."

He turned, and he wanted to kiss her. Really kiss her. It was a prelude to everything that would follow between them. She saw it in his eyes, and she wanted it, too, but they knew it was too soon. She put a finger on his lips, holding him back. The next step would take time, but it would come.

"I'm glad you told me," she said.

"I am, too."

Stride began to get up from the bench, but Serena held him back.

"One more thing," she said.

"What?"

"Maybe this is important, maybe it's not. Ten years ago. When you found the bodies. Did anything feel wrong to you about the crime scene?"

He was puzzled. "What do you mean?"

"Michaela was dead. Marty was dead. He killed her, he killed himself. You're a cop, you know crime scenes. Did anything feel wrong? The angle of the gun, the position of the bodies, anything."

"No," Stride said. "It felt like what it was. Why?"

Serena shrugged. "I don't know. It's just a thought. A panicked little girl can reinvent things under hypnosis, but what if Cat really did hear something that night? What if someone else was in the house when they died?"

Stride and Serena heard curses from the hotel room on the third floor of the Lakeshore Inn. Inside, the bottom half of Curt Dickes jutted out from under the bathroom sink. A leaking pipe had soaked his overalls, and a fine mist made a cloud like a vegetable spritzer.

"Shit!" Dickes bellowed.

His arms worked frantically, twisting a wrench. The spray of water diminished, then disappeared. He slid himself out onto the tile floor, shaking water from his hands. When he spotted Stride and Serena over him, he jerked up and banged his head on the underside of the counter.

"What the fuck?" he said, rubbing his skull. "You want to give me a heart attack?"

"I knocked," Stride said.

"Yeah, well, I'm in the middle of something, huh?" Dickes stood up and threw a couple of white towels onto the puddle on the floor. His greasy black hair was mussed into spikes. In the tight space, his cologne was choking. "Did you tell the guy at the desk you were looking for me?"

"Yes."

"Shit, thanks a lot. That's what I need, a visit from the cops while I'm at work."

"It'll be worse if they find out you've been setting up their guests with hookers," Stride said.

"You think I'm stupid? I don't shit where I eat." Dickes tugged at his wet shirt and noticed Serena for the first time. "Hey, you're keeping pretty good company, Stride."

"I'm with the Itasca County Sheriff's Department," Serena said.

"Yeah, yeah, I know who you are. Chick cop by way of Las Vegas. You don't think word gets around? So what do you guys want, anyway?"

"Let's talk outside," Stride said.

They backed out of the bathroom, and Dickes sat down on the end of one of the two queen beds in the hotel room. Both beds were perfectly made and creased into sharp corners. The television was on, its volume loud, and Stride took the remote and switched it off.

"Saturday night," he said. "Where were you, Curt?"

"This about the two murders? I heard about it. Brandy, huh? Sucks. She was a crazy bitch, but she got plenty of repeat business. She was talented, if you like it rough. Not that it's my scene, you know?"

"I said, where were you?"

"What, you think I had something to do with it? Forget that. Me and my new Fusion, we hit the highway on Saturday. I was at the casino half the night. That's half an hour away, and their cameras will have me on tape the whole time. You can check it out."

"Is there any talk on the street about who killed Brandy?"

Dickes shook his head. "Nah, but I hope you get this guy soon. Some of the girls are getting freaked, you know? Like there's some serial killer going after them."

Stride sat down next to Dickes. "Cat says you set her up with some rich guy at a resort on the north shore. This was about a year ago. I want to know who this guy was."

Dickes shrugged. "I've got a bad memory. Customers like it like that."

"Curt, this isn't about pimping anymore. This is a murder investigation. Don't play games with me."

The kid's eyes bounced back and forth between them. "Do I get a free pass if I talk?"

"I'm not handing out deals for anything," Stride told him. "I'm trying to keep you out of prison for twenty-five years. If this guy had anything to do with these murders, you're in the middle of it."

Curt blanched. "Look, Lieutenant, I really can't tell you anything. I don't know who the guy was."

"You didn't get a name?"

"I got nothing. Never saw the guy, never saw the driver."

"So how'd you set it up?"

"For posh jobs like that one, I get a text with the specs. What kind of girl, where she gets picked up, what sort of entertainment they need. I text a photo back for approval. If it's a go, an envelope with cash shows up in my PO box. I get the girl where she needs to be, end of story."

"You don't know who's texting you?" Stride asked.

"It's a different number every time. I figure they're using pay-as-you-go phones. No tracks."

"What about the limos?"

"Always unmarked. Smoked windows. Mud over the plates. I can't tell you who's behind it, because I don't know."

"Did you get any details from the girls? Where they went, who they saw? Any faces they recognize?"

"As far as I can tell, it's never the same place twice. Hotels, motels, resorts. Whoever's running this is careful, and I don't ask questions.

As for the girls, nobody ever came back and started bragging about whose mushroom they swallowed. I don't have any names."

"How often do you get a job like this?" Serena asked.

"Not often. Wish I got more, the money's great. It's only been six, eight times in a year. That guy with Cat, he was one of the first."

"How come you didn't mention this to me a couple days ago?" Stride asked. "You talked about bachelor parties and bald Swedes, not limos and secret cash. You've been holding out on me."

"Come on, you think I'm going to get any more calls if people know I'm talking to you? As it is, I'm probably screwed. My phone hasn't rung all weekend. And hell, I never thought anybody would wind up dead."

"If you get another text, I better be your first call," Stride said.

"Yeah, sure, whatever."

"I'm hearing about STDs making the rounds among the Duluth one-percenters. Any of your girls need a doctor?"

"You think they'd tell me about it?" Dickes asked. "Most of the girls insist on condoms, but some of them will go bareback for a few extra bucks. I don't want to know the gory details."

"I need names of the girls who went on the posh jobs," Stride said.

"You already got two. Cat and Brandy. The other two are real private. College girls who don't want to advertise, you know?"

"Names," he repeated.

Dickes swore. He gave Stride the names of two more girls. "Are we done?"

Stride gestured at the cell phone in his pocket. "Your phone, too. Give it to me."

"Fuck no! Are you crazy?"

Stride looked at Serena. "Did you hear him admit to solicitation a minute ago?"

"I did," Serena said.

"Hey, come on, you said you didn't give a shit about that!" Dickes protested.

"I changed my mind. Now give me the phone."

Dickes yanked it from his pocket and slapped it on the bed. "Here, fine. You're killing me. Now get out of here while I still have a job."

Serena sat down on the other side of him. "Not quite yet. We're not done. First tell me what you know about Margot Huizenfelt."

"I had nothing to do with that! I don't know what happened to her!"

"You ever talk to her?" Serena asked.

"Yeah, once. That was months ago."

"What did she want?"

Dickes hesitated. He bit his lip.

"Don't start having memory lapses, Curt," Stride told him.

"Look, she was asking about the same shit as you. Whether I knew about rich guys looking for escorts."

"What did you tell her?"

"I told her to get the hell out of my face. I told her jack shit, that's what I told her."

"When did you last see her?" Serena asked.

Dickes squirmed. The blanket on the bed was wet now, because of his sodden clothes. "I don't remember."

"Do you not get what's going on here?" Serena demanded. "Margot's missing. She may be dead. If we find out you know something and you didn't tell us, do you have any idea what trouble is going to rain down on your head? It'll make solicitation look like shoplifting a candy bar."

"I told you, I don't know what happened to her."

"You know something."

Dickes's nervous eyes flicked to his cell phone. Stride didn't miss the glance. "Who'd you talk to, Curt?"

The kid was sweating. He smoothed his hair, and it popped back up. "It was the truck, man! I saw Margot's truck! I just wanted to make sure he knew who she was. That's it. He told me not to worry."

"Who?" Stride asked.

"Lenny! I saw Margot driving a new SUV from Lowball's place on Miller Hill."

Stride looked at Serena, who nodded. "Margot bought a new Explorer a couple days before she disappeared. I talked to the woman who sold it to her."

"Well, we better talk to her again," Stride said.

"I'm telling you, it's nothing!" Dickes insisted. "Lenny told me not to sweat it! Margot bought a truck. That's all. She didn't ask anything about hookers!"

"So I take it Lenny is a regular client of yours," Stride concluded.

"Oh, shit. Oh, shit, I am so screwed."

"Focus, Curt," Serena told him sharply. "When did you see Margot in the new truck?"

"Like a month ago? I don't know. It was a Saturday, I think. There was a big concert at the DECC. Lots of business."

"Jason Aldean?" Stride asked.

"Yeah, that was it."

"Where did you see her? What time?"

Dickes rubbed his face in frustration. His sweat mixed with his cologne. The combination was lethal. "I don't know, in the evening. Six, seven o'clock? I was coming out of the Duluth Grill. I saw her in the parking lot, and I made myself scarce, you know? I saw the dealer sticker, though, so I called Lenny."

"Was Margot alone?" Serena asked.

Dickes shook his head. "No, she had a woman with her."

"Who?"

"Do I know every fucking woman in the city? I don't know! She was short. Skanky. Fake blonde hair."

Stride was pretty sure he knew who it was. He stared at Serena.

"Dory Mateo," he said.

35

Dory slid her naked body into the bathtub until the scalding water reached her chin. Her skin felt like flame. She gripped the porcelain sides of the tub and endured the heat as sweat poured down her face. When she inhaled, moist steam coated her nose and throat. She kept the lights off in the tiny Seaway bathroom, and there were no windows to the outside. She liked to bathe in the dark. When she was there, she could have been anywhere. A fine hotel. A cruise ship. A house of her own. Not a flophouse bathroom.

She pushed her fingers around the edge of the tub until she found a wafer of soap. She extended her arm and ran the soap along her skin, making it slippery. She did her other arm, then her legs, her breasts, her stomach, and her mound. Touching herself brought no arousal. Her desires were long dead.

The water slowly cooled as she lay there. She shivered. She wished Michaela were here with her, so they could talk. So she could explain. In the darkness, she imagined that she could hear the sound of her sister breathing. Her soft laugh. The rustle of her clothes.

"I betrayed you, *bonita*," Dory murmured to the dark room.

Her sister spoke.

"You? You could never do that."

Dory was silent. She couldn't say it, not even to a ghost. The secret was toxic. She'd confessed to Margot, and now Margot was gone, as if the truth were a deadly virus, killing everyone it touched. She half-wondered if it was Marty. Even dead, he was still destroying lives. Controlling those he hated. Wreaking havoc.

"I wanted to tell you back then, *bonita*, but I was too ashamed. And then it was too late. You were gone."

"Tell me now, and I will forgive you."

"No. You won't."

"Where I am now, there is nothing but forgiveness."

"No."

Dory stood up, dripping water from her body into the tub like rain. She found the towel she'd draped over the sink and used it to dry herself. She stepped out onto the cold floor. Her face brushed the string hanging from the light fixture and she pulled it, squinting at the harshness of the bare bulb. She was alone. Michaela wasn't there. When she looked down, she saw a millipede crawling near her toes. She kicked at it with her foot, and the bug slithered through the scummy grill of the floor drain.

She stepped into the same panties she'd removed before her bath. She pulled on her jeans and shrugged into a sweater that was scratchy on her bare skin. The leather of her boots was cold. Fully dressed, the fringes of her hair damp, she sat down on the edge of the bathtub.

She'd thought that telling Margot would ease her conscience. When they'd met for dinner at the Duluth Grill, she'd blurted out her secret. She'd told her everything. What she'd done. Why. Her shame, her guilt. Margot hadn't been surprised at all, not one little bit. Like it made all the sense in the world. Like it was the key to a lock.

For Dory, her confession hadn't changed anything. All she could think about were ways to wipe her mind clean.

She exited the bathroom into the hallway. It was empty, except for one old man, unconscious and smelly, sprawled in an open doorway. After a while, you didn't even notice. You held your nose and stepped over them. There was no one else, just him and her. Mornings were quiet here, because everyone was sleeping off the nights.

Dory made her way down the hall. She had the last room, near the window, where gray light streamed from outside. All the doors around her were closed. She reached for the door handle to her apartment, but she stopped without touching it. She didn't even know why she stopped.

She heard her sister whispering in her head, like a warning. "*Don't go inside.*"

Dory took a soft step backward and held her breath. Her room was as silent as a church. Beside her, through the hall window, she could see the alley below her. Papers whipped along the street, pushed by a lake wind. That was the problem. Silence. When she went to take her bath, she'd left her bedroom window open to clear out the smoke. She heard no breeze moving about the room now. The window was closed.

Someone was inside, waiting for her.

She backed up from her door. She avoided the drunk in the hall. She passed the bathroom again, moving through the warm steam. She kept going backward, and when she reached the stairwell, she finally turned around and ran.

In the lobby, she hugged herself and hurried onto Superior Street. She didn't wait to see if anyone came through the doors behind her. She ignored the greeting from the blind beggar in the lawn chair. She dodged traffic and ran toward the bank across the street and then sprinted when she was out of sight of the building behind her. Behind the bank, she cut into a pothole-filled parking lot and zigzagged through the cars. She crossed Michigan Street and found herself in the dead fields under the freeway. The car tires over her head sounded like stinging wasps.

She kept running. She didn't look back until she was lost among the railroad tracks near the harbor and she was finally safe. She had no idea where to go, but she knew what she had to do.

She had to tell Cat the truth. And then she had to disappear forever.

PART THREE
NO GOING BACK

36

Leonard Keck swung his Nike VR Pro seven-iron with a fierce chop and shot an imaginary golf ball through the tricky crosswinds toward the seventeenth green at Pebble Beach. In high-definition clarity on the eighty-inch plasma television hung on his office wall, the orange ball shot crisply across a California blue sky, shanked left toward the end of its flight, and dropped with a tiny splash into the surf of the Pacific Ocean. A groan of disappointment from the computer-animated crowd burbled out of the Bose speakers built into the wall.

"Son of a bitch!" Lenny shouted. He waved at Serena and Stride in the office doorway. "Hey, come in, guys, don't stand on ceremony with me. Jeez, Pebble is an evil course. Doesn't matter what kind of day I'm having, I always go in the water at seventeen."

Lenny swirled the melting chips of ice in his drink and swallowed it down. He wiped his lips with his hand. "I guess you guys are too young to remember the '82 Open, huh? Watson chipping in from the rough to beat Nicklaus? Best shot ever."

"I remember," Stride said.

Serena smiled. "Golf's not my game."

"Oh, golf's not a game, sweetheart," Lenny told her. "Golf's a twenty-two-year-old black widow with big tits. You know she's going to eat you sooner or later, but you can't stay away. Now come on, sit, sit."

Serena and Stride sat in two plush armchairs in front of Lenny's desk. Lenny took several more practice swings with his club and then paced around the office with the iron braced behind his neck. He seemed incapable of sitting still. He wore a chocolate brown tracksuit and golf shoes with cleats that left dotted impressions on the carpet. He peeled off a golf glove as he walked and stripped a tan visor from his head. He didn't dress or act like a man with money, which told Serena that he had more than enough money not to care. The only luxury item she saw on his body was a gold diver's watch.

Lenny was medium height, burly, with a modest paunch at his waist. Too many steaks and too much beer, she guessed. He had messy graying hair, a high forehead, and a tanned face freckled with age spots. His office at the back of his Miller Hill dealership showed off his influence and connections. He had framed photographs of himself with most of the state's top politicians and one, in the middle, taken at the White House with President Bush. His credenza featured awards from the city and state chambers of commerce, sales trophies from Ford, and Lucite deal cubes celebrating the closing of multimillion-dollar real estate finance projects throughout the region. He had an oil portrait of his wife on one wall; she was a severe woman, small and thin, wearing a full-length lavender ball gown, nosebleed heels, a gaudy ring twisted with diamonds and emeralds, matching earrings, and blonde helmet hair that would have stood up to a Jared Allen tackle. Her pinched frown said: I'm a country club wife, and don't you forget it.

Lenny finally sat down. He kicked off his golf shoes and propped his stockinged feet on the desk. When he pushed a button under the drawer, the thick curtains on the south wall parted, revealing a row of windows looking out on the auto showroom, where customers browsed among the trucks and hybrids. He studied the action on the floor.

"One-way glass," Lenny said. "I like to watch my salespeople. They never know when I'm checking them out. Keeps them on their toes.

Right now, I can tell you we've got two people ready to buy, that twentysomething young couple and the middle-aged black guy, and the rest are browsers. After a while, you know it as soon as they walk in the door."

The auto dealer picked up a signed baseball from his desk and tossed it up and down like a juggling ball. "Herbie signed this for me after the '91 Series. Had it on my desk ever since. I got a box at the new stadium, so anytime you want tickets, I can hook you up. Ms. Dial, I like that Mustang you drove in here. If you want a new one, I can give you a hell of a deal."

"I'm more interested in an Explorer," Serena said.

"Yeah? Well, great, I'll bring it home at cost."

"Specifically, I'm interested in the one you sold to Margot Huizenfelt."

"Oh." Lenny frowned and pursed his lips like Mick Jagger. "Huizenfelt? She the lady who went missing last month?"

"That's her."

"Okay, sure. XLT, cinnamon metallic, comfort package. Fantastic ride. I remember the truck more than the customer. That's the way it usually is. Real shame to have that vehicle sitting in an impound garage."

"The real shame is that its owner is missing and possibly dead," Serena said.

"Well, yeah, of course."

"Margot bought the Explorer two days before she disappeared. Did you talk to her while she was here?"

"I talk to everyone who buys one of my vehicles, Ms. Dial. Her lead salesman was Phyllis Bowen, but I thanked Ms. Huizenfelt personally for patronizing my establishment. That's my rule, been that way ever since I opened. I may not see customers for a decade or more, but they'll come back to me sooner or later, and in the meantime they'll send me their family and friends. That's the way it works. It's a service business."

"Margot?" Serena repeated.

"What about her? What do you want to know?"

"What did you two talk about?" Serena asked.

"We talked about what a great truck she was buying."

"Anything else?"

"Not much. I'm a politician, Ms. Dial, and Ms. Huizenfelt is a reporter. As far as I'm concerned, everything I say around a reporter is on the record, so I'm mighty careful about what I say. As I recall, Ms. Huizenfelt spent a lot of time admiring some of the things I have here in my office, and she made a few comments about the money I've earned in my life. I gather she isn't a big fan of people with money, and that's okay. I started out with nothing and now I'm one of the wealthiest people in the state. I got here through hard work and street smarts, and anyone else in this country is welcome to do the same. Meanwhile, you won't find me bitching about the pensions we pay for public servants such as yourselves. You earn every dime, and Jesus loves you for what you do."

Stride leaned forward and put his elbows on Lenny's desk. "We were thinking that Margot had other things on her mind when she talked to you," he said.

"And what would that be, Jon?"

"Prostitution."

Lenny rolled his eyes. "You're still on that wild goose chase? I thought K-2 would have talked to you about that. Look, I'll be the first to say that I have a fairly libertarian philosophy about what a woman chooses to do with her own body. My feeling is, if a woman wants to make money with the parts that God gave her, I say more power to her. As for the men, that's between them and their wives. I don't really see that it's any of my business. Or yours."

"Solicitation is still a crime," Stride said.

"So is murder," Serena added.

Lenny took his feet off the desk. He gave up on his salesman's face and adopted his politician's face instead. He could be intimidating when he wanted to be. "Are you suggesting I had something to do with this lady's disappearance? She accused me of buying hookers and I got rid of her? That's crap. You drag my name into this and you will regret it."

Stride glanced at Serena. "I don't think Jesus loves us anymore."

"I guess not," she said.

"Look, Jon, we've butted heads over the years," Lenny went on. "Doesn't mean I don't like you. I do. You and me, we've got a lot in common. We're both Duluth lifers. We both lost women we love. We've both been hunting with K-2, and we know the police chief of this great city couldn't shoot a shotgun straight to save his life. When I come down hard on you, it's not personal. It's politics. And in this case, I'm telling you both that you are making a mistake, and I don't want it to blow up in your faces."

"We're not here to accuse you of anything, Mr. Keck," Serena said. "We've just got a chain of events that makes us uncomfortable."

"How so?" Lenny asked.

"Let me spell it out for you. A few months ago, Margot wrote an article about an underage prostitute. From what we know, this girl has been in bed with at least one man with serious resources, someone who wouldn't want the world to find out he's been sleeping with a teenage girl. He may not be the only one. In fact, there are rumors of a prostitution ring operating among wealthy professionals in the city. Have you heard anything about that?"

"Not a word," Lenny replied. His face was stone.

"Just over a month ago, Margot came here to buy a new truck. She didn't go to a dealership close to home. She came to you. Two days later, she began trying to find Cat, the same girl she interviewed a few months ago. In fact, she was with Cat's aunt on a Saturday evening in Duluth, and the kid who saw her there, Curt Dickes, called *you* when he saw Margot that night. The very next day, Margot disappeared, and someone started coming after Cat. Just a few days ago, someone chased Cat as she was leaving a party that you hosted. Do you see why we have questions?"

"Sure I do," Lenny agreed. "It sounds fishy to me, too. All I can tell you is that Margot bought an SUV from me. That's all. As for this unfortunate young girl, I've never met her, and I sure as hell have never slept with her."

"She was at your party," Stride said.

"When I left that party, the only girl there was my own saleswoman, Phyllis, and Phyllis is not exactly the hooker type. If this Cat arrived later, or any other girls, it's none of my concern. I'd strongly suggest that it not be any of your concern either, Jon. Call that friendly advice, okay? When I have to, I can play dirty, because politics is a dirty game. Before you play against me, think about who's living under your roof."

"You're well informed," Stride said.

"Better believe it, Jon."

"So you didn't arrange for any girls at the party? You don't know who they were?"

"No and no."

"Curt Dickes says he set it up for you."

"Well, if Curt and one of my boys spread a few bucks around to grease the party, they did it without telling me. Anyway, I'm sure it wasn't for sex. My boys are smooth. They don't need to pay for it."

"What about Curt? What's your relationship with him?"

"I've known the boy for years. I know his family. Good people. Curt's had some tough breaks, and I help kids like that whenever I can. I haven't forgotten that I grew up with nothing. I pay Curt to hand out flyers in Canal Park. He sends customers my way. That's the extent of our relationship."

"He's driving around in a brand-new Fusion that you gave him," Stride pointed out. "Is that standard compensation for handing out flyers?"

"I loaned him a car for a few days. Big deal. His own beater is in my shop. Look, Curt's a boy who likes to brag. If someone brags about my cars, that's a good thing. You shouldn't take him seriously about anything else."

"Why did he call you when he saw Margot driving one of your trucks?" Serena asked. "He says she'd been asking around about rich men and prostitution in the city. It's interesting that he'd feel the need to warn you about that."

"Curt gets some strange ideas in his head, but I'm a big boy, Ms. Dial. I can take care of myself. I already told you, Margot and I talked about her new vehicle. Whatever happened to her after that had nothing to do with me. Now if you want to talk about upgrading that convertible of yours, I'm happy to spend the rest of the afternoon with you. Otherwise, I still need to hit another tee shot at Pebble and try to keep it away from the goddamned water."

Serena and Stride both stood up.

"Thanks for your time," Serena told him.

"For a woman who looks like you, sweetheart, I always have time. And Jon, it's always a pleasure. I meant what I said. I like you. I'd hate to see you get into trouble. K-2 feels the same way. You get my message?"

"Loud and clear," Stride said.

"Good. Real good. Give me a call when the weather warms up. We'll play eighteen."

37

"You golf?" Serena asked, as she sprinkled chocolate on the skim foam of her cappuccino.

Stride smiled. "I found a body on a golf course once. Does that count?"

"I don't think so."

"Cindy golfed. She bought me clubs, but I only used them twice. They're still in the attic."

"Was she any good?"

"Cindy? Oh, yeah, she was on the golf team in college. She used to play with K-2 and Steve all the time. I don't think they ever beat her."

The two of them found a table in the food court of Miller Hill Mall. The crowded space smelled of caramel corn and Chinese food. Oldies from the 1980s played from overhead speakers. Stride checked his watch; it was nearly three o'clock. He sipped black coffee and watched a squealing pack of toddlers chase each other between the tables.

"So what happened to Lenny's wife?" Serena asked. "He's got the big painting on the wall, and he said you both lost women you loved."

"That's true," Stride said. "Rebekah's dead."

"Did you know her?"

"No, I met him when she was killed. Lenny was just getting into politics back then. I have to give him credit, he was genuinely supportive when Cindy died a couple years later. I thought things would be different after that, but politics is politics for Lenny. Not long after, he was throwing up roadblocks for me again."

"What happened to her?"

"She was killed during a home invasion. She and Lenny were on some Ford junket in the Keys, but Rebekah got food poisoning and came home early. She stumbled right into the burglary, and a Hmong immigrant named Fong Dao shot her in the head."

"Awful."

"Yeah, say what you want about Lenny, he was devastated. The two of them got married young, long before he made his money. Most of his friends said she was the one with the business savvy. Rebekah was the one who pushed him into politics, too. He was launching his first city council campaign when she was murdered. At first, he said he was going to bow out, but then he changed his mind and won by a landslide."

"When was this?"

"Ten years ago, right before Christmas."

"Was that the same winter Michaela died?"

"Yes, Marty killed Michaela about six weeks later."

Serena frowned. "Is there any way there could be a connection?"

"I don't see how. By the time that happened, Fong was already under arrest. He'd done time for half a dozen burglaries in Saint Paul, and he was on our radar after a couple similar crimes here in the city. We found the money and jewelry from the burglary in Fong's apartment, plus the gun that was used to kill Rebekah."

"What about accomplices?" Serena asked.

"Fong was a loner, except for a girlfriend. If Fong thought he could cop a better deal by ratting out an accomplice, he'd have done it in a heartbeat."

"Lenny never remarried after the murder?" Serena asked.

"No, but he obviously didn't take a vow of celibacy."

"You think he's lying about prostitution?"

"I do," Stride said. "Don't you?"

Serena nodded. "Yeah, if there's some kind of upscale hooker network operating in town, he's part of it. I also don't think it's a coincidence that Margot started hunting for Cat right after her sit-down with Lenny. She figured out something and wanted Cat's help in proving it. The question is, would a prostitution scandal really be enough to end Lenny's political career? It's embarrassing, but politicians have survived worse."

"Not if the prostitute was a kid," Stride said.

"Is that worth killing over?"

"Lenny's more powerful than the mayor up here. You think he'd give that up over a one-night stand with a teenage hooker? I think he'd do just about anything to save his neck, and it wouldn't be hard for Lenny to find somebody to do the dirty work for him."

Serena inclined her head toward a woman who was picking her way through the mall crowds toward them. "Well, let's see what Lenny's employees say about him. That's Phyllis Bowen, the woman who sold Margot the SUV."

The two of them stood up to shake Bowen's hand as she joined them. The saleswoman from Lowball Lenny's dealership eyed the people around her, as if she was afraid to be recognized with two police officers. When Stride offered to buy her a cup of coffee, she shook her head. Instead, she put a paper lunch bag on the table, but she didn't open it. She sat down opposite them and fidgeted in her chair.

"I appreciate your meeting us, Phyllis," Serena told her.

Bowen shrugged. It was obvious that she didn't want to be here. "I hope this doesn't take long. I took a late lunch."

"We just have a few more questions."

"I already told you what I know. Margot bought an Explorer from me, end of story. She drove her last truck into the ground; it had like two hundred and fifty thousand miles on it."

"Did she say why she came to you? I mean, why not shop closer to home? There's a Ford dealership five minutes from her place in Grand Rapids."

"Nobody can touch the deals here. We get buyers from all over. Everybody knows Lenny."

"Yes, they do," Stride said. "So tell us about him."

Bowen fingered the paper bag, making it crinkle. "Lenny says the dealership is a family. Family don't tell stories on each other."

"I appreciate your loyalty, but we're investigating a disappearance and at least two murders."

"I don't know anything about that."

"Maybe not, but you can help us. What's it like to work at Lenny's dealership?"

Bowen's lips bent into a frown. "It's a boys' club. Big deal."

"You're no boy."

"I'm the token woman," she said. "They don't want blonde bombshells working the floor. Too many male buyers go straight to them. I guess I was plain enough to fly under the radar."

Bowen wasn't unattractive, but Stride knew she wouldn't turn men's heads. She was in her early thirties, tall and skinny, with brown hair cut in a bob. Her nose was a bit too big for her face and had a slight hawklike droop at the tip. Her chin made a severe point. She would blend into a crowd, not stand out from one.

"You can see why I'd get the up when a woman like Margot turned up in the showroom," Bowen added.

"The up?" Serena asked.

Bowen smiled. "Customer walks in, one of the salesman gets up. Anyway, nobody wanted her. I got the last laugh, because I made the sale."

"You must do pretty well," Stride said. "You were at the party on the *Frederick* this past weekend for the top salespeople, right?"

"That's right. Most of the younger salesmen don't get the fact that car buyers aren't looking for slick. They want solid, steady, dependable, trustworthy. That's me."

"How was the party?" Stride asked.

She rolled her eyes. "Painful, but not optional. Booze. Dirty jokes. More booze. I was happy to get home to my husband and my kids."

"What time did you leave?" Stride asked.

"Eleven fifteen. I ate the steak dinner at the Radisson, and I stayed on the boat long enough to collect my trophy, and then I was gone."

"Did you hear anything about girls at the party?"

Bowen opened the lunch bag and took out a juice box. She stuck in a straw and sucked up apple juice, making dimples on her cheeks. Some of the juice spilled onto the table when she put the carton down.

"Look, these guys are my colleagues. I have to work with them. I'm not the kind to go running to a lawyer if things get rowdy. I don't want it getting back to them—or to Lenny—that I'm raining on their parade, you know?"

"We'll try to keep your name out of it," Serena said.

"Okay. Fine. Yeah, of course, there were girls. There are always girls. Everybody knows what to expect at the winners' party. That's why I make a discreet exit every year before the action starts."

"Does Lenny know about it? Does he set it up?"

Bowen squeezed her lips together. "I have no idea. I saw him leave early. Okay? For all I know, this is something the boys cooked up on their own."

"Hard to imagine anything happening at Lenny's party that Lenny doesn't know about," Stride said.

Bowen said nothing, but her eyebrows twitched upward slightly, as if to say: *No kidding*.

Serena leaned forward with her elbows on the table. "Phyllis, did Margot ask questions about any of this? Did she talk to you about Lenny paying for prostitutes?"

Bowen played with the straw on her juice box. She craned her neck to watch the mall crowds, but she still said nothing.

"Margot disappeared right after she bought that truck," Serena said.

"You think I want to risk disappearing too?" Bowen snapped.

"Are you scared? Did Lenny threaten you?"

The saleswoman exhaled in disgust. "Let's just say that Lenny had the same questions you did. He wanted to know what Margot said to me. I told him what I told you. She bought a new Explorer. We talked about gas mileage and air bags and towing capacity. That's all. Why would she talk to me? She knew she was going to see Lenny."

"She did?"

"You buy a car, you talk to Lenny. That's the way it works. Margot said she was really looking forward to meeting him."

"So she knew that walking in the door?" Serena asked.

"Oh, yeah. It was one of the first things she said. She wanted to make sure Lenny was around that day."

Serena and Stride shared a glance.

"What did Lenny say when the news broke about Margot's disappearance?" Serena went on. "It must have come up between you."

Bowen hesitated. "He made a joke."

"What joke?"

"He said, who would kidnap a woman like Margot and leave behind that great truck?"

"That's it?"

"That's it," she said.

Serena shook her head. "I feel like you're not telling us everything, Phyllis."

Bowen looked frustrated. "It's gossip. It's no big deal."

"What is?" Serena asked.

"Margot made an offhand comment. That's all. It's nothing. I didn't tell Lenny about it."

"What did she say?"

"We were closing the deal, and she said something about seeing Lenny at a restaurant with a girl who looked like she was straight out of a college dorm. She made a crack like, 'I guess he can afford the best.'"

"Did you say anything back?"

Bowen frowned. "It was stupid. I wish I hadn't said anything at all."

"What did you say?" Serena repeated.

"I laughed. I said, 'Yeah, the younger, the better.'"

38

Maggie parked her Avalanche in front of the Seaway Hotel.

She hopped down and spotted an old man who went by the nickname Tugtug in a lawn chair pushed against the building wall. He had a coffee can between his legs and a sheepskin throw wrapped around his shoulders. Tugtug, who was blind, wore wraparound sunglasses and a camouflage bandana, and his scraggly hair and beard were snow white. He spent half his life at the Seaway and the other half outside city hall, begging for handouts in both places.

"Afternoon, Sergeant," Tugtug greeted her cheerfully. "How's The World's Smallest Policewoman this afternoon?"

"You know, Tugtug, you say you're blind, so how come you always know it's me?"

Tugtug pointed at her truck by the curb. "I know that engine. You're like some kind of crazy-ass NASCAR driver. One of these days, you might think about braking before you actually get where you're going. I hear other drivers appreciate it."

"Uh-huh. So how are you? Been a while since I've seen you."

"Been even longer since I seen you," Tugtug replied.

"Well, I walked into that one. You warm enough? It's almost dark."

"Yeah, manager says I can slip into one of the empty rooms tonight."

"How's the coffee can business?"

"A little slow, since you asked."

"How about one of my coupons?"

"That would be much appreciated."

Maggie reached into her jacket pocket. She didn't give cash to beggars, because she knew it went straight into drugs and liquor bottles. Instead, she'd set up an account with a local diner, and she printed up special coupons for free meals that she passed out to the homeless around the city. Each month, the restaurant billed her. It was a private thing; she hadn't even told Stride about it. She dropped a coupon in his coffee can, and Tugtug gave her a brown-toothed smile.

Nobody knew where he got the nickname. He claimed not to remember himself.

"What brings you to our little Showplace by the Shore, Sergeant? I haven't smelled any dead bodies lately. Nothing but the usual puke, weed, piss, and BO."

"Actually, I'm looking for Dory Mateo," Maggie said. "You know her?"

"I do, but you won't find her here."

Maggie looked at him in surprise, but Tugtug was more reliable than a Garmin. "No?"

"No, I heard her whiz by me this morning. Breathing hard. She ran toward the bank and kept running. She ain't been back."

"You're sure it was Dory?"

Tugtug cocked his head, as if the question were an insult.

"She say anything to you?" Maggie asked.

"Not a word, and Dory usually has a couple coins for the coffee can, too. Not today."

"Was anyone asking about her?"

"Just you."

"How about strangers coming or going?"

"Well, it's not like visitors generally introduce themselves. One gentleman left in a hurry. Couldn't have been more than five minutes after Dory hightailed it. I said hello, but he didn't say anything back."

"Do you remember anything about him?"

"He smell a bit like de islands."

"What?"

Tugtug put a finger on the side of his nose. "I caught a whiff of coconut."

Maggie laughed. "Well, you'll catch a whiff from me, too, but that's shampoo, not Jamaica, *mon*. Anything more specific?"

"Sorry. I pay more attention to the ones that fill my coffee can."

"Okay, thanks, Tugtug. See you around."

"Wish I could say the same, Sergeant," he replied.

"Damn, I walked into it again."

Maggie headed into the Seaway lobby and jogged up the stairs to the second floor. If Tugtug said Dory wasn't there, then Dory wasn't there, but she wanted to check anyway. The hallway was empty, but she heard noises behind the doors. Loud television. Shouting matches. Sex. She'd always thought of this place as a crossroads for desperate lives, and it didn't surprise her at all that Dory had wound up here.

She remembered seeing Dory shortly before Michaela was killed. Dory was still no more than twenty years old then, living in a garage apartment in a house owned by friends of Brooke's parents. Somewhere, Dory had gotten money for a new stash of drugs, and she'd snorted until she was nearly catatonic, with blood running from both nostrils.

Even in her drugged state, Dory knew that something bad was coming. *I told Marty to stay away from her. I said she was sleeping with Stride, but he said he'd kill them both.* One day later, Michaela and Marty were dead. Like an awful premonition come true.

Maggie approached Dory's door. When she saw that it was half-open, she stopped and listened. The room was quiet, but she was cautious. Every Duluth cop was cautious about Seaway doors. More than twenty years earlier, a team of officers had tracked a suspect to a second-floor room at the hotel and faced a hail of gunfire as they tried to arrest him. One cop was wounded by a shot to the chest. Another died of a bullet to the head.

She nudged the door open with the heel of her boot. It was a tiny room, and it was empty; there was nowhere to hide. Dory hadn't taken anything with her when she left. Her clothes were strewn across the bed. The bottom drawer in the rickety dresser against the wall was open. The window to the street was closed, and the room smelled of stale smoke.

Maggie stood in the middle of the room with her hands on her hips. She had a bad feeling. Why did Dory run?

She went to the window and saw a dusting of cigarette ash on the ledge. Her eyes flicked to the open drawer of the dresser near the floor. It was only open six inches, enough to see a messy stash of cheap lingerie. Underneath a pair of white panties, a glint of rosewood jutted over the laminate surface of the drawer. Her breath caught in her chest. She squatted and pushed the underwear aside with her finger, and what she saw was the slight hook on the rosewood handle of a knife.

The handle was dark with stains, and beyond it, the steel blade was crimson with dried blood. She recognized the knife. It was a Victorinox chef's knife, part of an expensive set.

It was the knife that killed Kim Dehne.

39

Under cover of clouds, night fell like a stone.

The cold air resurrected winter, and wet April snow descended in streams from the black sky. He could hear its quiet hiss outside the open garage. Under the shelter of the roof, he could barely see the pines that grew near the old house, and the rural highway was empty.

It was safe to move.

He climbed into the Charger and revved the powerful engine. He backed down the rutted driveway, tires crunching, until he reached the highway. Martin Road was in the far north of the city. Most of the terrain around him was desolate woodland. The snow was heavy; soon it would cover his tire tracks and leave a virgin bed between the trees.

He turned right. In the mirror behind him, his tires kicked up a white cloud like a tornado. For four miles, he didn't see another soul. When he finally saw headlights he slowed, but the other vehicle was nothing more than bright eyes behind a curtain of snow. He reached Rice Lake Road and turned south toward the city. Traffic thickened, but to anyone other than the police, a black Dodge Charger was just another cool sports car. He felt secure as he closed in on the urban corridor. Cars around him slipped and slid through the intersections, and he was careful to give them plenty of space. He couldn't afford an accident.

He kept a tight grip on the wheel. His hands were covered in hospital gloves, and he wore leather gloves on top of those. His hair was completely covered by a wool cap. He was conscious of everything that might shed from his body. Every cough. Every flake of dry skin. Every mucus dribble from his nose. The odds of the Duluth police recovering trace evidence from the vehicle for a DNA match were slim. This was the real world, not *CSI*. He was cautious anyway.

The steep downtown streets, when he reached them, belonged in San Francisco, not in the Midwest winter. He glided downhill, coasting through yellow lights, keeping an eye out for patrol cars. This was the place where cops congregated, the place where he stood the greatest chance of being seen. Every cop was looking for a dark Dodge Charger. If the plates didn't match, it wouldn't matter. They'd follow anyway. They might even pull him over and spot the bloodstains on the leather interior. He couldn't let that happen.

He held his breath, but the storm gave him cover. He passed through the hub of downtown and crossed over the interstate toward Canal Park. Like a ghost in the snow, he took the backstreet to the lift bridge and across to the finger of the Point.

It was three miles to Stride's house.

"We have to find Dory," Stride told Cat.

The girl sat cross-legged on one of the twin beds in the small room facing the street. She squeezed the gold chain around her neck between her fingers. "I don't know where she is. I don't understand any of this. You found the knife that killed Kim in Dory's room?"

"Yes, we did."

"I don't know how it got there."

"Did you open the bottom drawer of the dresser?" Stride asked her. "Did you look inside?"

"I can't remember. I don't think so. I didn't put the knife there. Really, I didn't."

"What about Dory?" Serena asked from the other twin bed in the room. "Could she have had the knife?"

"No, why would Dory hurt Kim?" Cat said. "She wouldn't do that."

Stride stood over her. She was scared to see his face dark with suspicion and concern. She felt his distance. He was the same as everyone; he didn't trust her anymore.

"Maybe you're right," he said, "but we need to talk to her right away. Dory's sick. You know that. Drugs can change people in terrible ways."

"She always told me she was a bad person," Cat said, "but not like this. She wouldn't do this."

Serena got up from the bed. She knelt in front of Cat and stroked her hair. Serena was strong; there was something about her that drew Cat in the way a mother would. A connection. A need.

"Cat, listen to me. I know she's your aunt. I know you love her, but you have to think about this very carefully. Is it possible that something could be wrong with her? Is it possible she could be violent?"

Oh, Dory. Tell me it's not true.

"I—I don't think so."

"You don't sound sure," Serena said softly.

"I am. I'm sure. Dory didn't do this. Neither did I."

Stride sat down on the bed beside her. "We don't believe you did, Cat."

She hooded her eyes from both of them. "I know I've lied sometimes. I've kept things from you, and I'm sorry. I'm not lying now. Someone else is making this happen."

Stride slid a photograph from his pocket and held it in front of her. "Do you know this man?"

She stared at it. He was one of those middle-aged men who leered at her, like hundreds of other men. They were all the same, but he looked familiar. "I think I've seen him on television. Who is it?"

"His name is Leonard Keck," Stride said.

"Oh, Lowball Lenny. The car guy. Yeah, I've seen his commercials. When you're looking for a deal, Lowball It! That's him, right?"

"That's him. Have you ever met him?"

"In person? No."

"Are you sure?"

Cat stared at the photo again. "Pretty sure."

"You never had sex with him? He was never a . . . customer?"

Her eyes widened. "No!"

"You told me once you don't usually look at their faces. Is it possible you don't remember him?"

"Well, I try to forget faces, but him, I'd know him. I wouldn't forget. I never slept with him."

Stride stood up again, and Cat thought he looked disappointed.

"Do you think he did this?" Cat asked. "Is he the one who's trying to hurt me?"

"I don't know," Stride said. "I thought you might know something that could be a threat to him."

"I really don't think I've ever met him," Cat said. "I'm sorry if that's the wrong thing."

Serena stood up, too. "Don't be sorry. If you never met him, that's good."

Cat nodded. "Okay."

"If you need anything, we'll be right outside," Stride said. "Try to get some sleep."

Cat reached for Serena's hand. "Will you still take me to see Dr. Steve in the morning?"

Serena smiled. "I promise."

The two of them left her in the bedroom and closed the door. Cat wasn't tired, but she turned off the light. She preferred the darkness; she could hide inside it. On the other side of the window, snow danced in the wind. She climbed off the bed and stared outside. The grass was already white.

She opened the window and squeezed her head and shoulders into the night air. She wore a pink sweatshirt and pajama bottoms, and her feet were snug inside slippers. Snowflakes made moist drops on her cheeks. She felt them in her hair. A couple of houses had turned on their holiday lights, making the neighborhood look like

Christmas again. Not far away, a dog barked; it was small, with a tiny yipping howl, like a terrier pretending to be a Great Dane. It made her smile.

Cat looked at the ground and her smile bled away.

Beneath her window, there were footprints in the snow.

40

"I got a head start," Brooke told Maggie, holding up a glass of white wine that was nearly empty. "This is my second glass. I'm already a little buzzed."

Maggie slid into the booth beside her. "I'll catch up."

They were at Black Woods on the north end of London Road. It was Brooke's favorite spot. Maggie found her eyes drawn to an empty table for two near the window. She knew from her investigation that it was the table where Kim Dehne had spent Saturday evening with Cat. Her last evening.

"Bad day?" Brooke asked, watching the frown on Maggie's face.

"I have an uncanny knack for screwing up my life."

Brooke pushed her straight blonde hair back behind her ear. "Don't we all?"

The waitress brought Maggie a matching glass of pinot grigio, and Maggie finished half the glass with her first swallow. "I started the day by accusing my boss of murder."

Brooke choked on a slice of pepper-seared ahi. "What?"

"I saw a video of one of Cat's sessions with Roslak," Maggie said. "He tried to bring her back to the night her parents were killed. She made it sound like someone was there when Marty killed Michaela. That Marty didn't necessarily pull the trigger on himself."

"That's crazy."

"Yeah, well, I let my mouth get ahead of my brain and asked Stride whether he did it. Stupid. Mostly, I'm just pissed off at him. Plus, Serena's back in town. That doesn't help."

"Big surprise," Brooke said. "You had to see that coming."

"I know. It shouldn't bug me, but it does. I'm letting it get in the way of my new thing, too."

"Yes, I hear you're dating a cop," Brooke said, but when she saw Maggie slam down her glass of wine, she blanched. "I'm sorry, babe, is that supposed to be a secret? Because everyone knows."

"Damn that Guppo," Maggie said. "Do you remember Ken McCarty?"

"Sure."

"He and I have been hooking up."

Brooke's face registered her disapproval. "I'm not trying to interfere, but you don't exactly have a winning track record with men."

"No, you're right." Maggie finished her wine just as the waitress brought a second glass. "Listen, I need your help on something. We're hearing about an upper-crust prostitution ring in the city. Guys with money. Kind of like the Nice Guys ring in Minneapolis a few years back. You know, lawyers and execs who are willing to pay for high-end girls."

"Not too many high-end girls at my place," Brooke said.

"I'm thinking about college girls who need the money," Maggie told her. "Anyone like that drop in for an STD test?"

"Sure, but most of them don't give us a name."

Maggie frowned. "How about Lowball Lenny? Any rumors about him paying for upscale girls?"

"Lenny?" Brooke seemed genuinely shocked. "Where did you hear his name?"

"He hosted a party on the *Frederick*. Cat was there, along with some other girls. Paid companionship."

"Yeah, I knew about the party. The girls were talking about it last week. I didn't hear Lenny's name. I can't believe he'd risk getting caught up in a scandal like that."

"The cock wants what the cock wants," Maggie said.

"Why the interest?" Brooke asked. "What's going on?"

"Margot Huizenfelt may have been digging into this prostitution ring when she disappeared."

"And you think she got too close?"

"Maybe. Except now we have a new problem."

"What's that?"

"Dory Mateo," Maggie said.

Brooke put her glass down, and her brow furrowed with concern. "Dory? What about her?"

"I found a knife in her room that was used in one of the murders last weekend."

Brooke's long, slim fingers covered her mouth. "Oh, my God, no."

"She was also one of the last people to see Margot alive."

"Dory's not a murderer," Brooke said.

"Then why is she running? She left the Seaway in a big hurry. No one's seen her since."

"I—I saw Dory last night. She was scared. She thought someone was coming after her."

Maggie scowled at Brooke. "Why the hell didn't you call me?"

"She was strung out. I didn't believe her. She wasn't making any sense."

"What did she say?"

"She heard about Margot disappearing. She was afraid she was next."

"Next? Why?"

Brooke hesitated. "I can't—I can't say. Dory's my friend."

Maggie curled her fingers tightly around Brooke's wrist. The woman's skin was warm, and her pulse raced. "Brooke, if you think you're protecting Dory, you're not. You're just making it worse."

"I'm telling you, she was paranoid because of the drugs. She had it in her head that Margot disappeared because of something Dory told her. I told Dory she was wrong. There was no connection. There couldn't be, not after all this time."

"What did Dory tell Margot?" she asked.

"I shouldn't say anything. It's not my place. You need to ask her about it."

"Goddamn it, Brooke, I'm asking *you*. What did Dory tell Margot?"

Brooke stared at the table. Her pretty face was beet red. "It was years ago. It has nothing to do with today. Dory hated herself for it."

"*Tell me.*"

"It was just before her sister was killed," Brooke said. "Dory needed money for drugs. She was desperate. He knew she'd do anything for cash, so he—he paid her for sex. She never forgave herself."

"Who? Who paid her?"

"Marty," Brooke said. "It was Marty. Dory slept with him."

The footsteps led away from her window. Where they ended, Cat saw Dory in the middle of the lawn. She held a cigarette in one hand, and her other hand was wrapped around her stomach. The smoke from the cigarette mingled with the steam she exhaled into the cold air.

Cat squirmed out of the bedroom window and dropped to the ground. The snow was slick under the rubber soles of her slippers. She slid like a skier across the lawn to her aunt and threw her arms around her.

"Dory! I'm so glad you're okay!"

Dory hugged her back limply, and Cat saw that her aunt's face was as pale as the snow, with tears making icy streaks on her cheeks. Dory's eyes were bloodshot. Her entire body trembled.

"Oh, my God, what's wrong?" Cat asked.

Dory's lips had trouble forming the words. Her voice slurred. "I had to talk to you."

"You're freezing, come inside."

"No! I'm going away. It's better for you if I leave town for good."

"Are you kidding? Don't talk like that, Dory."

Dory put her bare hands on Cat's cheeks, and her fingers were cold and wet. A sad, crooked smile played on her aunt's face. "I wanted to see you before I left."

"Please come inside. Let me help you."

"No. I can't."

Cat's heart filled with worry. "Dory, you didn't do something bad, did you? Tell me you didn't. They found a knife in your room. It was covered in blood."

"A knife? In *my* room?"

"It was the knife that killed the woman I was with. Did you—did you hurt her?"

"I didn't! Cat, how could you think that?"

Dory held out her hands to embrace her, but Cat recoiled. All she could see in her head was the image of the knife. And blood. Blood everywhere. Blood making a spider on the floor. It was so vivid that her stomach churned, as if she were about to be sick.

"You have to believe me, I didn't!" Dory insisted. "I would never put you in danger. You know that. The only thing I've ever wanted is to protect you. To *rescue* you. That's what Michaela would want."

"But Dory, the knife—"

"Someone put it there! Someone was in my room waiting for me. That's why I ran."

Cat wanted to believe her. She'd sworn to Stride and Serena that Dory was innocent, but she would have said that even if it weren't true. Dory was her only family. You didn't betray family. If they needed your life, you gave it to them.

"If you didn't do anything, then tell Stride what happened," Cat said. "If you run, he'll think you're guilty."

"It doesn't matter what anybody thinks. I just want to get as far from this place as I can. Somewhere warm. Somewhere where the past doesn't exist anymore."

"What about me?" Cat asked. "You'd leave me alone? What would I do without you?"

Dory held out a hand. "Come with me."

"What?"

"Come with me. Listen to me, Catalina. The two of us, we can go together. We'll be safe. No one will ever find us. Can't you see it, you and me starting over? It would be like nothing ever happened before. We can forget all the people who have hurt us. Forget them! Like they never existed!"

Go away. Escape forever.

Cat wanted to say yes. A fresh start, a new life, sounded like paradise. She wanted to leave now, without another thought. They could live in a place where William Green didn't matter. Where Vincent didn't matter. Where the things she had done didn't matter.

The trouble was, she knew there was no such place.

She also knew that she had a new life already. Inside her.

"Dory, I can't leave. I need to stay here. I'm pregnant. I'm going to have a baby."

Her aunt's mouth fell open, half in shock, half in fear. Cat had no illusions about Dory. She wasn't strong. For something like this, she was little more than a butterfly in a hurricane.

"Well, I could help you," Dory said without a glimmer of conviction.

"I know you could," Cat lied, "but this is my choice, not yours. I have to do this myself."

She could see relief in her aunt's face. "If that's what you want."

"It is, but I wish you'd stay. I want you close."

Dory shook her head. "No, you're better off without me. Especially now. I just came here to tell you something."

"What is it?"

Dory's fists squeezed open and shut. She looked as if she were trying to drag words out of her chest. "It's about your father," she said. "He was shit. He was nothing but shit. I know you don't like me to talk like that, but I'm sorry, it's true."

Cat's face clouded over. "Stop it, Dory."

"No! No, you have to hear this. I have to tell you. Marty always said I was the one who turned Michaela against him. He said I was poison. He loved it when the drugs took over my life. When I dropped out, when everything went to hell, he'd come by to laugh and tell me how worthless I was."

Cat said nothing.

"That winter, that last winter, Marty came by in the night. I was at the end of my rope, Catalina. No money. No food. I was curled up in a ball like a little baby, and all I could think about was how was I going to get more drugs. That was the only thing I cared about. He stood there and he called me names. He said I was the most pathetic person on the planet, and I was. I was. He said he would give me money. Five hundred dollars! Cash! I needed that money, *bonita*, you have to understand, I needed it. All I had—all I had to do . . ."

Dory crushed her hands against the sides of her temples, as if she could squeeze the memory out of her brain.

"He made me . . . I mean, I had to let him . . . I had to let him . . ."

"You whored yourself with my father."

"I'm so sorry! God, Catalina, I've carried it with me all these years like a knife in my chest. And then to lose Michaela, to have him do that to her. I always thought . . . I always imagined he told her about it as he was killing her. He would have told her what I did, so it was the last thing she ever heard, the last thing in her heart as she died."

No no no no . . . oh God . . . oh God . . .

Please . . . I'm dying . . . I'm dying . . .

"He didn't," Cat said. "He didn't say anything about you."

"You remember?" Dory asked.

"Some things. It's been coming back to me for days. I wish it would stay away."

"Can you ever forgive me, Catalina?"

Cat opened her mouth, but she didn't have time to say a word. The cold night broke apart into the pieces of a kaleidoscope spinning in her brain. She was conscious of a car on the street, of a window opening. It was a black car, a death car. Dory took two steps toward her, spreading her arms wide for an embrace the way an angel spreads its wings. She didn't see the car behind her. She didn't see the mortal danger looming from a gun in the open window. Cat began to shout a warning, but it was too late.

She saw the desperate plea that lingered in Dory's face—*forgive me*—and in the next instant, the light snapped off in her eyes, turning them black. Her forehead exploded, showering Cat with blood and brain. Cat heard a scream gurgle out of her own throat, simultaneous with the blast of the gun. Dory spilled forward, crumpling against her body, taking Cat backward onto the cold ground.

Covering her. Protecting her.

The blasts went on, again, again, again, again, again. Snow and earth erupted around her. She screamed until she had no breath. When the bullets finally stopped, when the engine roared and the car vanished, Cat couldn't get up. She clung to Dory, who was motionless in her arms. No matter how hard she shook her, no matter how many times she called her name, Dory lay atop her like a dead weight. The remnants of her aunt's life were splattered on Cat's face. Dory's blood was warm on her skin, but in the frigid air it had already begun to cool.

41

"*Cat!*"

Stride bolted to his feet. The gunshots came in rapid succession, punctuated by screams, and then they stopped. No more than five seconds passed from beginning to end. He ran the length of the house and threw open the door to Cat's bedroom, but the room was empty, and the window was open. A gust of snow and wind blew through the wavy curtains.

"She's outside!" he called to Serena.

Behind him, Serena ripped open the front door and skidded onto the front porch. He heard her shout. "There's a body on the front lawn, and we've got lots of blood! Get an ambulance fast!"

Stride grabbed his phone from his belt and dialed 911 as he followed Serena into the snow. At first, he saw only one body lying prone and lifeless in the grass. Cat. Then he saw movement on the ground and heard Cat's voice calling a name over and over.

Dory.

Serena squatted beside them. She tugged on Dory's shoulder, but the woman's head bobbed forward like that of a limp doll. Dory's face was visible, and Stride saw the fatal exit wound that had carved away much of her skull. He eased Cat out from under her aunt's body. Cat whimpered and cried, unable to stand. Her face and clothes were a mess of blood, bone, and brain, and he couldn't tell, looking at her, if she'd been shot, too.

"Cat, are you hurt?"

The girl didn't answer. He laid her in the snow and did a careful review of her head, limbs, and torso, seeing no bullet holes in her clothes or wounds on her exposed flesh. "I don't think Cat's been hit, but she's in shock," he said. "What about Dory? Is she gone?"

Serena checked Dory's pulse and nodded. "It was a catastrophic wound."

"Take a look at the street," Stride told her. "Make sure we're clear."

Serena already had her gun in her hand. She crouched low as she jogged toward the road that cut like an arrow through the Point. Under the falling snow, the area felt oddly quiet and deserted. If his neighbors had heard the shots, they were staying safely behind their walls.

As he held her hand, Cat's eyes fluttered open. She jerked in fear, and he pushed her shoulders down gently. "It's okay, lie still."

"Dory," she said. "Dory's hurt."

"I know."

"Is she okay?"

"Just lie still."

Cat pushed herself up anyway and saw her aunt six feet away, dead in the snow. She wailed and buried her face in Stride's chest. He put an arm around her body and let her sob.

In the middle of the street, Serena shoved her gun in her belt.

"There are tire tracks in the snow," she called. "Looks like he fired from the car. He's gone unless we can get the bridge up in the next few seconds."

"I don't want to block the ambulance," Stride said. "I still want Cat checked out. With any luck we'll catch him as he reaches the city."

He didn't think luck was with them. When he listened for sirens, he didn't hear any in the distance. The storm had slowed down emergency responses across Duluth, and his team was stretched thin. When he checked his watch, he estimated that three or four minutes had passed since the shooting. The killer might already have escaped across the bridge at high speed, and once he made it beyond the streets of Canal Park, he could go anywhere.

Serena rejoined them on the lawn. "It's cold. You should get her inside. I'll stay here."

Stride eased Cat to her feet. Her knees were rubbery and he kept an arm around her waist.

"We should get inside," he told her.

"No, wait."

"I want you lying down, Cat."

"I need to say good-bye."

"There'll be time for that."

"No, I need to do it now. Please."

He helped her to the trampled ground where Dory lay on her chest, her face turned sideways, her hair matted with blood. The storm was turning her body white. Cat knelt beside her. Dory's eyes were open and sightless, and before Stride could stop her, Cat reached out and closed her aunt's eyes. She crossed herself, a gesture of faith that took him by surprise.

Cat brushed flurries from Dory's coat and kissed her shoulder. She put her lips near her aunt's ear and whispered. Her voice was soft, but he could hear what she said.

"*I forgive you.*"

Maggie sped south on the I-35. Her windshield wipers were choked with ice, forcing her to squint through wet streaks at the clouds of snow that poured through her headlights. She was alone on the highway, and the road was slick, even under the monster tires of her Avalanche. When she shot off the freeway at the Lake Avenue exit, she felt the truck skid as she feathered the brake.

She climbed toward the intersection and coasted through the red light toward the Point. When she checked her mirrors, she realized that she was the first cop to reach the area. Her truck barreled through the intersection at Railroad Street, and as her eyes flicked right, she caught a glimpse of taillights half a mile south. It could have been a phantom of the storm; the lights disappeared as she watched. A moment later, the buildings of Canal Park blocked her view, and the car, if it was a car, was gone.

She roared past hotels and shops. The late-night sidewalks of the tourist center were deserted, and most of the parking places on the street were empty. She turned right at the DeWitt-Seitz building, rear wheels slipping, and then left again on Lake Avenue. The tall gray tower of the bridge loomed ahead of her.

She thought again: *Taillights.*

She couldn't shake the phantom. She'd seen a car speeding away.

Maggie stopped in the middle of the street, momentarily paralyzed with indecision. She wished she hadn't downed two glasses of wine so quickly. Her reactions were slow. All she had now were her instincts, and her instincts shouted a message at her. She was making a mistake.

Turn around.

She swung into a U-turn and kicked up a cloud of snow as she charged back toward Railroad Street. She careened left, but the road ahead of her was dark and empty. She was too late; the car had vanished. She continued for a mile past the DECC and Bayfront Park, following the street toward the industrial section of the rail yard, where pyramids of taconite and wood were capped in white like mountains. She was alone with the storm; no one else was with her.

He was gone.

Maggie shouted a loud expletive inside the truck. She turned again and retraced her steps. As she neared Bayfront Park, she swung left over the freeway toward downtown and stopped at the peak of the overpass. There were a few cars braving the storm in both directions. The same was true of downtown; she could see stray cars pushing through the intersections.

Whoever she'd seen was a needle in a haystack now, impossible to find.

Her radio squawked. "Hey, Maggie, is that you in the big yellow boat on the Fifth Avenue overpass?"

It was Guppo.

"It's me," she said. "Where the hell are you?"

"Heading north."

She eyed the freeway traffic and saw the flashing lights of a patrol car approaching from the south. "I spotted a car that could have been the shooter coming off the Point, but I lost him," she said.

"Maybe not. I saw what looked like a black Charger going the other way. He got off on fifty-three heading toward the Hill."

Maggie's adrenaline roared back. She gunned the Avalanche and merged onto the southbound interstate at a crazy speed. Highway 53 climbed at a sharp angle toward Miller Hill, where it made a T at the intersection with Central Entrance, which was the main road through the flatlands in the north of the city. If he stayed on the highway, they could put him in a box by closing in from three sides.

"I'll come up behind him on fifty-three," she told Guppo. "You hightail it up Mesaba and come in on Central Entrance from the east. Get a couple cars near the airport to come down from the west."

"You got it."

She wheeled around a slow-moving Corolla in the right lane just as she left the interstate. Highway 53 rose northward in tight curves, and even the powerful engine of her Avalanche struggled for traction on the snow-covered road. Her speed was maddeningly slow. She cruised through stoplights near the Enger Tower and Lake Superior College, and finally the truck picked up speed as the incline flattened. Through the snow, she saw taillights ahead of her. She closed quickly on the vehicle from behind.

If he saw her, if he thought she was a cop, he didn't run. Coming up behind the car, she saw that it was a Dodge Avenger, not a Charger, and it was blue, not black.

"Guppo, you sure that was a black Charger?" she called into the radio. "I'm behind a blue Avenger up here."

"I'm sure," he radioed back. "That's not him."

Maggie spun around the Avenger and continued until she reached the T intersection at Central Entrance. She eyed the slow-moving traffic in both directions, but she didn't spot the sports car. From the northwest, two patrol cars sped toward her. She didn't see Guppo from the other direction.

"Guppo, tell me you've got something. We've got nothing up here."

"Ditto, sorry."

"Keep coming my way, I'll head toward you. Let's get the other cars patrolling the side streets west and east of fifty-three, in case he turned off before he reached the Hill."

"Roger."

She turned right and wove between the cars inching along the slick road. Half a mile eastward, she spotted Guppo's patrol approaching from the opposite direction, and she pounded the wheel in frustration.

They'd lost him.

She flashed her brights at Guppo.

"What now?" he radioed.

"Check the mall. Maybe he's switching cars. I'll start running the streets to the north."

She watched his car fade into the snow in her mirror. They were shooting blind. When she reached the light at Arlington Road, she turned left. In the opposite direction, Arlington was one of only a few roads that intersected Highway 53, so the driver of the Charger could have used it as a shortcut to Central Entrance.

On Arlington, she crawled. The farther she traveled, the more deserted the road became, heavily wooded on both sides. Twice she spotted taillights and followed them quickly until she confirmed that they weren't the car she was hunting.

Her radio crackled to life again.

"We just got a 911 call on a cell phone. A dark sports car burnt through the red light at Arlington and Arrowhead. Could be our guy."

"Which direction?"

"North on Arlington toward Rice Lake."

"I'm on Arlington now," Maggie told Guppo. "Back me up, and see if we have anybody in Rice Lake Township who can come down from the north."

"I'm five minutes behind you, on my way."

Maggie accelerated northward. The land north of Arrowhead was largely rural, and there were few roads cutting through the undeveloped land on which to escape. Unfortunately, the lack of roads also made it difficult to box him in from other directions. She also knew that in a battle of horsepower between the Charger and the Avalanche, the Charger would win. Her best option was to find him, tail him, and not spook him.

She drove crazy-fast, as fast as she could make the Avalanche go, feeling as if she were hydroplaning on a river of wet snow. The flat, straight road headed into nothingness. She passed two crossroads leading west toward the airport, but she bet that he would have chosen a faster route if the airport was his destination. Instead, she stayed on the same northbound course, and as the road crested a shallow hill, she spotted twin red lights at the extreme end of her sight line.

It was him. It had to be him.

"I may have our guy," she radioed Guppo.

"Where are you?"

"Passing Norton Road, he's maybe half a mile ahead of me."

She was doing eighty, and if he looked in his mirror, he'd spot her bearing down. She eased off on the accelerator, closing the gap slowly. They neared the stop sign at Martin Road, and she saw brake lights flash. She turned off her lights, trying to make him think she'd pulled off the road. He stayed where he was, not moving, and she drifted to a stop, playing a game of cat and mouse across a quarter mile of pavement. In the storm, without lights, she hoped she was invisible.

Suddenly, ahead of her, she heard the blistering roar of an engine. The rubber squeal of the Charger's tires cut through the storm, and the car swung into a hard right turn, accelerating wildly.

"Damn, he spotted me!"

Maggie turned her lights back on and jammed the accelerator. At the intersection, she turned the wheel so hard that her wheels left the ground and then thudded back to the pavement. The car ahead of her was greased lightning; it was already disappearing. Her chassis quivered around her like a rocket, but even at extreme speed, the Charger widened the gap. A mile later, its taillights winked out into the darkness.

"I lost him, I lost him—*oh, shit!*"

Through the fog at the end of her headlights, she saw a dark shadow. It could have been a deer; it could have been a child. Instinctively, her foot slammed to the brake, and like a dancer, the Avalanche swirled on the sheet of snow. It spun in a Tilt-A-Whirl circle, once, twice, three times, and then the right-side wheels of the truck skidded onto the shoulder and spilled into the shallow gully. The truck toppled onto its side, and kept toppling, over and over, rattling Maggie's body with the shudder of each impact. Windows broke; glass flew across her skin; snow and dirt spat through the interior of the truck. She felt the world spin, and by the time it stopped spinning, it was black.

42

She was upside down.

When Maggie opened her eyes, she saw a face as round as Charlie Brown's staring in through the broken window. It was Sergeant Max Guppo, squatting beside the overturned Avalanche. He yanked open the driver's door, which groaned as he fought against bent metal.

"I thought you were dead," he said.

"If you're an angel, heaven has a lot of work to do," she mumbled in reply.

Before he could say anything, Maggie unhooked her safety belt and dropped six inches to the roof beneath her. "Ouch."

"You shouldn't move," he said. "You could be hurt."

"Oh, I'm fine. This thing's a tank. Help me out of here."

Guppo slid his beefy forearms under her shoulders and slid her out of the truck. Her legs wobbled as she stood, but she propped herself on his shoulder and waited for the dizziness to pass. With a huge breath, Guppo pushed himself up beside her. He didn't squat easily, and he had an even harder time unsquatting. She heard an unmistakable sound behind him, and a foul aroma overwhelmed the cold night air.

"Oh, hell, Guppo, what is that? Are you kidding me?"

"Sorry. Chili cheese fries. You sure you're okay?"

"Quit babying me."

"You're bleeding," he said, pointing at her face.

"So get me a frickin' Band-Aid. Come on, we have to find this guy."

"You should go to a hospital. Stride will kill me if he finds out I didn't get you an ambulance."

Maggie grabbed a fistful of Guppo's shirt and pulled him closer. "Now listen to me very carefully. Fuck Lieutenant Jonathan Stride!"

"I think you have a concussion."

"I don't. Let's go."

"Yeah, except where do we go? He's gone."

"He was on this road for a reason. Maybe he's hiding out near here. We start checking houses one by one, and we get as many cars out here as we can to do the same thing. We wake people up, we don't take any shit about how late it is. Okay?"

"You're pretty crabby."

"Yeah. I'm pretty crabby. My truck is totaled, and I feel like somebody's been using me as a punching bag."

Maggie turned too quickly and felt dizzy again. Guppo grabbed her before she fell. She shook him off and scrambled up the embankment to his patrol car, which was parked on the shoulder. Looking down, she saw her Avalanche, wheels in the air, its frame twisted. Her insurance guy was not going to be happy with her. Again.

She bandaged the cut on her face, and the two of them headed east. It was a lonely road, with few houses. Where they stopped, no one was happy to see them, but they crossed houses off their list one by one. Some they skipped, where the driveways were empty of tire tracks. Three other patrol cars joined them, and they hopscotched their way past Gnesen Road and then to Vermillion Road. The snow had stopped, but the desolate land was black under the clouds and they had to go slowly to find properties bordering the road. By the time it was two in the morning, she was almost ready to quit for the night and go to the hospital.

He'd beaten her, and she didn't like it.

"We done?" Guppo asked.

"Let's do a couple more," she told him. "By the way, I never thanked you for blabbing to the whole fucking world about me and Ken."

"I told Serena, that's all. She sent me snickerdoodles."

"You sold me out for cookies?"

"Well, they're really good. You know, cinnamon and all."

She knew there was no point in being angry. Guppo was Guppo.

They crawled along the highway. Where Martin Road curved southeast, Maggie spotted a narrow dirt driveway almost invisible between the trees. The snow was beaten down with tire tracks coming and going. When they turned their searchlight toward the woods, they saw an old rambler set back from the road. The house was dark.

"Those tracks look fresh to you?" Maggie asked.

"They do."

"Pretty late to be out and about."

"Yeah."

"Come on," she said. "Let's check it out."

Guppo parked on the opposite side of the road. Maggie opened the passenger door. Inside the warm car, she felt fine, but when she climbed outside, her muscles tensed in agony. As she crossed the street, her face twitched with the spasms in her neck. Guppo studied her with concern, but she waved him off.

"Call in the other cars," she said. "I want backup on this one."

He hailed the other cops on his radio, and she bent down to examine the tire tracks with a flashlight. "Definitely fresh. The snow has hardly covered them up. I'd say no more than half an hour old."

"There are two sets of tracks," Guppo said, bending slightly at his massive waist.

Maggie doused the light. They stayed on the shoulder of the driveway as they approached the house. The trees around them were thick. At the end of the driveway, they saw a detached two-car garage, its door closed. Tracks came and went on both sides. Twenty yards from the garage, a single-story house, with painted red siding, was carved into a clearing in the trees. A snow-covered cord of wood sat propped against one wall. The walkway from the garage to the front door showed no footsteps.

"Looks deserted," Guppo said.

Maggie hiked through the virgin snow to the front door. A picture window faced the woods and she peered inside, using her flashlight to illuminate the interior. The living room was furnished with an old-fashioned sofa with a faded rose pattern, a rocker, a straight-backed Shaker chair, and a big-box television from the 1980s. It was an old person's house.

"This place look familiar to you?" Maggie asked. She searched her memory, which didn't take long. "This is the Linnerooth place. Wally and Ruth. Remember?"

"Oh, sure, the lefse people."

Every year, the Linnerooths baked lefse at their winter home in Arizona and sent a big box to the Duluth police as a Christmas thank-you gift for their service to the city. In return, cops always stopped in to see Wally and Ruth during the warmer months to help with household chores and play Scrabble.

"It doesn't look like they're home yet," Guppo said.

"No, it doesn't. So who's using the garage?"

Maggie slid her gun into her hand. So did Guppo. They retraced their steps to the detached garage. On the far side of the dirt driveway, two other officers joined them. They closed in on the garage door from both sides.

She pointed at the metal handle on the door and gestured one of the younger cops toward it. He positioned himself and bent down, ready to throw it open. She lifted three fingers and counted them off—one, two, three—and the cop yanked the garage door open on its metal tracks. They pointed their weapons at the interior, but the garage was dark and quiet.

A single vehicle was parked in the left-side stall.

It was a black Charger, still wet with mud and snow.

Maggie approached the car on the driver's side. Her head throbbed, as if someone were beating on it with a hammer. Her legs felt weak. She steadied herself against the cold metal of the chassis. Guppo took the other side of the car and they simultaneously shot beams of light inside the Charger. It was empty. No one was inside the vehicle.

When she studied the leather on the front seat, however, she saw dark, dried stains. Blood. Kim Dehne's blood. He'd carried it on his clothes as he escaped that night.

"Think he's still here?" Guppo asked.

"No, he left the Charger and made a getaway in a vehicle we wouldn't recognize. Smart."

"He had to leave quickly. Maybe he left evidence behind."

"Maybe," Maggie said, but she wasn't expecting this man to give them any lucky breaks. It was his safe house, and she assumed that he kept it safe. He had to know that any time he left, he might not be able to come back.

"Turn on the light," she told Guppo. "Careful for prints."

Guppo found a switch near the rear door of the garage and turned it on with a pencil. The bright light made her squint and sent ripples of pain behind her eyes. The nerves in her neck stabbed her when she moved. Her ribs ached where the safety belt had locked against her chest in the accident. Her stomach had begun to churn, and she thought she might throw up.

"You're not looking good," Guppo said.

"Really? Because I feel terrific."

"I'll call that ambulance now."

"Great idea."

She studied the garage. It was impeccably organized, a handyman's garage, with steel shelves lining the walls and supplies neatly stacked together. Gloves. Birdseed. Gasoline. Oil. Antifreeze. Boxes labeled for Halloween and the Fourth of July. She saw a riding mower, a white overflow freezer, and a rusted snowplow attachment for a pickup truck. Near the side door, she saw a pegboard carefully arranged with an elaborate set of tools, saws, and drill bits. Wally Linnerooth was an old-fashioned Norwegian who had a place for everything and kept everything in its place.

Except for the food. The food wasn't right.

"Oh, shit," Maggie said.

Guppo looked at her. "What is it?"

She pointed at the set of metal shelves beside the freezer. The top shelf, at arm level, was stacked with Tupperware containers, boxes of Banquet chicken, Lean Cuisine meals, and links stuffed with home-made sausage.

"Oh, shit," Guppo echoed.

They both made a beeline for the freezer. It was a chest freezer, five feet wide and three feet deep. Maggie used the tip of her glove on the corner to force the lid open. A cloud of frost leached from inside.

Ice crystals clung to a fully clothed body squeezed into the tight space like a side of beef.

The body was faceup, its skin bone white. Eyes closed. Frozen blood traced the woman's cheeks from a wound near her temple, and a large plastic bag had been taped around her neck, suffocating her after she'd been assaulted. She was heavy, dressed in a flannel shirt and jeans. Her hair was cut short, mannish and flat.

It was Margot Huizenfelt.

43

The medical team had extracted Margot's body from the freezer, but the corpse was still frozen solid, her bent limbs jutting into the air in a pose that was unnatural and obscene. The thawing was slow, but under the heat of the crime scene lights, melting ice had begun to soak her skin and clothes like sweat.

Stride and Serena watched the activity through the open garage door. He understood the depth of loss and anger he saw in Serena's face. The longer a missing person stays missing, the more you know that he or she is never likely to be found alive. Even so, when you finally stare at that person's body, you can't escape the sense of defeat.

"Time of death will be almost impossible to determine," he said.

Serena's eyes were fixed on Margot. "The clothes match what she was wearing when she was last seen in Grand Rapids on that Sunday. If she was alive after she disappeared, it wasn't for long."

"Dan and his team will be working the scene for hours, but so far, he says it's clean. We're not going to get much here."

"The house?" she asked.

"It doesn't look like he even went inside. No trash, no food. The water's not turned on. He was careful."

She frowned. "Why take the body here?"

Stride kicked at the earth with his heel. "Ground's still frozen. So are the lakes. He couldn't bury it or dump it."

Serena turned away from the bright lights of the garage. They pushed through the snow of the front yard. Red and blue lights from the emergency vehicles flashed on the highway, and the evidence technicians streamed back and forth to their white crime scene van. Although the snow had stopped, the air was bitter cold. No one liked winter bodies.

"Margot was in Duluth on that Saturday looking for Cat," Serena said, rehashing what they knew about her movements that final weekend. "She talked to Bill Green. She talked to Dory. Maybe others, we don't know yet. As of midnight, she was down in the graffiti graveyard, still trying to find her."

"She never did," Stride said.

"Do we know where Cat really was that night?" Serena asked.

"Yes, she bumped into a girl she knew from Denfeld up at Miller Hill Mall. The girl let her crash at her parents' house. Maggie confirmed it."

"So at some point, Margot gave up for the night and went home to Grand Rapids. Early Sunday morning, she had breakfast at a local diner. The waitress said Margot was scribbling notes in a legal pad and made some comment about looking for someone to help her break a big story. No details about who or what. Margot left, and a day later we found her brand-spanking-new Lowball Lenny Ford Explorer parked near the Swan River. No legal pads, no notes, no computer in her house, nothing. The only real clue I ever found is that she got a call that morning from a pay phone at a rest stop in Floodwood."

"The killer setting up a meeting with her?"

"That's been my theory all along. She had to be meeting someone at the river. Unfortunately, he didn't leave prints on the phone or the coins."

"So he meets Margot," Stride went on, "kills her, cleans out evidence of what she was working on, and comes here to dump the body. He's already got the stolen Charger, so we assume that's what he's driving. And then he starts doing exactly what Margot was doing."

"Looking for Cat," Serena said. "Why?"

"Maybe Margot mentioned Cat when they met, or maybe she was listed in her notes."

"Or maybe one of the people that Margot talked to on Saturday tipped off the killer," Serena suggested. "Remember, we can't be sure that this guy is working alone. This place is pretty remote, so how did he get here? The buses don't come up this far. There were two cars in the garage. He couldn't drive them both."

"We're canvassing the neighbors to see if anyone saw the Charger coming or going. There aren't a lot of people up here, but that means neighbors tend to notice things."

Serena studied the modest rambler, which was now ablaze with lights as the crime scene team explored the house. "Why'd he pick this house, anyway?"

Stride shrugged. "Half the people in Duluth know that Wally and Ruth are snowbirds and that their house is empty all winter. Wally has been on the Rotary for decades. Ruth's been a hospital volunteer at St. Luke's as long as I can remember."

Serena shook her head. "We've got nothing. Nothing except bodies. This guy is two steps ahead of us everywhere we go."

Stride couldn't disagree with her. He felt as if someone were playing games with them, throwing up red herrings and misdirections to lead them everywhere but where they needed to go. This man was inside their heads. Kim Dehne gets killed with a knife, like Vincent Roslak. The knife vanishes and then shows up in Dory's apartment. The evidence leads them away, while the killer calmly goes back to finding Cat.

Why?

He saw Max Guppo waddling toward them across the frozen lawn, looking like an oversized version of the mayor of Munchkin City. Same comb-over. Same mustache. Same thunderous waistline. He'd known Guppo as long as he'd been with the Duluth police, and he didn't think he'd ever met a kinder soul. He also knew that Serena had Guppo wrapped around her pretty finger. Whenever he smelled snickerdoodles in the office, he knew that Duluth police secrets were spilling across the county line to Grand Rapids.

"How are you, Max?" Serena greeted him. "Hey, you've lost a little weight, haven't you?"

Stride rolled his eyes at her. "Shameless."

Guppo's face, which was already red from the cold, brightened at the compliment. He was a happily married father of five, but he was a sucker for Serena's smile. "Actually, I'm down ten pounds."

"Good for you! How are the kids?"

"They're super. The oldest, Gina, is playing Division One volley-ball at Iowa State."

"You guys must be really proud."

"Uh, Max?" Stride said, interrupting the lovefest. "You want to tell me what's going on?"

Guppo tugged at his uniform, which was snug despite any weight he'd lost. "Oh, sure, the girl? You know, Cat? The hospital released her. One of our people was going to take her back to your place, but she refused to go. She insisted on coming here. She's in the back of your truck."

"How is she?"

"Pretty shaken up."

"I'll go talk to her," Stride said.

Serena wiggled her fingers at Guppo to say good-bye as the over-sized cop retraced his steps to the crime scene. Stride zipped up his leather jacket and took a look at the highway through the trees. His Expedition was parked on the shoulder behind Guppo's patrol car.

"You want me to come with you?" Serena asked.

"No, I'll do it. You know, I never get flattery from you. How does Guppo rate?"

"Well, he's much sweeter than you are, Jonny."

"That's true."

Stride hiked up the driveway in the trampled path that had been made by his officers. When the wind blew, snow sprayed from the evergreen branches overhead and trickled down his back in cold streaks. At Martin Road, he crossed to the opposite side and opened the rear door of his truck and slid inside. The interior was cold, and Cat sat in the far corner, wrapped in a tan Mexican blanket that Cindy had given him almost twenty years ago. The girl's skin was pink and scrubbed; her hair had been washed. There were no traces of her aunt's death clinging to her body.

Her eyes were distant and sad.

"You found Margot?" she said.

Stride nodded.

Cat sat in silence and chewed her nail, staring at the lights and the silhouettes of the police officers moving back and forth through the night like soldiers. Flares and parked squad cars closed the road in both directions. Finally, she said, "Are you afraid of dying, Stride?"

"I'm not looking forward to it," he replied.

"I saw Dory die. Right in front of me. She was alive, and then she was dead."

"I know."

"I can't stop thinking about it. I keep seeing her face."

He didn't know what to say. He'd been in her shoes many times, watching life become death. There was no way to comfort her.

"What do you think it's like?" she asked. "Being dead, I mean. Is that all there is?"

"I wish I knew, Cat."

"My mother used to tell me about heaven. She said if I was good, and I prayed, I would go to heaven. She made it sound so beautiful. Do you think my mother's in heaven?"

"If there's a heaven, I'm sure Michaela is there," Stride told her.

"But you don't think it exists."

"I hope it does, but I let God worry about things like that. I worry about the world down here."

"Even if it does exist, I'll never get in," Cat said.

"Why do you say that?"

"Me? I'm just a whore."

He reached out and cupped her chin with his hand. "What you were is behind you. You're young, and you're going to have a child, and you have your whole life ahead of you."

Cat sniffled and wiped a hand across her face. "It doesn't matter. I don't think it exists, anyway. There's no heaven. It's just a lie that people tell. I think death is nothing but a cold nowhere."

Stride slid across the seat. He wrapped Cat up in his arms. Her eyes were open, but she'd run out of tears.

"My mother's gone. My father's gone. Now Dory's gone, too. I have nobody."

She said it matter-of-factly. That was what made his heart break. It had become so commonplace to her. He took a deep breath and thought about Cindy. Her voice was still vivid to him, when she woke him up in the middle of the night. So earnest. So sure she'd found the answer. *Maybe we were meant to rescue someone else's child.*

"I won't let you be alone, Cat. That's a promise."

Cat said nothing. She didn't know what it meant for him to say those words. She couldn't afford to believe him, anyway. This was a girl for whom promises were empty.

"Get some rest if you can," he told her. "We'll be here for several more hours. Serena will take you to see Steve in the morning. Your baby's the most important thing. Okay?"

She nodded with her head against his chest. He felt her relax just a little. When he eased away from her, she held on to his hand.

"Do you think you can be a good person and do something really bad?" she asked.

"I hope so. I've done some bad things myself."

"Me too. I was so angry with Dory, but then I thought, who am I to judge her? She always protected me. It doesn't matter what she did in the past. I guess I was just angry at my father all over again."

Stride frowned. "Your father? Why him?"

"Dory told me something. He paid her a lot of money to sleep with him. She kept it a secret from me all these years, because she felt so guilty. If it were me, I probably would have done the same thing. If someone gave me five hundred dollars, you think I'd say no? I'm not sure I would."

"When was this?"

"Right before my mother and father died." She saw the grimness take hold in Stride's face, and she said, "What? What's wrong?"

"Nothing," he said.

"Do you think it means something that Dory slept with my father?"

"I think it meant something to Dory. She had trouble living with it. Beyond that, no. I heard you say that you forgave her for what she did. That's the end of it. You can let it go."

"Okay."

"Get some rest," he repeated.

He eased her against the cushions of the seat, and she was asleep before he even adjusted the blanket on top of her. Her face was angelic. He smiled, looking at her, but he didn't feel like smiling at all. He was suddenly deeply troubled.

It didn't matter that Dory had slept with Marty. It didn't even surprise him. It was exactly the kind of cruel, manipulative thing that Michaela's ex-husband would do, just for the pleasure of demeaning another human being. What troubled him was that he knew Marty Gamble inside and out. He knew everything about him. He could practically account for every minute of his days. Where he worked. Where he ate. Where he drank. The clothes he wore. The money going in and out of his checking account. He knew it all.

There was no way—no way—that Marty Gamble should have had five hundred dollars to pay Dory for sex.

44

Steve Garske poked Serena in the shoulder. "Wake up, sleepyhead."

Serena blinked. Moments earlier, she'd been reading a copy of *People* magazine in the clinic lounge as Cat went inside to the examining room with Steve. Looking at the clock, she realized that nearly an hour had gone by, and she was stretched out on the sofa with her head on a throw pillow. Her long hair was a rat's nest.

"Is it still April?" she asked.

"Last time I checked," Steve said, "although you wouldn't know it from the weather. It's eighteen degrees out there. So much for global warming."

"I moved from Las Vegas for this paradise," Serena said blearily, covering a yawn with her hand. "How's Cat?"

Steve still wore his lab coat, with a stethoscope slung around his neck. "Physically, she's fine. Mentally, well, that's another story. She's really upset."

"She had a bad night," Serena said.

"I heard."

Serena pushed herself up on the sofa and stretched her arms over her head. She saw the Caribbean glow on Steve's skin. "Nice tan," she said.

"I don't tan. I burn. Anyway, it's fading already. Soon I'll be a white ghost like everyone else around here." He added, "It's good to see you, Serena. I've missed you down at Amazing Grace this winter. I always throw in a Terri Clark song just for you."

"Yeah, sorry, I haven't been in town much."

"But you're back?"

"I'm here now," she said.

His face had a sly smirk. "So what's new with you?"

"You mean, like, are you getting enough fiber in your diet? Are you still renting DVDs from Netflix? Or do you mean, what's up between you and Jonny? You are an incorrigible gossip, Dr. Garske."

"I am," Steve agreed, "but since you brought it up, are you guys a couple again?"

"We're talking. We're working together. We'll see how it goes. I won't deny that it's nice to be with him."

"Have you slept with him yet?"

"Jesus, Steve!"

"Hey, if you can't tell your doctor, who can you tell?"

"You're not my doctor."

"Fine, I'm his doctor. It's a professional inquiry. Sex is good cardiovascular activity."

"If you remember, lack of sex wasn't his problem," Serena said sourly. "It was who he was having sex with."

"Point taken. Sorry. If it weren't for the whole do-no-harm oath, I would have kicked his ass when he told me about it. Speaking of your romantic rival, I heard that Maggie was in a car accident last night. Is she okay?"

"She's fine. You can only kill the undead with a stake through the heart." Serena yawned again and realized what she'd said. "I'm sorry, did that come out as bitchy as it sounded?"

"Pretty much."

"Well, she's fine."

"I'm relieved," Steve said. "I love her, but I knew she and Stride were a train wreck. I'm really glad you and he are trying to work things out."

"You never quit, do you?"

Steve mussed his blond hair. "Nope. Dr. Lovelorn, that's me."

"Uh-huh. Don't quit your day job, Doc. Can I go get Cat?"

"Sure, go on back."

Serena stood up. "Tell me something, Steve. Back when Jonny and Cindy were trying to have kids, was he really on board with it? Or was it what Cindy wanted?"

"Sorry, kiddo, I can't say anything about that. They were both patients."

"I know. Never mind."

"What about you? Did you and Stride ever talk about kids?"

"I can't have kids."

"I realize that, but that's not the only way."

Serena shrugged. "We didn't really talk about it. It was easier not to talk about a lot of things. That was part of our problem."

"I hear you, but it doesn't have to stay that way forever. You know, Stride wasn't always closed off the way he is now. He used to be pretty cocky. Much more like a cowboy. When Cindy died, he didn't feel invincible anymore."

It was like playing a record with a skip in it. The same note, over and over in her ears. "Yeah, I know, Cindy was the love of his life. Me, I'm Nancy Kerrigan, skating for the silver medal."

"That wasn't what I meant at all," Steve said.

"Doesn't matter. It's true."

"Actually, it's a big load of self-pitying crap, Serena Dial."

She laughed. "Yeah, maybe."

"Look, I've known Stride practically my entire life. I knew him with Cindy. I knew him with that disaster of a second wife of his, Andrea. I've known him with you. Was he happy with Cindy? Absolutely. It's pretty damn easy to be happy when you're young. But to be happy again, to fall in love again, after you've been through what he went through? That's a hell of a steep climb. And that's what I saw with him and you."

Serena patted him on the cheek. "You're a smoothie."

"Yes, I am."

"You need a girl, Steve."

"What makes you think I don't have a little beach bunny down in Nassau?"

"Do you?"

"Nah, I just go for the piña coladas and the music. I'm married to my work. And my guitar."

"Next gig, I'm there," Serena promised. "I have to get Cat."

She squeezed Steve's shoulder and headed for the examining room. She knocked, but there was no answer from inside so she pushed the door open. Cat sat on the edge of the table, her stockinged feet dangling. She was dressed in a medical gown, open in the back, revealing the bare curve of her spine. She obviously hadn't moved since Steve left the room.

"Cat? You okay?"

The girl didn't answer. Serena slipped inside and shut the door behind her.

"Steve says you're doing great. That's good news."

Cat shrugged. "I guess."

"Are you thinking about Dory? I'm sorry. It was an awful thing to go through."

"It's not just that," she said.

"Then what?"

Cat pointed at a chair against the wall, where her clothes were neatly folded. A large, overstuffed manila envelope sat on top of her sweatshirt. "Dr. Steve gave me a bunch of brochures and books and stuff. What to eat. What not to eat. Vitamins and exercises. What's happening inside my body. He told me what to expect month by month."

"It's a lot to absorb," Serena said.

"I'm not sure I'm up to it. Me having a baby? I'm crazy to think I can do it on my own. Maybe it would be better if I just—you know. Ended it."

"You're feeling overwhelmed. That's natural."

"It would be a lot easier if I didn't go ahead with it, though, huh?"

"Why the big change, Cat? You were excited."

"I know, but I've been thinking it's not fair to a kid to have a mother like me." Cat stared at her feet. "I'm just scared. Losing Dory, it made me realize I'm all by myself in this."

"No, you're not. You'll have help."

"Thanks. You and Stride have been great. Sooner or later, though, it's over, you know? It's nice that Stride says I won't be alone, but what can he do? Find me a foster home for a couple years? Come see me sometimes? It's not that I'm not grateful, but it would suck to be a mom like that."

"Stride said you wouldn't be alone?" Serena asked.

Cat nodded.

"He doesn't say things like that lightly."

"Well, it's not like I can stay at his house forever."

Serena didn't say anything. She wondered whether Stride had really thought about the road ahead for Cat. And for himself. She also wondered where, if she had her desires, she fit into that equation with the two of them. If she fit at all.

"Let's worry about that later, okay?" she told Cat. "Why don't you get dressed? We can do a quick breakfast somewhere. What's your favorite breakfast?"

"Hot dogs," Cat said.

"Seriously?"

"Yeah, Dory took me to the state fair once a couple years ago. I was able to get a hot dog at like seven in the morning. A big foot-long chili dog with onions. It was great."

"Well, Coney Island is open. Let's see if we can get you a breakfast dog."

Cat grinned. "Cool!"

She hopped down from the examining table. She shrugged out of the sleeves of the gown and stood on the floor in nothing but white socks. She was casual about her nudity, but in a way that was childlike rather than cynical. She didn't act like a street girl who had been naked around too many men. She was a beautiful young woman who had no clue how beautiful she was. Serena had been that way once, too, but it was so long ago that she couldn't remember the feeling.

Cat stepped into white panties and then pulled up her gray sweatpants and tightened the drawstring. Half-dressed, she reached into one of her boots and took a gold chain into her hand. She slid the chain over her head and under her flowing hair to nestle at her neck. The gold dangled down her chest, and at the end of the chain, between the girl's breasts, Serena saw a pretty, jeweled ring.

"What's that?" she asked.

Cat cupped the ring in her palm. "Oh, that. My father gave that to me. It's the only thing I have from him, so I always wear it."

"May I see it?"

"Sure."

She removed the chain from around her neck. With the tiniest hesitation, she put it in Serena's hand, where the ring sat in the middle of a coiled nest of gold. Serena took the ring and pinched it between two fingers and held it near her eyes, where it sucked light like a magnet from the entire room. The ring itself was actually two rings twisted together, one with prongs cradling diamonds, the other with prongs cradling square-cut emeralds.

"Your father gave this to you?" Serena murmured.

"Yes."

"When did he do that?"

"A couple of nights before he died. Mother didn't know about it. He would sneak into my room sometimes late at night, because that was the only time he could see me. He wasn't supposed to come near us. He said if anyone knew, they'd send him away again, and I didn't want that. So it was our secret. That last time, he gave me the ring. He said I couldn't show it to anyone, but this way, I would always have something to remind me that he loved me. I suppose I should have thrown it away after what he did, but I couldn't."

Serena stared at the ring. The light from the jewels, with all their reflections, was hypnotic. The ring teased her and laughed at her, as if to say: *See? I was here all along.* She didn't think she'd ever had a moment in her life of such shocking clarity. A moment where something cloudy and confused became so simple. She also knew, without any doubt, that the ring in her hand was cursed. It was evil. Without some kind of exorcism, it would destroy more lives.

"It's pretty, isn't it?" Cat went on, unaware of the strange dance between Serena and the ring. "I know it's ten-dollar Walgreen's paste, but I love it. I'd be lost without it."

Serena's fingers closed around the ring in a tight fist, as if it could be suffocated from lack of air.

"It's not paste," she told Cat, "and I've seen it before."

45

Lowball Lenny opened the door for Stride and Serena at his mansion in the Congdon Parkway.

His home was a mammoth, Tudor-style house from the Duluth robber-baron days, at least a century old, with brick walls and sharp gables crisscrossed with wooden beams. The roof was lined with red clay shingles. Chunks of snow and ice made the flagstone sidewalk treacherous. Mist clung to the frigid morning and made the house look as if it were hovering in the clouds.

Stride remembered Lenny's home perfectly. Even ten years later, he could map its rooms and staircases and its odd maze of hallways in his memory. He'd spent dozens of hours here in the wake of Rebekah Keck's murder.

"Hey, you guys," Lenny said. "Back so soon?"

"May we come in?" Stride asked.

"Yeah, of course."

Lenny waved them between the Corinthian columns on the porch through glass doors that led to the foyer. The interior was dark and laden in dust, like a Gothic house of horrors. The ornate wallpaper hadn't been updated in decades, and portions of it were bubbled and peeling. Stride saw heavy antiques, mostly in cherrywood. Lenny had eclectic, expensive collectibles, too. A Kieninger grandfather clock. Limoges china. A Civil War bayonet mounted on the wall. It was sad to imagine one rich old car dealer living alone in this dense, depressing splendor.

Stride saw a single modern electronic device near the doorway. The house had an alarm panel with a keypad for entering a security code. He wondered if Lenny had changed the code after the home invasion. The numbers stuck in his head from the murder investigation. Sometimes the oddest details refused to vacate his brain.

1789.

That was the code. Most people used birthdays or anniversaries, but not Lenny. He'd told them the code was absolutely random, four numbers he'd drawn from the air. That had been the one mystery in a case that seemed to have no mystery at all.

Where did Fong Dao get the security code?

"You guys want anything?" Lenny asked, leading them into a wood-paneled study. A fire roared in the fireplace, spitting and growling like an angry bear. The room was hot, and Lenny's forehead glowed with sweat.

"No, thanks," Stride said.

"You sure? Juice, Danish, whatever? Hell, a mimosa if you want it."

He shook his head and Lenny took a seat in a huge leather armchair by the fire, where he'd been reading the sports section of the *News Tribune*. He shoved the paper onto a circular coffee table and waved them to a lavish old sofa, with white fluff spilling out where the upholstery was worn. Everything in the house was expensive, but much of it was in disrepair.

Lenny wore a tracksuit, as he had in the office, but this one was navy blue, not chocolate brown. He wore fluorescent sneakers rather than golf shoes.

"So what's up?" he said with a wary smile.

Serena reached into her pocket and extracted a plastic evidence bag. "Do you recognize this ring?"

"You're too far away for these old eyes, honey," Lenny said.

She crossed the room and held the ring close to Lenny's face. Even inside the bag, the fire and the Tiffany lamp on the coffee table made the stones glitter. He held out his hand to take it, but as he studied the ring he pulled his arm back. The smile washed away from his face.

"Where did you get that?" he asked.

"Do you recognize it?"

"It looks like a ring I gave my wife many years ago."

"Was it custom?"

"Yes, Rebekah designed it herself. It was one of a kind."

"This is the ring your wife is wearing in the painting in your office, isn't it?" Serena asked.

"That's right. I'll ask you again, where did you get it?"

Stride leaned forward, his elbows on his knees. "For the last ten years, a girl named Cat Mateo has been wearing it on a chain around her neck. Her father gave it to her."

"Is her father this Hmong immigrant who killed Rebekah? Fong Dao?"

"No."

"So how did he get it?"

"That's a very good question," Stride said.

Lenny picked up a flowered china cup that was filled with steaming coffee. He took a sip and licked his lips. "Keep me posted. I'll be interested in what you find out, of course."

Serena returned the plastic bag to her pocket. "You're pretty calm about this, Mr. Keck. We thought you'd be upset."

"Finding Rebekah's ring doesn't change what happened," he said. "My wife is gone. You'll forgive me if I'm not anxious to revisit that ugly period in my life, Ms. Dial. It's over."

"No, I'm afraid it's not," Serena told him. "Not anymore."

"What do you mean?"

"Margot Huizenfelt was in your office two days before she disappeared," Serena said. "Then she immediately started looking for this girl Cat. We've been struggling to find a connection, and now we think we know what it is. Margot saw the painting of your wife on your office wall. She saw the ring and she remembered that very distinctive piece of jewelry hanging around the neck of a young prostitute she interviewed a few months ago. Needless to say, a reporter like Margot would have smelled a story. A big story. We think that story got her killed."

"I don't know what to tell you," Lenny said. "This is all news to me."

"Did Margot comment on the painting of your wife when she was with you?" Serena asked. "Did she ask you about the ring or about what happened to Rebekah?"

"No, she didn't. Like I already told you, we talked about her new truck. That's all."

Stride could see the anxiety in Lenny's face. The sweat on his skin from the hot fire became drips running down his cheeks and neck. The more he tried to hide his reaction behind a mask of calmness, the more obvious it became that the car dealer was terrified to see that ring again.

"You're holding out on us, Lenny," Stride said. "What's going on?"

Lenny put down his china cup and folded his arms across his chest. "I'm telling you, Jon, I don't know what the hell is going on. If I knew anything at all, I would clue you in, but I don't."

"Have you seen the ring since it disappeared in the burglary?"

"Obviously not, if this girl had it."

"Did anyone mention to you that they'd seen a ring like Rebekah's?"

"No! Don't you think I'd call you if I heard something like that?"

"Actually, I'm not sure you would. Maybe you'd try to get it back yourself instead. Maybe you'd start looking for the girl who was wearing it. Is that what happened?"

"I didn't do anything like that. No one told me about the ring."

"Cat has been with some wealthy men," Serena reminded him. "That may include some men who are friends of yours. People who've been in your office or knew your wife."

"She was also at your party on the *Charles Frederick*," Stride said, "along with a dozen salesmen who've known you for years."

"Nobody said anything about the ring!" Lenny repeated. "Nobody. Look, everybody who buys a car from Lowball Lenny winds up in my office. Okay? That painting of Rebekah is up there for the whole world to see. So maybe I've got a customer whose wife isn't so hot for blow jobs and he likes to get some outside action from time to time. See where I'm going with this? He sees the painting when he's in my shop buying a Focus, and he thinks, hey, I've seen that ring before, around the neck of that little hottie I paid fifty bucks for a suck last month. Next thing you know, he's trying to find her."

"How much is the ring worth?" Serena asked.

"At least seventy-five thousand bucks. Probably a lot more now. People would do nasty things for that kind of dough."

Stride exchanged a glance with Serena. He didn't trust Lenny, but the car dealer was right. Anyone who set foot inside his office was a suspect. Anyone who slept with Cat might have seen the ring.

He examined the dark study in the century-old mansion. When he'd come here for the first time, Lenny had been in the same chair, drinking, crying, his face a hollow mask of grief. Rebekah was still on the floor in the upstairs bedroom, where he'd found her. Lenny had come home from the Keys to discover his wife's body, cold and dead. A bullet in her brain.

"There's another motive we have to consider," Stride said.

"What is it?" Lenny asked.

"Someone may be covering up a murder. Rebekah's murder."

"You already got the guy who did that," Lenny said.

"We thought we did, but it looks like someone else was part of the plot. Somehow, a man named Marty Gamble wound up with this ring after the burglary. He had cash, too. Clearly, he had a connection to Fong Dao that we didn't know about back then."

"So ask him."

"Marty's dead. So's Fong. The thing is, we didn't find anything in Marty's place to link him to Fong or the burglary. Nothing. No cash. No jewelry. Someone cleaned up after him. Someone else was part of the plot."

"Look, guys, I wish I could help you, but I can't."

Stride let the silence draw out. All they heard was the crackle of the fire. Lenny kept sweating.

"After we searched Fong's apartment, we did an inventory of the cash and jewelry we found there," Stride said. "You told us we'd recovered everything that had been taken."

"Yeah, so? I'm sure I told you that the ring was still missing."

Stride shook his head. "You didn't. If we'd known it was missing, we would have kept looking for it."

"Well, what do you want from me, Jon? My wife was dead. My world was over. I was kicking off a fucking political campaign. I had things on my mind."

"What about the cash? Could more money have been taken than what we found?"

Lenny shrugged. "I don't have a clue how much cash is in my house. I've got a lot of money. Maybe there was more than I thought."

"Did you know this man Marty Gamble?" Serena asked.

"I don't know the name. Who knows, maybe he bought a car from me."

Stride slid a photograph from inside his pocket. "What about the face?"

He passed the picture to Lenny, who studied it and shook his head. "Mean-looking SOB, but I don't know him."

"Would you remember him if he was a customer?"

"Do you know how many thousands of customers I see every year? Give me a break."

"Marty was a construction worker," Stride said. "Did you have any building projects going on during that time?"

"I'm sure I did. Office buildings, condos, whatever. If he was part of a team working on one of my buildings, you'd have to talk to the general contractors. Look, this guy might know *me*, because I'm a celebrity around these parts. I'm on TV commercials, understand? The papers write about me. The point is, I didn't know *him*."

Stride didn't think that Lenny was lying about Marty, but the car dealer also wasn't telling them the full story about the burglary. A sharp businessman like Lenny didn't forget about a seventy-five-thousand-dollar ring. No way. He'd known all along that they hadn't recovered it, and he'd deliberately concealed the fact that it was still missing.

Why?

"Just curious," Stride said, "did you ever change your security code? Is it still 1789?"

"Of course I changed it." Lenny tapped his head. "I keep it right up here. Nobody except me knows what it is."

Stride nodded. "That's what you said back then, too, but Fong obviously had the code."

"I told you, Rebekah probably screwed up and told someone what it was, or she wrote it down or something. She was forgetful. The alarm kept going off because she'd get inside and not remember the code. She was always calling me to ask what it was. Didn't you guys say you thought you knew how Fong got it?"

"Fong was a nurse's aide at St. Luke's," Stride acknowledged. "He was working there while Rebekah was having plastic surgery done. We assumed that somehow he learned the code while she was there."

"Yeah, so?"

"So we couldn't prove it. We couldn't prove that Fong had ever been in her room. Fortunately, there was enough other evidence that the jury overlooked it."

"He figured it out. Isn't that the main thing?"

"No, we can't assume anything anymore," Stride told him. "We need to look at everything again. Fong, Marty, Margot, everything. I think we missed something big on this case, and someone's willing to kill to keep us from taking another look."

46

"You're alive," Serena said.

Maggie sat in one of the chairs in Stride's office. She had a fresh white bandage on her forehead, tucked under her black bangs. When she swung her head, she winced in pain. "Yeah, sorry about that. Maybe you'll get lucky next time."

"Promises, promises."

Stride sat down behind his desk. "Sure is nice to have the gang back together again," he said ironically, as both women smiled at each other with faux sweetness. "Seriously, Mags, what are you doing here? Shouldn't you be at home recovering?"

"Jeez, you and Guppo. I'm aces. Leave me alone."

"Whatever you say." Stride leaned back in his chair. His eyes shot between the two of them, which was like studying tigers in side-by-side cages, both with sharp claws. He opened his mouth to say something, but he figured anything he said would make it worse. He let it go.

"So what do we know?" he said. "Originally, we thought Margot was interested in a high-class prostitution scandal. Maybe that's why she went to Lenny's in the first place, but now we think she connected Cat and Lenny via his wife's ring. Is that a reasonable conclusion? Or are we getting ahead of ourselves?"

"It's too much of a coincidence not to mean something," Serena said.

"I agree with Angie Harmon here," Maggie said, drawing a withering stare from Serena. "Margot knew about the ring that Cat wore. She specifically mentioned it in the article she did about Cat a few months ago. I think if you see that ring, you don't forget it."

"It also explains why Margot was asking Bill Green about Cat's parents on that Saturday," Serena added. "She was trying to figure out how Marty Gamble got his hands on the ring."

"So how did Margot wind up dead?" Stride asked.

"Somebody figured out what she was doing," Maggie said. "Somebody didn't want her asking questions about that home invasion."

"Lenny?"

Serena shrugged. "He's scared of something. You can see it in his face. I'd like to know why. If Margot spotted the ring, she must have mentioned it to him. Even an offhanded comment to see how he reacted. Lenny also knew that Margot was talking to Dory Mateo on Saturday. Curt Dickes called him."

Maggie stretched her arms like a yoga instructor. Her flying elbows came dangerously close to Serena's head. "Why would that raise red flags? We never connected Fong and the burglary to Marty, Michaela, Dory, or anybody else. They'd be strangers to him."

"That's true, unless Lenny knows more about the burglary than he's telling us," Serena said.

Stride shook his head. "We can speculate all day, but it's not going to get us any closer to finding out what happened. We've been investigating in the present, but I think we need to go back to the past. Ten years ago, the trail to the burglary ended with one person."

"Fong Dao," Maggie said.

"That's right. We thought he did it alone, but obviously we were wrong."

"How did Fong die?" Serena asked.

"He was involved in a prison fight three years ago," Stride said. "He got his head bashed in. Obviously, he can't tell us anything, but we know what we're looking for now. We need a connection between Fong and Marty Gamble, or someone close to Marty."

"There was a girlfriend," Maggie said. "Fong was dating a black girl. Twenty years old back then. Name's Djemilah Jordan."

"Is she still in Duluth?" Stride asked.

"No, I looked her up. She did a stretch in Shakopee for check fraud a couple years ago. After release, she stayed in the Cities." Maggie waved a piece of paper in the air. "I have her address and job info. I'm going to drive down and talk to her."

"Okay."

"I thought I'd check out the place where Vincent Roslak got stabbed, too. Roslak and Cat were sleeping together. Chances are, he saw the ring around her neck. Maybe this little worm figured out the connection before everybody else did and got sliced and diced for his trouble."

Stride frowned. "Fair enough. Just get back here tonight. Nobody's going to bed until we tie Marty Gamble to Fong Dao."

"Got it. See you later."

Maggie pushed herself out of the chair. She nodded at Serena, who nodded back, but neither one of them said a word. Maggie limped as she left the office.

When they were alone, Stride said, "Is it going to be a problem? You two?"

"Not for me," Serena replied. "How about for you?"

"I have to work with her. That's all."

"Ditto."

Stride knew better than to push her further. "I've got Guppo pulling the archives on Fong Dao," he said. "Credit card receipts, phone records, employment history, arrest records, everything. Before we knock on any more doors, I'd like to know what we missed."

"I'll get coffee," Serena said. She stood up, but then she turned back and leaned across Stride's desk. "You know, Jonny, this discovery about the ring changes a lot of things. Not just the burglary. Have you thought about that?"

Stride nodded. "Michaela and Marty."

"It's an awfully big coincidence, them winding up dead so soon after the home invasion."

He saw the bodies in his head again. Marty, the burnt wound in his temple, the gun near his hand. Michaela, floating amid her spilled blood. "If someone else was in the house that night, they knew what they were doing," he said. "They didn't leave any evidence behind."

"Maybe not physical evidence, but we have a witness," Serena reminded him. "Cat."

"Cat doesn't remember anything," he said.

"Or she doesn't want to remember. The question is, can we unlock what's in her head?"

"Roslak tried. It didn't tell us much."

"Maybe Cat needs to revisit the scene of the crime," she suggested.

Serena turned around. As she did, she nearly ran into Kyle Kinnick, who stood in Stride's doorway, listening to them, his hands on his scrawny hips. She towered over the short, floppy-eared police chief, who wore a slightly baggy brown suit. He gave her a coffee-stained smile.

"Serena Dial," K-2 announced in his quavering voice. "It's good to see you around these parts again."

"Good to see you, too, sir."

"Oh, I'm not a sir to you, just to him." He nodded at Stride. "I need a couple minutes alone with this man, if you don't mind."

"Of course," Serena said. She gave Stride a quick wink, then disappeared.

K-2 pulled Stride's door shut behind him. The chief didn't sit down; instead, he wandered around the office, tapping on the unpacked boxes on the floor with his brown shoes and staring out the window. Eventually, he leaned on the window ledge, and Stride swung around in his chair to face him.

"I like Serena," K-2 said. "She's better than you deserve."

"I won't argue with you."

The chief scratched his nose. "Pretty and smart. Like Cindy. Don't mess it up, okay?"

Stride said nothing. He waited.

"I got my balls squeezed again today," the chief went on. "Feels like déjà vu to me, Jon. Does it feel like that to you?"

"Yes, it does."

"Seems to me I asked you to give me a heads-up before you start messing with Lenny Keck. And guess who just called me and suggested in pretty strong terms that I think about firing your ass?"

"You do what you have to do, Chief," Stride said.

K-2 dug in his ear and studied the results. "Oh, hell, Jon, I'm not going to fire you, but neither one of us needs the city council on our backs. They can make our lives miserable. I don't need to tell you that. I'm not exactly going to glide to reelection if the council turns against me."

"I realize that."

"You're dredging up painful times for Lenny. I thought you of all people would be sensitive to that. Do you and your lady friend really need to rush into his house like storm troopers and start grilling him about the night that he lost his wife? For God's sake, Jon, the man's not a suspect in anything, is he? He was the victim back then."

"I'm not so sure anymore," Stride said.

K-2 whistled through his teeth. "I'm telling you, regardless of what you think about his business dealings or his politics, Lenny's a good man. I've known him for years."

"I know you have."

"So I'm asking you a favor. Cut him some slack."

"I can't do that," Stride said.

"Do you want me to make it an order instead?"

"It won't make any difference. I'm going to follow this wherever it takes me."

"Look, Lenny likes you, and he likes me, but that's not going to make a damn bit of difference if he feels threatened," the chief reminded him. "We are talking about one of the richest, most powerful men in the state. You do not pick a fight with that kind of man, particularly when you don't have squat to back it up. You need more than your gut. You need evidence."

Stride shook his head. "This isn't just about my gut. Lenny knew we hadn't recovered everything from the burglary. He knew that his wife's ring was still missing, and I'll bet that wasn't the only thing. A lot more cash probably walked out of his house, too. He didn't tell us.

He kept it a secret. He let us think this started and ended with Fong Dao."

"You sure about that?"

"Pretty damn sure. People died because of something he's hiding."

"If this blows up in your face, I can't help you."

"Do you want my resignation?" Stride asked. "Because otherwise, I'm going to keep pushing."

"I want your common sense. You still have some of that, right?"

Stride smiled and got out of his chair. He eased against the wall next to K-2 and thought about the early years, when they were both young. He remembered him in the Northland clubhouse, scowling in mock dismay as he paid off a golf bet to Cindy. He remembered K-2's embarrassed grin every time Cindy kissed him under the mistletoe at the department Christmas party. He remembered the chief's arm around his shoulder at Cindy's funeral.

"We go back a long way, Chief," Stride said. "I've earned your trust."

"Yes, you have, and I've earned yours, Jon. Don't forget that."

"I know. You've stuck out your neck for me more times than I can count. Sometimes when I didn't deserve it."

K-2 chuckled. "So now you want me to stick my neck out again, is that what you're saying?"

"That's what I'm saying."

The chief rubbed his smoothly shaven chin and shook his head. "Exactly what is it you want me to do, other than commit political suicide?"

"I need you to lean on Lenny. I need you to make him understand that he has to come clean with me. He's a friend. He'll listen to you."

"I think you overestimate my power of persuasion," K-2 said.

"No, I don't. Look, Chief, one way or another, Lenny has to realize that this is all coming out. Everything. I don't care about the consequences. I'm going to get to the bottom of this. He doesn't want to get in my way when I'm investigating multiple homicides. Whatever he knows, he needs to tell me now, because it's only going to get worse."

K-2 shoved himself off the wall and smoothed the lapels of his suit coat. "You're a piece of work, Jon, you know that?"

"Will you talk to him?"

"Oh, hell, I will, for whatever good it'll do me. I'll get him drunk first, but I'll talk to him. Then I suspect you and I will both be looking for new jobs."

47

Maggie made the two-and-a-half-hour drive to Minneapolis in less than two hours in her rented inferno-orange Corvette. Driving the sports car, she began to wonder if it was finally time to give up her Avalanche and buy something that was built for speed. The growl of the engine, and the vibration under her seat as she hit ninety miles an hour, made her horny. Or maybe it was the pain medication. Or maybe it was Ken. She couldn't be sure.

She exited I-35W near the Metrodome and made her way east to the Seven Corners area. This was her old stomping ground. She'd spent her college years at the University of Minnesota, where she was a Chinese exchange student majoring in criminology. As she drove, everything on the street reminded her of those years. The students on the sidewalks looked exactly like her, except for their cell phones and iPads. Crazed Minneapolis bicyclists still did fearless battle with the cars. She saw pro-Palestinian graffiti on the brick wall of an apartment building—different era, same politics. She passed a twenty-four-hour greasy spoon where she'd spent hundreds of hours gobbling up American hamburgers with her nose buried in her books.

She never partied back then. She never drank. She didn't have sex. She just studied. She would have had more fun if she'd gone to school now.

Maggie found a parking place in front of a Chinese restaurant near Nineteenth and Riverside. The parole officer for Djemilah Jordan had told her that Fong Dao's ex-girlfriend was now a hostess at the Lucky Pearl, and it looked like the girl had gone clean after her stint in prison. Maggie got out and plugged the meter. The drab concrete towers of the Riverside Plaza loomed behind the low roofs of the retail strip. She smelled stir-fried beef through the vents of the restaurant, and it smelled good. She realized she was hungry.

Inside the restaurant, most of the tables were empty, except for a couple students hanging out over cold tea. It was too late for lunch and too early for dinner. A black woman of about thirty, with beaded hair and a nose ring, looked up from an accounting textbook.

"Table for one?" the woman asked, smiling behind thick lips. She was tall and bony, and she wore a Lucky Pearl T-shirt and drainpipe orange corduroys.

"Yeah. Way in the back, okay?"

"Sure."

The woman led her to a table in a dark, deserted section of the restaurant, near the door to the kitchen. Maggie felt warm steam and heard Asian voices chattering behind the swinging doors. There were fake gold masks hanging on the walls and cheaply framed posters of Tiananmen Square.

Maggie waved away the menu. "Give me some salt-and-pepper chicken wings. Do you do shrimp cake with baby bok choi?"

"Uh-huh. It's real good."

"That's what I want."

"You're easy," the woman said, smiling.

"I get that a lot. So are you Djemilah Jordan?"

The woman's smile vanished. "Cop?"

Maggie flipped the lapel of her leather jacket to reveal her badge. "Duluth."

"Duluth? I ain't been there in years."

"I know. I've got some questions that go way back."

"I'm straight now. I'm in college."

"So I hear. Good for you. I still have questions. Your parole officer assured me you would be a model of cooperation."

"About what?"

"First, chicken wings," Maggie said. "I'm starving."

Djemilah disappeared behind the doors of the kitchen. She returned five minutes later with a plate of salt-and-pepper wings, steaming hot, with chunks of chopped jalapeño and pepper flakes clinging to the crispy skin. Maggie disassembled one of the wings and gnawed meat from the mini-drumstick.

"These are great," she said. "Have a seat, Djemilah. Let's chat."

The woman eyed the front of the restaurant. There were no customers. She pulled out a chair and sat down, positioning herself so she could watch the door. "What do you want?"

"Tell me about Fong Dao," Maggie said.

Djemilah frowned. "He's dead."

"I know. That's why I'm talking to you. You were his girlfriend back then, right?"

The woman dug into her pocket for her wallet and pulled out a wrinkled photograph and slapped it on the table. The picture showed a young boy, ten or eleven years old, with cropped black hair and a serious face. "That's my son. Maybe you want to come back to my apartment and explain to him how you people killed his father."

"Fong was never getting out of prison," Maggie said. "I feel bad for you and your son, but when you shoot a woman in the head, your life is over. Fong did this to himself. If he had a kid, he should have known better."

"Fong didn't kill that woman," Djemilah said.

"I'm not here to argue with you. I just need information."

"Yeah? Why do you even care after all these years?"

"Back then, we thought Fong did this all by himself. Now we think he had an accomplice. Probably more than one. We need to know who."

"You're wrong."

Maggie sighed. She had a photograph in her coat pocket, and she showed it to Djemilah. It was a close-up of the diamond and emerald ring that had hung around Cat's neck for years. "You ever seen this ring before?"

"Pretty," Djemilah said. "No, I never seen it before."

"It belonged to the woman who was killed in the home invasion. Ten years ago, this ring was in the possession of a man named Marty Gamble. Does that name mean anything to you? Did you or Fong know him?"

"No."

Maggie removed another photograph from her pocket. "This is Marty Gamble. Does he look familiar?"

Djemilah shook her head. "No."

"Take a good look."

The woman picked up the photograph and studied it. "Never seen him. If he had the ring, then he must have killed that woman, not Fong, right? That's what I've been telling you."

"This man worked construction in the Duluth area. Did Fong ever do anything like that to pick up extra money?"

"Construction? No way. Fong wasn't made for shit like that. He was small. Smaller than me."

"Who did Fong hang out with?" Maggie asked.

"He didn't have a lot of friends. He was quiet. I liked that, you know? Me and him, we hung out alone most of the time."

"Where did you hang out?"

"My place, mostly. I lived with my aunt."

"Did you go to bars? Did you ever go to Curly's?"

"Are you kidding? That's a good way to get a bottle in the head, you know? I wasn't into that. Neither was Fong."

Maggie picked up another chicken wing, but she found that she was losing her appetite. Plus, her neck was throbbing, and she had a headache behind her eyes. "Djemilah, I'm not trying to hang anything on you. It sounds like you and Fong were close. I'm sure he wanted to protect you. The thing is, Fong didn't do this job alone."

Djemilah leaned across the table. The beads in her hair clicked together. "He didn't do it at all."

"We found jewelry and cash from the burglary at his place. Plus the gun."

"You guys planted it."

Maggie shook her head. "Come on? Seriously? That's your story?"

"Well, somebody did. Fong was framed. He didn't do it."

"Fong did a year for half a dozen identical burglaries in the Cities before he moved to Duluth."

"Not with a gun," the woman retorted. "He never used a gun. He never even owned a gun. I would have known."

"Six months before the Keck shooting, there were two unsolved burglaries in Duluth. We found merchandise from those crimes in Fong's apartment with his fingerprints on them."

Djemilah sucked her lower lip between her teeth. "Okay, look, that summer, I found out I was pregnant. Understand? We were barely making ends meet with the two of us. So Fong, yeah, he did those couple jobs, just like you said. I didn't know. He was looking for money to make it easier for us, and when I found out, I blew my top. I said if he ever did anything like that again, I'd kick him to the street with one of my heels up his ass. I'm telling you, you don't want to see me mad, and I was mad. He swore he would never do it again, and he *didn't*."

"So he committed the first two burglaries, but not the third?"

"That's the way it was."

Maggie shook her head. "Sounds to me like he kept you out of it when he planned the Keck job. He didn't want you getting mad at him again."

"Hey, I did get mad after he was arrested! I figured he was guilty, but he swore up and down he didn't do it, and I believed him. Somebody set him up."

"Even assuming that's true, who could have done that to him? Did he give you any names?"

Djemilah shrugged. "It could have been anybody. Fong had a job at the hospital, you know? People at the hospital, they all knew about his past. Doctors, nurses, staff, whoever. It was easy to blame him. Somebody gets robbed, everybody looks at the ex-con."

"There's a reason for that," Maggie said. "Most of them reoffend sooner or later."

"Not Fong. He was done with that. And definitely not with a gun. Let me tell you something: if I thought he did what you people said, I'd spit on his grave. I wouldn't lie for him. My life went to hell after he got locked up, and I'm only digging out now. But you people were wrong."

Maggie held up the photograph of Marty Gamble. "Look again, Djemilah. This man was involved in the burglary that killed Rebekah Keck. If Fong is guilty, then he had ties to this man. If Fong is innocent, then this man knew enough to pin the crime on him. Somehow their lives intersected. Do you have any idea how they could be connected?"

The front door to the restaurant banged. Two Asian college students came inside and waved. Djemilah stood up from the table.

"I gotta go," she said, "and the answer is no. I don't know that man, and neither did Fong."

48

The sun was nearly down.

Stride, Serena, and Cat stood outside Michaela's old house on the remote hilltop of the Antenna Farm. In the intervening years, the evergreens had soared, making the house look even smaller than it was. The paint was the same, yellow and peeling. The porch beams were warped and faded, in need of stain. The weeds in the lot were overgrown, with patches of snow clinging to the fields like white islands.

"It looks abandoned," Cat said.

"The owners lost it to foreclosure last year," Stride told her. "The bank has it now. The house will probably be torn down if the lot sells."

"Oh." She sounded sad at the prospect.

Stride's Expedition was parked in the rutted driveway. They stood near his truck, twenty yards from the house. Cat hung back, looking afraid. Serena reached out and took her hand.

"Have you been back here since it happened?" she asked her.

"No. Not once."

"We don't have to do this if you're not up to it," she said.

"No, it's okay. I want to. You said it might help."

Cat started toward the house. Her boots cracked a puddle of thin ice like a broken window. Stride and Serena followed, letting the girl walk by herself. It had been Serena's idea to bring Cat here, to see if the visit triggered any memories, but now he wondered if they were making a mistake.

The girl stopped and looked at Stride. "Was it cold?"

"That night?"

"Yes."

"Bitter cold. You were freezing when I found you."

She nodded. "I remember being cold."

Cat climbed onto the porch. The loose wood sagged under her feet. Stride found himself overwhelmed by the vividness of his own memories. When he took hold of the railing, he recalled how it had felt under his hands ten years earlier when he'd stood there with Michaela. He remembered the steam making a cloud in front of her face with each breath. He felt the touch of her hand.

Serena watched him carefully, as if she knew what he was thinking.

"Do you remember how you got under the porch?" Serena asked Cat.

"Mother came to my room and woke me up. She opened the window on the back of the house and lowered me into the snow. She said to hide there and not to come out until she came and got me. She made me say it over and over, that I shouldn't come out, no matter what I heard. Over and over."

"Why did you have to hide?"

Cat stared at the driveway, where the truck was parked. "There were lights. A car. Someone was shouting."

"Who?"

The girl bit her fingernail. "My father."

"Are you sure it was him?"

"Yes. He'd been drinking. I wanted to go to him and tell him not to be mad, but I—I went under the porch, like my mother said."

"Was he alone?"

Cat's mouth opened and closed. Her eyes glazed over. "I—I don't know."

They let her stand in the cold. Cat put her face up against the frosty glass of the front window and peered inside. Stride stood next to her.

It was hard to see through the maze of ice crystals. Serena lingered behind them on the porch.

"Do you want to go inside?" he asked.

"Can I?"

"Sure."

He had a key from the bank, and he undid the lock. Inside, the house was a wreck, much worse than he expected. The furniture, except for a toppled three-legged chair, had been removed or stolen, and the carpet had been ripped out. Sometime over the winter, the furnace had failed, and pipes had frozen and burst, leaching over the floor and flooding the walls. Vandals had come inside. So had animals.

"Sorry, it's not safe to be here," Stride said. "I didn't realize it was so bad."

"Please, just a minute," Cat said.

She picked her way into the empty center of the floor. Stride saw ice, trash, and rat droppings. Water stains made ribbons on the ceiling.

"We should go," he said.

"Please."

He didn't want to be here. It was too painful. He could see where the Christmas tree had been, on that night when Michaela had tried clumsily to seduce him. He could smell sugar and hear music. It was all unreal; it was all long gone.

"Her window was open," Cat said.

"What?"

"In my mother's bedroom. She always left the window open, even when it was cold."

Stride remembered the crime scene and the open window. He recalled thinking that Michaela liked the night air, the way he did himself. "Yes, it was."

"The window is over the porch." Her lower lip quivered. "I heard them."

"I know."

"I heard everything, didn't I?"

"Yes, I think you did."

"I—I just don't remember."

"It's okay, Cat."

"You found me there? Under the porch?"

"Yes, I did."

"I wish I could remember that."

He said nothing, but he was thinking that it was better if she remembered nothing at all. He'd been frantic. Heartsick. Mute with rage. He'd searched the whole house, which took no time at all. His panic had grown when he couldn't find her. He'd gone outside and shone his flashlight under the porch, and at first he saw nothing, but when he shouldered his body all the way into the crawl space, he found her squeezed into a corner. Her knees were tucked under her chin, eyes shut, face soaked by tears; she was paralyzed with fear. He'd eased her out and kept her in his arms, and she hadn't said a word as he held her. She barely breathed.

Now here she was in front of him again. This teenager was the same little girl with whom he'd shared that awful moment. It felt like a lifetime ago.

"You saved my life," she said.

"I just found you."

"No, I think if you hadn't come when you did, I'd be dead."

"Why do you think that?"

She frowned. "I don't know, but I think it's true."

"We should go, Cat," he said softly.

"Another minute, okay? I need to see her room. I need to see where it happened."

"Maybe it would be better if you didn't."

"No, I need to do this. This place won't be here much longer. If I don't do it now, I never will."

"If that's what you want."

He moved to join her, but Cat held up her hand. "Could you let me do it by myself? Alone?"

"I don't like leaving you here."

"Please. Just for a minute."

Stride hesitated. "One minute."

He was about to leave, but she called after him. "Stride?"

"Yes?"

"Do you really think someone else was here that night? Is it even possible?"

He nodded. "Possible? Sure, it is."

"Wouldn't I remember?"

"Maybe you do. You say you dream about it. Is there someone in your dreams?"

Her face was confused. "In my dreams, I always think about you."

She turned toward the hallway that led to the bedrooms. The floorboards shifted, as if they would sink through to the cold ground beneath them. He thought about following her, but instead, he backed through the open door to the porch. Serena stood at the railing, dwarfed by the forest surrounding the large lot. He came up beside her. She was right where Michaela had been so many times. Just as close. Just as attractive.

They stood next to each other in silence. There was no more sun, just shadows. April felt like December.

"I was a little in love with Michaela," he admitted.

Serena gave him a sad smile. "Of course you were. It's who you are."

She slid her arms around his waist. They were face to face, an inch apart. Her eyes were two bright emeralds. She leaned into him, and he leaned into her, and they kissed, their cold lips turning soft and warm. His fingertips caressed the down on her neck. Her arms rose on his back, holding him tightly. It felt like months of ice melting. It felt like spring coming.

When their lips released each other, they stayed cheek to cheek. He felt her breath on his face and the caress of her hair. They didn't move or speak; they just held each other and remembered how it felt. It was like listening to the notes of a song you once knew by heart, letting it become familiar to you all over again.

They didn't even hear Cat.

She was there in the doorway when they finally broke apart. Her face was contorted in terror, her eyes wide and white. It was the face of a lost six-year-old child.

"Cat, what is it?" he called to her.

Her mouth dropped open. They could hear her panicked breathing. She shook her head over and over.

"Where's the girl?" she said.

He didn't understand. "What?"

Her jaw worked, but no words came out. Her lips formed an O of fear. Like a startled rabbit she bolted forward and threw her arms around Stride, nearly launching them both off the deck.

"That's what he said," she cried. "That's what the man said when he came inside to kill my father. *Where's the girl?*"

49

Maggie waited impatiently for the light to change at Hiawatha and Twenty-Sixth. She drummed her fingers on the Corvette wheel to the screaming thump of Def Leppard. Beside her, the light-rail train blocked traffic. The trolley clanged south toward the airport, its chimes as placid as church bells, and when the barriers lifted at the tracks, she turned right onto the side street. She drove half a block to the house where Vincent Roslak had been stabbed to death eight months earlier.

It was a two-story concrete house that had been subdivided into apartments. Five satellite antennas were mounted in a row on the flat roof, with wires draping down the front wall into windows. Hairline cracks ran through the concrete walls. The postage-stamp lot was fenced, and the unlocked gate hung askew. Maggie let herself in, and at the front door she pushed the buzzer for the manager's apartment.

"Mr. Walton?" she said, when the man answered the door. "I'm Sergeant Maggie Bei. I called you about the Roslak place."

"Yeah, yeah, come in."

Bennett Walton was in his late twenties, with thinning red hair and thick black glasses. He wore a long-sleeved jersey and athletic shorts. He was tall and had a basketball player's physique, with square shoulders and knobby knees. He wore Converse sneakers with no socks, and Maggie could see his big toe sticking out the front of one of his shoes.

Walton led her into a hallway painted in dingy white. There was a staircase at the back, and they climbed to the second story.

"So the place hasn't been rented yet?" she asked.

Walton shrugged. "Nah, nobody likes a murder scene, you know? People get creeped out."

"Do you own the building?"

"My mom does. I keep the tenants from calling her night and day."

He opened a door on his left, its loose knob rattling, and let her inside. Roslak's apartment was a narrow studio, running the length of the house. A kitchenette was immediately on her right. Through the bay windows facing the street she could see her rented Corvette parked at the curb. The apartment was unfurnished, and it had been repainted and recarpeted.

"You had to tear everything out?" she asked.

"Oh, yeah. Had to paint the ceiling downstairs, too. Blood soaked through. Pretty nasty."

Maggie wandered toward the front of the apartment. "Who found the body?"

"Me. People started complaining about the smell. It was July and really hot. When he didn't answer, I let myself in. I nearly crapped my shorts."

"How was the body situated when you found it?"

"He was on his back next to the sofa," Walton said, pointing at the floor. "Eyes open. Blood everywhere. Yuck."

"Did you see the knife that killed him?"

"Nope."

"Any idea what he was doing when he was killed?"

"Well, his pants were around his ankles, and his dick was hanging out. That give you any ideas?"

Maggie nodded. "I get it."

"What a way to go, huh?" Walton told her, wincing as if someone were holding a pair of scissors to his testicles. "You're getting busy, everything's hot, and then the chick goes all *Basic Instinct* on you. Ouch."

"How well did you know Roslak?" she asked.

"I barely knew him. He paid the rent on time, that's all I cared about."

"Did he have a lot of people coming and going from his place?"

"Oh, yeah. All the time. At first, I thought maybe he was a dealer, you know? Or a man whore. He was a sexy-looking guy, and it was mostly women coming to visit. Then somebody told me he was some kind of shrink."

"You see anyone regularly? Like a girlfriend?"

Walton shook his head. "Nope."

"How about a Hispanic teenager? Small, dark hair, very attractive."

"Like I said, I stopped paying attention. I'm a gamer. *Call of Duty.* If I'm home, I'm not looking out the windows."

"The police thought he'd been lying here for a couple days," she said. "You see anything or hear anything weird around that time? Shouting, arguments, screaming?"

"Arguments happen all the time in this place, but the walls are thicker than you think. We don't get a lot of noise between the apartments unless people have their windows open. It was so hot that most people had their window ACs running, and those things are really loud."

"I don't see a window unit here."

"People yank them during the winter," Walton told her, "but this place never had one. In the heat, his body pretty much fermented, you know?"

"Yeah." She dug in her pocket for a photograph of Margot Huizenfelt. "You ever see this woman around here?"

"Don't think so."

"Okay. Thanks for your help, Mr. Walton. Mind if I hang out here for a few minutes?"

"Knock yourself out."

Walton left her alone, but he left the apartment door open. She stood where the body would have been found. She smelled fresh paint, and the new carpet was springy under her heels. The apartment was sterile now, but she tried to imagine a sofa against the wall, with Roslak engaged in intercourse. Pants and underwear pooled at his ankles. The girl beneath him.

Somewhere in mid-fornication, she changes her mind. Or maybe she never consented. She attacks him, stabs him, drives him backward to the floor, and keeps stabbing. He's too surprised even to scream. His lungs fill with blood, and he can't talk. He just dies.

The cops never found the knife. She took it with her. Did Roslak have the knife when they started? Was he threatening her with it?

Or did she have the knife all along?

Maybe it was close by. In her boot. The way Cat always kept it.

Maggie decided that she had learned one thing by coming here. Roslak's death didn't smell like a murderer bent on keeping a decade-old secret from being exposed. He had been up close and personal with his killer. Very close, very personal. They knew each other; they were intimate. This was about sex gone bad, suddenly and violently. It didn't feel as if it had anything to do with a stolen ring hanging around Cat's neck.

She opened a window facing the street. Cold air blew inside, and bare branches knocked together from the tree in the yard next door. Distantly, with the wind, she heard the light-rail trolley on Hiawatha. Back then, on a blistering July day with no air conditioning, Roslak would have opened a window. If anyone were passing on the sidewalk outside, they would have heard the noises of sex rippling from the apartment. Or murder.

Maggie slid down to sit on the carpet with her hands wrapped around her knees. It was nearly dark. She sat in the deepening gloom without moving. She was convinced she'd overlooked something important. Even with no furniture, with nothing to remind her of the crime scene, the apartment spoke to her, but it was in a language she didn't understand.

What was she missing?

Outside the apartment, she heard heavy footsteps. She assumed it was Bennett Walton coming back, but then she saw the face and burly body of Ken McCarty grinning at her from the doorway. She found it hard to muster a smile in return.

"Hey, you," he said. "I got your text."

"Hey."

Ken strolled through the apartment and slid down next to her. He sensed her bleak mood. "You okay? Guppo told me you rolled the Av."

"I'm fine."

He nudged her in the ribs with an elbow, and her torso was tender. "You don't look fine."

"I'm fine," she repeated, with a hint of irritation.

"Okay. Just asking. Nice wheels outside."

"It's a rental."

"Yeah, when I rent, I don't get a 'Vette. Are you sticking around overnight? You want to come over to the love shack?"

"No, Stride wants me back up north."

"Too bad. Did you learn anything down here?"

"Nothing that ties Roslak's murder to Duluth. Nothing that ties Marty Gamble to Fong Dao. I talked to Fong's girlfriend, and she's convinced that Fong was set up. He wasn't involved in the Keck break-in at all."

Ken chuckled. "Sure. Him and all the other innocent men with multiple burglary convictions."

"I know, stupid, right? The crazy thing is, I think I believe her."

"Maggie Bei doubting herself? That's new."

She shrugged. "I was too sure of myself in those days. Too cocky. I should have asked more questions."

"Sounds like twenty-twenty hindsight to me. We got a tip, we got a warrant, we nailed him. They should all be so easy."

"Maybe it was too easy," Maggie said. "Djemilah says the people at St. Luke's knew about Fong's criminal record. Any one of them could have pointed us at him. Once we found the stash in his apartment, I was ready to close the book."

"Not just you. Stride was convinced, too. So was K-2."

"Yeah, but I sold it. I said we had our guy. I looked for an accomplice and didn't find one, so that was that. Except obviously, I screwed up the whole case. Think about it, how could I find an accomplice in Fong's life if Fong wasn't even involved in the crime?"

"Come on, don't dump on yourself because of what this girl told you. If we convicted men based on the stories they tell their girl-friends, the jails would be empty."

"You're right about that."

"Of course I am." He checked his phone and read an incoming message. "Anyway, duty calls, babe. I gotta run, but I'm glad you let me know you were in town. Shame you can't stay."

"Yeah." She leaned across and kissed him. Plenty of tongue. "You coming this weekend?"

"I'm practically coming now."

"Go," she said.

Ken pushed himself to his feet and left her alone in Roslak's apartment, which was now nearly pitch black. She lingered in the darkness, thinking about Fong Dao and his conviction for murder. She'd led the raid on his apartment herself. She'd been the one who found the box, opened it, found the jewels, found the cash, found the gun. It was all laid out for her. Open and shut.

Too easy.

No matter what Ken said, and no matter what she told herself, she couldn't shake a sick feeling in her gut. Something was wrong. Everything was wrong.

She was beginning to think she'd made a mistake ten years ago that had cost a man his life.

50

Stride checked his watch. "He's late."

They were miles from the heart of the city. The bone-white Catholic church building dated back to 1896, with a copper dome and cross atop its steeple. It was located on a lonely road in the township of Gnesen, in wooded land tucked among the northern lakes. A handful of graves rested in the quiet lawn surrounding the church, dwarfed by evergreens.

Serena cast her eyes around the deserted churchyard. "Why would he ask to meet us here?"

"He doesn't want anyone to see us together," Stride concluded.

It was dark, but there was a streetlight near the church, and the light cast shadows into the cemetery. They sat on a bench in front of a stone grotto. The rough stones were dusted with snow. Inside the cave created by the rocks, Christ clasped his hands in prayer. Behind the grotto, agitated crows hidden in the trees warned them away. Serena sat close to Stride, their bodies touching, his arm around her shoulder to keep her warm.

"Cindy came here with K-2 for services sometimes," Stride said.

"Did you?"

"Me? No. You know I'm not religious the way she was." He listened to the peaceful solitude. "I always thought, though, that if you had to spend eternity somewhere, this wouldn't be a bad place."

"It's just frozen ground, Jonny."

Stride said nothing. He knew that Serena, growing up the way she did, had no belief in God. There had been a time after Cindy died when he'd felt the same way, bitter and certain that he was alone in the world. Now, he was content not knowing whether there was any kind of guiding hand. There were moments when the universe felt random and cruel. There were other moments that felt predestined and made him feel arrogant not to believe.

Like finding Cat in his bedroom closet.

Like kissing Serena on Michaela's porch.

He stood up from the bench. "Come on, you're freezing. Let's wait inside."

She smiled. "Me in a church? God might smite me at the threshold."

"I'll go in first and take the hit."

Serena stood up and took his hand. Her long, slim fingers were cool. They walked through the graveyard to the double church doors, which led inside to the nave. Three modest stained-glass windows lent colored light to the floor from the streetlight outside. Rows of empty pews lined the space. The sconce lights on the walls glowed like candles.

Halfway to the altar, Stride slid into a pew and Serena sat beside him. She took a hymnal from the bench in front of her and turned the pages. The binding was broken and worn. She closed it carefully and put it back.

"Cat was really shaken," Serena said. "I'm sorry I did that to her. Bad idea."

"Maybe she needs to remember that night," he said. "That's part of the healing."

He thought about the drive back to his cottage. Cat had said little. There'd been no more memories or revelations. She'd stared out the window and resisted their efforts to draw her out. When they'd left her with a policewoman for the evening, she'd stretched out on her stomach in front of the fire. Her face had been far away.

"Is any of it real?" Serena asked. "Can we trust what she told us?"

"For now, let's assume we can. She thinks that someone else was there that night. If that's true, whoever it was probably shot Marty."

"And Michaela?"

"No, Marty definitely killed her," Stride said. "He was covered in her blood. It wouldn't have taken much to gin him up to butcher her. Someone simply pushed him over the edge."

"But why?"

"Because Michaela's death made the whole story work. If Marty got murdered, we'd start digging into his life to find the answers. But to snap and murder Michaela? And then shoot himself? That made perfect sense. We all saw it coming."

Stride shook his head. He'd been played. They'd all been played. They'd been given a scenario that fit their expectations, and they'd swallowed it whole. Marty was the perfect fall guy. So was Fong Dao. A home invasion and then a murder-suicide. Both crimes solved, with no one the wiser.

"Someone walked away from that heist free and clear," Serena said.

"Until that ring showed up," Stride said. "You think you're safe for ten years and then all of a sudden there's Margot Huizenfelt putting Marty in the middle of Rebekah Keck's murder. Whoever it is must have been desperate to keep the connection from being exposed."

"Once you've gone that far, there's no going back," Serena said. "Everyone involved in the home invasion was guilty of murder. Get caught, and your life is over. Kill, and stay free. The question is, who's still out there? Did Fong and Marty work with an accomplice? Is that who we're looking for?"

"That assumes Fong was involved in the burglary at all," Stride said. "Maggie says she's not so sure anymore. We *looked* for an accomplice in all of Fong's activities back then, and we didn't find one, so we assumed he pulled the job himself. One perp. End of story."

"Don't blame yourself, Jonny."

"I don't like being fooled," Stride said. "Whether Fong was guilty or not, Marty didn't do this alone. How did he get the alarm code? How did he know that Lenny and Rebekah were out of town? He needed a lot of information to pull this off. He needed someone close to Lenny to help him."

"Or Lenny," Serena said.

"Yeah. Or Lenny."

Serena said what he was thinking. "We have to face a nasty possibility here, Jonny. This might not be a burglary at all. The theft may simply have been a cover-up to draw the investigation away from what it really was."

"Murder," Stride said.

"That's right. Everybody assumed that Rebekah Keck stumbled into a home invasion and got killed, but maybe this was all about making her murder look like an accident. She comes home, Marty's waiting for her. He shoots her and ransacks the house. A few weeks later, everything's recovered at Fong Dao's place, and Fong goes away for life. Meanwhile, Marty winds up in the middle of a murder-suicide that looks completely unrelated. No loose ends."

"You think Lenny arranged for Rebekah's death," Stride said. "He got Marty to pull it off and then killed him."

"I think it's possible. Don't you?"

He didn't answer. Instead, they heard a loud voice at the front of the church.

"*You're both wrong.*"

Leonard Keck, in a royal-purple tracksuit, stood by the stained-glass windows with his hands on his hips. His gray hair was a mess, and his tanned, blotchy face was angry. Behind him, Police Chief Kyle Kinnick stood in the open doorway of the church. The cold air made a draft past the chief.

Lenny marched down the aisle in his tennis shoes.

"You are both wrong," he repeated. "I didn't know this man Marty Gamble. I didn't have anything to do with what happened to Rebekah. I loved her, and that's the truth. I don't care what the two of you think of me. I may be a son of a bitch, but I didn't do this. I didn't kill my wife."

PART FOUR

GRAFFITI GRAVEYARD

51

"So what are the ground rules, Chief?" Stride asked.

They stood at the back of the church. K-2 wore a black fedora and a heavy brown trench coat over his suit. His dress shoes were wet with snow. His ears jutted out from the side of his head, and the ends were pink from the cold. At the other end of the aisle, Leonard Keck sat in the front pew with a Styrofoam cup of coffee in his hand.

"I told him that we wouldn't use anything he says in a prosecution against him," K-2 said. "Hence the private meeting."

"That ties my hands."

"Just be glad he didn't bring along his lawyer, Jon."

Stride ran his hands back through his hair. "What if he confesses to murder?"

"He won't."

"If he stonewalls, the deal's off."

"He knows that. It cost me a hundred-dollar bottle of scotch to get him here, so you owe me big."

"I doubt it was that easy."

K-2 shrugged and scratched his ear. "Yeah, I had to threaten to call the city council, the US attorney, and the chair of the state Republican Party. He knows he may lose his council seat when this gets out, but there are always second acts in politics. Particularly in Duluth. Besides, he's rich. He can still buy all the influence he wants."

"You know what he's going to tell us?"

"Most of it."

"How bad is it?"

"Bad enough, but mostly stupid. Stupid screws up more investigations than anything else. You know that."

Stride nodded. People lied to the police the way that they lied to their doctors. They felt embarrassed. They felt guilty. They didn't want to admit doing something foolish. He'd wasted weeks of time and watched criminals go free because of lies that had nothing to do with the real crimes.

He gestured to Serena and the two of them joined Lenny at the front of the church. The car dealer sat with his legs apart and his knees bent. Steam rose from the white coffee cup. He stared up at the altar, a frown on his face.

"Feels odd, huh, being in a place like this," Lenny said. "Talking about sins."

"Do you want to go somewhere else?" Stride asked.

"Nah, get it over with. If the Catholics are right about purgatory, I'm screwed anyway."

He could hear the slur of the scotch in Lenny's voice.

"You said you didn't arrange for Rebekah's murder," Stride said. "Convince me."

Lenny's face twitched. He sipped his coffee. "What do you guys want? It's not like I can prove it. All I can tell you is, I didn't have a motive in the world to kill Rebekah. We were rich. We were happy. She was there with me when I didn't have money, and she was there with me when I did. It's not like I had some mistress waiting in the wings to take her place. I never got married again, because there was no one else in the world for me except her." He glanced between Stride and Serena. "You two, you're lucky. You found each other after Stride lost his wife. I never had the same experience, and believe me, it's not for lack of women trying to convince me otherwise."

"Tell us about the last trip you took," Serena said. "Who knew you were leaving town to go to the Keys?"

Lenny shrugged. "Who didn't? Everybody at the dealership knew. Most of the politicos. I'm sure Rebekah told dozens of people. We weren't trying to hide it. Hell, I told K-2, so he could arrange some extra drive-bys while we were gone. Would I do that if I was planning to stage some kind of phony robbery? Get serious."

"Exactly what happened on the trip?"

"Nothing happened," Lenny said. "It was the usual convention stuff. Boring speeches and a lot of parties, booze, and shrimp. We were having a ball until Rebekah started spewing out bad lobster from both ends. She decided to go home early. I offered to go with her, but she insisted I stay and finish out the convention. I got a limo to take her back to Miami, and she flew home. By the time she got to Minneapolis, she felt good enough to drive our car back to Duluth. She made it home around midnight. That's when she got shot."

"Who knew she was coming back early?"

"Nobody except me and a few people at the convention, unless she talked to some of her friends. You've got her phone records, you tell me. She called me while she was driving home to say she was okay. That was the last time I spoke to her."

"When did you get back?" Stride asked.

"A day later. I got a limo to drive me home from MSP."

"Weren't you concerned when you couldn't reach Rebekah?"

Lenny shrugged. "I was busy with the convention. I tried a couple times and got the machine. No big deal. I figured she was doing one of her social or charity things. Or she was shopping."

"Can you think of any reason why someone would have wanted her dead?" Serena asked.

"Rebekah? No way. Was she tough? Sure. Did she have a bitchy side if you crossed her? Absolutely. I mean, hell, she was a rich Jewish housewife, what do you expect? But nobody had any reason to kill her. I'm telling you, some bastards thought we were gone, they broke in to rob me blind, and Rebekah showed up at the wrong time. That's what happened. If I came home with her, I'd be dead, too."

"Okay," Stride said. "Let's talk about the ring."

Lenny glanced at the front of the church, where K-2 stood with his arms crossed across his scrawny chest. The car dealer tugged on the waistband of his tracksuit. "What about it?"

"You knew it was missing. Why didn't you tell us about it?"

"I told you, I thought I did."

"You're lying. You never filed an insurance claim."

"It must have slipped my mind. Hell, my wife was dead. You think I was worried about insurance money?"

Stride zipped up his leather jacket. "We're done, Lenny. My next stop is at the *News Tribune* to find a reporter to write the story."

"Lenny!" K-2 called from the front of the church. "I already told you how this has to go. If you've got something to say, you better say it."

Lenny squeezed his fists together. "All right! Yeah, all right, I didn't tell you about the ring. I just wanted the whole thing to go away."

"Were there other items of jewelry missing?" Stride asked.

"Yeah, some big earrings. A couple bracelets and necklaces. Expensive stuff, but it's not like I could describe it. I knew I'd given her things that weren't in the stash you recovered."

"What about cash?" Stride asked. "We found about five thousand dollars in cash at Fong's apartment. Back then, you said that was all of it. Was that a lie?"

"There was more," Lenny admitted. "A lot more."

"How much?"

"Upwards of fifty thousand dollars," he said.

Stride exhaled in disgust. "Unbelievable."

"Why did you have that kind of cash in your house?" Serena asked.

"Let's just say that in my business there are some transactions that are best handled in cash, okay?"

"Bribes," Serena said.

"Incentives. Bonuses. The fact is, if I told you people how much money was really taken back then, you'd have started asking questions that I didn't want to answer. My political career would have been over before it started, and the IRS would have started nosing around, too."

Stride shook his head. "So instead, you said nothing. You knew there had to be accomplices in your wife's murder, and you gave them a free pass."

"Rebekah was dead and nothing was going to bring her back!" Lenny retorted. "She would have told me to do exactly what I did. She would have said I was crazy to screw it up just to put a couple thugs behind bars."

K-2 strolled down the church aisle toward the three of them. "This is all under the cone of silence, Lenny, but don't think I'm going to forget it. If your act isn't clean right now, you better clean it up fast. Is that crystal clear, my friend?"

"I hear you," Lenny muttered. "Are we done? Can I go now?"

He started to get up, but Serena put a hand on his shoulder. "Not so fast, Mr. Keck."

"What? What else do you want? I've told you everything."

"We still have a problem."

Lenny looked plaintively at K-2. "This is nuts. Come on, Kyle, get me out of here."

The chief studied his friend's face. "Why don't you hear the lady out?"

Lenny scowled and laced his hands together in his lap. "Fine. What's the problem?"

"If Fong *was* involved in the burglary, then the split's wrong," Serena said.

"Huh?"

"We found five thousand dollars," Serena explained. "If they stole fifty, Fong should have had a lot more money in that box. Particularly if he had the gun and did the job himself. Where's the rest of it?"

"What are you asking me for? Maybe he stashed some of it somewhere else. He had a girlfriend, right? He probably gave it to her. Or maybe he was just a patsy and somebody framed him."

"If Fong was a patsy—if he was really innocent—then we have an even bigger problem," Stride told him.

Lenny squirmed in the pew. He looked at K-2 for rescue again, but the chief's face was stone. "What do you mean? I don't get it."

"Why frame someone if the police are going to keep looking for accomplices?" Stride asked.

"I don't know what you're talking about," Lenny said.

"If this was a setup, then someone *planted* five thousand dollars in Fong's house for us to find," Stride said, leaning in close to the car dealer's face. "Why bother? They had to know we'd keep looking for the rest of the money. And the jewelry, too. What could they gain by framing Fong if you were going to turn around and tell us that we'd only recovered a fraction of what was stolen?"

"Unless they *knew* you wouldn't say a word," Serena said.

Lenny chewed his lip. His tanned face turned red.

"What about it, Lenny?" K-2 asked. "Did you forget something during our little chat?"

"This is over," Lenny said. "I'm leaving."

"You leave and our deal's off," K-2 told him. "I start an investigation tomorrow into every business transaction you've conducted in the last ten years."

"Is that the problem?" Serena asked. "Was the heist masterminded by someone who knew all about your *incentives* program? Did they threaten to expose everything if you didn't keep your mouth shut?"

"It had nothing to do with money," Lenny snapped.

"Then what was it?"

Lenny put his hands on top of his head and yanked at his messy hair. "I can't believe this."

"You might as well tell us," K-2 said. "It's all coming out. You can't run from it."

"I was launching my first political campaign! My wife had just been murdered! You think I wanted shit like this in the papers? You think I wanted everyone to know? I would have been humiliated. Ruined."

They waited. The silence was excruciating. Lenny looked like a guilty little boy.

"Look, here's the thing. Rebekah wasn't exactly interested in sex the way I was. Understand? So when I got rich I figured I deserved to get some of what I was missing."

"Prostitutes," Stride said.

"They were more like escorts. High class, expensive. When Rebekah was away, sometimes I'd arrange to have some fun, okay? They were young, beautiful college girls, and they would do anything I wanted. What guy could say no to that?"

"Except somebody found out about it," Serena concluded.

"Yeah, somebody set me up. They had photos from a motel I'd visited. Very explicit, very embarrassing photos. Serious fetish stuff. The pictures were waiting for me when I got home from the Keys and found Rebekah. Bad enough to have my wife lying there dead, but then to know I'd be a fucking laughingstock, too? They said if I talked to you guys about what was taken, the pictures would go to the press. I didn't know why they cared until I heard about the search at Fong's place. Then I figured . . . I figured it was a cover-up."

"Lenny, you let an innocent man take the fall?" K-2 demanded. "You just sat on your hands while we put him in prison?"

"Innocent, hell. Come on, Kyle, he was an ex-con. A low-life crook. You found loot from other burglaries at his place, too, right?"

"He was convicted of murder, Mr. Keck," Serena said. "It was a murder he almost certainly didn't commit. Were you really okay with the idea that the people who killed your wife were still out there? That they never paid for what they did?"

"I didn't have a choice," Lenny said. "Don't you get it? I had my whole reputation to think about."

Stride shook his head. "Tell us about the girls," he said. "You said they were college girls."

"Yeah, very pretty, very smart. That was part of the attraction. They weren't low-life street girls."

"Did you ever take them to your house?"

Lenny nodded. "Sometimes."

"So they could have seen you enter your alarm code," he said.

"I—I suppose so."

"We need names," Stride told him.

"You think I had their real names? They didn't tell me, and I didn't ask."

"How did you find them?" Stride asked. "Who set it up?"

"There was—there was one girl. A business major. I spoke at her class, and she came up and talked to me afterwards. We went for coffee, and—I don't know, I made a pass at her. She said if that's what I wanted, fine, but it wasn't free. She gave me a price, and I said sure, why not. That's how it started. When I wanted more, she introduced me to other girls who were willing to do the same thing."

"Who was the girl?" Serena asked.

"She wouldn't have been part of a plot like this. Not her."

Stride squatted in front of him. "*Who?*"

52

Brooke Hahne stared at the knife on the passenger seat.

She'd taken the knife from the kitchen drawer in her apartment. It was stainless. Sharp. She picked it up and clutched it in her hand and studied the blade, which glinted under the dome light of the Kia. The handle felt cold. When she tensed her wrist, she saw the radial artery bulge from her skin. She touched the flat edge of the blade to the swollen artery. With a vertical flick, she could open it up. Blood would spurt, warm and bright red, like a poinsettia.

It wouldn't take long for her to die. Not long at all. It would be swift and painless.

She'd driven aimlessly in the darkness for two hours, and now she'd finally parked. She sat in the chill of her car and wondered how everything had gone this far. How the past had spiraled out of control. She should have put an end to it ten years ago, but she'd fooled herself into thinking she could do penance and make it right. Every day at the shelter, saving lost lives, was atonement for her sins.

Except that was a lie.

In reality, she was a coward, afraid of spending her life in prison. She'd been scared and selfish, unwilling to face what she'd done. Now more people had died because of her, one after another, like a bad dream that wouldn't stop.

People she'd never met. And people she'd loved.

"Oh, Dory," she murmured. "What did I do?"

A photograph of the two of them dangled from her rearview mirror, where she'd taped it. They sat on top of the stone runs known as the Cribs just off the boardwalk, in their bikinis, cheek to cheek, arms around each other's waists, silly grins on their faces. A few seconds later, she remembered, they'd dove into the cold lake water hand in hand. They were roommates and college freshmen then, giddy about everything that was ahead of them. If only they'd known.

For Dory, drugs were ahead of her. Misery, addiction, shame.

For Brooke, it was Leonard Keck. That was how it all started.

Back then, it hadn't seemed like a big deal. She needed money, and he had money, and all she had to do was disconnect her body from her mind. She wasn't the only one doing it. Some of the other girls talked about it in hushed tones, behind closed doors. A party. A nice dress. It was like a date, but the happy ending came with cash. Two hundred, three hundred, sometimes five hundred dollars. A fortune.

Lenny had hit on her after class like a rich old fool, and she'd thought, *This is my chance.* Why not? You can fuck me, but it'll cost you. It was business, like selling a car. They both got what they wanted out of the deal. She could smile and fake it as he did whatever he wanted to her, and the end justified the means. No student loans. No mountain of debt.

It was her body. Her choice. Everybody said it was a victimless crime.

No one was supposed to get hurt.

No one was supposed to get killed.

He pawed her everywhere with his old, clumsy hands. His fingers fumbled with her silk blouse, and he popped the buttons, ripping the flaps apart and yanking the cups of her lace bra down to expose her breasts. He covered them with his mouth, sucked on her pale pink nipples, and squeezed her small mounds until he left fingerprints.

"Shit, look at you," he panted, his eyes wide, feasting on her nude flesh.

It was the same every time they were together. Like she was a museum piece. Like he couldn't believe she belonged to him.

Lenny still wore his tux from the university fundraiser. The studs on his white shirt rubbed her bare skin as his body crushed her. She could feel his hardness through his trousers, aching to be released. He already had her skirt bunched above her hips, her panties around her ankles, and her knees spread like butterfly wings. She watched his back arch as he sank down her body. He buried his face and tongue between her legs, lapping at her slit like a dog at a water bowl.

She squirmed away and grabbed his face and kissed him. Her fingers ran through his hair, and she took one hand and rhythmically squeezed the pole under his zipper. "Let's go inside. I want to be naked in your bed tonight."

"Oh, yeah."

Lenny half-pushed, half-kicked open the rear door of the car. He staggered into the cold December night. Brooke slid her panties from her ankles and stuffed them in her purse. She disentangled herself from her bra and let her blouse hang open in an expanse of smooth skin. She followed him out of the car. He was so drunk he could barely stand. He dropped his keys on the driveway and got down on all fours in the snow and snatched them into his fist. Breathing hard, he rocked back on his heels and stared up at her.

"You are gorgeous," he said. "Shit, I want to be inside you."

"Yeah? Well, come on, lover."

She helped him to his feet. The knees of his trousers were wet and dirty. He steadied himself with an arm around her waist as they staggered up the walkway to his front door. She kept her eyes open for traffic and neighbors, but no one was around to recognize her. There was no streetlight. They were invisible.

She'd been here many times in the past year, but this time was different. This time she was scared.

He jabbed the key at the lock but couldn't get it in. She peeled the keys from his hands.

"Let me do it."

"Hurry up. I want you so bad. No condoms tonight, huh? I hate condoms."

"Bareback, sure, if that's what you want."

"You still on the pill?"

"Duh," she grinned.

He pushed the silk sleeve off her shoulder. "I'm not going to have to worry about STDs, huh? I can't afford to get fucking herpes or something."

"Don't worry, I'm clean, baby."

"You sure? You seen a doctor lately?"

"Oh, yeah. I've got a doctor. Don't worry about that."

She twisted the key in the lock and Lenny spilled inside as she opened the door. The house smelled musty and rich. The lights were off. On the wall, a white alarm panel flashed, and she saw the countdown on the screen. They had twenty-five seconds to deactivate the security system before the alarm sounded. He was too drunk to do it himself.

"What's the code, Lenny?"

"Huh?"

"The alarm code, baby."

"Oh, shit. It's. . . what the hell is it? One. . . one seven. . . one. . . "

Brooke tapped buttons with the pads of her fingers. Her red fingernails glowed under the LED light. The alarm flashed an error. "That's not right, baby. Try again. You don't want the police coming, do you?"

"One. . . seven. . . it's one seven eight nine. Yeah, that's it."

She tried again, and the panel flashed a message: Code Accepted.

Brooke smiled in triumph and relief. "Are you ready, lover? Let's go upstairs."

She took Lenny by the hand and led him into the shadows of the hallway. He groped her body in unpleasant ways as they climbed the stairs, but she didn't care. She wasn't thinking about what he was going to do to her. Not tonight.

She was thinking: This is the last time.

She was thinking: 1789.

Brooke wondered if Lenny knew. Somewhere in his head, he had to know that she'd been the one to set him up. Thanks to her, his wife was dead, but oh God, oh God, *it was an accident.* No one was supposed to be home.

If Lenny suspected, he'd never said a word.

Whenever they met now, they pretended to be nothing but business acquaintances. On most days, she could forget what she'd done, but not when she saw his face at the city council meetings. Those were the unbearable moments. She'd sit in the front row before she had to speak, and he would be there on the elevated platform, behind the microphone. She would swear each time that she wouldn't look at him. She'd repeat it to herself: *Don't look, don't look, don't look.*

Even so, sooner or later, she always did. He would be staring at her; their eyes would meet. She'd suffer that little smirk on his face and know exactly what he was thinking. He was undressing her. Remembering all the times he'd been inside her. Getting hard behind the council table as he thought about her mouth swallowing him.

He had to know the truth, but if he did, he'd pushed it out of his mind. He'd never made any attempt to get revenge or to punish her. Even now, if she'd let him fuck her again, he would have done it. If she'd whispered a price, he would have paid it. That was what made her sick. To him, she was still nothing but a whore.

The knife.

Brooke pressed the point of the blade into her wrist, deep enough that she winced in pain. She didn't imagine the pain would last long. Just a sting, like a needle prick, if she did it fast enough. Once the blood began to flow, she would grow light-headed. Eventually, she would pass out before her breath grew ragged and her heart stopped beating.

She stared at herself and Dory in the photograph. Sweet, naive kids.

"I'm so sorry," she said. "I never meant for any of this to happen."

The knife slipped in the sweat of her hand. She was scared. None of this was going the way she had planned. Her mind fought with itself and refused to let go. She was still a coward, unable to end it. When she tried again, the knife dropped from her fingers to the floor of the car. She left it there.

Beside her, on the passenger seat, her cell phone buzzed with a text message. She knew it was him. She thought about ignoring it, but he'd always controlled her. She couldn't resist.

Where are you? I need to see you.

It was never over. She was right where she was ten years ago. Under his thumb. Nothing had changed. She texted back: *No.* And then before he could reply, she added: *I'm done. I can't do this anymore.*

Her phone buzzed again. *WHERE ARE YOU?*

She felt his rage, and even now it terrified her. She barely knew where she was. The car had seemingly driven itself. When she looked at the land around her, she realized she was in a deserted park by the harbor waters. Her windows were clouded with steam and frost. The car rocked with the lake wind. *I'm on the Point.*

He texted again. *Stay there.*

Stay there. Don't move. He was coming to get her. She wrote back what she was thinking: *It's too late for that.*

Brooke turned off her phone before he could reply. She didn't want to hear from him again. This was the end. If she stayed, if she did what she'd planned to do, then he would be the one to find her. He would make her disappear and no one would ever know what had happened. The thought was appalling.

If he found her here alive, he would kill her. That was why he was coming to find her. She was the only link now between him and the truth. She was the last witness.

She couldn't bear to let him win again. Not after all these years, not after the way he'd haunted her. She couldn't let him escape. She had to do what she should have done ten years ago. The only way to make peace with her past, the only way to make him pay, was to confess everything.

53

"I can't find Brooke," Maggie told Stride. "She's not at her apartment. She's not at the shelter."

"Keep looking."

"Are you sure about this, boss?" she asked. "Brooke?"

"I'm sure. Lenny gave her up."

"But Brooke and Marty? I can't picture her mixed up with a thug like that."

"We don't know where she fits in the chain, Mags. The link to Marty may be one of the other girls who was involved with Lenny back then. Let's just find Brooke and see what she says."

He heard the awkward silence on the phone.

"I've got her cell number. I'll see if we can ping it."

"Fine, do that."

He hung up the phone. Serena looked at him. "One of the other girls?" she asked. "Do you really think so?"

"No," Stride said grimly. "Brooke was involved, and she's still involved. Margot must have talked to Brooke when she was trying to find Cat on that Saturday, and she said something that panicked her. That's what got Margot killed."

"I don't see Brooke as a cold-blooded killer," Serena said. "She can't be doing this alone. Someone else was working with her back then. And with Marty. He's trying to cover their tracks."

Stride pointed at the house across the street from where they were parked. The garage door was open and the overhead light was on. They saw the ample backside of a man bent over the propped hood of a Coupe de Ville. "If anyone can tell us who was tight with Marty, it's Bill Green."

They got out of the Expedition. It was late evening, and the temperature had plummeted below freezing. A violent wind, as cold as a sharp slap, kicked litter and dead leaves down the street. Its roar sounded like the thunder of rushing water, and the dormant trees yawed with the gusts. He shuddered involuntarily as the wind hit his face. Serena's hair swirled.

The two of them marched across the empty street toward the open garage. Inside, the wind whistled, and a space heater with a noisy fan blew warm air across the cement floor. A halogen flashlight was clipped to the hood of the Cadillac, casting a hot bright glow. Bill Green had his boom box playing the same radio station as the last time Stride had confronted him here. The song was "Wanted Dead or Alive" by Bon Jovi.

"Hey," Stride called over the noise of the music.

Green reared back from the car. He wore overalls and a flannel shirt and unlaced work boots. His face and hands were smudged in black and he held a wrench between his fingers. His long hair was untied and hung loose at his shoulders. The man eyed them and switched off the radio, leaving no sound but the wind.

"You guys again?" Green asked. "What the hell do you want now? Leave me alone!"

Stride slid a photograph of Rebekah Keck's ring from the pocket of his coat. He held it in front of the man's face. "Do you recognize this ring?"

Green squinted at the picture. "Yeah, sure, looks like Sophie's engagement ring. I gave her the tiara and the crown jewels for our anniversary."

"I'm not in the mood for jokes," Stride said.

"Okay, fine. It looks like the fake ring that Cat wears around her neck."

"You've seen her wearing it?"

"The girl lived in my house for ten years," Green retorted. "Of course I've seen it. So what? Marty gave it to her. What's it worth, fifty bucks?"

"More like seventy-five thousand bucks," Serena said.

Green couldn't fake his reaction. His face screwed up and he threw the wrench to the ground with a sharp clang. "Bullshit!"

"It's real," Stride said.

"You are fucking kidding me. That girl's been walking around all this time with stones worth that kind of money? Where the hell would Marty get something like that?"

"He stole it," Serena said.

Green shrugged. "Well, yeah, I didn't think he won the lottery or something. Who'd he rob, Donald Trump?"

"You tell us."

"I don't have a clue."

"I can't believe Marty would set up a big, high-risk burglary and not say a word to you about it," Stride said. "Frankly, it seems like something you guys would plan together."

"Me?" Green shook his head. "Forget it. Wherever Marty got this ring, I had nothing to do with it."

"A lot of money from the theft was never recovered," Stride said. "Marty's apartment was clean when we searched it. He had a partner."

"Yeah, well, if there was something to find, somebody else found it. Hell, if I was part of a job like that, do you think I'd still be busting my ass on highway repairs every day? You think I'd let some little girl walk around with jewels like that around her neck? Get real."

"Marty never bragged about the job to you?" Stride asked.

"No, he didn't. It doesn't smell right anyway. Marty was muscle, not brain. He liked to get drunk and beat people up, not do break-ins. Hard to believe he could have pulled this off."

"We think he had help," Serena said.

"Not from me."

"Then who?" Stride asked.

"Hell if I know."

"You probably knew him better than anyone else."

"That ain't saying much," Green told them. "Being close to Marty usually meant getting your jaw busted."

"What about friends?" Serena asked. "Or girls?"

"Marty didn't have many friends, and there was only one girl. You know that. Marty was fucking obsessed with Michaela."

"What about after the divorce?"

"Oh hell, then it was even worse. No way he was going to let Michaela throw him out with the trash. It was going to go one of two ways. Either he'd beat the shit out of her until she took him back, or he'd kill her if she started fucking somebody else. Which is exactly what he did."

"What did he do for sex?" Stride asked. "Did Marty use hookers to let off steam?"

"Who knows? Probably. So some guy gets a little action in a doorway. The only people who get bent out of shape about it are the cops and the politicians, and most of them are doing it, too."

"Did Marty know any college girls?"

Green rolled his eyes. "Come on, that's not the kind of action you find down at Curly's. A girl like that's not looking for a fifty-dollar blow job, you know?"

Stride frowned. "Do you know Brooke Hahne?"

"The gal who runs the shelter downtown? Yeah, sure. Sophie talked to her about Cat."

"Did you know her ten years ago?"

"Ten years? She must have been a kid then." Green's eyes widened. "Holy shit, are you saying that Brooke—?"

"Just answer the question. Did you know Brooke Hahne ten years ago?"

"No."

"Did Marty ever mention her to you? Or did you ever see him with a girl who looked like her?"

"Hell, no. A classy girl like Brooke wouldn't be hanging out with a guy like Marty. She'd be with some rich guy, hoping his heart explodes."

Stride thought: *She was*. She was in bed with Lowball Lenny, but that didn't explain how Marty Gamble wound up with Rebekah Keck's ring. Somewhere, they were still missing a connection.

"Do you remember a home invasion right around Christmas ten years ago?" he asked Green. "The victim was Leonard Keck. His wife was killed."

"The car guy? Yeah, I remember something about that. It was big news." Green whistled. "Are you saying that Marty did the job? No way. I don't buy it. It's out of his league."

"Did he have a gun?" Serena asked.

"Sure he did. More than one."

"Did he say anything that would connect him to the burglary? Did he say anything about Lowball Lenny or the murder?"

"I don't remember him saying a word, but that doesn't mean anything. Marty and I weren't exactly talking to each other back then. I didn't want to have anything to do with the son of a bitch."

"Why not?" Serena asked.

Green pointed at the two-inch scar on his forehead. "Because he nearly killed me, the asshole! We got pissing drunk and got into a big fight behind Curly's. It was a couple weeks before Christmas. Late, like one in the morning. He was on and on about Michaela, and I said he should just forget her and leave her alone, you know? Well, he lost it and started whaling on me. Fucking scary. He shoved a gun in my face and whacked me across the head with it. I was bleeding like a pig! You bastards sent me to a clinic and let him walk, like usual. Me? The doc gave me twenty stitches. After that, I didn't have two words to say to Marty. We were still on the outs when he blew his head off."

Stride nodded. They were at a dead end with Bill Green. He had nothing more to tell them. The only lead they had left was to find Brooke Hahne and get the truth out of her. She had all the answers, if she hadn't already skipped town. If she was still alive.

The two of them stalked out of the garage into the darkness. The wind found them immediately, howling down from the skyline. It nearly drove them off their feet with its ferocious blows. The Duluth wind knew how to fight; it was a mean drunk, like Marty.

Stride stopped in the driveway. He heard a roaring in his head, but it wasn't the wind. He felt cold, but the cold was deep inside his chest and empty, like a midnight cemetery.

A mean drunk.

He turned back to the garage and walked all the way up into Bill Green's face.

"What did you say?"

54

Brooke pounded on Stride's door.

She wasn't dressed for the cold, and the Point was alive with winter wind. She wrapped her thin arms around her chest and backed up to the porch steps and stared down the length of Minnesota Avenue. Down the long road leading toward the city, she saw no headlights.

Where was he?

She'd parked her Kia on one of the stubby lakeside streets, hoping he would miss it. Her face and clothes were dusted with beach sand blown down from the dunes. On the other side of the house, she heard the windblown lake roaring like a tiger.

The door to Stride's cottage opened slowly, and she saw a police-woman in uniform, her hand close to her sidearm. She was shorter than Brooke and just as thin. The young cop's eyes were suspicious. Brooke ran to the door, trying to untangle her blonde hair from her face.

"Is Lieutenant Stride here? I need to talk to him right away."

"Who are you?"

"I'm Brooke Hahne. I run the downtown shelter. Can I come inside?"

"No one comes in."

"Please, just call him. Can you do that? Or call Maggie—Sergeant Bei. She's a friend. This is urgent."

"What is this about?"

Brooke hesitated. "I just need to talk to one of them."

Over the policewoman's shoulder she saw Cat stroll into the living room from one of the interior bedrooms. The girl noticed her and ran to the door. "Brooke! What are you doing here?"

"Hello, Cat."

"What's going on?"

"I need to see Stride." She swallowed hard and added, "I—I know who's doing this to you."

"You do?" Cat tugged on the policewoman's sleeve. "Let her in, please."

"Stride said nobody comes in," the cop protested.

"I know Brooke. You can't leave her out in the cold."

The policewoman's eyes traveled over Brooke's body. It was obvious, in her blouse and skirt, that Brooke had no weapon. She'd left the knife and phone in her car. She shivered with a new gust of wind, and the cop reluctantly moved aside and let her inside the house.

"Thank you," Brooke said.

"I'm calling Sergeant Bei," the cop told her.

"Yes, do that, please."

"Stay where I can see you, and don't use the phone."

"Of course."

Cat's brown eyes were serious and concerned. She was as pretty as ever, with her golden face and flowing hair, but she didn't look like a child now. She'd grown up. That was what death did to you. Cat instinctively threw her arms around Brooke in a tight hug, and Brooke felt guilty. She didn't know if she could say what she needed to say to Cat.

It was me.

I'm the reason someone has been trying to kill you.

I'm the one who told him Margot was looking for you.

I'm the one who told him how to find you.

She couldn't believe what she had done to protect herself. It was as if she were another person, someone from ten years ago, young and stupid. Since then, she'd tried to make her life about protecting girls like Cat, but instead her past had roared back to life, like the wind on the lake.

"I'm so sorry," she whispered in Cat's ear.

Brooke studied Cat's face. The girl could see her guilt. The truth couldn't hide anymore, and Brooke was tired of keeping it concealed. Cat knew that Brooke had done this to her, but there was no blame in her eyes. Just a deep, beautiful sadness.

"Sit with me," Cat said.

Brooke heard the policewoman calling Maggie. She heard Maggie's voice in reply. Fifteen minutes. Maggie would be there in fifteen minutes. She felt equal parts fear and relief, because this was the beginning of the end. Soon enough, it would all be done. She'd be arrested; her life would be over. It didn't matter. She felt liberated.

Cat took her hand. It was odd, the girl leading the woman. Cat wore a bulky wool sweater, jeans, and cowboy boots. She pulled Brooke into the dining room and they sat down at two of the chairs pulled out from the table. They were inches apart. Cat leaned forward and put her hands on Brooke's knees. "Tell me what's going on."

Brooke felt tears slipping from her eyes. "I don't know where to begin."

"Just talk."

Just talk. If only it were that simple. She thought about her parents. At least they were both gone; they wouldn't suffer the shame of learning the truth. She wondered what would have been worse for them, to know that their daughter had been involved in crimes that led to murder, or to know that it had all started when she'd begun sleeping with rich men for money. Lenny had been the first, but not the only one. For a girl growing up with religious parents, she'd found it strange that she felt no qualms about selling her body. It wasn't anyone else's business. No one knew.

Until him.

Until he found out what she was doing.

"I didn't have a choice," Brooke murmured.

"About what?" Cat said.

"He would have exposed me. I would have been kicked out of school. My parents—my parents would have known what I was doing. It sounds like nothing now, but back then it felt like the end of the world. All I had to do was get the code. The alarm code. That was it. He swore no one would get hurt. I figured, who cares if a rich bastard had some things stolen?"

"Lenny?"

"Yes. It was supposed to be easy and safe, but everything went wrong. I couldn't believe it when I saw the news that night. His wife was dead. Shot. Murdered. *Because of me.* All it was supposed to be was a stupid robbery, a few thousand dollars, and instead, I was a murderer. That was it, the rest of my life ruined. It didn't matter whether I was there. I knew they'd convict me, too."

Brooke heard the door of the house open and the angry whistle of the wind. Maggie was here for her. She hated to face her friend, but now that she'd begun to talk, it was amazing how easily the words flowed. She'd waited a long time to unburden her soul. She remembered two years earlier when she'd spoken to inmates at the women's correctional facility in Shakopee. It had occurred to her then that it was only a matter of time before she found herself behind those walls. She'd always known that she couldn't hide forever.

"I was panicked," she went on, "but he told me it was under control. He knew someone he could set up to take the fall. I was sure that Lenny would tell the police about me, but he said he had it covered. He had some ugly pictures of Lenny with one of the other UMD girls. Sure enough, Lenny never opened his mouth. Then a few weeks later, they arrested some poor Asian boy. They found things from the burglary in his apartment. It seemed like it was all going away. I began to think no one would ever know."

Cat bowed her head. "That wasn't the end, though, was it?"

Brooke took Cat's hands, but let them go when the girl flinched. "No. I'm so sorry."

"Why my parents?"

"You have to believe me, Cat, I didn't know what he planned to do. He said he couldn't do the job himself. He needed an alibi. So he got your father to do the break-in. He never said he planned to kill him, but with Marty gone there wasn't any way to tie it back to us. I just never, ever thought that anything would happen to your mother."

"She didn't know?" Cat asked quietly.

"She knew nothing. She was just a victim. Like you."

Cat got up. Her chair made a scraping noise on the floor. Brooke reached out for her, but Cat turned away. The girl stood at the dining room windows, looking through the slats of the blinds. This was the way it had to be. Cat couldn't forgive her. No one could.

Brooke opened her mouth to explain, but the hiss of the wind in the living room was so loud that she thought it would drown out her voice. Cold air bled through the house, raising goose bumps on her skin. The uneven floor beneath her feet groaned. The entire cottage shook under the assault, as if they were swirling inside the cone of a tornado.

Something was wrong.

Brooke rushed into the living room, but the policewoman had vanished. The room was empty. The door to the porch was open, letting in the elements. The open door banged like a hammer on the wood of the window frame. *Bang bang bang.*

Brooke stared at the doorway. The darkness beyond froze her with fear. Her face swung to Cat. "We have to get out of here right now."

She hunted for something she could use as a weapon, but it was already too late. When she looked back at the door, there he was, standing on the porch, blocking their escape. His easy smile was gone, and in its place was cold death. He had a gun in his hand as he walked into the house.

"Where's the girl?" he said.

55

Stride slapped his palm against the computer monitor mounted to his dashboard. "Did I mention how much I hate technology?"

Serena rotated the keyboard and monitor toward herself. "Let me do it before you put a fist through the screen. What are you looking for?"

Stride ran his hands back through his hair. He didn't want to believe what he suspected. "Bill Green says Marty beat him up in an alley near Curly's," Stride said. "It was a couple weeks before Christmas ten years ago. I want to see if there was an incident report."

"Near Curly's? That doesn't narrow it down."

"Limit it to assault and gun reports," Stride said. "And check victim names against Green."

"What about Marty?" Serena asked.

"No, you won't find him in there."

Serena was puzzled. "Why not? Are you sure?"

"I'm very sure."

She didn't argue, but she ran a search for both men and said, "There's nothing in the system on either name in that time frame. Maybe there was no ICR."

"Green said the police responded. It has to be there."

Serena took her fingers off the keyboard. "You want to tell me what I'm really looking for, Jonny?"

Stride felt the Expedition shudder. The wind was wild. Debris cascaded across the windshield. "Green said we let Marty walk," he said.

"So? It sounded like a bar fight. That's going to be a judgment call on whether the cop takes them in."

"Not if a gun was involved. No way we let that slide. Besides, it doesn't matter. It was *Marty Gamble*."

"Meaning what?" she asked.

"Marty was on probation. He'd finally done time after he nearly killed Michaela, but he was back on the street. I was sure he was going to come after her again as soon as he had the chance. I wanted him. He was my top priority, and every one of my cops knew it. They knew his name. They knew his face. If he so much as took a leak against the side of a building I wanted him hauled in so we could get him revoked. If we could have nailed him for assault—*with a handgun!*—he would have been busted back for the rest of his time and probably another couple of years. The cop who brought him to me would have been a hero. I would have pinned a medal on his chest."

"No one did," Serena said.

"No one did. Marty never hit the system."

"So Green's lying. Or he never admitted that Marty was the one who beat him up."

Stride said nothing.

Serena looked at him and her face darkened as she realized where his mind was taking him. "Or you had a bad cop," she said.

He pointed at the screen. She scrolled through the ten-year-old incident reports in silence, and he waited. It was still possible that Green had made up the story. It was still possible he'd kept quiet about Marty out of fear of his cousin's retribution. But Stride didn't think so. This was worse. This was one of his own. Someone inside would have known that Marty could be leveraged to do just about anything to stay out of jail. Someone inside would have known about Fong Dao's burglary record. Someone inside would have known how to stage a murder-suicide without raising any questions.

"December sixteen," Serena said. "There was a 911 call about an assault in progress. The time and location fit."

"How was it resolved?" he asked.

"That's what's odd. It came in as assault but the report was converted to drunk and disorderly, accidental injuries. No info on an assailant, no ID on the vic, definitely no gun. According to the follow-up, the vic declined medical treatment and disappeared. That's it. Incident closed." She added, "This might not be the right report."

"Who responded?" Stride asked. He thought: *This was the call. Marty assaulted Bill Green. Someone buried it.*

"Do you remember your officer codes from ten years ago?"

"No, but the table should be in the system."

Serena clicked on the code. He watched her close her eyes. Her breath left her chest.

"Who?" he said softly.

"It was Ken McCarty," she told him.

"I'm nearly at your place," Maggie told Stride as she sped down the Point in the Corvette. "Brooke's waiting there."

"Mags," he said.

She knew in the tone of his voice that something was very wrong.

She listened to him talk.

She listened to what he said.

She didn't react. When he was done, she simply said, "Understood," and hung up the phone, cutting him off in mid-sentence.

Ken McCarty.

Her lover. Her friend. The baby cop she'd hired. Ken was dirty. Worse than dirty.

It was odd, how calm she felt at the news. How none of her emotions churned. She saw it for what it was; she'd been seduced and conned. There was no coincidence in Ken showing up in her office, no accident in his inviting her to dinner and charming his way into her bed. She was his pipeline. He was in town hunting for Cat, and he was using his old boss to keep tabs on what the police knew.

She'd let a bad cop, a thief and a murderer, fool her with his lies. She'd had wild sex with the very man she was hunting.

Still she felt nothing. Not anger. Not shame. She was dead inside. There was only one thing to do.

Find him.

Maggie dialed his cell phone, but the call went to voice mail. He'd turned it off to avoid the footprints of cell towers tracking him through the state. She knew what that meant. He wasn't in Minneapolis anymore; he'd followed her north. He'd been going back and forth between the two cities for days, hiding out in a cold garage and driving a stolen black Charger.

Hunting. Killing.

He was here.

She parked south of Stride's cottage on the bayside. When she got out, the wind cut through her burgundy jacket, but she didn't feel the cold. She was almost in a trance. Across the street, in one of the cross-alleys that ended at the lakeside dunes, she spotted a white Kia Rio. Brooke's car. She jogged across the street and checked it out, but the car was empty.

She spotted a picture of Brooke and Dory hanging from the mirror. A kitchen knife sat on the floor of the car.

"Goddamn it, Brooke," she murmured.

It wasn't hard to figure out how it started. Before Ken joined the Duluth police, he'd been a campus cop at UMD. He knew the students and administrators; he knew the lay of the land. If someone had wanted the police to talk to one of the girls about escort trafficking on campus, Ken would have gotten the call. Keep it discreet. Keep it out of the headlines and the police logs. Just make it go away.

She wondered whether Ken simply blackmailed Brooke. Or whether he slept with her. Or both. Ken had a gift for manipulation. A girl like Brooke would have been scared to death to have a cop confronting her about turning tricks for tuition money. She would have done whatever he said. The perfect pawn.

It wasn't even hard to figure out why Ken had risked everything for a big score. Maggie knew Ken back then. He was in love with money, but he didn't have much. There had been rumors about his spending habits getting out of control, about debts, even about loan sharks, but when she grilled him about it, he'd promised that he had it covered. As far as she knew, he'd dug himself out, because the rumors stopped. She just never realized that his golden parachute involved Brooke, Lowball Lenny, and an ex-con named Marty Gamble.

He must have thought it was the perfect plan. It all would have worked if Rebekah Keck hadn't come home early. If Marty hadn't panicked and shot her. She told herself that Ken wasn't violent, that he wouldn't have harmed anyone if the burglary at Lenny's hadn't gone south in a bad way.

The trouble was, she didn't believe it. Ken chose Marty for a reason. He could eliminate him, and no one would ever ask questions. Right from the beginning, Marty and Michaela were going to die.

Maggie stayed on the lake side of the street, hugging the trees, which swirled around her as she closed in on Stride's house. Snow clung to the lawns and sidewalk and blew up in silver sprays under the streetlights. She looked for Ken's car but didn't see it, but she slid her gun into her hand anyway.

As she ducked between the trees, she saw a body near the corner of the house. Heel marks in the snow showed where the body had been dragged out of view of the street. She ran closer and realized it was the policewoman she'd assigned to protect Cat. The young woman lay sprawled in the snow. Her brown hair was matted in blood where someone had struck her. She was unconscious, but Maggie checked her pulse and was relieved to find that she was still breathing.

She grabbed her phone and called for an ambulance. As she did, the woman began to revive on the wet ground. Her eyes fluttered. She groaned in pain and tried to get up. Seeing someone above her, she instinctively tried to fight, but Maggie grabbed her wrists.

"Don't move," Maggie told her. "It's me. Help's on the way."

The policewoman settled back into the snow. Her eyes stayed open and began to focus.

"Someone hit me from behind," she murmured.

"I know. I have to check inside. I'll be back."

Maggie saw that Stride's door was closed. She crouched low and led the way up the porch steps with her gun. At the door, she twisted the handle; it was unlocked. She pushed it open and slipped inside. The living room was empty. A lamp was knocked over; there had been a struggle. She eased around the doorway and cleared the first bedroom on her left, where Cat had been sleeping. From there, she quickly moved to each of the other rooms.

The house was cold and deserted. There were no more bodies, but there was no one here.

Distantly, above the howl of the wind and the roar of the lake, she heard a siren wailing down the Point as the ambulance raced closer. She dialed Stride as she ran back to the front of the house.

"It's me," she said.

"We're on our way downtown. Do you have her?"

"No, they're both gone. He's got Brooke. And Cat, too."

56

Ken McCarty waited with the headlights off. Sweat trickled down his forehead from his buzz cut, and his eyes danced back and forth over the mirror, watching for cars. It was late; they were alone. He kept his gun in his left hand, pointed across the steering wheel at Brooke. Cat squirmed in the backseat behind them, her mouth, wrists, and ankles bound with duct tape.

They sat behind the guardrails at the lift bridge. All the while, he talked. That was one thing Brooke remembered about Ken. He liked to talk. He talked about his parents, his dog, his car, his girlfriends, his stereo, his apartment, his clothes, his sunglasses, and his penis. He talked when he was threatening her. He talked when he was fucking her.

Now, when he was getting ready to shoot her, he was still talking.

"What are the odds, huh?" he said, his knee bouncing nervously inside the car. "That son of a bitch Marty Gamble swipes a ring, and he has to pick the only thing that would ever blow up in our faces. Jesus, if only I'd had more time to find the girl that night."

"You'd have killed Cat?" Brooke murmured. "A little girl? I can't believe even you would do that."

"Loose ends, Brookie. You see what happens when you have loose ends? It's not pretty."

"You planned to kill Marty all along, didn't you?"

Ken craned his neck to stare up at the bridge. The deck hovered above them at the top of the span. She wondered if they could feel it sway up there, as the wind blew through the canal. In front of them, she saw ship lights. It wouldn't be long now. She was running out of time.

"Hey, everybody knew that he'd go off the deep end sooner or later," he said. "I just helped it along. I took him out for a drive to celebrate Fong's arrest and got him so drunk he could hardly walk. That's when I started telling him about Stride and Michaela and how Stride was bragging about his affair with her. Marty would have believed anything I told him. Next thing I knew he was screaming at me to drive over there. I let him go inside and I could hear him whaling on her. When I went inside, he was sitting against the wall, and she was bleeding from like a million holes."

In the backseat, Cat kicked viciously at Ken. The car shook with her fury. Her bound legs reared up and landed a glancing blow on his head, dizzying him. Brooke grabbed for the gun, but she was too slow. Furious, Ken spun around; he held Brooke back with a hand around her throat and pointed the gun over the seats at Cat's face.

"Hey! Knock it off, you little bitch! Do you have any idea how much fucking trouble you've caused me? One little teenage hooker! Unbelievable! Believe me, we're going to have some fun before you disappear, baby, because I've earned it."

He thumped back into his seat, breathing hard. He was losing control. The gun bounced in his hand as he drummed the steering wheel. He shouted at the bridge. "Come on, goddamn it! Come on!"

Brooke saw flashing lights beyond the open gap of the canal. She hoped it was a police car, but it was an ambulance, and she knew where it was heading. She wondered if the policewoman at Stride's house was dead, if he'd killed her, if she had another victim on her conscience. How many was this now? She'd lost count.

"For a long time, I wondered if you'd kill me," Brooke said.

"I thought about it."

"Why didn't you?"

Ken grinned. "Hey, I always liked you, Brookie. Let's face it, you were a great fuck, too."

He reached across the car and squeezed her breast like it was a stress ball. She winced inside at his touch, but she didn't show him her revulsion. The sex between them had gone on for years. She never knew when he would show up or what he would do to her. Each time, she wondered if it was the last—if he would fuck her and then strangle her and make her disappear. The sight of him terrified her; the touch of his hands made her want to leap out a window and kill herself. Even so, she couldn't say a word to anyone.

"I didn't need people poking around in your background if you disappeared," he said. "Besides, I figured you had as much to lose as me, right? A girl who fucks rich old goats for tuition money knows the sacrifices you have to make, and you weren't going to give it all up. I was right, too, wasn't I? When Margot showed up talking about Cat and the ring, you called me. I knew you'd never let that pretty face rot in jail. Good girl, Brookie."

Good girl?

She'd thrown open Pandora's box. She had no soul.

"What happens now?"

He shrugged. "That's up to you. It doesn't look like I can trust you. You were ready to rat me out."

"People keep dying," she murmured.

"You think I wanted it that way? Sometimes you do what you have to do."

"The police are going to figure it out. They probably already have."

"That's your fault. You should have kept your cool. Now they know where to look."

"You won't get away."

"You think I don't know how to disappear? You think I haven't made plans? No one's going to find me. You can come along for the ride or you can wind up in a hole somewhere." He jerked his thumb at the backseat. "Right next to her."

"You'd let me come with you?"

He didn't answer. He eyed the bridge again and pumped his fist. The bridge began to come down, not just on the canal, but on ten years of her life. He turned on the engine, which purred. Soon they would be out of the city, on the rural back roads. He probably already had his route planned. There would be a cabin waiting for them on the Wisconsin side, near a pretty lake. Secluded. Quiet. She had no illusions that he would let her live beyond the first night, no matter what he said. He would fuck them both, and then he would kill them both.

Even so, she wanted him to think that she believed him. That they were partners.

"Time to go," he said.

He let the ambulance roll past them in the opposite direction, and then he drove across the bridge as if nothing in the world were wrong. The gun was pointed at her chest again. He drove into the empty streets of Canal Park, and the wind made it look like a desert ghost town, blowing snow like dust and tumbleweeds across their path, from Grandma's Restaurant toward the old brick factories.

"Do you remember the first time?" she asked.

He looked at her.

"You and me," she said.

He grinned.

The first time. He'd left a message on her phone to meet him in a campus parking lot near one of the athletic fields. A cop in an unmarked sports car. At night. She'd had her heart in her mouth, wondering what he wanted, but there was no mystery in that. He knew. This young cop, barely older than her, knew all her secrets. He'd followed her and photographed her; he had everything it would take to expose her hidden life. She'd bawled like a kid, and then he'd said, with that sly grin, "It doesn't have to go that way."

He'd unzipped his fly, and she understood the way it would go. She didn't care. She'd serviced him for months, and she'd thought of it as nothing more than an insurance policy, until he came to her on a snowy December night with a different plan. *You need to do something for me.*

A week later, she gave him the alarm code at Lenny's house. 1789.

Ken stopped at the light. He waited to turn left on Railroad Street, which led south beside the concrete overpasses of I-35. She knew the road; it took them past Bayfront Park into the industrial zone, where the ships loaded and unloaded and the ore-filled railcars rattled over the tracks. From there, the Blatnik Bridge arched over the bay into Superior, Wisconsin, in a part of the state that was mostly a wilderness of single-lane roads and deep forests.

You can wind up in a hole somewhere.

"Are you tense?" she asked, with a faint smile on her lips.

His head swiveled. "Huh?"

"You know." She touched his thigh.

"Hell, yeah."

"You're right, I don't want to sit in jail," she said. "I want to come with you."

"Show me how much."

He unzipped. It was like the old days. The light changed, and he accelerated. She slid across the seat and bent her torso over him. Ken waggled the gun at her.

"Don't be stupid."

She removed his shaft from his jeans and stroked him with her nails, getting him hard. His breath caught in his throat. She knew how to get a reaction. Beneath her, the car engine growled; he was going faster.

Faster.

She took him in her mouth, tasting salt and sweat. Underneath her bobbing head, her hands massaged the wrinkly skin of his scrotum and the firm chestnuts floating inside. He moaned. His hand pushed her head down, so far that she felt herself gagging. He had one hand, his gun hand, on the wheel. She felt the veer of the car; he couldn't steer straight.

Faster.

Brooke knew it was now or never. She snapped her fingers shut like a hawk's claw, digging her sharp nails into his testicles, eliciting a primal scream. Simultaneously, she cracked her head upward into his chin, rifling his neck backward. She threw her left hand into his skull and drove it into the cold, hard window of the car. With her other hand she let go of his balls and spun the wheel, wrenching the car into a sharp turn. The car, still going forty miles an hour, shot off the road onto the dirt and ice of the grassy field beside the freeway.

The car hit a light pole, which broke with a screech of metal and hit the hood like a falling body. Brooke flew forward, hitting the dashboard, bouncing backward. With a chemical sear, the air bag exploded into Ken's face and the car lurched to a stop. Disoriented, Brooke found herself facedown near his feet. Something hard and heavy—the gun—grazed her skull and disappeared under the seat as if sliding on ice.

Her head spun, but she pushed herself up and yanked the handle on the passenger door. It opened and she tumbled outward, falling into snow and weeds. She spotted Ken slumped in the driver's seat, already groaning and recovering. With no time to waste, she opened the rear door and dragged Cat outside into the cold. The girl was bruised from the impact, but she wasn't hurt. Brooke tore at the duct tape around the girl's ankles and as the tape split, Cat thrust her legs apart, freeing herself. Brooke didn't take the time to work on the girl's hands. She helped Cat stand.

"*Hurry*," she hissed.

As they began to run, Brooke saw Ken's eyes inside the car. They were open now, and there was murder in them.

She and Cat sprinted along a snow-covered line of railroad tracks only steps from the twin overpasses of I-35. The roar of engines above their heads was a constant throb. They were no more than a hundred yards from the streets of downtown Duluth on the other side of the freeway.

People would find them there. People would rescue them.

She pulled Cat across the tracks toward the city. The crushed rock under their feet was slick. The ground sloped downhill toward the freeway foundations, and they made tiny, dancing steps on the frozen earth, skidding to a stop at the giant wall of the northbound overpass. Dead brush around them was wet with snowdrifts. They hugged the wall, inching sideways on a slippery stretch of concrete no more than a foot wide. Where the wall ended, they reached a narrow creek that tunneled between the two overpasses. The water was glazed over with ice. Lights on the highway overhead cast long shadows. They could see a Soo train parked on the tracks of the depot, and beyond it the city loomed, bright and close. Freedom was a quick skate across the water.

Brooke stepped onto the creek. So did Cat. The ice gave way with a crack; their feet landed in three inches of murky, numbing water. Before they could take another step, a loud crack boomed above the noise of the cars. The wall on the other side of the creek exploded in dust.

Another crack. Another.

He was shooting at them. The next bullet was so close that she felt a sting on her ear. When she touched her hand there, her fingers came away with blood. Brooke was paralyzed, but Cat yanked her under a concrete arch that made a roof over the frozen creek, where they were blocked from view. They were below the freeway, like pygmies in a giant land, with miles of roadbed stretching no more than four feet over their head.

A one-sided iron ladder, propped against the wall, led out of the water and into the secret no-man's land between the two sides of the interstate.

"Come on," Cat urged her. "We'll hide in the graffiti graveyard."

57

"Gunshots," Stride said.

They headed north into the city on Michigan Street. When he heard the distinctive pop-pop of shots in quick succession, he braked sharply and pulled to the curb near the depot. As they listened, the gun went silent.

"Where?" Serena asked.

"Somewhere near the tracks."

He turned into an alley that led to the railway yard. His wheels bumped over the maze of tracks. The alley dead-ended at I-35, and he followed a gravel road beside a lineup of old passenger cars and Wisconsin Central engines. The freeway above them was lit by streetlights, but the area around the tracks was black. He turned on his high beams, giving the train cars a white glow. The loose rock under his tires was loud as he inched through the rail yard.

He stopped, leaving the lights on. When he opened his door, the wind ripped it out of his hand. Serena got out on the other side. They both slid their weapons from their holsters.

Stride followed the wall of the freeway overpass and gestured to Serena to remain on the other side of the alley, in the shadow of the trains. The two of them crept south, the wind fighting them, drowning

out the noise. Cars shot by on I-35 a few feet over his head. He saw
Serena clearing the space between each railcar.

They were alone.

Then he heard it, distant and muffled, as if coming from inside
a wall. A young girl screamed, and the scream cut off sharply into
silence. He was sure he recognized the pitch of the voice.

It was Cat.

Serena ran across the road to join him. Thirty yards ahead of them,
the wall beside the interstate ended and the weedy ground sloped
downward under the roadbed. On the other side of the freeway was
the harbor.

"Do you know where they are?" she whispered.

"Sounds like the graffiti graveyard."

He led the way to the end of the freeway wall and stole a look
around the corner. He was conscious of his truck headlights illuminating him from behind and throwing his shadow like a giant. The
sunken area between the freeway beds was dark. He heard water dripping. The winter branches of a bent tree scratched his face as it fluttered in the wind.

Stride inched his way down the slope. Serena followed. He reached
a dirty creek, which stretched like a ribbon between six-foot walls
under the southbound lanes. The creek water was frozen. Boulders
and rusted debris jutted out of the ice. He saw a ladder leaning on
the east wall. Where light from the freeway spilled over the maze of
concrete, graffiti art bloomed in a wild, psychedelic tangle of colors. It
was everywhere, covering everything.

He listened and heard nothing, but somewhere over the wall, a
cone of light speared through the darkness. A flashlight. He cupped
his hand over Serena's ear and whispered. "Stay with the creek."

Stride crossed to the opposite side of the canal, wincing as the ice
broke, flooding his shoes with frigid water. Serena stayed behind him,
almost invisible, following the wall on the fringe of the creek. He bal-
anced a wet boot on the slippery steel of the ladder and pushed up
one step. The ladder vibrated. He climbed two more steps and then
shunted over the top of the wall. With a squishy thud, he dropped
into snow and mud.

In the land ahead of him, a shot exploded through the darkness.

Cat watched the flashlight go on and off as Ken McCarty crept closer to them. She pressed her lips shut, trying not to scream again.

The graffiti graveyard was a grassy shelter tucked between the north–south overpasses. The ladder up the stone wall from the creek was the only way in, but once inside, the enclosure stretched for hundreds of yards, with drivers speeding north and south just overhead, unaware of the odd playground beneath them. The homeless came here, along with druggies and artists. The ground was littered with hypodermic needles, broken glass, and aerosol cans. Every wall and column was covered with elaborate spray-painted designs, like a multicolored museum.

Cat squeezed herself behind one of the concrete pillars that propped up the roadbeds. Brooke stood behind another pillar ten feet away. There were other people around them. Despite the cold, she saw blanket-shrouded bundles huddled against the walls. In the occasional flash of light, their eyes glittered at her like cats'.

The flashlight swept the ground on either side of the pillar where she stood. She pushed her ankles together to keep the beam from finding her. She heard another shot, and the noise was deafening inside the concrete jungle. She knew what he was doing. He wanted them to move, to run, to show themselves. She clapped her hands over her ears and held her breath.

Each flash of light, on and off, teased her with examples of graffiti art around her, making the paintings on the concrete look scary and alive.

Flash. A smoking monkey with suspicious, squinting eyes.

Flash. A green-and-blue chain of spiked barbed wire.

Flash. A row of bone-white skulls with black eye sockets.

Flash. A fanged spider.

Flash. A single sentence scrawled in drippy red, covering up a golden devil-robot. *Alone we are nothing.*

Cat stared at Brooke, who pointed a finger northward. Ken was getting closer; they had to move or they would be trapped here. When the light went off, they skidded across icy ground, jumping past three more pillars and ducking into cover just as the flashlight shot across their feet, nearly exposing them. Each time the light came from a different angle. He was zigzagging as he tracked them north. Soon he would be so close that they would be able to hear his footsteps.

They were more than a hundred yards from where they had started. It was cold, and they clung to each other, shivering.

"He won't stop," Brooke whispered in Cat's ear. "He'll find us, and he'll kill us."

"We have to double back," Cat said.

She knew there was only one way to escape. They had to cross the graveyard to the southbound overpass, climb the wall, and drop down into the frigid creek. They could slip past him in the water, back toward the railway yard and the downtown streets. They would be safe, unless he heard them and found them there. If he did, there was nowhere to run.

"The creek," Cat said.

Brooke nodded.

The graveyard was dark. His flashlight was off. They didn't hear him coming; he was somewhere in the field of concrete, waiting and watching. Above their heads, a highway light made crazy shadows and lit up the graffiti. As cars passed, the light flickered like a strobe. They had to cross a stretch of dead grass to move from the north-bound to the southbound lanes, and there was no way to dodge the light. If he was looking when they ran, he would see them like black silhouettes. They had to risk it.

Maybe he was a hundred feet away.

Maybe he was right there, with the gun.

They dashed across the snow. Their running footsteps through the wet drifts sounded loud. The light stretched out their bodies on the ground. They crossed from the shelter of one crossbeam to the next crossbeam in no more than two seconds, and they stopped, listening. Cat expected to hear him running. She expected to feel the flashlight beam dazzling her eyes. Instead, there was silence.

"Come on," she said.

They crossed to the wall bordering the creek. Cat pulled herself up, scraping her hand on sharp gravel. She swung her legs around, dangling them over the water below her. Brooke had trouble with the climb, and Cat extended one of her hands to help her. When they were both on top of the wall, they took a breath and jumped. It wasn't far, but the ice cracked like a bullet and cold water splashed up to their ankles. The bed of the creek was slimy and uneven with hidden debris.

The walls bordering the creek were barely eight feet apart and six feet tall. No light made it down there; it was like an underground tunnel. They couldn't see the archway far ahead of them; they walked in nothingness. The only thing real was the touch of Brooke's hand; their fingers were laced tightly together.

The wind didn't reach the creek, but they heard it above them, wailing like a wounded animal. The air was freezing, and the ice bath made a bitter chill that traveled up Cat's body. Her bones shook; she couldn't stop herself from trembling. After a minute in the water, she no longer felt her feet, and she began to stumble in her boots. Each step broke through the glaze of ice, and no matter how quiet they tried to be, she felt as if they were shouting their presence to him.

Suddenly, she was blinded.

The flashlight beam, ten feet away, lit them up, turning night to day. They froze and covered their eyes. Running was pointless; they couldn't escape. Cat squinted and tried to see behind the light; at first, all she could see was a hand holding a gun, pointed across the short space at her chest. She thought about her baby. She wondered if her mother was right and if there was a heaven somewhere.

The light tilted up and Cat saw the face of the person behind it. Not Ken McCarty. Not someone evil. It was Serena.

Silently, Cat leaped across the short space and felt herself wrapped up in Serena's arms. She wept into her shoulder with relief. Serena kept the light on Brooke and the gun leveled across the water. Cat took her wrist gently and pointed the gun down.

"It's okay, she's okay, she helped me."

Brooke raised her arms in the air in surrender.

"Where is he?" Serena whispered.

"Up there somewhere. Is Stride here?"

"Yes. Come on, let's get out of here."

Serena turned. Her flashlight swung with her, and in its glow they all saw a hunched figure on top of the creek wall, ready to spring. She raised her gun, but it was too late to aim and fire. Ken McCarty jumped with arms spread, flying down through the air like a vampire bat, landing squarely on Serena's chest and driving her backward into the water.

The gun dropped. The flashlight dropped.

The creek was black again.

58

"Stride!"

Ken McCarty's voice boomed through the graffiti graveyard, calling him closer. The shout came from below, fifty yards away, in the belly of the creek. Stride ran through the snow, dodging the concrete pillars. When he reached the creekside wall, he crouched and switched on his own flashlight, expecting a bullet over his head.

Nothing happened.

He left the flashlight on top of the wall and crab-walked ten feet forward, where a rusted set of bedsprings was propped against the stone. He pushed himself up on the metal frame, high enough to swing his torso over the top of the wall and point his gun down toward the water.

Ken stood in the ankle-deep creek. The light captured his cocky grin, which hadn't changed since he was a baby cop. He stood behind Serena with one muscular forearm locked around her throat. His other hand held a gun against her temple. Three feet behind him, Cat and Brooke stood in frozen silence.

"It's been a long time, Lieutenant," Ken called.

"Let her go, Ken," Stride said. "Let her go, and put the gun down."

"I don't think so."

Stride didn't have a shot, and Ken knew it. Half the cop's face was hidden behind Serena. He saw Serena struggling to breathe as Ken's grip choked off her air.

"Ken, you know it's over. The police are surrounding this area right now. You're not going anywhere. If you want to stay alive, let her go, and drop the gun."

Ken jammed the gun into Serena's face and she struggled in his grasp. "Actually, Lieutenant, my odds just got better. I have a hostage. Someone you care about. I don't think you're going to let anything happen to her."

"You're not walking out of here."

"No? Then shoot me. Go ahead, take the shot. I hope you've spent time on the range lately. It's dark. The angle's bad. Chances are, you blow your girlfriend's head off instead of mine. Are you willing to take that risk? I'd hate to think of you grieving about it the rest of your life. How many women are you willing to lose, Stride?"

Stride said nothing. They both heard sirens on the streets outside the graveyard.

"They're coming for you, Ken."

"Then get on the radio and tell them to back off! Serena and I are getting out of here right now. No cops, no guns. If I die, she dies in the cross fire."

"Where do you think you're going to go?" Stride asked. "You won't last a day on the run."

"I got away for ten years, Stride. I'll get away for ten more. I don't need much of a head start. Let me go and I'll release Serena when I'm safe."

"That's not going to happen," Stride said.

"Then you better shoot me."

Stride's hand tensed on his gun. He saw Ken's forehead lined up in his sights, but the cop's body jerked, going in and out of focus. It was too dark, too far, too cold. Serena's green eyes gleamed in the light, and he knew she wanted him to shoot. She'd wrench away and give him a split second, but he couldn't do it. He tried to tell her with his eyes. *No.*

Ken took a step and pushed Serena forward with him. She was going to bolt; she was going to wrestle away. The ice crushed into white frost. Stride had to make a choice.

"Stop!" he called.

"I'm getting out," Ken said. "Keep your girlfriend alive and let me go."

Stride aimed the gun again. His finger slid on the trigger. As he searched for a moment to fire, he spotted movement in the shadows directly behind Ken. His eyes flicked to Cat and saw the girl's face wrenched with emotion. Tears ran down her face. Her mouth was slack with fury and horror.

As Stride watched, Cat knelt down and slid her hand into her boot. She came out holding a knife.

STOP STOP STOP STOP STOP STOP.

No no no no . . . oh God . . . oh God . . .

Please . . . I'm dying . . . I'm dying . . .

Cat clutched the knife in her hand. She could hear her mother's voice ringing out in agony, as clear as it had been that night. Even when she'd clasped her hands over her ears to drown it out, she could still hear it. The knife going in and out of her body. Her mother. Crying. Bleeding. Dying.

This man caused it. This man standing in front of her. This man took them all away. Her mother. Her father. Dory. Now he was holding Serena. He was going to take her away, too.

She couldn't let it happen. She had to stop it. *Please, Mother, give me the strength to stop it.* All she had to do was stab him. Raise her arm, drive the knife down, penetrate his flesh, take away his life. Pay him back for what he'd done, plunge in the blade over and over and over and over the way he deserved. It would be so easy, so right. Kill him. Stab him.

Cat could see the dimple in his back, underneath his neck, where she would strike him first. Blood would spurt. She'd seen it before. He would cry in pain, and she would have no mercy. She would pull the knife out, slash again, pull the knife out, slash again, pull the knife out, slash again. She would count. Ten times, twenty times, thirty times, forty times, until the black creek was red with his blood.

Raise her arm, drive the knife down, penetrate his flesh. *Mother, make me strong.*

Michaela was silent from the grave. Cat realized she was calling out to the wrong parent. It was her father who would guide her, her father who would teach her to be brutal and ruthless, to call out the devil in her soul. Marty Gamble wouldn't hesitate to do what had to be done. He would take the knife and cast out every weak emotion and rain down death and pain and blood.

I must stop him, Father. Show me how.

Mother, forgive me.

But it didn't matter how long Cat stood there. She couldn't do it. She stood paralyzed, wracked by trembling, the knife quivering in her fingers, and she couldn't do it. She told her arm to move, and it wouldn't move. No matter how much she wanted to, no matter how much she needed to, she couldn't lift the knife; she couldn't sink it in another person's body. This man, this murderer, was going to get away because she was weak.

Cat felt cool fingers on her hand, the hand that held the knife.

It was Brooke Hahne, standing beside her. Brooke's eyes were calm and determined.

She peeled the knife away from Cat's hand and in a single motion, a graceful arc, she buried the blade to the hilt in Ken McCarty's neck.

59

It happened fast, and it happened slowly.

Ken howled in pain, and his body spasmed as the knife sliced through his nerve endings and severed his artery. Blood erupted. A red fountain. The arm he held around Serena's neck gave way, and she spun out of his grasp. She slipped on the ice and went to her knees. Ken swayed, his gun arm shot skyward, but as he collapsed against the wall, the gun was still locked in his hand.

A mortal threat.

Stride saw it happening and couldn't stop it. He shouted. He screamed. He took a shot himself in the same split second, but his bullet struck the wall above Ken McCarty's head and ricocheted harmlessly up into the crossbeams of the freeway.

He heard the wind. He heard cars racing.

His flashlight beam lit up Ken's drunken dance and glinted on the metal of the gun, and the gun danced, too, danced and swung. With the tiniest twitch of Ken's finger, it fired. The gun spat flame. The shot was like a bomb.

The bullet drove into Serena.

Flashbacks.

Stride didn't remember throwing himself over the wall into the creek. He knelt over Serena and saw the faces of the other women he'd lost, as if they lay beside her. He was at their deathbeds, when it was too late to change anything, when they were already out of his grasp.

"Michaela."

His finger in the blood of her neck. No pulse.

"Michaela!"

His voice choked and ragged.

Her eyes closed, angelic. He put his hands on her cheeks; they were still warm, as if life had only just left them. Minutes earlier, she'd begged for his help, but in the time it took to reach her, he was already too late. He'd already failed her.

He was conscious of Ken McCarty limping toward the archway. He didn't chase him. Ken had nowhere to go.

Serena was on her back. The dank, frozen water puddled around her. Her upper body was matted in blood, so much blood. More blood than one body should give up. Her eyes were open, but she was looking over his shoulder, at the angels, seeing visions of things to come.

"Don't look there," he told her. "Look into my eyes. Stay with me."

"Cindy."

The shell of his beautiful wife.

He heard her breathing catch. Each breath was a labored effort. Each one came a little harder and a little farther apart.

Her lips moved. Cindy murmured something he didn't understand. Stride leaned closer. The sight of her skin, and the smell of disease lingering on her body, crushed him. It wasn't his battle to fight. He was a bystander in the worst event of his life.

She tried again. He tried to hear her.

"It's okay, Jonny."

It was a whisper that didn't sound like her at all. He didn't understand. She couldn't be telling him that everything was all right, because nothing was all right. But for an instant, he saw a glimmer in her eyes that reminded him of who she was.

She spoke again. It was a terrible effort.

"It's what I want now."

He nodded. He could never accept it, but she could. She had to. There was no other choice.

He brushed his lips against hers. When he moved back, her eyes were closed again. The gasping, painful sound of her breath was gone, replaced by peaceful silence. The color left her face. He sat there, staring at her, and he found he could talk again. He told her how cold it was. He reminded her of that camping trip in the spring and how they had laughed together. He told her how beautiful she was and how much he loved her. He was still talking when the doctors came and led him away.

"Serena, look at me," he begged her. "Look at me. Stay with me. Help's coming. Help's almost here."

He leaned in, kissed her, stroked her wet, dirty hair in the creek.

"I love you. Don't go."

Ken McCarty coughed. Blood spattered from his mouth. He didn't have to make it far. His car was near the freeway where he'd crashed it. He still had that cabin near Solon Springs waiting for him. He could hide there while he healed.

He put a hand on the wall and it left a bloody print. It didn't matter.

Outside the graffiti graveyard, the night looked darker than it had before, as if the darkness were in his eyes. The rocks on the slope under the freeway looked funny. He realized it was because he was on all fours. Crawling. The mud and snow squished through his fingers.

He coughed. Liquid dripped from his neck. More blood made little pearls dotting the rocks, like a spatter painting. It would be easier to sleep. Sleep here, rest here, then get in the car and head across the bridge into Wisconsin in the sunshine of the morning. Tomorrow. Tomorrow.

No. He had to keep going. He couldn't wait for daylight.

Ken pushed himself to his feet, an effort that felt impossibly hard. He saw his car. The light post was on top of it. The doors were open. He could reach it; he could run; he could escape. He took a wobbly step and sank to his knees again. Something cold pressed into his head. It was a feathery touch, but it nearly knocked him over. The barrel of a gun.

"Hello, Ken," Maggie said.

Somewhere behind her, he saw flashing lights. He heard sirens. Police cars. Fire trucks. Ambulances. People running. People hurrying past him into the graffiti graveyard. Shouts. Radios.

"I was hoping to shoot you but it doesn't look like I need to bother," she told him.

"Huh?" Nothing made sense now.

"You have a knife sticking out of your neck," she explained. "Looks like it got your carotid. Payback's a bitch."

"Think I'm dying," he said.

"I think so."

"Help me."

"Not much to help, Ken."

"Come with me."

"Not where you're going."

"Serena," Stride said.

He saw the lights and heard the stampede of boots. They were coming for her.

"Serena," he repeated.

She didn't answer. She was still looking beyond him, as if she could see things that living persons shouldn't see. He wanted her frozen green eyes to move. He wanted her to see him kneeling over her.

"Don't you dare leave me," he told her.

Brooke Hahne sat in the dirty, icy water six feet away. She shivered uncontrollably, her knees pressed together. Her fists were clenched in front of her face. She didn't say a word; there was nothing to say, even though she had led them here to this place. He wanted to hate her, and he couldn't.

Cat knelt beside him. Their eyes met, and in that moment she might as well have been his own daughter. His own flesh. He loved her; he needed her. The girl took his hand and squeezed it fiercely. She pulled Serena's hand out of the water and clutched it, too, like a chain among the three of them. Cat's eyes closed. Her head tilted toward an invisible sky.

He heard her murmuring, praying, over and over, the same words.

"Do not take her, do not take her, do not take her, do not take her, do not take her, do not take her."

The medics were on top of them. They moved to gently push them away.

Stride took Serena's other hand as they gathered around her. He and Cat held on to her, refusing to let go, as if blood and warmth could pass through their bodies. He prayed, too. The same words, aloud, in unison. *Do not take her.* Not after Michaela. Not after Cindy. There could be no more loss.

He held his breath, and out of nothingness something changed, like a miracle happening. He saw her eyes shift, finding his face, recognizing him again. She turned away from the angels and let them go.

There was life in her hand.

60

"You know what would go great on this pizza?" Cat said. "Peanut butter."

Stride stared across the dining room table in disbelief. "You really are pregnant, aren't you?"

Cat skipped into the kitchen in her socks. She came back with a jar of peanut butter and a knife and spread a dollop onto one of the tiny squares. When she popped it into her mouth, she rolled her eyes. "Oh, yeah. You really have to try this."

"I'll pass," Stride said.

Serena laughed at the two of them, but she paid the price, wincing as pain jolted her chest. She smiled anyway. "You see, Cat, you're violating the purity of a Sammy's sausage pizza. For Jonny, that's like painting a mustache on the *Mona Lisa*."

Cat held out the jar to Serena with questioning eyes, but Serena shook her head. The girl shrugged and tossed her hair back, and she wagged a finger at them. "You guys don't know what you're missing."

She hummed as she adorned more of the pizza, but Stride knew that her cheerfulness was an act. She was nervous and scared; he could see it in the little darts from her brown eyes as she tried to read their faces. He'd already told her that the two of them needed to talk to her.

There wasn't much pizza left now, and she was busy pretending that she didn't have a care in the world.

"So the car guy," Cat said. "He's history, huh?"

Stride nodded. "Lenny resigned from the council today."

"Rich men don't go to jail."

"No, probably not," Stride admitted. "He's got lawyers, money, and leverage. He'll probably walk."

"He kept his mouth shut back then. He should pay."

"He should. We'll see. If we get him for anything, it'll be his connection to this upscale prostitution ring in the city. We think Steve was right about that. We're still digging into it."

"I heard about Brooke, too," Cat said. "That's bad, huh?"

"It could be worse," Stride said.

"I guess."

Three weeks had passed since the events at the graffiti graveyard. Serena had spent a week in the hospital, but the bullet had spared her major organs. The immediate danger of blood loss had passed after treatment on the first night in intensive care, and the lingering effect now was mostly the pain of broken ribs and torn muscles. She wasn't moving well; she would be out of work for at least two more months.

For Brooke Hahne, it had been three weeks of behind-closed-door legal maneuvering.

"If she'd gone to court, she would have faced multiple counts of first-degree murder," Stride went on. "That's life without parole. As it is, they pled her down to murder two because she wasn't personally responsible for any of the homicides. She'll still spend twenty-five years behind bars."

"I don't know how I feel about that," Cat said. "She saved my life."

"But not before putting it in danger," Serena pointed out.

Cat nodded. "Yeah."

"Listen," Stride said.

The girl's knee bounced nervously under the table. "Yeah?"

"We need to talk about someplace for you to live," Stride said. "It's been more than a month."

"I know." Cat played with a piece of pizza on her plate, pushing it back and forth with her fingertip. "Hey, it's been fun. I'm really grateful. You'll never know how much."

"You need somewhere permanent," Stride said. "You deserve more than a temporary solution."

"Yeah, I get it." She got off the chair with a shrug that belied her sadness. "Foster parents, huh? I know how the system works. I guess I better go pack. So where's it going to be? Who are they?"

"Cat, I want you to stay here with me," Stride told her.

She stopped. "With you?"

"Yes."

"Really?"

"Really. If you want to, that is."

The girl shoved her hands in her pockets. "Why, because you feel guilty about my mother?"

"No. That wouldn't change how I feel at all."

"Then why?"

"Because the more I thought about you being somewhere else, the more I realized I wanted you here," Stride said.

Cat sat down again. "For how long? A few months?"

"As long as you need to stay. Until you're an adult and on your own. I want to be your new legal guardian."

"I'm going to have a baby. It's going to be crazy."

"Probably," he said.

"A cop with a teenage hooker? How will that look?"

"I don't care how it looks."

She didn't want to smile. He realized that, to her, it felt like a candy cane on a string, and when she reached for it, someone would pull it away. Her eyes went back and forth between him and Serena. "You two are getting back together. I'll be in the way. You don't want me here."

"We both want you here," Serena said. "We talked about it."

"Will you stay here, too?"

"I thought I'd stick around while I recuperate," Serena said, winking. "It's easier than going back and forth to Grand Rapids. You and

I can get to know each other better. When you're not in school or doing homework, that is. Besides, if you and Jonny were alone here, all you'd ever eat is Sammy's pizza."

"You say that like it's a bad thing," Stride said.

Cat giggled. She couldn't hold it back anymore. She smiled. It was the smile he remembered from the first night, as glorious as a sunrise. "Well, maybe I could stay for a little while," she said.

She got up and began to clear the table, stacking the plates, making a clatter of china and silver. As he watched her in the kitchen, he felt Serena watching him. He had no idea if he was ready to have a teenager in the house. And then a baby, like an instant family. He and Serena hadn't even talked about each other yet and where their own relationship was going. There was time for that. He only knew that it felt right, the way it did when you examined a missing puzzle piece from every angle and finally found the one that fit.

As much as Cat needed someone in her life, he thought he needed her more.

When Cat finished the dishes, she came over to him, drying her hands on a kitchen towel. "I thought I'd go for a walk on the beach, if that's okay," she said. "It's safe to do that now, right?"

Stride glanced at Serena, who couldn't hide a tiny grin. From this moment forward, every day would test his limits. It was odd how quickly he could think like a parent and a cop at the same time. The evening was dark, and there were monsters outside. Always monsters.

"It's safe," he told her, "but be back in an hour."

61

Cat stood by the dunes, breathing in the lake air that floated over the hill. April had given way to May, and winter had finally given way to spring. The breeze was mild. The long grass swished and bent. She climbed the trail to the top of the sand and saw the great expanse of Lake Superior stretched out in front of her. It was midnight blue under the stars, but there were whitecaps agitating the waves.

She hadn't told Stride why she needed to go outside, but she wondered if he knew. She had to say good-bye. Good-bye to her parents. Good-bye to Dory. Good-bye to who she was.

Her past was finally behind her.

"Catalina Mateo," said a voice from the shadows.

Cat jumped. When she looked down the stretch of dunes, she saw two rusty old deck chairs stuck in the sand. Maggie Bei sat in one of them.

"Oh!" Cat exclaimed. "You startled me. What are you doing here?"

Maggie shrugged. She had a bottle of wine in her hand. Even at night, she wore sunglasses. Cat could see that the woman was a little drunk. "I like to come out here sometimes and watch the lake. I've done it for years."

"So you can be close to Stride?" Cat asked.

The Chinese cop laughed. She was cute and as tiny as Cat, but she had a hardness about her. "Don't try to psychoanalyze me. It doesn't work. Besides, the last shrink I visited shot himself in the head."

Cat swallowed hard. It was an odd thing to say.

Maggie patted the empty chair with the base of the wine bottle. "Sit by me," she said. "I want to talk to you."

"Okay."

Cat didn't want to stay, but she stayed anyway. She sat in the deck chair beside Maggie, and the two of them stared at the lake water under the night sky. Maggie didn't say anything. Cat kicked at the weeds with the toe of her boot.

"Stride asked me to stay with him," Cat said.

"I heard."

"Serena, too."

"Peachy."

"I know you don't like me," Cat said.

"I like you fine, Cat, but I don't trust you."

Cat squirmed in the chair. "Why not?"

Maggie's head swiveled. She didn't take off her sunglasses, and Cat couldn't see her eyes. The cop had a tiny diamond in her nose. She didn't explain anything to her. Not yet.

But it didn't matter. Cat knew exactly what she meant.

"Those are two people I care about in that house," Maggie went on. "Stride's my best friend in the whole world. He always will be. For a while, I thought maybe, maybe, it might be something more than that, but who was I kidding? As for Serena, well, I still like her. One of these days maybe we'll figure out how to be in the same room without killing each other."

Cat waited. "I'm not sure—"

"You being there with them is either going to bring them together or drive them apart," Maggie continued. "I'll probably regret saying this, but I'd rather you bring them together, okay?"

"Okay."

"If you give them shit, you will answer to me."

"I understand."

Cat began to get up, but Maggie shook her head. "I'm not done," she said.

Cat sank back into the chair. She waited for Maggie to talk, but the cop sat there in frustrating silence, and the silence felt like a balloon, getting bigger and bigger until all it could do was pop. Finally, when she couldn't stand the tension anymore, she blurted out, "What do you want from me?"

"The truth."

"About what?"

"You know what."

Cat did, but she couldn't say. Now the silence was hers. She said nothing at all. Her whole body felt cold.

Maggie finally took off her sunglasses. "I was down in Minneapolis just before everything went to hell," she said. "Can you believe Ken McCarty had the balls to come see me? What a bastard he was."

"I'm sorry."

"I don't need you to be sorry. I didn't feel a thing for him when he was alive. I don't feel a thing for him now that he's dead."

"I don't believe you," Cat said.

"See, you sound like a shrink again, Cat. Don't do that."

"Sorry," she repeated.

"Speaking of shrinks, did you kill Vincent Roslak?" Maggie asked, so suddenly it felt like a scab being ripped off her skin.

Cat began shaking. "No."

"No? That's your story? That's all you have to say about it? You see why I don't trust you."

She heard Vincent's voice, like an echo she couldn't get out of her head. She still loved him. *Is sex a violent act for you? Are there any sexual acts you won't do?*

"I didn't kill him."

Maggie nodded. "You never saw him after he moved to Minneapolis, right? That's what you told Stride."

Cat said nothing.

"Except you did see him down there, didn't you?" Maggie said. "I knew something was wrong when I visited his office, and it took me a while to figure out what was driving me crazy. You know what it was? The bells. Just like Quasimodo. The bells, the bells. It was the light-rail line that goes by Roslak's apartment. I'd heard it before, and you know where? It was on a tape that Roslak made of one of his sessions with you. I could hear the light-rail chimes in the background. It was in Minneapolis, Cat. Why would you lie about that if you didn't have something to hide?"

Do you think you could kill someone, Cat?

"I—I didn't want anyone to think—"

"You didn't want anyone to think you killed him. Sure. By the way, I showed your photo to a Jefferson Lines driver who does the bus route between Duluth and Minneapolis. He remembered you really well. That's the problem when you're such a stunner. Men don't forget you. He said you made that trip every week. How many times, Cat? How many times did you see Roslak down in the Cities?"

Cat couldn't lie anymore. "A lot. I loved him."

"So what happened? Did you realize he was just abusing you and all of his other patients? Did you realize he was just interested in sex? He didn't give a shit about you, Cat."

"I didn't kill him," Cat repeated.

"So who did? Ken? That's what I thought at first. Roslak must have figured out about the burglary. He saw the ring, or you said something under hypnosis, and he somehow made the connection to Ken. It would be easier if we left it like that, but I don't think that's what happened."

"I didn't kill him!" Cat shouted again. "How can you say that to me? I couldn't even put the knife in your boyfriend's back! I stood there as he was about to shoot Serena, and I couldn't do it! Is that the problem? Do you wish you'd killed him yourself? I could never do that to another soul. I know what knives do. I've seen it."

"You've seen it?"

Cat bit her lip. "My mother."

"You didn't see your mother."

"Leave me alone!"

"Who killed Roslak?"

Cat sat down again and inhaled loudly.

"If you cry, so help me, I'll slap you," Maggie said.

Cat swung around angrily. "I won't cry. Not in front of you."

"Who killed him, Cat?"

Please. It's hot in here.

I'll open a window.

She twitched. She could still feel him behind her. It hurt so bad, but it was what he wanted, and she would let him do anything, just so that he kept loving her. "She heard what he was doing to me," Cat said. "I was crying. She thought he was raping me. She misunderstood."

"Who?"

"Dory." Her voice was devoid of emotion, as if she had pulled a plug and let it drain away like dirty water in a bathtub. "She drove me down to the city that day, and she waited for me outside so she could smoke a cigarette. The window was open. It was loud."

Maggie was silent.

"She burst in on us. I was—I was bleeding back there. He was still inside me, and she pulled him off. My knife, the one I always kept, it was on the floor near my boots. Dory didn't give me time to explain. I wanted to tell her it was okay. I was letting him do it. It was what he needed. He loved me. She took the knife and she stabbed him, and she kept stabbing him. I wanted her to stop, but she just kept stabbing and screaming at him."

Cat slowly pulled her legs underneath herself and folded her hands in her lap. "When it was over, we took one of his coats so Dory could wear it, and no one would see the blood. We drove home. We stopped along the way to throw the knife in one of the lakes. When we got back, I helped her take a shower and clean herself, and then we bundled up all the clothes in a garbage bag and put it in a trash can. We never talked about it again."

Maggie got out of the chair. She put her sunglasses on again in the darkness. "Is that the truth?"

"It's the truth," Cat said. "Dory was all I had. She protected me. So I protected her."

Maggie turned around and hiked down through the trail in the dunes.

"Are you going to tell Stride?" Cat called.

There was no answer. Maggie kept hiking through the long, swaying grass until the darkness swallowed her up and Cat was alone again with the roar of the lake. She didn't take a walk in the wet sand the way she'd planned. She didn't say good-bye to everyone who had died. She realized that she'd been wrong. The past was the past, but it was never really behind her.

The house was quiet after midnight. Serena's hair was wet, and he toweled it dry, using soft touches to avoid stress on her wound. They stood on the slanted floor of the house's third bedroom. A floral blanket covered the bed. A flickering lavender candle lit and scented the space. Serena was fragrant from the soap in the shower, and her skin was damp under the silk robe.

"Sharing a bathroom with two women," she murmured. "You're a brave man, Jonny."

"I'll adjust." He squeezed the strands of her hair in the thick towel.

She turned around, and the candle cast his shadow across her face. "Do you mind if I sleep here? Not in your bed?"

"It's fine."

"I'll get there, Jonny. I just need time."

"I know."

"Will you undress me?"

His fingers tugged at the bow of her robe. The strip of silk came undone, and the robe parted an inch down her body, exposing a shadow of skin below her neck. He nudged the fabric from her shoulders and it spilled to her feet. She was naked and perfect in his eyes, but she wasn't healed. The gauze on her chest reminded him of what she'd suffered. He ached to touch her, but there was something just as arousing to see her standing there under his gaze.

"There's a nightgown in the closet," she said.

"You?"

She smiled. "We have a child in the house now."

He found the black nightgown on the hanger and bunched the fabric and gingerly slid it over her body, covering her in lace. Clothed, she was even more beautiful, drawing his eyes to the swell of her breasts and her bare legs stretching from her mid-thighs to her feet. Behind her, the bed was turned down.

"I'm so tired," she said.

"Of course."

"It hurts."

"I know."

He tucked her in and blew out the candle, causing a finger of smoke to curl into the air. Almost as soon as she closed her eyes, he heard her breathing change, growing steady and regular as she slept. He closed the door softly, leaving her alone. He was tired, too, but he couldn't go to bed yet, feeling as he did. Life had changed. He was a guardian of the future. He was a watchman protecting things of infinite value. So be it. There were other times to sleep. He sat down in the red leather chair near the fireplace and kept vigil on the night.

JOIN BRIAN'S COMMUNITY

You can write to me at brian@bfreemanbooks.com. I welcome e-mails from readers and always respond personally. Visit my website at www.bfreemanbooks.com to join my mailing list, get book club discussion questions, read bonus content, learn about events in your area, and find out more about me and my books. You can also "like" my official fan page on Facebook at www.facebook.com/bfreeman-fans or follow me on Twitter at @bfreemanbooks.

ACKNOWLEDGMENTS

It was a great pleasure coming back to Duluth for the return of Jonathan Stride. The people of Duluth and Superior always give me and Marcia a warm welcome, for which we are very grateful. A special thanks to Sergeant David Greeman and the members of the Duluth police for the detailed tour of their facilities and visits to many interesting corners of the city. Thanks, too, to the staff of the DECC, the lift bridge, and the county emergency response center for taking me inside their operations. Chuck Frederick, Ken Browall, and the team at the *Duluth News Tribune* have been great supporters of me and my books, as have Sally Anderson at the Bookstore at Fitger's and Laura Selden at Mix 108.

Isanti County attorney Jeff Edblad was his usual helpful self in trying to explain intricacies of Minnesota criminal law and sentencing procedures to me.

In the publishing industry, I have been extremely fortunate to work with agents Ali Gunn, Deborah Schneider, Diana Mackay, and coagents around the world. I'm also very grateful to everyone at Quercus in the United Kingdom and the United States, with particular thanks to David North, Charlotte Van Wijk, Nathaniel Marunas, Eric Price, and Rich Arcus.

Matt Davis, Paula Tjornhom Davis, Mike O'Neill, Alton Koren, and Terri Duecker provided thoughtful suggestions on many different aspects of this book. Somewhere in the middle of a bottle of wine (or was it two?), Matt, Paula, Marcia, and I also came up with the book's title. I honestly don't even remember who first said it.

Marcia always gets the first two words in every book, but she gets the last words, too. Thank you for everything, sweetheart!